Meet Charles de Montforte,
an English soldier wounded in
battle on American soil and
rescued by the one woman
he can never have . . .

Amy imagined him towelling himself dry. She imagined him feeling about for his clothes. And she imagined him donning his new shirt, lying so intimately against his clean, warm skin—

"Miss Leighton?"

She jumped guiltily and yanked open the door. There he stood, barefoot and bare-chested, clad only in his breeches and nothing else. With his fingers he had slicked back his wet hair, and there was a smile on his face.

Amy swallowed hard and stared at Lord Charles de Montforte. *Oh please God, don't let me be thinking of him the way I'm thinking of him. He has a fiancée who loves him; this is wrong, wrong!*

But she couldn't help the direction of her thoughts. Not with him looking the way he did . . .

Other **AVON ROMANCES**

ENCHANTED BY YOU *by Kathleen Harrington*
HER NORMAN CONQUEROR *by Malia Martin*
HIGHLAND BRIDES: HIGHLAND SCOUNDREL
by Lois Greiman
THE MEN OF PRIDE COUNTY: THE REBEL
by Rosalyn West
PROMISED TO A STRANGER *by Linda O'Brien*
THROUGH THE STORM *by Beverly Jenkins*
WILD CAT CAIT *by Rachelle Morgan*

Coming Soon

KISSING A STRANGER *by Margaret Evans Porter*
THE MACKENZIES: PETER *by Ana Leigh*

And Don't Miss These
ROMANTIC TREASURES
from Avon Books

A RAKE'S VOW *by Stephanie Laurens*
SO WILD A KISS *by Nancy Richards-Akers*
TO TAME A RENEGADE *by Connie Mason*

Avon Books are available at special quantity discounts for bulk
purchases for sales promotions, premiums, fund raising or educa-
tional use. Special books, or book excerpts, can also be created to
fit specific needs.

For details write or telephone the office of the Director of Special
Markets, Avon Books Inc., Dept. FP, 1350 Avenue of the Americas, New York, New York 10019, 1-800-238-0658.

THE BELOVED ONE

DANELLE HARMON

AVON BOOKS ◆ NEW YORK

AVON BOOKS, INC.
1350 Avenue of the Americas
New York, New York 10019

Copyright © 1998 by Danelle F. Colson
Inside cover author photo by Bryan Eaton
Published by arrangement with the author
Visit our website at **http://www.AvonBooks.com**
Library of Congress Catalog Card Number: 98-93120
ISBN: 0-380-79263-X

First Avon Books Printing: November 1998

AVON TRADEMARK REG. U.S. PAT. OFF. AND IN OTHER COUNTRIES, MARCA REGISTRADA, HECHO EN U.S.A.

Printed in the U.S.A.

WCD 10 9 8 7 6 5 4 3 2 1

To Antony,
who knew Charles better than I did.

With special thanks to Lauren,
who is three thousand miles
too far away;
to Helene, who always
makes me laugh;
and to Andrea,
who knows me better
than I know myself.

Acknowledgments

There are many to whom I am indebted for their contributions to this book. I would like to thank my editor, Lucia Macro; my agent, Nancy Yost; and Christine Zika, who not only suggested the de Montforte series but allowed Charles to survive. I would also like to thank Dr. Jack Bowers; my cousin Lorraine Leathers, who was happy to read the unpolished manuscript and offer suggestions that I found invaluable; Sterling Udell for the "catapult idea"; John Seitz and Mary Jo Putney for their advice on eighteenth-century military matters; Brian Gatcombe, who inadvertently inspired the "fire scene"; Roscoe and Poppy for keeping me thin in the face of a freezer full of British chocolate; and of course, and as always, my beloved husband, Chris—a hero in the truest sense of the word.

And finally, a very special thank you to all those readers who wrote asking me for Charles's book . . . here it is!

Prologue

The moon was rising.

Earlier in the day, and throughout much of the previous one, it had been raining. Now, the last clouds filed swiftly out to sea, riding above trees still bare of leaves and allowing the moon to turn the steeples, roof-tops, and cobblestoned streets of Boston to silver. In the harbor, the bows of the great warships swung slowly to the west as the spring tide began to come in. In timber-framed houses all across the town, lamps glowed at doors, faint candlelight shone from behind windows, chimneys spewed wood smoke toward the stars. All was peaceful. All was quiet. The town was settling in for the night.

Or so it seemed.

History would remember two lanterns hung in the Old North Church, the midnight ride of Paul Revere, and at daybreak, the battle of Lexington and later, Concord, that would open the American Revolution.

But there were some things it would not remember.

On the second floor of Newman House, whose owner resentfully let rooms to the king's officers, a captain in the proud scarlet regimentals of the Fourth Foot sat at

1

his desk, finishing the letter he'd begun earlier to his family in far-off England . . .

Newman House,
18 April 1775

My dear brother, Lucien,

It has just gone dark and as I pen these words to you, an air of rising tension hangs above this troubled town. Tonight, several regiments—including mine, the King's Own—have been ordered by General Gage, commander in chief of our forces here in Boston, out to Concord to seize and destroy a significant store of arms and munitions that the rebels have secreted there. Due to the clandestine nature of this assignment, I have ordered my batman, Billingshurst, to withhold the posting of this letter until the morrow, when the mission will have been completed and secrecy will no longer be of concern.

Although it is my most ardent hope that no blood will be shed on either side during this endeavour, I find that my heart, in these final moments before I must leave, is restless and uneasy. It is not for myself that I am afraid, but another. As you know from my previous letters home, I have met a young woman here with whom I have become attached in a warm friendship. I suspect you do not approve of my becoming so enamoured of a storekeeper's daughter, but things are different in this place, and when a fellow is three thousand miles away from home, love makes a far more desirable companion than loneliness. My dear Miss Paige has made me happy, Lucien, and earlier tonight she accepted my plea for her hand in mar-

riage. I beg you to understand, and forgive, for I know that someday when you meet her, you will love her as I do.

My brother, I have but one thing to ask of you, and knowing that you will see to my wishes is the only thing that calms my troubled soul during these last few moments before we depart. If anything should happen to me—tonight, tomorrow, or at any time whilst I am here in Boston—I beg of you to find it in your heart to show charity and kindness to my angel, my Juliet, for she means the world to me. I know you will take care of her if ever I cannot. Do this for me and I shall be happy, Lucien.

I must close now, as the others are gathered downstairs in the parlour, and we are all ready to move. May God bless and keep you, my dear brother, and Gareth, Andrew, and sweet Nerissa, too.

> *Charles*

"Captain? I'm sorry to trouble you, sir, but everyone's waiting downstairs for you. It's nearly time to leave."

"Yes, I am sensible to it. I shall be down directly, and do thank everyone for their patience with me, Ensign Gillard." The captain scanned his letter. "Not worried about tonight, now, are you?" he asked conversationally, not looking up as he folded the correspondence.

"Well, not exactly worried, sir, but . . . well, do you have a bad feeling about this mission?"

Lord Charles raised his head and regarded him quietly for a moment. "And here I thought it was me," he admitted, his expression both amused and reassuring.

"Everything will be all right, won't it, sir?"

"Of course, Gillard." The smile broadened. "Isn't it always?"

"Yes. Yes, I suppose it is." Gillard grinned back. "I'll leave you now, sir."

"Thank you. I shall be down in a moment."

Gillard closed the door, and dipping his quill in the ink once more, the officer wrote his brother's address across the front of the letter:

> *To His Grace the Duke of Blackheath, Blackheath Castle, nr Ravenscombe, Berkshire, England*

There. It was done.

Putting down his pen, Lord Charles Adair de Montforte rose to his feet, picked up his hat and sword, and, leaving the letter propped on his desk, strode boldly out of the room, down the stairs, and to his fate.

A fate so tragic that even Gillard's premonition could not have foreseen its very horror.

The waiting was terrible.

Fourteen-year-old Will Leighton lay stretched out flat on his stomach behind a stone wall, his musket propped between two boulders and trained on the ominously still road along which the king's troops would come.

Easy! he told himself, his heart pounding. *You're a man now! A grownup!* But he was so tense he felt sick. So jittery he kept forgetting to breathe. Off to his right, several others, all members of the Woburn militia under Major Loammi Baldwin, also lay hidden. None of them looked as nervous as he felt. Eyes flinty beneath their tricorns, they stared toward the road.

Waiting.

Will tried to imitate their gritty expressions, but all he could hear was the fierce pounding of his heart. His elbows dug into the spongy, rain-soaked earth. Dampness seeped up through his clothes, chilling his skin, making him shiver. In the maple above, a chickadee flitted from branch to branch, trilling its innocent song: *chickadee-dee-dee; chickadee-dee-dee.*

And from fifteen feet away, Baldwin spoke the words they'd all been waiting for:

"Here they come. Get ready, boys, to let 'em have it."

And now Will felt a sensation like needles prickling all up and down his spine as he heard it too: Dogs, barking an alarm from somewhere down the road. Distant shouts, sporadic musketfire, the steady rattle and stamp of hundreds of approaching men. Will's hand began to shake. Any moment now, the king's troops, on their way back to Boston after what everyone said was terrible fighting at Concord, would come around the bend and into view.

He swallowed, the taste of fear metallic on his tongue. Nearby, his cousin Tom narrowed his eyes, spat, and brought his musket to full-cock.

"Oh, we'll let 'em have it, all right. Come on, you bastards . . . We've been waiting for this moment for *years.*"

And come they did. Will's eyes widened and his heart quailed as the troops, nearly a thousand men strong, streamed around the bend like a river of blood. They were an awesome and terrible sight. Mounted officers in scarlet coats rode amongst them waving swords and barking orders. Sunlight flashed from bayonets, gorgets, and pewter buttons. But closer scrutiny revealed the signs of battle. Many, limping painfully, had all they could do to walk; others were borne on litters and in carts, and still others were so bloody that their breeches, snow white only hours earlier, were as red as their wool coats. There was exhaustion in their eyes. Desperation in their faces.

But Will, who'd heard all about what had happened at both Lexington and Concord earlier this day, felt no pity.

And neither did Baldwin as he roared, "*Fire!*"

From both sides of the road, a barrage of musket shot slammed into the unsuspecting troops, catching them in a deadly crossfire. Horses, screaming, bolted in terror. Soldiers fell dead as colonial muskets banged out, instantly cutting them down. Redcoat officers, shouting commands, sent their horses charging to and fro, trying to restore order and organize the troops into fighting formation, and soon answering volleys of shot were plowing into the surrounding trees and enveloping the rocky pasture and woods in thick, acrid smoke.

Discharging his musket and retreating behind a massive oak, Will reloaded, his hands shaking so badly that he spilled half his black powder down his leg. He rammed the ball and wadding home, his nerves shot as all around him yelling minutemen ran past, diving behind rocks and trees to aim and fire and reload once more. He brought his musket up again, just in time to see a wild-eyed young ensign break rank and sprint toward them from out of the drifting smoke, yelling at the top of his lungs, "Come out and fight fairly you cowards, you damned rebel wretches! Show yourselves and do battle like brave men, not skulking Indians!"

"Gillard, *get back*!" shouted a redcoat captain, splendid in scarlet and white, the blue facings of his uniform proclaiming him to be one of the King's Own—and sent his horse charging down on the runaway ensign at a full gallop.

Tom narrowed his eyes and raised his musket. "He's mine, the son of a bitch."

And fired.

Will would remember it for the rest of his life: Tom's musket roaring. Half the young ensign's face going up in a fountain of blood. His body seeming to trip and somersault, rolling over and over in the just-greening grass before it slammed up against the granite wall that Will had just vacated.

"Got 'im!" crowed Tom, thrusting his musket skyward a second before a ball sliced through his neck, instantly killing him.

Will had no time to react, for at that very moment the captain's horse exploded out of the smoke. Five feet from the stone wall where the ensign lay screaming in agony, the captain pulled the animal up and leaped from the saddle. Ignoring the lead whining about him, he ran to the young soldier, lifted him in his arms, and carried him back toward the trembling horse.

Will stood transfixed. Never had he seen such steely courage, such selfless devotion to a subordinate. The captain's hawkish face was hard, his eyes the December-ice clarity of aquamarine, and as he turned his back on Will and gently hoisted the soldier up into the saddle, Will knew he was going to have to kill him.

He leaped out of hiding.

Fired.

And *oh my God* missed.

The captain turned his cool, level stare on Will, one pale, arched brow lifting with the sort of surprised annoyance that any well-seasoned warrior might show a colonial bumpkin trying to irritate the finest army in the world. Will's stomach flipped over. Nausea strangled his throat. Too terrified even to reload, he froze as the captain picked up his ensign's musket and trained it dead-center on Will's chest. The blue eyes, so competent, so self-assured, so very, very dangerous, narrowed a second before the redcoat would have blown him into eternity.

''Don't shoot!'' Will squeaked, and his voice cracked, revealing his age—or rather lack of it.

The captain realized Will's youth at the same moment the weapon discharged and jerked the musket skyward, trying to deflect his fire. Flames roared from that long and terrible muzzle, shooting straight over Will's head. The gun's fierce kick, combined with the unnatural angle at which it had been fired, threw the officer off balance. As he stepped backward to regain it, his heel sank into a hollow in the soft April earth and he fell straight into the wall of granite, the musket flying from his hand and the back of his skull striking one sharp, lichen-caked boulder with an awful, thudding *crack*. For a moment, he seemed to gaze up at Will in astonishment as he lay there spread-eagled against the rocks; then the pale blue eyes lost focus and clouded over, their thick lashes coming down like a curtain on the last act as his head slid sideways, leaving a smear of blood on the boulder behind him.

For a moment, Will stared at the dead man in horror. Then he turned and fled.

Letter from General Thomas Gage, Commander-In-Chief of His Majesty's forces, to Lucien de Montforte, His Grace the Duke of Blackheath. . . .

My dear Duke,

I regret to inform you that whilst on a mission to Concord to seize arms that the rebels had secreted there, your brother, Captain Lord Charles de Montforte, was engaged in fighting and fatally injured. From all accounts, His Lordship fought bravely and selflessly, bringing glory to his family's name and tears throughout his regiment upon confirmation of his death.

Enclosed herein is the regimental gorget taken from Lord Charles's body immediately prior to burial in Concord, along with a letter that his servant, Billingshurst, found propped on his desk the day of his death. His dress regimentals will follow. I hope that these will bring you some comfort in this darkest of hours. Your brother was greatly respected and admired by both superiors and subordinates; he was ambitious and supremely confident in his own abilities, but like the best-loved commanders, never crossed that fine line into arrogance. He was an asset to this army, to his country, and a beloved friend to all who knew and served under and with him.

Respectfully yours,
Genl. Thomas Gage

Chapter 1

❦❦❦

"Make sure you whip the butter well when you churn it this morning, Amy. And for goodness sake, do add more salt this time," sniffed Mildred Leighton as she strode huffily past her sister. "There's nothing worse than bland-tasting butter, and you never do seem to get it right."

"Oh, and Amy, since you're doing the washing today, don't forget my blue petticoats. There are mud stains on the hem and they look positively dreadful," added Ophelia, coming downstairs and going straight to the looking glass on the wall.

"Yes, Ophelia. Yes, Mildred," sighed the thin figure, stooping nearly double beneath the lintel of the keeping room's massive fireplace. Pushing the iron crane off to one side, she tucked a loose strand of hair behind her ear, and, kneeling on the sooty bricks, began shoveling ash from out of the pit beneath the bake oven.

Ophelia, vainly fluffing her blond curls until they haloed her face, turned from the looking glass and regarded her half-sister with disdain. "And make sure my petticoats are ready by tomorrow afternoon. Matthew Ashton

10

has promised to take me for a drive, and I want to look my best.''

''Matthew Ashton?'' hissed Mildred, outraged. Already a bold and enterprising young sea captain, Matthew would someday inherit his father's Ashton Shipyards—and was probably one of the best catches in Newburyport. ''How dare he ask you and not me!''

Amy thought it fine time to interrupt before things degenerated into a cat fight. ''Perhaps Matthew will ask you next week, Mildred,'' she soothed.

Mildred turned on her. ''Just because your one and only friend on this earth happens to be Matthew's sister—that bad-mannered little hoyden, Mira—don't think that makes you an authority on Matthew.''

''Or an authority on men,'' added Ophelia.

''Amy? An authority on men?'' Mildred shrieked with laughter. ''The only men Amy might ever become an authority on are the sort that work along the docks and ogle her!''

Both Mildred and Ophelia guffawed, pitiless as Amy's cheeks reddened beneath their sooty glaze of ash smoke.

''I don't know how you can stand there and laugh, when Will's still not back from Uncle Eb's and for all we know, something awful might've happened to him,'' she said, thinking of the rider who had galloped through Newburyport late last night with the news that fighting had finally broken out down at Lexington and Concord between the redcoats and local militia groups. ''Cousin Tom was in the Woburn militia. They were in the fighting, and you know as well as I do that where Tom leads, Will is sure to follow.''

Her half-sisters stared at her coldly. ''My, my, aren't *we* the righteous one,'' sneered Mildred, hands on her hips. ''Instead of fretting over Will, why don't you worry about poor Ophelia and me *and let out my jacket*!''

"If she wasn't down at the harborfront dreaming of places she'll never go and men she'll never meet, she'd have gotten it done yesterday like she was supposed to,'' said Ophelia, with a haughty glance at the gaunt figure still on her knees on the ashy firebox. "You'd better get your head out of the clouds, Amy, because you have a better chance of snaring the moon than you do a respectable man, and don't you forget it.''

Amy went silently back to her chores. They were right, of course. She was wasting her time, dreaming about things that would never be. But how could she *not* dream, when reality was nothing but boredom and drudgery? She was resigned to the fact that she would live and die a spinster, just as she was resigned to the fact that, for the remainder of Papa's life, she—less than a daughter, yet more than a servant—would keep house for him, cook his meals, and help him write his sermons now that his eyesight was beginning to fail. In return, she would always have a place to live. Hers wasn't such a bad lot, really; after all, she had a roof over her head and decent food in her belly. But lately, she found herself wanting more, and long after the household went to bed, she would lie beneath the covers and dream of what her life would be like if only she were pretty and respectable like her sisters.

If only she was like the other young women of Newburyport, entitled to the same dreams that they had . . .

Finally, breakfast was ready. The Reverend Sylvanus Leighton, pale and haggard from an obviously sleepless night, joined them in the keeping room and gave thanks for the meal, adding a special prayer for Will's safe return. Then, painfully aware of the empty place that Amy had set for his one and only son, he stared dejectedly out the window. The cornmeal mush, fried to a rich, golden brown and cut into slices, lay undisturbed on his plate, floating in the maple syrup like boats at low tide.

Amy could not stand seeing him suffer so. She reached out and impulsively put a hand over his, knowing, even as she did, that he would probably pull away.

He did.

She drew her hand back and pasted a smile on her face to hide her hurt. Why should she have expected any different when it had always been this way? "Eat, Papa," she said gently, tucking the offending hand between her knees and trying to pretend the incident hadn't happened. "Starving yourself won't bring him back to us any sooner."

Ophelia snapped, "Maybe he *would* eat, if only he had some fresh butter for his breakfast—"

At that very moment, Will's dog Crystal—who'd been sulking ever since Will had left for Woburn to help Sylvanus's brother Ebenezer with the spring planting— shot out from beneath the table, and, paws skittering for purchase on the wide-boarded floor, tore through the parlor. Barking joyously, the dog flung herself against the door.

"Will!" Amy cried, leaping up and nearly upsetting the table as her half-brother ran inside, Crystal barking and tripping up his feet. All out of breath, he charged into the keeping room.

"Where have you been?" Sylvanus demanded, worry and relief making his voice harsh.

"Look at you, you're covered with dirt!" shrieked Ophelia.

"And *blood*!" wailed Mildred, clapping her hands to her cheeks.

"I was in the fighting yesterday," he panted, grabbing his father's hand and pulling him back toward the still-open door. "You've got to help me, Pa, got to send Amy to fetch the doctor! I brought a friend home with me and if we don't do something to save him, he's going to die!''

"Should've called the undertaker, not me,'' said Dr. Plummer, as he watched Sylvanus and Will carry the man through the door. "That young fellow's deader than dead.''

"He ain't either!'' cried Will, head twisted round to look behind him as, his arms locked beneath the stranger's armpits, he backed into the keeping room where Ophelia and Mildred, busily crunching bacon, gave shrieks of horror and leaped to their feet.

"William Leighton! How dare you bring that . . . that *man* into this house!'' they screeched. Neither rose to help, and neither moved their chairs out of the way to ease the trio's progress to the table.

That task fell to Amy, who did it hurriedly and without needing to be told. Standing back, she glanced anxiously at Will's friend as they brought him near. His hair, which had been combed back and tied at the nape with a black taffeta ribbon, had come loose and now hung in bloody swatches over his face, concealing all but the tip of his nose from Amy's curious gaze. He wore muddy breeches of white leather, and a sleeveless waistcoat of ragged olive-green homespun was loosely buttoned over a bloodstained shirt. His frame was lean, his build powerful, wide across the upper body, narrow at the waist and hips, and so long in the leg that she knew his feet would hang over the edge of the table when they set him down. Probably a farmer, she thought, accustomed to hard work.

But as they carried him past, his dangling hand brushed her skirts, and Amy's eyes went wide. No farmer *she'd* ever met had hands that looked like that. Long, elegant fingers. Clean skin devoid of dirt and

scars. Short, well-scrubbed nails that were filed smooth
and obviously well cared for.

Her gaze lifted to Will's—but he and Papa were already hoisting the fellow up onto the table. As they set
him down, the lolling head fell back over Will's arm
and revealed a face that took Amy's breath away. Her
hands flew over her mouth.

He was breathtakingly handsome.

Absolutely, positively, indisputably, beautiful.

Dr. Plummer, however, took no notice of the fact.
"What happened to him?" he asked, bending over the
man's face, lifting one eyelid and peering into the sightless, rolled-back eyes.

Blue, Amy thought, noting their extraordinarily clear
color before Plummer let the eyelid slide shut once
more. *Oh, God, don't let him die—with those looks, he'll
make all the beautiful angels in heaven envious and
there'll be war up there all over again.*

"He—he f-fell during the fighting and hit his head,"
Will stammered.

"How?"

The boy shrugged, his gaze darting away. "Don't
know."

"How long has he been out?"

"Since yesterday, when it happened."

"*Yesterday!?*"

Will reddened. "Y-yes, sir."

"This man should've been seen to immediately! Why
the devil didn't you get him to a local doctor instead of
lugging him all the way up here?"

For answer, the boy only swallowed and hung his
head. He looked absolutely miserable.

Ophelia, however, had no pity for either her brother
or his injured friend. "Really, Will, I don't know what's
got into you, bringing him here when you should've just
let him there to die. After all, America needs good, com-

petent men defending her, not clumsy oafs who injure themselves at first opportunity.''

"Maybe he injured himself so he wouldn't *have* to fight," scoffed Mildred. "The coward."

"He wasn't a coward!" Will exploded. "He was a fine man, with more courage than a dozen lions!!"

Dr. Plummer impatiently motioned for them to be quiet, then laid his finger on the injured man's wrist, feeling his pulse. He straightened up, frowning. "Well, he's alive all right, but if I can save him I doubt he'll be a-thankin' me for it. Come, come, let's turn him over so I can have a better look at the back of his head. What's your friend's name, anyhow?"

"Er, Adam. Adam Smith."

"Well, let's get Mr. Smith settled comfortably on his stomach with his head turned slightly to the left. Yes, that's good. Perfect. Now, someone get me a candle so I can better see what I'm a-doin' here."

Adam, his right cheek pressed against the oak table-top, did not look quite so handsome from the back. In fact, he looked downright terrible, and Amy gasped as they all got a good look at the wound that had felled him. Low down on the back of his head and slightly off center to the left, a gash, nearly three inches long, was still oozing blood out into the tangled blond hair and down his neck. Plummer drew his bushy brows together and began probing the wound. A moment later he straightened up, wiping bloody fingers on his leather apron.

"I'll have to trepan him," he declared. "His skull is fractured and chances are there's blood pooling just beneath the break. If we don't drain it off the brain, he'll die."

There was a temporary silence as everyone digested Plummer's words.

"Maybe we ought to just . . . let him die in peace,"

Will mumbled, his cheeks coloring as he heard the callousness of his own words. As Amy and Sylvanus turned horrified stares upon him, he added, lamely, "Especially since he isn't going to make it, anyhow . . ."

Plummer blew out his breath. "Well, Reverend?"

"I say trepan him—and let the decision rest with God, not us, as to whether he lives or dies."

"He won't be the same as he was before this happened to him," Plummer warned, resting a possessive, almost affectionate hand over the gaping wound as though he couldn't wait to get started on it. "You know that, don't you?"

"We have to give him the chance. After all, the poor fellow did do what he could for America, didn't he?"

Amy was the only one who saw her brother wince as though he'd been struck. Ophelia and Mildred were too busy making their exit. Sylvanus was still looking at the stranger. And Dr. Plummer was laying things out on the table: a linen rag, a razor, two long metal retractors with hooked ends, and the trephine—a small, ring-shaped saw with a handle in the center and deep, jagged teeth designed for grinding a small plug out of a person's skull. Amy looked at it and felt her knees go all wobbly.

Don't you dare get squeamish! she berated herself, fiercely. She gazed down at Adam, whose long eyelashes just brushed the table. Poor Adam with the blue, blue eyes that might never open again.

Her heart ached with pity for him. "I'll help you if you need me to, Dr. Plummer," she said quietly. "Just tell me what I have to do."

Five minutes later, Sylvanus, who couldn't stand the sight of blood, made his excuses and Amy found herself pressed into service. Under Plummer's direction, she fetched a bowl of warm water and a pillow from her bed while Plummer went outside to have a few pulls on his pipe—no doubt to steady his own nerves, Amy thought.

Racing back downstairs, she gently lifted Adam's head, put the pillow beneath it, and then eased him back down so that his brow was cradled on soft down instead of oak. Involuntarily, her hand smoothed the hair back from his temple, as though she could comfort and encourage him for the ordeal that lay ahead; then she dampened a rag and washed the wound, trying not to look at the blood and water running in halting pink streams through his pale hair.

Plummer returned, rolling up his sleeves and grimly eyeing his patient as though trying to determine the best way to approach the task ahead of him. Amy's heart began to pound with apprehension.

"Stand at the head of the table, Amy, and put your hands on either side of his head to steady it," the doctor directed. "Good." Wiping the razor on the leg of his breeches, he shaved the area around the wound with as much skill as any barber. Amy watched the soft clumps of hair tumbling forlornly down over her knuckles, falling on the pillow, the table, the floor. Finally Plummer set the blade aside. "There. That ought to do it. Now, brace his head real steady, Amy, and don't let it move." And then, noting her pallor, he added, "You don't have to watch if you don't want to."

She didn't want to—but she could no more look away than she could stop breathing. It was as though by finding the courage to watch, she was somehow going through this ordeal right along with him. To look away and abandon Adam to such a thing, to allow him to suffer it all by himself, seemed cowardly. She would be brave—for him. And so she held his head and held up her own and forced herself to take deep, steadying breaths as she watched Plummer draw his scalpel and make his first cut. As the doctor progressed, first with scalpel and then with the trephine, Amy found herself gently talking to the unconscious man as though she could somehow soothe him.

"He'll not hear you," Plummer grunted, leaning his weight into the trephine and rotating it, "but if it makes you feel better, go ahead and talk to him."

"It *does* make me feel better. And maybe he *can* hear me . . . after all, who's to say that he can't?"

"What a fanciful girl you are," Plummer said, amused. "But the best assistant I ever had. Now, keep your wits about you. We're almost there."

Amy no longer wanted to look. She squeezed her eyes shut and locked her knees together and it was then, as she stood there holding so tightly onto Adam's head that her arms began to ache, that she noticed his breathing had changed. Her eyes flew open.

"Dr. Plummer?"

"For God's sake, girl, not now."

"His breathing—it doesn't sound the way it did a moment ago . . ."

Still gripping the trephine, Plummer paused only long enough to note that Amy was correct.

"Tarnal hell, I'm losing him."

Amy, fingers entwined in Adam's hair to better anchor his head, the terrible grinding vibrations of the trephine coming up through her palms, shut her eyes and prayed like she never had in all her seventeen years. *Please don't die*, she begged silently, pressing her palms to Adam's ears and willing her own life into his fading body, *please, please, don't die . . .*

But Adam's soft respirations were coming more and more slowly, growing ineffective, growing faint.

Please God. Oh, please, give him a chance, I beg of you—

"Pay attention there, Amy!" barked Plummer, his upper lip beaded with sweat as he tossed the trephine down on the table. It began to roll away. Impatiently he slammed it back down. The trephine rolled again, this time falling off the table and hitting the floor. Plummer swore and left it there. And now Adam was no longer taking shallow little breaths, but gasping desperately, trying to draw air into his dying lungs. Tears stung Amy's eyes, burned in her sinuses. She had seen fish in buckets die like that; to see a man going the same route, especially one as strong and handsome as this one, filled her with an unbearable agony.

"The devil take it," Plummer swore, grabbing up the scalpel and prying the plug of bone loose. "Damnation!"

And now even the erratic gasps were coming slower and slower. Amy sniffed back the tears. Oh, God help her, this was awful, awful, awful—

"Come on, damn you, breathe!" Plummer all but yelled, his voice rising in urgency as Adam gave a final, heavy sigh and fell still. He watched the trickle of red, red blood oozing up and out of the gaping wound. *"Breathe!"*

But as each moment filed past, Adam did not move, did not breathe, and Plummer's frozen, rapt expression began to melt into despair. He stood staring down at his patient, hands clenched and a myriad emotions crossing his face, before his shoulders finally sank and, looking haggard and old, he swore beneath his breath and turned away in defeat.

"Call in the undertaker, then," he said bitterly. "I've lost him."

Chapter 2

⌒⌒⌒○○○⌒⌒⌒

Will fled. Plummer wiped his brow and trudged off to tell Sylvanus the bad news.

And Amy was left alone with Adam.

She stood there with him for what seemed like a long time, her hands caught in his bloody hair, her palms still pressed to his ears as though she could keep the life from leaving him. As she stared down at his body, its fragile warmth still caught between her hands, its still face buried in her pillow, her throat closed on a harsh sob. He couldn't be dead, he just couldn't, he was too young, too strong, too handsome—

But he was.

Gently turning his head and coming around to his side, she bent, bringing her cheek to his cheek, her temple to his temple, and let the tears come.

And it was then, with her damp face pressed to his, that she felt the tremulous fluttering of a pulse, soft as a butterfly's wings, beating in his temple.

She pulled back.

"Adam?" she whispered, barely daring to speak.

Another moment passed. And then his shoulders rose on an inhalation of Herculean proportions, rising up, up, up, only to settle back down on an equally huge exhalation.

"Breathe, Adam! Oh, please, breathe!" And then, when he didn't, Amy put her lips next to his ear and yelled, straight into his head, "*Breathe!*"

Adam breathed. Plummer came charging back in, Sylvanus right behind him. Seeing the rise and fall of Adam's shoulders, Plummer hurried forward, opening his bag as he went. Adam was coming back to life— literally—beneath Amy's bloodstained fingers. She returned to the head of the table, put her cheek next to his, and unable to contain her excitement, unable to stop the tears from coursing down her face, coached each slow, gathering breath by matching it to her own.

"Breathe . . . breathe . . . breathe . . ."

Each respiration was stronger than the last. Whispering words of encouragement, Amy stroked the sides of Adam's head with her thumbs, marvelling at the strength and will of a man who could come through what this one just had, and live. She looked up at the doctor and laughed with joy.

"Oh, Dr. Plummer—you did it, he's breathing!"

"*We* did it," he corrected with a wry smile, and reaching into his bag, extracted a handful of lint. He was just pulling off a wad of it when tremors began moving through Adam's body, ending in twitches of his fingers, a jerk of one leg.

"What's wrong with him now?" Amy cried in alarm.

"Nothing." The doctor smiled. "He's just waking up."

"Waking up?"

"Yes. Once I took the pressure off his brain by releasing the blood clot, it's only natural that he regain consciousness. That is, if God wanted him to live."

"Obviously, God *does* want him to live!"

A groan of pain came from deep within the pillow.

Quickly, the doctor plugged the wound with lint and threaded his needle, preparing to stitch it shut. Adam was flexing his fingers now. Trying, weakly, to raise his head. Plummer pulled the wound shut, pinched it with one finger, and stabbed the needle through.

Adam's whole body jerked, his hand flailing blindly before hitting Plummer's wrist with nearly enough force to break it. The needle went flying, only to be yanked back by the thread. Plummer let out a curse, and Adam began thrashing about.

Amy couldn't hold him down.

"Keep him still, Amy!"

She threw her full weight across him, trying desperately to restrain him. He fell back to the table, struggling, as both Will and Sylvanus added their weight. Her heart pounding, Amy leaned down and put her lips against Adam's ear. "It's all right," she soothed. "You're going to be just fine, but you have to be still! We're not trying to hurt you. I know how frightened you must be, but the doctor must do this in order to save your life."

A muffled groan came from deep within the pillow.

"Dr. Plummer?"

"What, Amy?"

"He's suffocating; can we at least let him turn his head so he can breathe?"

Plummer pushed back. "Aye, go on."

Gently lifting Adam's head, Amy turned it so that his right cheek lay on the pillow. The pale blue eyes were wide and staring, the handsome face flushed and damp with sweat. "Just give him a moment," Amy pleaded, noting Plummer's impatient scowl. She dipped the rag in clean water and tenderly wiped Adam's cheek and brow. "That's not too much to ask, is it?"

Plummer nodded his assent and allowed Sylvanus to draw him off into the parlor. No sooner had they left than Amy noticed Will, his face like paste, standing nearby.

"Will, what *is* the matter?"

"Nothing," he whispered, staring down at his friend. "Nothing a'tall."

Amy gave him a sharp glance, then returned her attention to the man who lay on the table. "It's all right, Adam," she murmured, stroking the damp hair that still adorned all but the back of his head. "Just relax."

Adam stared fixedly at the wall, his lips just grazing the bloodstained pillow. "Not Adam . . . Charles."

It came out *Chaaahles*, on a deep and startlingly elegant drawl that left the "r" from the name and marked him as anything but the rebel they'd all assumed him to be.

Amy's jaw dropped open and, horrified, she whirled to stare at her brother. "He's a—"

"Redcoat." Will went green and shot a terrified glance at the door through which the doctor had just passed. "An officer, if you must know." He hugged his arms to himself and stared at Amy, his lower lip thrust out, his eyes both fearful and defiant. He looked like the frightened child he was. "What would you have me do, leave him out in a field to die?"

Amy, paling, grabbed Will by the sleeve. "Do you realize what you've *done*?"

Will looked as though he were about to cry. "Now you know why I was half-hoping he wouldn't make it."

"Why on earth did you bring him home?"

"I felt guilty."

"For heaven's *sake*, Will!"

Beneath them, the officer lay quietly on the table. In despair, Amy realized he must've heard every word— and known they were his enemy, long before they could say the same about him. Lying gravely wounded and separated from his countrymen, his army, and everything familiar to him, helpless and at the mercy of the very people who'd declared themselves to be his enemy, he must be terrified. Waking up to what he had, he probably thought they were practicing some wicked torture on him.

She touched his brow and gently smoothed his hair back. "Charles."

"Oh, Juliet, forgive me," he whispered—and hooking an arm around Amy's neck, pulled her roughly down against him. Caught off balance and completely off guard, Amy all but tumbled across his chest. As she flung out an arm to stop her fall, his lips found hers, and in the next moment, he was kissing her with a desperate passion, one arm locked around her back like a vise.

Will ripped her from his embrace. "Don't you touch my sister, you damned lobsterback, you!"

"Will!" Amy cried. "Can't you see he's mistaken me for someone else? Leave him be, he's clearly out of his head!"

"Juliet . . ." The officer sounded confused, groggy, his voice rising in worry. "Juliet, where am I?"

With a nervous glance toward the door, Amy leaned down to whisper in his ear. "Listen—" Her cheeks were flushed, her pulse pounding madly; heaven help her, her legs were weaker now than they'd been all during the surgery! "I don't know who this Juliet is, but I'm not her. I'm Amy. *Amy.* Can you understand that?"

He hesitated. "Amy?"

"Yes, Amy. Now listen to me. We're rebels and you're a king's officer, and you must say nothing to the doctor about who you are or it'll be the end of us all!"

"I am not . . . such a fool as that," he murmured thickly. "But if you would be so kind . . . as to bring me a candle . . . I shall take great comfort in being able to see you."

Amy exchanged glances with Will. The candle was three feet away from his staring eyes.

"You see, it is frightfully dark in here . . . and I . . . I am afraid . . . that your doctor cannot see what he's doing."

Will blurted, "But the candle *is*—"

Amy clapped her hand over Will's mouth and slowly shook her head from side to side, warning him not to say any more.

"Don't worry, Charles," she said gently. "When the doctor comes back, I'm sure he'll have a candle for you to see by."

His hand found hers and pulled it down to his lips. "You . . . my dear angel . . . are a great comfort to me."

"Amy, quick, Plummer's coming back!" Will cried.

"All right, let's get this over with," muttered the doctor, composed once more as he and Sylvanus strode back into the room. "At this rate I'll be here 'til dinnertime."

Amy pulled her hand from Charles's. Then, with gentle pressure, she guided his head back to center so that his brow lay once more in the cradle of the pillow, which she adjusted so that he could breathe. A redcoat. Not just *any* redcoat, but an officer who was probably, judging by those beautifully groomed hands and the elegant cadences to his speech, a member of the upper ruling classes, no doubt with blood as blue as his eyes. God help them! What were they going to do?

But injured though he was, he had enough presence of mind not to betray himself or the two youngest Leightons by speaking in front of Plummer—and for that Amy uttered a silent prayer of relief. He didn't move a muscle as the doctor resumed stitching up the wound, merely suffering his fate with stoic resolve and never realizing that just above him, Amy was reliving that brief, desperate kiss that he had claimed. He never saw her flushed cheeks, never knew that her tongue had come out to touch and taste the lips that he had mistakenly claimed. And in that moment Amy, remembering his hard strength, the roughness of his cheek against her own, suddenly wished that *she* was the owner of the name he had uttered . . .

Juliet.

She was daydreaming again. Mentally chastising herself as Plummer tied off the last stitch, Amy realized that the splendid body beneath her had relaxed, seeming to sink down into the table as the officer fell unconscious once more.

His irrepressible strength had finally failed him.

Two minutes later, it was all over, and the poor ravaged head was wrapped in a bandage and left to rest on the bloodstained pillow. With a trembling sigh of relief, Amy bade Dr. Plummer goodbye and watched as Sylvanus walked him to the door, thanking him for his services and resting a hand on the doctor's shoulder.

Then she turned to Will.

"You, my brother, have some explaining to do," she murmured, and taking his arm, hustled him outside.

Chapter 3

From far, far away, Charles became aware of the smell of wood smoke, coming to him through the darkness in which he lay. He wasn't sure if it was a dream or not. It was a pleasant smell, maybe cherry, maybe apple they were burning, and he could hear the sizzling snap of the log, feel its warmth hot and dry against his face.

Eyes shut, he lay there on his stomach facing the fire, floating in a state that wasn't quite sleep, wasn't quite wakefulness. Back and forth between the two he drifted. He sensed the passage of time, and people around him, and more time passing, and someone tending to him. He slept. He dreamed. And eventually consciousness came within reach, teasing him with its elusiveness, flitting away, floating ever nearer until he was able to wade his way into the midst of it.

"Billingshurst?" he whispered, calling for his batman.

Silence.

"Billingshurst . . . where are you?"

But there was no Billingshurst, nothing familiar, no one here. Charles raised his head, only to suck in his breath in agony. Stabbing pain lanced his skull, as though he had a hundred hangovers all concentrated into one killer headache, but that made no sense to him at all. He liked a glass of port or sherry once in a while, or even an ale with the villagers back home in Ravenscombe, but he, unlike his younger brother Gareth, wasn't a three-bottle man.

Confused, he tried to make sense of things. There was a thin mattress beneath his body, and beneath that, a hard floor. Thirst ravaged his mouth, and a host of scents invaded his nostrils; drying herbs and baking bread, a pudding boiling in a pot, and over everything, a heady wash of tar, fish, tidal marshes, and clean salt air. He heard the distant tolling of a church bell and wondered if it was Sunday. Or who had died. Or if he had perhaps died, and this was what hell felt like.

"Billingshurst . . . anyone . . . oh-h-h-h, *damn*."

Nothing but the chattering of a flock of sparrows somewhere outside.

He turned onto his side, his shirt bunching and twisting beneath him. There was a blanket covering his body, a pillow beneath his ear, and a strange, naked chill against the back of his aching head. And yes, he could feel the blazing warmth of the fire against his face, making the skin feel tight and dry—

But he could not see it.

He opened his eyes.

And still could not see it.

He ignored the sudden butterflies in his stomach and chastised himself for a fool.

I am dreaming. Something monstrous has happened to me, and if I lie here long enough, I shall remember what it is . . . meanwhile I shall close my eyes and go back to sleep, and when I wake everything will be as it was, with Billingshurst shaking my shoulder to rouse me for the day. Yes, I shall just go back to sleep, and when

I wake, everything will be just as it should be.

He drew the blanket over his head. He was probably just having a nightmare. It would pass soon. Until then, he would rein his mind into obedience and force himself to think of things that brought him comfort and happiness. England . . . his family . . . and Juliet, whose eyes had filled with joyous tears when he'd got down on his knee and asked her to marry him. Had it only been last night? How far away it seemed now, almost as though it had never happened—but he could feel the empty place on his finger where his signet ring should have been, and saw again, in his mind's eye, the way her hand had trembled when he'd taken the ring off his own finger, slid it over hers, and then brought her finger to his mouth and kissed it. He thought of the joy on her face, the twang of her colonial accent, and the baby she would give him in a mere six months. That was the only part of the whole thing that seemed unreal, but he knew it couldn't be: after all, the baby was the reason he'd asked her to marry him, wasn't it? Marrying her so that she would have a husband, and the baby, a name, had been the right thing to do.

And Charles always did the right thing.

God help him, but his head hurt. It hurt so badly that the pain was shimmying down the back of his neck and spine, seeping into his gut even, and making him feel faintly nauseous. This was no dream. It wasn't even a nightmare. It was worse. He wished he could go back to sleep, but that blissful state eluded him, and the consciousness he had fought so hard to reach now held him securely in its grasp and would not let him go.

And now footfalls approached, reverberating beneath his ear. They were soft and tentative, making a board squeak here and there but otherwise trying to pass behind him without disturbing him. Charles tensed, eyes open and staring into the gloom beneath the blanket as he waited for the unknown person to continue on. He felt exposed. Caught off guard. Defenseless.

The footsteps stopped. Then they continued toward him, very slowly, very carefully. He sensed the person's nearness as he—or she—crouched down behind him and put a hand on his blanket-clad shoulder.

It was a she. He could tell that just by the softness of the hand and the sharp, sweet scent of something—bayberry, was it?—that drifted from her clothing as she knelt.

"Are you awake?" the "she" asked, proving her gender without a doubt.

She sounded much like Juliet; same provincial drawl, same inflections to her speech and the way she pronounced her words. But her voice was of a slightly lower pitch, soft and a little breathy. It wasn't Juliet. His heart fell.

"Yes," he murmured.

She hooked her fingers over the edge of the blanket and slowly pulled it down over his shoulder. He threw an arm across his eyes, unwilling to face the truth. She touched his cheek, and impatiently, irritably, he shrugged her off. If she wasn't Juliet, she had no business touching him.

"My name's Amy," she said gently. "Amy Leighton. I've been taking care of you for the last week. Do you remember me?"

Amy . . . Amy . . . He frowned, trying to recall a memory that was just beyond his grasp. "I . . . I am unsure."

"You woke for a little while this morning and spoke to me then."

"I . . . do not remember."

"Do you recall the surgery, then?"

"No."

"What about your name?"

He didn't answer.

"Please, sir, can you tell me you name?"

He groaned, the expenditure of even this much mental energy taxing him beyond the limits of his strength. "I . . . would rather not."

She pulled the blanket back up to his shoulder and said gently, "I already know that you're a king's officer who fell during the fighting near Concord."

"And *I* know that you're a Yankee . . . probably a rebel."

"Yes. But that doesn't mean we want to harm you, keep you prisoner here, or make you suffer any more than you already have. Heaven knows you've been through enough. We're good people, sir, and wish only to restore you to health." The girl paused a moment, as though having a difficult time trying to decide what to tell him next. "Please—you suffered a terrible injury. I only want you to tell me your name so I can be assured that you are . . . well, functioning as you should be."

"Miss Leighton . . . I am very weak. My head aches. It hurts to think, even. Hurts even more to speak. I . . . I am not up to an interrogation."

"I'm sorry, I didn't mean to be thoughtless. I was just concerned, and, well, anxious after your well-being . . ." Her hand briefly touched his shoulder, then she pulled back, away from him. "Shall I leave you to sleep, then?"

"I suspect I . . . have probably slept enough." He lay there, drained of strength, his eyes pinned shut beneath the weight of his arm. "How long was I out?"

"Eight days."

"Eight *days*!"

"The doctor said you were in a coma."

He lay there, too weak to even think about all that must've gone on in those eight days since tensions had finally exploded between the army and the Yankees.

"And where am I?"

"Newburyport, about forty miles north of Boston."

That made no sense at all to him. His memory struggled to piece together the maps he had seen of the colony. Wasn't Newburyport on the seacoast, and a significant distance from both Concord and Boston at that? If he'd fallen at Concord, what the devil was he doing up here?

She accurately interpreted his silence for confusion. "My brother was in the fighting at Concord, too. He brought you home to us after you were injured," she explained. "This is where we live. My father's the minister of the Church of All Souls."

"I . . . see," he murmured, not quite seeing at all. Who were these people? Why wasn't he with the troops in Boston? What the blazes was going on here? He lay there for a moment, arm still draped over his eyes, trying to make sense of things that made no sense at all.

"Will you tell me your name, sir?"

Oh, bugger it. She was a persistent little thing, and he was of no mind or strength to resist her determination. "Charles," he rasped, turning over onto his back. "Charles Adair de Montforte." And then, hoping to head off any more questions he was too weak to answer, he added, "I was born in the year 1752, my home is in Berkshire, England, and I am a captain of infantry in the Fourth Foot." He paused, exhausted simply by the effort of speaking. "Does that satisfy you that I am still in control of my faculties, madam?"

"Oh yes," she breathed, and he heard the smile and relief in her voice. "Oh yes, indeed!"

But Charles was beginning to fear that he didn't have much to smile about. He had yet to open his eyes. And he wanted to be alone when he did.

"I . . . am grateful to you for your kindness, Miss Leighton, but I feel frightfully unwell, and I would like to be left alone for a while."

Silence.

"That is, if you do not mind."

"Are you going to go back to sleep?"

"No, I shall get up and stretch my legs, I think."

"Then . . . I don't think I'd better leave you. Not yet, anyhow. You might need me."

Need her? How presumptuous—he didn't *need* anyone. Irritated, he lowered his arm from his face, pushed himself up on one elbow—

And saw nothing. Just darkness that was like a night without stars, a well without bottom, a horrible expanse of nothingness without depth, without texture, without anything.

Charles went very, very still. Everything inside of him—his heartbeat, the course of blood through his veins, his very thoughts, even, seemed to stop.

"Miss Leighton?"

"I'm here."

"Why can't I see you?" he asked, greatly confused. "Why can't I see this fire I feel against my face, or the birds I hear outside, or this room in which I find myself? Is there something in my eyes?" His looked around, stunned. "By God, woman, what has happened to me?"

He heard the rustle of her skirts, smelled bayberry as she knelt down beside him and took his suddenly cold hand within her own. He rubbed his eyes and stared, blinking, into the blackness, trying to see beyond it. But it was there when he turned his head to the right. It was there when he turned his head to the left. It was there when he opened his eyes as wide as they would go and looked where she should be, and it was there no matter where he directed his open, staring gaze. A deep, involuntary shudder drove through him, and cold sweat broke out all along his spine, turning his insides to ice. He yanked his hand from hers and reached blindly up and out into the darkness.

"There is nothing wrong with your eyes, Charles," she said quietly. "You fell and hit your head on a rock and were left for dead. My brother went back after the fighting passed, saw that you were alive, and brought you home to us, thinking you could be saved." Her voice grew even more gentle. "The doctor has been visiting every day . . . he warned us that if you ever woke at all, it was likely you might not be able to see . . . that your eyes would be fine, but your brain might not be able to tell what they were seeing. Does that make sense to you? It doesn't to me, but then, I'm not a doctor . . ."

"No. No, I cannot accept this . . ."

"You had a blood clot beneath your skull, and the doctor said that if he didn't release it, you'd die. He had to trepan you." Again, she took his hand, squeezing fingers gone as cold as marble. "I'm sorry. We did everything that could be done."

"This—this is unreal, it cannot have happened to me, there is no room in my life for this!"

"Is there anything I can do? Anyone I can contact, write a letter to, summon for you?"

"No—dear God, no . . ."

"Please, calm down," the girl murmured, her hand stroking his shoulder as he stared blindly about him. "You've had a terrible shock and now you must rest, get your strength back—"

"Get my strength back? For what? I'm blind, *blind*, what the hell good am I if I can't *see*?!" He lunged to his feet, pushing this way and that with his hands in a frantic attempt to get his bearings. He took a step, lost his balance and fell, crashing heavily to the floor. There he lay, fighting the panic, the emotions that were rushing down on him.

"Shhhh. It's all right." She was there, crouching down beside him, her irritating little hand on his arm, his back, stroking him as though he was a baby. Soft fingers brushed the hair off his forehead, rubbed the back of his neck in a sweet, soothing motion. "Just be still. You're not alone. I'm here."

He was sharply aware of the floorboards, hard beneath his cheek and smelling faintly of dust and pine. He was embarrassingly aware of the fact he wore only a long, nearly knee-length shirt. And he was very aware of her hand, soothing him, stroking him. Normally he would have resented such womanly coddling—even from Juliet—but in his shock and grief he was powerless to do anything but lie there and allow it.

The girl Amy tried to put a hand on his shoulder in comfort.

"Leave me!" he said hoarsely, embarrassed by his shameful display and angrily twitching his shoulder to throw her off. He buried his face in his hands. "Oh, please, just go away and leave me to die."

The girl said nothing, which made him all the more angry, all the more afraid, all the more frustrated by his sudden helplessness. He hated himself for it. Hated himself for this shocking loss of control. But most of all, he hated himself for what had happened to him because it was, after all, his own damned fault.

Cruel, cruel memory! He remembered the boy jumping out and shooting at him. He remembered jerking his musket up at the last moment so that he wouldn't kill the lad, and then losing his balance, falling backwards and hitting something so hard that a million lights had exploded in his head. What a clumsy fool he was. What an inept excuse for a soldier. He'd always wanted to go out in a blaze of glory. Well, he'd gone out, all right.

In a blaze of humiliation.

Sitting up, he gazed miserably into the darkness, trying to get used to it and knowing he never could. *Imagine, an entire life with nothing before you but this. No light, ever again. No colors, ever again. No faces of*

*those you love, no knowledge of what your baby will
look like, no career, no future, no independence, nothing.*

He took a deep, shaky, bracing breath.

Ever again.

Outside, the sparrows were still chattering; for them,
for the girl beside him, for just about everything on
God's earth, life went on as usual. How could everything
be so complete and utterly normal, when for him, things
would never be the same?

He heard liquid pouring into a vessel of some sort,
and then the girl's voice, subdued, sympathetic.

"Here, drink this. It'll make you feel better."

"Nothing will make me feel better."

"Please, Captain. I know you've had a shock, but you
should be grateful that you're alive."

"Grateful? *Grateful?* Did it ever occur to you that I'd
prefer to be dead?"

"I'm sorry. I . . . I cannot imagine what you must feel,
right now."

"Indeed, you cannot. I am a captain in the King's
Own. I had a fine career, people who depended on me,
and the sweetest girl in Boston just accepted my hand
in marriage. Now I doubt whether I can so much as feed
myself without mishap—let alone lead my troops into
battle or suffice as anything resembling a husband or a
father. No, madam, you cannot imagine what I feel right
now. You cannot imagine it at all."

"But these are early days."

"Right. Early days. I suppose the doctor thinks I will
recover my sight tomorrow, eh?"

"The doctor thought you'd never wake up. The fact
that you have is a miracle in itself."

"You will understand if I don't quite consider it a
miracle."

He dug the heels of his hands into his eyes, and rested

his head thus, his fingers splaying up through hair that felt thick and disgustingly greasy. His fingertips encountered a bald spot, and, pushing his hand further back and over his crown, he discovered that an area the size of his fist had been shaved, and was now cloaked with soft, downy fuzz.

And there—*ouch*—stitches, swelling, soreness. Ah, yes. Of course. They would've had to shave his hair off in order to cut a plug of bone out of his skull. The very idea was horrifying. Bitterly, he wondered if he'd lost his sight before the doctor—no doubt some inept, ignorant provincial—had got to him, or after.

Despondently, he asked, "What happened after Concord?"

She gave a heavy sigh. "Your army retreated to Boston, suffering heavy casualties along the way. The countryside is still in an uproar, post riders have been racing through, and God only knows what will happen next." She paused. "Would you like something to eat?"

"No."

"A little water to drink, then?"

"I do not want anything."

"But you must be hungry . . . thirsty . . ."

"Please, child. Just leave me alone."

He needed to grieve in privacy, to try to come to terms with what had happened to him, to think what to do next. He needed to contact his commanding officer, Lieutenant Colonel Maddison; he needed to get a letter off to Lucien in England; and oh, God, he needed Juliet. Badly. He dug his knuckles into his eyes to stop the sudden threat of tears. Oh, so very, very badly—

He wiped a hand over his face, and as he did, his elbow hit the tankard the girl was just bringing up, sloshing its contents all down his chin and neck.

Charles's temper, normally under as tight a control as everything else about him, exploded.

"Plague take it, woman, just leave me the devil alone! I am in torment enough without someone trying to nanny me!"

"I'm only trying to help—"

"Then go away and leave me be, damn you!" he roared, plowing his fingers into his hair and gathering great hunks of it in his fists. "Go away, go away, *go away!*"

Stunned silence. And then he heard her get to her feet.

"I'm sorry, Captain de Montforte. I guess I should have realized that you'd need time to come to terms with what's happened to you." A pause. "I'll leave this jug of hard cider next to you in case you get thirsty. It's not as potent as rum, but maybe it'll let you escape from your troubles for a while." Her voice had lost its sparkle, and Charles knew then—much to his own dismay and self-loathing—that she was a sensitive little thing beneath that cheerfulness, and that he'd hurt her feelings. He suddenly felt like a monster, especially when her voice faltered and she said, "I'll be just across the room, peeling vegetables for supper . . . if you need anything, just call and I'll be right there."

She walked away, and he dug the heels of his hands into his useless eyes and let self-disgust consume him. With vivid clarity, he saw the face of his brother and heard again the words with which Lucien had proudly seen him off to America: "*Godspeed then, Charles, and return to us crowned in laurels. You are a de Montforte. I expect nothing less than glory from you. Especially from you.*"

Laurels. Glory. He hadn't even seen proper action. He bit savagely down on the inside of his cheek and felt sick with shame, for he had never failed anyone before.

Ever.

Now, he'd failed not only his family, but his country, his reputation, his men. He had ruined his life and nearly killed a young boy as well. It was beyond unbearable. He tried to block out his last, painful memories, but all he could see was poor Ensign Gillard charging into that rebel-held pasture and straight toward his death.

Over and over again.

Behind him, he heard the sound of a pail being set down on the floor, and then the rapid *scrape-scrape-scrape* of a knife over vegetables.

He remained where he was, suffering in silence.

The scraping went on. Stopped. Became a rapid *chop-chop-chop*. Stopped. There was the sound of vegetables being tossed into a pot. More scraping. More chopping . . .

And absolutely nothing from the girl.

With a weary sigh, he lay down on the pallet and pulled the blanket back over his shoulders. "My apologies, Miss Leighton. You are kinder than I deserve, and my anger is not with you, but myself."

He heard the thunk of more vegetables landing in the pot. "There's no need to apologize, Captain. After what's happened to you, no one's expecting you to behave as you normally would."

"Had I behaved as I 'normally would,' I would not be in this predicament," he said bitterly. "Furthermore, it is humiliating to find myself so dependent on people who are not only unknown to me, but who owe me nothing."

"You are wrong, Captain. We owe you everything."

"I am a 'redcoat,' Miss Leighton. No longer your protector, but your enemy."

"And I am the sister of a fourteen-year-old boy who thought war was the way to prove his manhood. *He* was the one who shot at you, Captain de Montforte. He was the one whose life you could have snuffed out in a heartbeat, but decided instead to spare at the last moment, and for that, sir, we owe you *everything*."

"You mean to tell me that your *brother* was the one who—"

He broke off as a door slammed and sudden, impatient footfalls reverberated across distant floorboards.

"Amy? Amy, where are you?" shrilled a young woman's voice.

He heard Amy catch her breath; a second later the footfalls stormed into the room.

"Amy! Oh, there you are, tending to that horrible drain upon our resources again. I wish he'd just hurry up and die so that you'd get back to *our* needs. I told you I needed you to dress my hair since I'm going out this afternoon, but you haven't even got out the curling iron, have you?"

"I've been busy with other things, Ophelia."

"Yes, that stupid oaf Will dragged in! *I want you to fix my hair!*"

"And *I* want her to get supper going!" snapped another female, her voice as sharp and impatient as the first. "Here it is, nearly three o'clock, and you *still* haven't collected the eggs, made the beds, or even started the stew—"

"I'm doing it now—"

"You aren't either, you're down here fawning over your pet man again!"

"And why not, he's the only one she's ever likely to get!"

"Why don't you get yourself a dog instead, Amy? At least you'll get some response!"

Vicious laughter rang out and Charles, who hadn't moved, felt Amy's humiliation as keenly as if it were his own. His heart started a slow, angry *tha-dump*, and his fists clenched involuntarily as he stared into a fire he could not see.

"Please, stop," he heard her plead. "You don't know what you're saying—"

"But I know what I'm seeing. Always got your silly head in the clouds, haven't you? I'll bet you're sitting down here daydreaming, gazing at that useless creature and pretending he's your suitor!"

"Ha! That sure does explain why she's barely left his side, doesn't it? You know you're scraping the bottom of the barrel when you have to start pretending someone who's too senseless to know any different is your lover, ha ha ha!"

Charles had had enough. He raised himself on one elbow. "I *beg* your pardon?"

Behind him came a shriek and a splintering crash as one of the two newcomers dropped something to the floor.

"Heaven above, he *spoke*!"

Charles kept his back toward them so they couldn't see his blindness. "Yes, I believe I did," he said in his frostiest drawl. "I also believe I heard you maligning this dear angel in a way she does not deserve."

He could sense Amy's cringing embarrassment.

The two females were speechless with shock.

"Will you not apologize to her?" he asked with deadly softness.

"Apologize? *To Amy?* Whatever for?"

"Captain, please—my sisters, they . . . they don't know what they're saying."

"The devil they don't. You deserve an apology from these two termagants and I will see that you get one."

"Termagants?! How *dare* you!" Angry footsteps came right up behind him. "Just who do you think you are, anyhow? Imposing on us, partaking of our Christian charity and now putting on airs and insulting us! Why, just listen to that impossibly fancy accent of his, Mildred! He thinks he's above himself!"

"Thinks he's above *us*!" cried the other, mimicking Charles's expensively educated, aristocratic speech. "So where *are* you from, anyhow? Regardless of what Will said, I can tell right now that you're no farmer, and you're not from Woburn, either!''

"You are correct. I'm no farmer, and I am not from Woburn.''

"Who are you, then? Answer me!'' The girl stamped her foot. "*Answer me now!*''

"No! Don't tell them!'' gasped Amy.

"Shut up!'' snarled the one called Ophelia, and Charles heard the sharp crack of a hand meeting flesh, and Amy's cry of pain. Everything inside of him went cold with a deep, black rage. How dare they hurt her. *How dare they.*

His back toward them all, he summoned his strength and rose slowly to his feet.

"You tell us who you are right now or I'm going to go get Papa!''

Charles kept rising, the blanket sliding off his shoulders, too angry to care that he wore nothing but this long shirt.

"You're not even from around here, are you? *Are you?*''

"How very astute you are. For a provincial, that is.''

"You're as much a provincial as we are!''

He laughed softly. "I think not.''

"What?''

"Go get your father.'' And then, when no one moved, "*Now.*''

The girl fled the room. "Papa!'' she cried in a piercing shriek that made Charles's head ache all the more. "*Pa-paaa!*''

Sylvanus, sitting outside beneath an apple tree and trying to work out a theme for Sunday's sermon, jerked his head up as Ophelia, bawling like a cow needing to be milked, came flying to the open door. Raising his eyes to God in a silent plea for patience, he put down his notes.

"For the love of heaven, what's going on in there?"

For answer, she burst into tears and ran back inside.

Sylvanus abandoned his sermon and followed, dragging his feet all the way. The first person he saw was Amy, hands steepled over her mouth. She stared at him like a rabbit caught in a snare, and it was then that he saw Ophelia and Mildred near the keeping room fireplace and shrinking back from—

Praise the Lord! Will's friend was conscious and on his feet. His spine, as straight as the back of a pew, faced them all, and his bearing was one of pride, outrage, and the sort of well-bred elan not often found amongst people of Sylvanus's acquaintance. Barely able to contain his excitement, Sylvanus came up behind him.

"Ah, Mr. Smith, thank the Lord you're awake! Will is going to be absolutely delighted that his friend has finally returned to the land of the living!"

The young man's profile was severe, his jaw clenched with impatience as he fixed his gaze straight ahead. "Will?"

"Yes, Will! Don't you remember?"

"I beg your pardon, sir, but I am not acquainted with anyone named Will, and my surname is certainly not *Smith.*"

Sylvanus blinked, slightly undone by the anger in the man's tone. "Well, of course it is . . . Will said so himself . . ."

"What *madness* have I woken to?" The stranger pressed his fingertips to his temples, as though his patience with the lot of them had finally reached its end. "My name, sir, is Lord Charles Adair de Montforte. I am a captain in His Majesty's army, my home is in Berkshire, England, and my brother Lucien is the fifth and current duke of Blackheath.'' The proud head turned to regard him, the clear blue eyes staring straight over Sylvanus's right shoulder and through the wall behind him. "And who, pray tell, are *you?*"

Chapter 4

A redcoat. A *blind* redcoat. A blind, *aristocratic* redcoat. Oh dear, oh, dear, oh dear . . .

"Amy. Go find Will and bring him to me immediately."

"Oh, Papa, please, be easy on him, he only did what he thought was right—"

Sylvanus kneaded his brow. "Don't argue with me, Amy. Just go get him, *now*."

Amy found her brother together with his ever faithful dog, Crystal, outside in the barn. He was gathering the eggs she should have collected this morning, trying to help her with duties that, because of the captain, she could no longer keep up with. Amy's heart went out to him. Poor Will was ravaged by guilt from all corners. He took one look at Amy's face and froze with his hand beneath a hen's breast, earning a vicious peck on the back of his hand for his hesitation.

"It's time, Will," said Amy, taking the basket from him. "The captain's awake, and Papa wants to talk to you."

Her brother swallowed, made a brave but pitiful attempt to square his shoulders, and followed her back into

46

the house, Crystal following at his heels. Sylvanus was
waiting by the door. He gestured for Will to precede
him into the keeping room where Lord Charles, his back
to them all, sat on his pallet before the fireplace, decently
covered in one of Sylvanus's old banyans. Ophelia and
Mildred stood with folded arms in the corner, and the
air was so thick with tension that Amy almost expected
a lightning bolt to slam down out of the ceiling.

Sylvanus poured himself a mug of hard cider and took
a seat. Then he looked up at Will, his face confused,
saddened, mirroring betrayal. "Out with it, son. Before
your family, before this fellow you brought home, and
before God."

Will took one look at the expectant faces around him,
and, his eyes filling with tears, blurted out the story for
all to hear.

"I didn't know what else to do, Pa!" he said, stroking
the dog's head and gulping once, twice. "I couldn't just
leave him there, not after he saved my life! He was
dying, and no one should have to die alone!" And then,
between apologies to his father, to the stone-silent captain, and even to God for sneaking off to fight without
Uncle Eb's knowing, Will finally broke down in great
wracking sobs that testified to the anguish in his soul,
burying his face in Crystal's neck.

Amy glanced at the captain. He hadn't said a word
throughout Will's confession, neither batting an eyelash
nor moving a muscle, merely sitting there on his pallet
with his back to them all. It was as though he'd already
given up on life, already given up on hope, and that what
had happened in his past was now irrelevant. Glancing
at him, Sylvanus raked a hand through what was left of
his hair; then, ushering Will to his feet, he sent the boy
to bed.

An awful silence remained in his wake.

Sylvanus picked up the poker and stabbed at a burning

log. "I just don't understand it. He's never given me a spot of trouble. Always been a good lad, always did the right thing, and now . . ." He took off his spectacles and rubbed wearily at his eyes. "And now, I don't know what to do with him. I just don't know . . ."

"After what he did to Lord Charles? Punish him, I say!" snapped Ophelia, her eyes softening as she gazed at the silent figure on his pallet. "Poor, poor Lord Charles!"

"Yes, what a noble sacrifice our brave friend has made!" Mildred gushed. "His eyesight for Will's life. Oh, Lord Charles, how *ever* can we thank you?"

Amy wasn't surprised when he didn't answer them. A half hour before, he'd been a drain upon their resources. A half hour before, they couldn't wait for him to hurry up and die. Now that he was *Lord* Charles, everything had changed. As a handsome and undoubtedly wealthy aristocrat, he was marriage material, an object of competition between them both, the ultimate prize to be won. The two were out to impress him, and they wanted blood to do it. Will's blood.

"What are you going to *do*, Papa?" Ophelia demanded, trying to pressure her confused and hapless father into a decision.

"I . . . I don't know."

"Please, Papa, have mercy on Will," said Amy, interceding. "After all, he's only fourteen. He was alone and scared, and he didn't know what else to do . . ."

Ophelia rounded on her. "How can you defend him so? Haven't you any thought for poor Lord Charles? If Will had taken our gallant captain to Boston and handed him over to the king's troops instead of bringing him all the way up here to Newburyport, he would've been treated for his injuries that much sooner! He would've woken up to find himself amongst people he knows and trusts, instead of strangers whom he must think of as the enemy. Your concerns are with the wrong person! Lord Charles is the injured party here, not Will! Will ought to be whipped for what he did, no ifs, ands, or buts about it!''

''What do you mean, Will? *Amy's* the one who deserves to be whipped!'' hissed Mildred, eyes gleaming as she, too, turned on Amy. ''I'll bet *you* knew who Lord Charles was from the start, didn't you?''

''I knew he was a redcoat, yes, but I didn't see a need to say anything—''

''Didn't see a need to say anything! You stupid, unthinking, idiot, Newburyport is a rebel town! We even had our own tea party last year! What happens if someone finds out we're harboring a king's officer? And what about when Dr. Plummer comes back to check on him? All Lord Charles has to do is say hello, how do you do, and the doctor's going to know immediately that he's no rebel a'tall! *You've* put us in as much danger as Will has, Amy, for keeping your silence!''

''And unlike Will, *you're* old enough to know better!''

Amy bit her tongue to hold back her angry retort. Of course she hadn't said anything to Sylvanus, but that was because Will had begged her not to. Unbidden, her mind drifted back to that desperate, tearful conversation she and Will had had in the barn, just following Charles's surgery . . .

''Swear you won't tell Pa, Amy! Oh, please Amy, don't tell him, he won't understand and since the captain will probably die anyhow it doesn't make a bit of difference—''

''Will, why did you even *bring* him here?''

''I had to,'' he'd said miserably, his eyes filling with tears as he sank down on a bale of hay, his head in his hands. ''Oh, Amy . . . I thought war was going to be glorious. I thought it would feel good to kill one of those bastards, to know I'd done my part for America, but when it came down to it, and I saw people on both sides dying horribly all around me . . .''

"It suddenly wasn't so glorious anymore," she'd finished.

"It was awful," he'd sobbed, tears squeezing out between his fingers.

"Tell me what happened, Will."

And he had.

"I wanted to hate the redcoats, Amy, I wanted to kill one, but how can you hate and kill someone you feel nothing but admiration for? When that young soldier ran away from the safety of the troops, the captain was just like the shepherd who leaves his flock to save a single lost sheep, heedless of all the bullets flying around him. I've never seen courage like that, Amy. . . . And just as he was putting his soldier up over the saddle, I got a hold of myself and thought, here's my chance to kill one, to kill a really important one and do my part for America so that everyone'd be p-p-proud of me."

Tearfully, he'd told her what had happened next, how the captain must have noticed his youth and in the last moment, spared his life, only to fall backwards against the wall. He told her how, long after the fighting moved on and the fields and woods had gone quiet, he'd gone back. "I had to"—he'd choked back a sob—"had to see for myself j-just what I'd d-d-done to him."

"It's all right, Will. Don't cry . . . you're too big to cry now and besides, it's not your fault."

"But it *is* my fault, Amy! It's like when you go hunting and you kill something for the supperpot. You know you have to do it, and you get all excited when you pull the trigger, but when the bird goes up in a little puff of feathers, or the beautiful deer stumbles and goes down, there's a big part of you that hopes that when you get there, you were just imagining that you hit it . . . that it'll have recovered and got away . . . or that you killed it cleanly so it didn't suffer.'' He'd passed the back of his sleeve across his nose. ''The captain didn't get away, and I didn't kill him cleanly. He was still lying there, right where I'd left him, with blood from his head all over the lichen on the rock behind him. And the worst part of it was, that horse of his never did leave him, and was still standing there guarding him like some big dog, with the dead soldier still lying across the saddle right . . . right where the c-c-captain had p-p-put him. I couldn't just leave him out there to die, Amy. I just couldn't . . .''

''But how did you get him home without anyone stopping and questioning you?''

''One of our men was lying dead nearby, so I swapped the captain's red coat, gorget, and hat for the other fellow's waistcoat. Oh, Amy, what am I going to do?''

She had pulled him to his feet. ''*We* are going to go right on letting everyone believe the captain's a rebel,'' she'd said briskly, thinking, like Will, that he would probably die anyhow. ''It'll be our little secret.''

And it had been—until now.

And now the chance for defending herself was past; with the captain awake and listening, it seemed cruel and insensitive to admit that they'd pretty much expected him to die. No. She'd take whatever punishment was coming her way, if only to spare his feelings. He'd been through enough, the poor man, still sitting on his pallet with his gaze turned toward a fire he could not see and his mind as far away as England's misty shores. Totally oblivious to everything. Totally uncaring.

Sylvanus put down the poker. ''Will's guilt is punishment enough for what he's done. But Amy—,'' his voice turned plaintive, ''—Amy, you should have known better. You should have come to me immediately. Why didn't you?''

"I'm sorry, Papa. Will begged my silence, and I—I thought that he should be the one to tell you, not me.''

"*I thought that Will should be the one to tell you, not me*,'' mimicked Mildred, nastily. "If something bad comes of this, it's going to be all your fault, Amy! Papa's right, you *should've* known better!''

"Nitwit!''

"Imbecile!''

Tears stung Amy's eyes. She was accustomed to getting abuse from her sisters, but oh, lordy, it felt a hundred times worse to get it in front of the captain. She glanced up at Sylvanus for help, but she should have known better than to look for it there. He stood confused and uncertain, unwilling to make a move in any direction, and treating this problem as he did all others that involved the raising of his children; that is, by ignoring whatever he found unpleasant in the hopes it would go away.

But Ophelia didn't go away, and neither did Mildred. The former shot Amy a look of loathing, then crouched down before the captain. "Now, you mustn't worry, Lord Charles,'' she crooned, in a voice that was meant to be reassuring but, addressed as it was to a proud king's officer, came out sounding patronizing. "I know you must feel very sad and sorry for yourself right now, but we'll take care of you, and you can be certain that no harm will come to you here. Everything will be just fine.''

The captain ignored her.

"Did you hear me, Lord Charles? I believe I'm talking to you.''

He only stared straight ahead and blinked, the exaggerated sluggishness of the action only emphasizing the extraordinary length of his lashes, the aquamarine clarity of his eyes. He did not turn his head to look Ophelia's way, or even acknowledge that she had spoken.

This was a situation Sylvanus *did* know how to deal with. "Leave him alone, girls," he said gently. "The poor fellow has had a shock and needs to rest. Can you not see that?"

Ophelia shot her father an angry look. Then, sweetly addressing Lord Charles once more, she cooed, "Well then, perhaps I can get him something with a bit of laudanum in it so that he can sleep."

Mildred pushed her sister aside. "No, no, Ophelia, *I* can get that for him."

"*You're* going to Lucy Preble's poetry reading, you don't have time to see to Lord Charles's wishes as *I* do."

"And *you're* going out driving again with Matthew Ashton!"

Sylvanus said, "I think Amy can see to Lord Charles's needs just fine."

"Now Papa, you *know* that Amy has so many other things to do, she doesn't have *time* to see to him," Ophelia protested. She gave her father her sweetest smile, but above it her eyes were harder than stone. "We only want to help her out."

"Yes, help her out," put in Mildred, not wishing to be outdone.

"Divide his care between the three of you then," he said wearily. "But if there's anything, er, *delicate* that needs doing, leave it to Amy. There are some things the two of you just shouldn't be seeing."

Ophelia and Mildred giggled. Sylvanus turned away. On his pallet, Lord Charles remained unmoving, and as Amy looked from him to her sisters, both of whom were regarding her, she saw that their eyes gleamed with malice and loathing. *Don't think we're going to let* you *take care of him*, those glittering eyes warned. *He's ours now.*

He's his fiancée's, Amy wanted to retort, taking a certain delight in anticipating their response when they found *that* out.

Sylvanus eased himself down into a chair. "And now, I'd like to speak to Captain de Montforte in private," he said, reaching for his cider. "Mildred, go get ready for your reading. Ophelia, you've got an outing with Matthew Ashton to prepare for."

"But Papa—"

"Come now, girls, go. I wish to speak to our guest alone."

"What about Amy? Why does *she* get to stay?"

"Because she's making supper. Now hurry up, or you'll be late."

They pouted. They pleaded. But for once Sylvanus didn't give in to them. As soon as they stormed from the room in a huff, he turned to the lone figure sitting before the fire.

"I *am* sorry, Captain de Montforte," he said. "This cannot be easy for you, and you have my sympathies for your plight."

There was no response from the captain.

"Dr. Plummer will want you to rest for the next fortnight, but after that, we need to think about getting you back to the army in Boston," Sylvanus continued. "If you ask me, your spirit's taken a far worse blow than the back of your head, and I think it would do you a world of good to be with your own people." His voice gentled. "You need to be with friends, not strangers."

The captain only blinked again in that slow, exaggerated way he had, and continued staring into nothingness.

Sylvanus, growing worried, glanced at Amy, who shook her head and motioned with her hands to let the man alone. But out of guilt for his son's part in this tragedy, Sylvanus persisted. "I know you must be eager to return to Boston, and as much as I'd like to take you

back there myself, I just can't leave my flock, I can't
spare my son, and it is, of course, unthinkable that I
allow my two daughters to bring you ... though I suppose I *could* always send Amy.''

The captain, still staring straight ahead, spoke for the
first time. ''Is Amy not your daughter also?'' he asked
flatly.

''Er—well, uh ... she bears my name, yes. But she
doesn't have a reputation to consider, as do Ophelia and
Mildred.''

''*All* young women have reputations to consider.''

''Yes, but Amy is—well, never mind, Captain. Suffice it to say that, unlike her sisters, Amy's reputation
does not demand careful care and protection.''

Amy wanted to die.

The captain's jaw hardened.

And Amy, seeing it, quietly stirred the stew in its big
black kettle. ''Papa, if Lord Charles wants to go to Boston, I can take him anytime he wants to go—''

''*No!*'' barked their guest, startling her with the ve-
hemence of his tone. He glared sightlessly into the
flames, his fists clenched. ''I will allow it.''

Sylvanus began, ''Really, Captain, Amy's a very capable young woman—''

''Precisely that, she is a *young woman*, and Boston is
a den of rascals, sailors, blackguards, and scum. It is no
place for her, and since I've been rendered useless in
my ability to protect her, I will remain here until someone can come up from Boston to collect me. I will not
see her life or virtue risked on my account. *By God, I
will not!*''

Sylvanus's brows shot straight to the roots of his
sparse white hair. And Amy, who had never before had
anyone defend her in such a gallant way, had never
thought of herself as a woman worthy of ''protection,''
and had never been the focus of such gentlemanly con-

cern, widened her eyes and put her hand to a suddenly fluttering heart.

"Papa," she said, trying to mediate, "Lord Charles has just woken up. He is exhausted, upset, and needs time to rest. Time to come to terms with things. Maybe you should have this conversation with him later."

Sylvanus, his face white, nodded. He made a comment about getting back to his sermon and hastily exited the room, leaving an awkward silence in his wake.

Once he had gone, Charles's shoulders rose on a great sigh of weariness, then fell. There was no pride to maintain now. No reason to show strength where none was needed. He put his head in his hands and stayed that way for a long time, not saying a word while the girl moved about the room, quietly performing her slave duties. But he could not get her out of his mind. Her humiliation had been, and still was, nearly palpable. The way her sisters had attacked her, the way her apathetic father had failed to defend her, the way her cowardly brother had allowed her to shoulder blame that was his and his alone, gave him a tangible outlet for anger which heretofore had no other but self-pity. They were a pack of wolves after a little fawn. They were horrible. And as she silently went about preparing supper, Charles decided that he had never disliked anyone as much as he did these people who called themselves her family.

The stew was thick and bubbling, the bread a lovely golden brown, and the fragrance of beef, onions, and herbs filled the keeping room before he finally spoke.

"Miss Leighton."

He heard her crossing the room, the brush of air against his face as she knelt down to his level, taking the hand he held out to her in silent apology. "Yes, Lord Charles?"

"I am sorry for embarrassing you so. Forgive me."

"Oh, there's nothing to forgive," she said, squeezing

his hand and then releasing it. "I know you're not angry with my family, but with your circumstances—"

"On the contrary, Miss Leighton, I am furious with your family. I do not know if I can suffer them for the remainder of my stay here."

"I don't mind bringing you back to Boston, then, if you want to go—"

"Damn it, girl, don't fuel my fury with such remarks!" Charles dug his fists into his eyes and then, in a calmer, quieter voice, murmured, "I need you to do me a kindness."

"Certainly."

"Can you read and write?"

"Yes."

"Providence smiles on me at last. I need someone to pen three letters for me. Will you do that?"

"Oh, yes. We can do them right now, if you like. Supper won't be ready for a while, and I'm just tidying up a bit, that's all . . ." He heard her jump to her feet. "I'd be happy to write your letters for you, Captain de Montforte, even post them for you in the morning—"

"No. You have more than enough to do. Let your sisters post them."

"I don't mind, really—"

"I mind. Let them do it."

"Well . . . all right." He heard the whisper of her petticoats, caught the tantalizing scent of bayberry mingled with warm, soft *female* as she came close. His senses heightened, his skin warming at her nearness, and Charles frowned, disturbed by his reaction to her. "Now, if you'll take my hand, I'll bring you into Papa's study, where there's pen and paper."

He extended his hand up toward her voice, unaware that she, at the same time, was beginning to lean down. His fingers plunged through cloth and into the plush softness of a breast, and he heard her surprised gasp as he jerked his hand back, curling his fingers into his palm, into a fist, and cursing himself for his inadvertent liberty.

"Miss Leighton, I am *dreadfully* sorry—"

"N-no, you couldn't see what you were doing, there's nothing to be s-sorry about," she managed, in a somewhat breathless voice.

"Shall we try again?"

"Yes"—a nervous little laugh—"yes, let's."

He tentatively extended his arm. God help him, the feel of her breast, so soft, so firm, so ripe, was still seared on his fingertips, imprinted on his brain. Charles didn't even realize his hand was still fisted until he felt her gently prying apart his fingers.

It was all he could do not to pull her down into his arms, to put his hands all over her so that he could see, through his touch, the face of this woman who had done so much for him, who was the only light in his world of darkness, who seemed to intuitively understand and protect for him those things he needed most. Dignity. Rest. Space to heal.

But he could not put his hands on her, of course. He could not go about touching people. He could not, would not, go about touching young women, especially those to whom he wasn't engaged to be married. And so he rose to his feet, taking care that he didn't put undue pressure on her hand and thus throw her off balance, and then stood there swaying a little with disorientation, weakness, and a renewed pounding of his head.

"Can you manage this, Lord Charles?"

"Yes—just give me a moment." He took a few deep breaths to steady himself. She remained very still beside him, just holding his hand, letting him get used to the feel of being on his feet once more.

"I am ready now," he said.

She squeezed his hand and took a step. He, in his stockinged feet, followed. How very strange it felt to move through this impenetrable blackness. How very strange it felt to entrust your steps, and more importantly, your direction, to another. And how strange it was to put such confidence in this small, albeit strong, little hand. She did not try to hurry him, but merely stayed with him, holding his hand and reassuring him by her very presence that he was not alone. He kept moving. His head swam with dizziness and his skin prickled with apprehension that he would bump into something and fall, that he would trip over something and bring them both crashing to the floor. But no. He tripped over nothing, and she stayed right beside him.

"We're at the door to the study now, Lord Charles. It's open. If you shuffle your feet, you'll find the door-jamb and it won't trip you up."

He did, and there it was, just as she'd warned. He lifted his foot, walked over the tiny obstacle that, in his infirm state, would have been enough to send him sprawling, and began to move a little more confidently. The girl kept pace beside him. He felt like a big, blundering fool for clutching her tiny hand as though it was the only thing in the world worth hanging onto, but he couldn't help it.

It was.

"We're here," she said. "If you turn to your right and back up a bit, you'll find yourself against Sylvanus's favorite chair. It would be a good place for you to sit and dictate to me, I think."

He did as she suggested, and there it was, the stuffed edge of a chair, pressing against the back of his legs. Suddenly weary, he put out one hand, found the arm, positioned his body, and very carefully lowered himself down. It was amazing how much thought was needed for acts to which he wouldn't have given the merest consideration before. But the chair was deep, the stuffing soft and lumpy with age and use, and it swallowed him

up like a mother's arms might a babe. Charles sighed
and leaned his aching head back, and it was only then
that he rather reluctantly released the girl's hand.

"Are you all right, Lord Charles?"

"My head," he murmured. "It's killing me."

There was a slight hesitation; then he caught her scent
as she leaned toward him, felt the warmth that surrounded her body a second before her fingertips moved
gently over his brow, his temples. Instinctively, he
leaned his head into that cool, soothing touch, but caught
himself just as his cheek met the palm of her hand. Stiff-
ening, he pulled back—to throbbing pain and a desperate wish to feel that caring touch once more.

A desperate wish that he didn't want to acknowledge.

She moved away. He heard the sound of a chair being
pulled out, a drawer opening, an ink bottle being un-
capped, papers being slid about.

"I'm ready," she said. "Are you?"

"Yes." He sighed and let his cheek rest against the
threadbare back of the chair. It smelled of old man. Old
fabric. Old horsehair. He could fall asleep here, and
when this was done, he probably would. "The first is to
my commanding officer in Boston," he said wearily.
"The second, to my brother Lucien in England. And the
third—" Shame sliced through him. Juliet had trusted
him to take care of her and her unborn baby, but with
that one stupid move in a rocky field near Concord, he
had let her down, just as he had let down his family, his
men, and everyone else who depended on him. He
couldn't take care of her and a baby, now. He couldn't
even take care of himself.

Somewhat hoarsely, he finished, "The third is to my
fiancée, Juliet."

He closed his eyes and in a detached, resigned voice

that revealed none of his anguish and grief, began to dictate.

She proved to be a wonderful letter-taker. Better, even, than Billingshurst. She didn't need him to spell the difficult words. She didn't ask him to repeat himself. And she didn't beg him to slow down, her pen only moving faster and faster to keep up with him. And as he heard his voice droning lifelessly on, and her pen dutifully scratching away, a sense of release, of calm, finally began to overtake him. He was finally setting things in motion. Tomorrow, the letters would be on their way, and his life would begin to look up. Lieutenant Colonel Maddison would send someone to bring him immediately back to Boston. Juliet would be there waiting to care for him. And when Lucien got his letter, neither hell nor high water, rebels nor revolution would keep the duke of Blackheath from coming straight to America to bring him back to England.

Home.

Charles heard himself dictating the final address; then the sound of her rapidly moving pen blurred into nothingness, and nothingness claimed his exhausted brain.

He slept.

And Amy, feeling a heavy sense of wistfulness as she finished the last letter, thinking what a lucky, lucky girl this Juliet Paige was to be affianced to such a worthy man as this, looked at the figure sleeping in her father's chair, his unkempt blond hair falling haphazardly over his brow, his neck at a most uncomfortable angle, and felt something catch in her throat.

He defended me as though I was a real lady. He stood up for me at risk to his own situation. He is brave and selfless and kind, and he actually made me forget who I really am.

Very quietly, she tiptoed across the room, picked up

the blanket that lay across the back of the sofa, and, returning to the captain, placed it gently over his sleeping body.

And then she left the room, taking care to close the door behind her.

Chapter 5

Captain de Montforte slept through supper. He slept through the Bible reading that followed it. He slept through a squabble between Mildred and Ophelia, through Amy quietly putting a final log on the fire that danced and smoked a few feet away from his stockinged toes, and finally, through a silent procession of family members creeping past him on their way up to bed.

As she passed her father's desk, Ophelia, carrying the cat, spied the captain's three letters propped against a candlestick. Swiftly, and when Amy's back was turned, she swept them up and hurried upstairs.

She had them opened and read before she even reached the landing.

Mildred was stripped down to her stays when Ophelia entered the room. The two sisters unlaced each other. Grumbling about how Amy had always used to come in with the bed warmer before Lord Charles's arrival, Mildred slipped beneath the quilts of the bed they both shared and gasped at the feel of the icy sheets against her skin. Ophelia quickly followed her in, and the two snuggled together for warmth, the cat under the covers with them. Downstairs, they could hear the squeak of the floorboards as Amy moved about. And they could envision her gazing dreamily at Lord Charles, and fancying him as she had no right to do.

The thought made them both angry and nauseated.

"Listen to her down there," Ophelia said hatefully. "Fussing over him, making him cozy, digging her way under his skin like a tick. I nearly strangled myself on that stupid string she's rigged up so he can find his way around. Next thing you know, she'll be sleeping beside him to keep him warm!"

"It makes me furious to see how nice he is to her. Can you believe the way he defended her this afternoon? I nearly fainted with shock and disgust. He treats her like she's some well-bred lady, whereas us—"

"Whereas us, he won't even speak to."

Mildred jerked the covers up to her chin. "If only he knew what she *really* was, he wouldn't even suffer her to talk to him, let alone take care of him."

"Not that it's going to matter one way or another."

"What are you talking about?"

"Our resident aristocrat already *has* himself a fiancée."

"What, some snob of a noblewoman over in England?"

"No, some hussy down in Boston named Juliet Paige." Ophelia leaned over and retrieved the letters she'd put on the night table. "Here, read these. They're the letters he had Amy write for him that *we're* supposed to post."

The chilly air outside the covers forgotten, Mildred sat up, pulled the candle close, and read each letter. She skimmed through the one to Lord Charles's commanding officer, showed markedly more interest in the one to the duke, and narrowed her eyes as she read the one to his fiancée. By the time she finished it, her face was twisted with spite and jealousy.

She hurled the letters across the room. "I wonder what she looks like, the little twit!"

"The tail end of a donkey, probably."

"I bet she's no better than *we* are . . . yet *she's* the one who'll get to be called *lady* . . ."

"And live in a grand house."

"And have clothes that cost the earth."

"And servants she can order about like an army."

"And a husband that looks like Lord Charles."

A charged, resentful silence stretched between them.

"Know something, Millie?"

"What?"

"I hate her."

"So do I."

"And I don't think we ought to post those letters."

"We have to. How else are we going to make him like us, if not by doing favors for him? Don't be a dolt, Ophelia, we have to post them."

"No, Millie, don't *you* be a dolt. Blind or not, Lord Charles is an aristocrat, and my sights are set a lot higher than the local fishermen, artisans, and seafarers! Do you think I'm just going to sit here and let him slip through our fingers so some stupid cow down in Boston can have him?"

Mildred shot a nervous glance toward the door. "What do you have in mind?"

"A plan. A plan so good that she'll *never* have him. A plan that will keep him here long enough for one of us to get our claws into him and a ring on our finger. Now listen up, and listen good . . ."

At two o'clock in the morning Charles, still in the chair, finally woke to a house that had gone dead quiet and the nearly unbearable weight of his own thoughts.

Someone had covered him with a heavy wool blanket. His skin was sensitive to the fabric—it made him itch—

and he wondered if it had been the blanket, or the vivid, disturbing dreams, that had finally roused him. They were still with him, those dreams. In them, his hand was once more plunging accidentally into Amy Leighton's breast . . . but this time her gasp was not one of surprise, but of desire. This time, she had responded by wantonly pressing herself into his hand, her nipple going pebble-hard against his stroking fingers, her flesh filling his palm, even as she'd slid her hand down his belly, her fingers touching, stroking, rubbing him until—

Zounds, he was hard. Hard! He shook his head, trying to clear it of such rubbish. What the devil was wrong with him?

Disgusted by the dream, his reaction to it, and yes, his disloyalty to Juliet for even having it, Charles stirred in the chair, trying to ease the heaviness in his loins. It was only when he forced himself to contemplate the bleakness of his situation—and his future—that the unfulfilled ache finally eased, succumbing to the mental pain that annihilated everything else in its path.

He rested his cheek against the back of the chair, thinking.

Thinking, perhaps, too much.

You've really gone and done it now, haven't you?

He had always prided himself on the fact that he was a man who did not make mistakes, but in the last three months—starting with what he had done to Lady Katharine Farnsley—he had made a lifetime's worth of them.

All his life he'd tried to be the best that he could be. He had won his mother's love and his father's admiration by constantly doing good, doing well, just plain *doing*. In his own mind, failure had not been allowed. After a while, failure was not expected. And he had known then, as he knew now, that failure was the one sure way to lose the respect and affection that others had for you.

And you've failed splendidly, man.

What would become of him now?

His life as he'd known it was over. From now on, he'd be hopelessly dependent upon others for his very existence. What would he do, where would he go?

They were frightening thoughts, but Charles met them with complete calm. It would be difficult, maybe even impossible, but he had to accept what had happened to him and get on with things. It wouldn't be easy, but he knew that if he looked toward the future, and found and focused upon a goal to get himself past this sudden calamity that had been visited upon him, he might survive. He would never be "Major" de Montforte, but he could work on making himself as independent as possible with the least burden to others. That alone would be a challenge—and a worthy accomplishment.

I will beat this thing, he vowed savagely. And he had plenty of people in his life to help him do it. He had Amy Leighton. He had Juliet.

And he had his family.

They would be there for him. They would help him get through this, to rebuild his life, to make him whole again.

He couldn't help but wonder how each of his brothers would react if this had happened to them. It was hard to imagine Lucien as blind; Charles wryly doubted that neither God nor the devil would dare saddle the duke with such an infirmity. What about Andrew, his youngest brother? Andrew aspired to be an inventor. Andrew had a clever mind and a wonderfully active imagination—no doubt he would invent some contraption to help him get through life with the minimum of discomfort.

And then Charles thought of Gareth, and a fond smile came over his face. Where Charles was serious and guided by ambition, Gareth, only a year his junior, had always shunned responsibility of any kind. He had run wild through childhood, through university, and now, through early adulthood, raising havoc from Lambourn to London as the leader of a group of equally dissolute friends calling themselves the Den of Debauchery. Gareth's carefree nature, his delight in daredevil pranks and reckless tomfoolery, was something that Lucien railed about in every letter Charles received from him, but despite that, he was the brother that Charles loved most— and the one whose nature he wished he could emulate in this, his hour of darkest despair.

Gareth wouldn't be sitting here feeling sorry for himself. He'd find a way to laugh at his problems. And whereas the idea of dining with his hosts distressed and unnerved Charles, to whom the thought of spilling food all over himself was horribly embarrassing, he knew Gareth would probably make a joke out of it, and delight in making a spectacle of himself.

Oh, if only *he* could be that way!

Well, at least he'd be home with them all soon, for he had little choice but to resign his commission in the army and take Juliet and himself back to England. But was there anything there for him? He envisioned himself once again at Blackheath Castle, ferociously guarded by Lucien, shielded from society, and living out the rest of his days as a recluse in the ancient home where he'd grown up. At least Juliet would have a happy social life there, in company with his sister Nerissa. Though Charles himself could no longer take care of her—or a baby—Lucien and his two other brothers certainly could—and would.

Gareth. Gareth would make life bearable.

Buoyed by thoughts of his family, Charles stirred, stretched, and winced at the sudden pain that blazed through his head. Blindness was bad enough; was he to have a damned headache for the rest of his life, as well?

"I think," he muttered beneath his breath, "that if I had a gun I'd put myself out of my misery."

"And *I* think," said a soft feminine voice, "that if you had something to eat, you'd feel a whole lot better."

Amy Leighton. With a violent start, he remembered his dream. *Dear God, had he said anything in his sleep? Had he called her name? And heaven help him, had she seen the jutting hardness of his erection?*

No. There was the blanket—thank God.

"Hello, Miss Leighton." He gave a faint, almost rueful smile, and just as a precaution, pulled the blanket more securely over himself. "You weren't supposed to hear that."

"And you weren't supposed to say it." There was a rustle of petticoats as she got up. "I saved some stew for you. Would you like me to fix you some?"

"Later."

"How about some hot water so that you can wash?"

"Not right now."

"Something to drink?"

"Actually, I would like—that is to say, I—," he faltered, scowling. "I need some privacy."

"Yes, of course," Amy said, in understanding. Unwilling to leave him alone so soon after his shocking discovery, she had been trying to pass the night in a nearby chair. Now, she went up to him, took his hand, and coaxed him to his feet. He was not yet able to judge his proximity to other people; as he straightened to his full height, his lips nearly brushed her face and remained only inches away, fully within that unseen but deeply felt area of private space that surrounds every person—that surrounded Amy. Her blood went hot. She stepped involuntarily back, assailed by memories of what that mouth had felt like against her own.

Oh, what she wouldn't give to have him kiss her again!

Amy! she scolded herself, shivering the thought away.

"Are you cold, Miss Leighton?"

"A little," she fibbed, not wanting him to know the effect he had on her. As it was, the mere warmth of his hand over her own was making jelly of her knees and butterflies of her heartbeat. She must ignore these—these *feelings*! Putting a safe distance between them, she led him back out to the keeping room, where she guided his hand toward the length of yarn she'd tied around a nail while he'd slept. She closed his fingers around it and stepped back.

"What is this?"

"Yarn. I've strung it from here, to the door, and from there, to the privy outside. I thought you might . . . well, I thought you might appreciate it," she finished lamely, as an odd, cold look came over his face. She hoped she hadn't offended or embarrassed him. She was only trying to help. To give him confidence to find his way through his strange new world with more independence than fate had dealt him.

"Thank you," he said tightly, and then, looking sleep-rumpled and faintly scandalous in his stockinged feet, worked his way down the rope and outside. Amy got out a bowl for his stew. She hoped he was all right out there. That he wouldn't trip over anything, or grow suddenly dizzy and fall. It was all she could do not to go to the door, but she knew she must not hover too much, nor be so helpful that she was stifling. Lord Charles did not need a nanny. What he needed was independence, and the realization that he wasn't as helpless—or useless—as he seemed to think he was.

And most of all, she thought fiercely, he needed to eat.

Two minutes later, he came back in. "I think I will

have that bowl of water in which to wash, now," he said, removing the banyan. "And then, if it pleases you, I will eat."

"Oh, yes, it would please me very much, Lord Charles!"

He smiled tightly. "I am only doing this for your sake, Miss Leighton. Not my own. If I had my way, I wouldn't eat, but you've gone to such trouble on my behalf, I feel obliged to repay your kindness."

She took the banyan from him and draped it over a chair. "I hope you don't mean that."

"I beg your pardon?"

"I said, I hope you don't mean that. I want you to eat because you're hungry. Because you need to regain your strength. If you don't do it for yourself, Captain de Montforte, then do it for your fiancée. After all, what would she think if we were to send you back to her all skin and bones?"

"God knows what she's going to think as it is," he said cryptically. "But you are entirely correct, Miss Leighton. I will eat for her sake—as well, of course, for yours."

"And *I* will get that hot water for you," she said, springing up and hastening toward the hearth.

"Please. There is no need to rush on my account."

"Yes, but—"

"Miss Leighton." He smiled grimly. "You may be your family's slave, but you are not mine."

"I'm not a slave."

"No?"

"Slaves labor but don't get paid. Slaves are often mistreated. Slaves have no time to themselves, exist to serve the needs of others, and are not appreciated."

"Yes. My point exactly."

Amy's cheeks burned with embarrassment. Though she was tempted to challenge the remark, and angrily at that, she didn't want him asking questions she had no wish to answer. Better that he didn't know the truth about her—then, at least, he'd continue to be kind to her, to talk to her, to treat her as though she was something precious and special.

Besides, he was bound to find out about her shameful beginnings, anyhow. Ophelia and Mildred would make sure of it. Quietly, she went about getting him his hot water.

"Miss Leighton?"

"Yes?"

"Have I offended you?"

"No." And then: "But I'm not a slave. I have a nice home here, and I have nothing to complain about, so please don't make my business your own, Captain. Now here's your hot water, soap, and a towel, and when you're finished, I'll see you eat that stew whether you want it or not."

His elegant brows rose in surprise and amusement. "I beg your pardon?"

Good heavens! Had she really been so rude? "I said, I'd like to see you eat something," she mumbled, embarrassed.

"My dear Miss Leighton. I daresay I liked it better when you were snapping at me!"

"I wasn't snapping . . . was I?"

His lips curved in a smile; a real one this time, and one so rich and warm and wonderful that it made the sun shine like July in Amy's heart, warming her from head to toe. "You were," he said mildly, "and I must confess I much prefer your temper over your meekness. Snap at me all you want. And snap at your sisters, too. If you'd only turn some of that mettle on them, perhaps they'd treat you with the respect you deserve."

She went quiet. Too quiet.

"Miss Leighton?" he asked, plunging his hands into

the bowl of water and then searching around for the soap. "*Now* have I offended you?"

"No . . . but they will never treat me with respect, because . . . well, because I don't deserve any."

"What an absurd thing to say! Why the devil do you think that?"

"Can we please change the subject?"

He sighed, found the soap, and bending his head toward the bowl of water, lathered his face, ears, neck, and nape. "Very well, then. If that's what you want, I shall endeavor to keep my curiosity, and my protests, to myself." He plunged his head into the bowl, vigorously soaped both his hair and his shorn scalp, and reaching blindly out for the pitcher, poured the entire lot over his head. "However," he said, sputtering as water ran down his face and into his eyes, "I will warn you right now that I will not suffer things as cheerfully as do you."

"Meaning?"

"Meaning that if I perceive an injustice toward you, I will not let it pass unremarked. Now . . . I wonder if we might trade favors, Miss Leighton?"

"Uh . . . what do you have in mind?"

"My stitches are tight and in need of removal. If you'll perform that humble task for me, perhaps tomorrow, I will devour every bit of the stew you set before me." He straightened up, gingerly towelling his head. "In fact, I might even force myself to take a second helping. Now, if I might have some privacy?" He grinned. "The rest of me needs washing as well."

Amy blushed. "Yes—yes, of course. Would you like me to fetch the tub?"

"No, I can make do with this, until tomorrow. There's no need for you to put yourself to the trouble of hauling in a bath for me."

"But—"

"*Miss Leighton.*"

She sighed. "Very well then, Captain de Montforte. I'll just get you some more hot water, then—and a clean new shirt."

"A heavenly suggestion, but I'm afraid that I only have one."

"No. You have three." She grinned and straightened the cuff of her short-gown as he turned toward her in surprise. "I was so sure that you weren't going to die that I've been doing some sewing this past week."

"What?"

"I made you two new shirts, and by the end of next week, you'll have a waistcoat, a frock, and a second pair of breeches."

He actually blushed. "Breeches? How did you . . . get the fit?"

If he was red, Amy was even redder. "I um . . . measured your leg while you slept."

"Did you now? Well . . . if I might have my original ones in the interim, it would make me feel a bit more . . . covered."

Her cheeks were blazing. "Of course—I'll be right back."

A moment later, she was handing him both a fresh shirt and the breeches that Will and Sylvanus had recently removed from his inert body, freshly cleaned and white once more. Hoping to save both of them further embarrassment, she quickly changed the subject as he placed the clothes on the floor beside his foot. "I hope you like the things I'm making," she stammered, trying to fill the awkwardness left by the recent turn of their conversation. "I know you're probably used to fine silks, velvet, and satins, but homespun and various sorts of wool are really about all we have, I'm afraid . . ."

"Miss Leighton."

"Lord Charles?"

He gave her that special smile that melted everything

inside her. "You are an angel. And don't forget it."

You are an angel. And don't forget it.

If the smile had set her heart a-twirl, then a compliment like that was enough to spin her off her feet. Thank heavens he couldn't know how the simplest things he did and said affected her! Leaving him to his ablutions, she slipped into the parlor, shutting the door behind her and leaning heavily against it. She tipped her head back and put a hand over her rapidly pounding heart.

She was all out of breath.

Beyond the door, she could hear him moving about. A curse as he bumped his elbow on something. And now, splashing. Pauses as he scrubbed himself. More splashing. Amy couldn't help it—her knees grew weak as unbidden, her mind conjured up deliciously wicked images of him, tall, strong, virile and—oh!—stark naked. Her blood went all hot and prickly at the thought and she put her palms to her suddenly warm cheeks. *Stop that!* she told herself. She shouldn't be fantasizing about Lord Charles; he already had a fiancée, and besides, he was so far beyond her reach that she might as well dream of touching the stars.

Presently, the splashing stopped, and there was silence. She imagined him towelling himself dry. She imagined him feeling about for his clothes. And she imagined him donning his new shirt, the tiny stitches she had made, the fabric she had cut, lying so intimately against his clean, warm skin—

"Miss Leighton?"

She jumped guiltily and yanked open the door. There he stood, barefoot and bare-chested, clad only in his breeches and nothing else. With his fingers, he had slicked back his wet hair, and there was an apologetic little smile on his face. He was holding the damp towel in one hand.

Amy swallowed and stared. *Oh, please God, don't let*

me be thinking of him the way I'm thinking of him. He has a fiancée who loves him; this is wrong, wrong!

But she couldn't help the direction of her thoughts. Not with him looking the way he did. Stray bubbles of soap still clung to shoulders that were wide and powerful, clung to upper arms strapped with muscle, clung to the damp gold hair on his chest and now rode a trickle of water down his concave belly and toward his waistband. Amy's gaze followed the trickle, arrived at that waistband—

And froze.

"You m-missed some of the soap," she said faintly.

"Yes, I know. Do you think you could wipe it off?" he asked, offering the towel.

Amy hesitated. Now that he was awake and capable of feeling her touch, now that she knew he had a fiancée, and now that she had these—these *thoughts* about him, she didn't think touching him was such a good idea. It was all right while he was unconscious and somewhat anonymous, but not now. Not now, with her body responding to him the way it was, not now with the knowledge that he had a fiancée who loved him. If she were Juliet Paige, would she want some other woman wiping soap off her man?

Certainly not!

"Miss Leighton?"

"Y-yes?"

He smiled. "My skin, perhaps because I am fair, is not as robust as the rest of me. It is sensitive to soap that hasn't been thoroughly washed off. Though I cannot see it, of course, I know that I haven't got it all off because I am starting to itch like the devil, and I'm afraid that if something isn't soon done about it, I shall end up looking as though I have the pox."

Amy gulped. "Do you think Juliet will mind?"

"Mind what?"

"Well, the soap . . . my wiping it off seems to be a rather intimate gesture, and I don't want to do anything that wouldn't be right . . ."

"Miss Leighton, what the *devil* are you on about? You've cared for me this whole past week and probably saw things no gentle maid should have seen, and now this? You're only wiping off soap, for heaven's sake, not kissing me—"

"I've already done that as well."

"*What?*"

"Well, *you* kissed me, I should say. Quite without my knowing you were going to do so, and while you were half out of your head and thinking I was your Juliet."

"I do not remember kissing you, so therefore, it doesn't quite matter, does it?"

It matters to me. "Well . . ."

"Miss Leighton?" He held the towel straight out. "Please. I am on fire. In another five minutes I shall be covered with tiny red spots. Surely, wiping excess soap from my skin is nothing more intimate than what you've been doing for me during the entire time I lay ill?"

"Yes, but then you were unconscious . . . and then, I didn't know you had a fiancée."

"My fiancée is not so jealous, or underendowed in confidence, that she would regard such a favor on your part as an intrusion or a crime," he said, beginning to sound impatient.

Amy bit her lip. "Very well then," she said, and reaching out, took the damp towel. She dipped it into what remained of the clean hot water, wrung it out, and gingerly touched it to his neck.

Suds glistened there, caught in the little grooves between tendons and muscle. He stood still and relaxed as she wiped them away, though Amy, racked by involuntary little shivers, was not so composed. He was just too close. He was just too handsome, especially with his wet hair slicked back and making the hawkish features of his face, dominated by that aristocratic nose and those deceptively lazy, clearer-than-water, blue eyes, all the more pronounced. He loomed above her in a way that made her feel both protected and awed, and his nearness made her breathless, hot, and prickly with awareness. She clamped her knees together. Could he hear the way her heart was suddenly pounding? Could he feel the heat that must be coming off her? And oh, Lord help her, could he guess her wicked, sinful thoughts?

Again, she dipped the towel in the bowl, wrung it out, and shakily drew it out over his collarbone. Down his shoulders and upper arms, her touch growing more confident, her gaze growing reverent, as she went. Oh, such muscles he had, sharp with definition and hard as marble, even at rest! Oh, how tall and very manly he was! Subconsciously, she licked her lips as she wiped the frothy suds from the inside of his elbow, then pulled the towel down his forearms and out over his wrists. What would those arms feel like around her? What would the touch of those fingers be like against her cheek?

Somewhat belatedly, she realized that he was no longer quite so relaxed, his body tensing, his stance going a bit rigid. Guilty panic filled her. Oh dear, she wasn't working fast enough; no doubt the soap was bothering him, and he was fighting to keep still.

"Almost done, Miss Leighton?"

"I'm—I'm getting there," she managed.

"Good . . . I'm, er, getting itchy."

Back into the water went the towel, and now Amy drew it down his chest, wiping up stray soap as she went. Damp gold hair sprang back in the wake of the towel, and she could feel his heartbeat just beneath her fingertips. Was it her imagination or was it pounding as rapidly as hers? And was it her imagination, or was he breathing just a little bit hard, like herself?

Hurry up!

Oh, God, it was an effort to make her respirations sound normal! She glanced up at his face, hoping he hadn't noticed, but he was still staring straight ahead, his firm, sensual lips so close she could easily have stood on tiptoe and kissed them. His jaw, which needed a shave, was only a few inches away. And his eyes . . . romantic eyes they were, of the palest shade of blue beneath long straight lashes, the outer corners slightly down-tilted and lending him a lazy, almost sleepy expression—though the clear, crystalline quality of their color banished any thought that the mind behind them was anything but sharp.

Wouldn't you love for him to kiss you again, Amy? Wouldn't you just love that, you wicked little creature?

Mortified, Amy tore her gaze away, rinsed out the towel, and ran it down his ribs. Only a few bubbles left, thank God. Only a few little trickles—

And one of them was going straight down the trail of hair that led from his navel and disappeared beneath the waistband of his breeches.

Amy, her hand and the towel on his stomach, froze at the same moment his hand shot out to grab her wrist.

She might have been imagining his pounding heartbeat. She might have been imagining the rigidness of his stance. She might even be imagining that his breathing sounded raspy and harsh.

But she wasn't imagining the huge bulge just beneath the waistband of those breeches, a bulge that swelled and strained the fabric and told her that everything she'd thought was imagination was not imagination at all.

She gasped and dropped the towel, her hand covering her mouth.

"I guess this wasn't such a good idea, after all," he said softly, bending to retrieve it.

"I . . . guess not," she stammered, horrified.

He offered a pained little smile. "Forgive me, Miss Leighton—I am only a man, and blind as I am, it is far too easy to imagine that your touch is that of another. I did not intend for this to happen. I did not mean to offend you."

"N-no offense taken."

For the sake of her modesty, he turned his back on her, quickly and discreetly ran the wet towel beneath his waistband to catch the trickle of soap, and then, turning, held it out to her.

Amy stared at it for a moment, her cheeks burning as she thought of where that towel had just been; then she took it and put it in the bowl, feeling weak and feverish.

"Miss Leighton?"

She gulped, swallowed, and did not allow herself to look at him. "Yes?"

"If you would be kind enough to hand me that fine new shirt you made me?"

Her face flaming, she grabbed it and thrust it into his hand before leaping back, careful not to look below the level of his chest. It took him a moment to get it over his head and once he did, he quickly pulled it down, leaving it loose outside his breeches for reasons that were obvious to both of them.

He smiled, the gesture both rueful and boyishly innocent. "Shall we forget this ever happened?"

"Yes, C-captain, I—I think that would be best."

His smile broadened and he offered his arm with a casual yet studied gallantry that melted what was left of her heart. "Good. Now, I think I will have some of that stew you promised . . . if the offer still stands?"

Chapter 6

H e might've been able to easily forget it, but Amy couldn't.

It was just as everyone had predicted. She had bad blood. Hot blood. Lustful, wicked, wanton blood. The sins of the father had come back to haunt her. She, like him, was a carnal savage. She, like him, was immoral.

She was a horrible person.

Oh, God, forgive me, please. I didn't mean to do what I did, I'm so sorry, I never wanted for that to happen . . .

"Miss Leighton?"

She led him to his chair, hoping he hadn't noticed her silent tears.

He remained standing. "Miss Leighton, are you all right?"

"Of course I am," she said briskly, hoping she sounded convincing. "Why wouldn't I be?"

"I pray you are not upset by what just happened between us."

"No, Lord Charles. Besides it was my fault, not yours—"

"Oh, for God's sake, it wasn't anyone's fault. A man is a man is a man, Miss Leighton, we respond to certain

81

stimuli and there isn't a blasted thing we can do about it. It's a physical reaction, nothing more, so stop blaming yourself, would you?'' He massaged the back of his head. '' 'Sdeath, if anyone's to blame, 'tis me. I should've known better.''

"Please don't be angry, Lord Charles—''

"My anger is not with you. And please, call me Charles. Given that you're the poor soul stuck with the tasks of bathing, babying, and all but bottle feeding me, we damn well ought to dispense with formalities, don't you think?''

He looked annoyed. Disgusted. Deciding it was wisest to say nothing, Amy ladled out some stew, fetched the bread she'd kept warm in the oven, and brought both, together with a mug of hard cider, to the table on a tray.

The captain was still standing.

"Aren't you going to sit down?'' she asked.

"Yes, but only after you take your own chair.''

"You don't have to wait for me.''

"I am a gentleman, Miss Leighton. I will wait for you whether you wish me to or not.''

Amy stared at him as though that terrible blow had robbed him of more than just his sight. No one ever waited for her to sit down. Everyone started eating the moment Sylvanus finished saying grace, and if Amy wasn't in her seat by then, they began without her. And now here was this son of a duke, this English aristocrat who was supposed to be their enemy, treating her with a respect and kindness she had never known. Treating her as though she were a real lady. She shut her eyes for a brief moment, savoring the feeling for the precious thing that it was.

Then, her heart beating just a little bit faster, she pulled out her chair and sat down, pressing her hands between her knees.

"Are you seated, madam?"

"I am."

He nodded and then pulled out his own chair. Amy, still reeling over his chivalrous treatment of her, gazed longingly at him and then, shutting her eyes for a moment, let her mind wander, allowing herself to pretend that she was the lady of the house, and he, her dashing, impossibly handsome husband . . .

Oh, Juliet Paige, you are the luckiest girl on earth!

She opened her eyes to reality and instantly sobered. The captain was frowning down at his tray. His face tense, he slowly felt about until he located the napkin she'd placed by his plate, and unfolded it in his lap. His uncertainty was apparent, his fear of making a fool of himself, obvious.

"Would you like me to leave you, Captain de Montforte?"

"No, I would like you to sit there and join me."

"But I'm not hungry—"

"Neither am I, damn it, but you asked me to eat and so I will." He swore bitterly to himself and rested his brow against the heel of his hand, the picture of remorse and self-disgust. "I'm sorry. That was uncalled for."

"It's all right."

"No, it is not all right." His hand went to the back of his head, rubbing the area distractedly; how much pain he was in, she could not even begin to imagine. "It is unlike me to be such a beast. I do not set out to hurt people's feelings, especially those of kind young women who are only trying to help me. Please forgive me, Miss Leighton. I have not yet come to terms with my fate, and I must confess that, much to my dismay, I am not handling this very well at all."

"You're handling it better than would most people I know," she offered, cheerfully.

"Regardless, I am not handling it to my own satisfaction. That, coupled with the fact it's my own blasted fault that I'm even in this predicament, is putting me in a very ill temper indeed."

"You blame yourself for this?"

"Of course I do."

"But it was an accident!"

"Regardless."

"You can't go back and change what happened, so why not just forgive yourself and try to make the best of things? Aren't you as deserving of forgiveness as anyone else?"

"No. I find it far more difficult to forgive myself for my mistakes, than others for theirs. They are allowed to make them. I am not."

He was still rubbing the back of his head. She watched his fingers sliding up through his damp hair, and wished she dared offer to take over that task for him.

"Your head hurts, doesn't it?"

"As well it should, considering the fact there's a hole in it."

"You'll feel better after you eat something."

"Do you think so?" He tried to smile. "I am not so sure about that. Besides, I rather suspect that feeding myself is going to be the supreme test of what remains of my abilities." He felt for, and found, his spoon. "You will not assist me, though. I will not allow it."

"I wouldn't dream of it."

"Good."

Amy knew that his pride would be better served if she kept silent. Still, she cringed when he tentatively explored the tray's contents with his fingertips, accidentally plunging one of them into the still-hot stew and, jerking back, nearly upsetting the mug with his wrist.

"Don't look," he said gruffly. "I am about to make a complete fool of myself."

"As long as you eat it, I don't care what you make of yourself."

"Oh, I'll eat it all right, if it bloody well kills me."

"It won't." She grinned. "I'm a good cook."

"Then I shall determine to do your stew justice, Miss Leighton."

"Amy."

He smiled tightly. "Amy."

And with that, he lowered his spoon, hit the side of the bowl, and nearly overturned it. He tried again and this time, found his target. Raising the dripping spoon, he paused and looked in her direction. His eyes were so clear, his gaze so direct, that for a moment, Amy thought he could see her.

"You're watching me."

"Yes. I want to see that you eat it, just as you promised."

"The only thing you'll see is me making a damned mess," he said irately.

"Maybe. But you'll get it right eventually, I just know you will."

He shook his head, dismissing her faith in him, and brought the spoon to his mouth. It tipped slightly, and broth trickled down his chin and onto his shirtfront. A very tight, very strained, very determined smile gripped one corner of his mouth, and Amy knew then that he was not a man to give up on something once he put his mind to it. He tried again. Spilled more stew. Swore roundly. And got it right the third time.

Amy's shoulders, which had been stiff with tension, relaxed.

"This is gorgeous," he said. "Thank you for keeping it warm for me."

"You're welcome." She watched him eat, admiring the shape of his fingers against the spoon, the easy, aristocratic grace of his movements, the way his hair, so thick and bright, was now drying in rich gleaming waves around his face.

"What is Juliet like?" she asked, a little wistfully.

He looked up. "Sorry?"

"Juliet. I was just wondering what she's like."

"Rather like me, I should say. Or rather like I was before I got hurt."

"You're the same man you were before you got hurt, Charles."

"Don't be fanciful, child, I'm not, and I never shall be." He dug his spoon into the stew, more forcefully than he had before. "As for Juliet"—he paused, as though the subject was a private one and he was unsure he wanted to discuss it—"she's a pretty girl with dark hair and fine green eyes. Your voices are similar, which is why I must have mistaken you for her when I, uh . . . when I kissed you."

I wish you'd mistake me again.

"You must love her very much," Amy said, wishing that *she* had fine green eyes instead of huge, brown, boring ones.

"I do. And still I got her with child. Fine way to show someone you love them, eh?" His face looked suddenly bleak. "I cannot imagine I'll make much of a husband, now, and even less of a father." He stopped, surprised at how much he had revealed.

"I think you'll make a *wonderful* husband."

Lord Charles looked up at her emphatic tone, and Amy blushed a hundred shades of crimson.

"And father," she added, lamely.

His unseeing gaze remained on her for a long moment. And then, with an amused little smile, he resumed eating his meal.

"I'm sorry," Amy stammered, blushing. "I—uh—I didn't—"

"Do you know, I think I shall have that second helping, after all," he said briskly, deftly cutting off her lame apologies and saving her from further embarrassment. Amy's heart swelled with gratitude even as she chastised herself for her impulsive words. Given what her sisters had said about him being her "pet man," and now the silent amusement in that one long gaze, he must certainly know the secrets of her foolish heart. Oh, what must he think of her?

"Miss Leighton?"

She nearly jumped out of her skin, terrified that he'd been able to read her thoughts.

"If you don't mind, I would love a bit more of this stew," he prompted gently.

Warm smile. Warm eyes. Warm heart.

Would those beautiful hands be warm as well, touching her in places that no man ever had before?

"Yes—yes, of course." Red-faced, she rose, fetched his empty bowl, and hurried to the kettle that still hung over the dying fire. "After all, we wouldn't want to send you back to Juliet looking as though we'd starved you. She'd think we Americans are a horrible sort."

"Oh, I doubt that. Juliet's as American as you are."

"She *is*?"

He looked up as Amy set the bowl before him, a faint smile on his face. "Of course. Did you think otherwise?"

"Well, yes . . . I mean, you're a king's officer . . . I thought she must've come over from England with you."

"Heavens, no. She's the daughter of a Boston storekeeper."

"Not an aristocrat like you, then?"

"No, thank God."

Amy giggled.

"What's so funny?"

"For being an aristocrat yourself, you don't seem to like them much."

"Oh, it's not that. I was just thinking of the woman I would have had to marry had I not, uh, got Juliet into trouble."

"*Had* to marry? Do you mean you got someone else in trouble as well?" Amy asked, her mouth agape.

"Good God, no!" And then, incredulously: "What sort of man do you think I am, anyhow?"

She went crimson. "I—I didn't mean it the way it sounded . . . but if you *did* get someone else in trouble, I wouldn't hold it against you, or like you any less—"

"I did not get anyone else in trouble, I can assure you." His lips were twitching, as though he found this whole discussion both ludicrous and amusing. "But as a second son, raised to take over as duke should anything happen to Lucien, I have certain responsibilities toward my family. One of these was that I marry Lady Katharine Farnsley, whose father's lands border our own. We were promised since birth, and a union between the de Montfortes and the Farnsleys would have been quite advantageous. But Boston is a lonely place for a man who's far from home. And Juliet"—he smiled, affectionately—"Juliet's a very pretty young woman. Shunning the destiny that was planned for me, and betrothing myself to a Yankee instead, was about the most rebellious thing I have ever done in my life— and I imagine it will not sit well at home when Lucien learns of it."

"What difference does it make what Lucien thinks?" Amy asked, confused. "Shouldn't you marry whoever you please?"

"I am not one to disappoint my family, or their expectations of me."

"Won't Lucien get to marry whom *he* pleases?"

"I doubt that Lucien is inclined to marry at all. He has yet to find a woman who is his equal." He bent his head and absently stirred his stew. "I was never happy about the idea of marrying Katharine, anyhow. She is heavily dowered, yes—but that asset is outweighed by the fact that she is also a shrew, and I must confess that I'd as soon wed her as I would one of your equally awful sisters."

"Lord Charles!"

He merely raised a brow, amused. "Yes?"

Amy couldn't help her little giggle. Charles grinned in return. And then he seemed to sober a bit as he went back to his meal. "Tell me, Amy, what do your neighbors think about the idea that your father is harboring a redcoat?"

"They don't know, and I don't think he plans to tell them."

He looked up in sudden alarm. "Oh, no. This will not do. He *must* tell them."

"I think he means to let everyone go on believing you're Adam Smith from Woburn, and as soon as it's convenient, have Will bring you back to Boston with no one the wiser. Sylvanus means well, truly he does, but I doubt he's aware of the consequences of keeping silent where you're concerned."

"Then I must convince him otherwise. By allowing them to think I'm someone I'm not, he is not only putting himself but his family in danger. What will his trusting flock think if they were to learn from anyone but your father that he, their minister, has been deceiving them all along?" He shook his head. "Far better, I think, that he tells them who I am immediately."

He went back to eating his stew.

"But—but Lord Charles—"

"Yes?"

"Aren't you worried about what the townspeople might do to *you*?"

"No." He gave a bitter, humorless smile. "Besides, my dear friend—what can they do to me that I have not already done to myself?"

Chapter 7

The week that followed was not easy for anyone.

Lord Charles was not in a good mood. Plagued by a persistent headache, worry over Juliet, and impatience with his condition, he soon fell into a black depression. Will slunk past him like a puppy afraid of a beating. Ophelia and Mildred fled the room in tears when their persistent efforts to gain his attention yielded them a verbal mauling that no one but a British aristocrat could have given so well. Sylvanus's attempts to give biblical solace were rebuffed, and even Crystal the dog avoided the silent figure who refused to eat with them, refused to communicate, refused to do anything but sit on his pallet and growl at anyone who dared try to speak to him.

There was only one person whose company Charles welcomed, and that, much to her sisters' confusion and wrath, was Amy, with whom he stayed up long after the others went to bed, quietly talking.

A week after he'd woken up, things finally came to a head.

Amy had roasted a joint of beef for supper. Sylvanus was at the sideboard carving it, and Amy had gone out to the larder for some milk when the captain got up from his pallet and approached the table.

Crystal thumped her tail against the floor and watched his progress. Mildred and Ophelia, already seated, exchanged hopeful, excited glances. Will grinned widely. Sylvanus turned around with the platter of meat and halted in surprise.

And no one said a word.

Amy came in, carrying a pitcher of milk. "Lord Charles?"

"I will dine with the family tonight," he said tersely.

Amy didn't miss the excited elbow jab that Mildred gave her sister. She set the pitcher down, and, slipping her hand into Charles's, guided him to his place. Her sisters' eyes narrowed with malice at the familiarity that she and the captain shared.

He stood stiffly by his chair as Amy hurried to the sideboard for a bowl of potatoes.

Ophelia was beside herself. "Oh, Captain, we're just *delighted* that you're finally joining us for supper! Why, it must have been horrible, eating all by yourself all these nights!"

"I have not dined alone, and the company was quite enjoyable, thank you."

"We're having roast beef tonight, Lord Charles," Mildred announced, as though the smell that wafted throughout the house was not enough reason for Charles to guess that fact for himself.

"I wouldn't have known."

"I just *adore* roast beef," she continued breezily. "It is one of my absolute favorite dishes."

"Mine too," Ophelia added. "Do you like roast beef, Captain?"

"I do. And did you cook it yourself, Miss Leighton?"

"Oh no, Amy makes all the meals around here."

"So I've noticed. She is a very accomplished cook."

"Oh, she's passably fair," Ophelia said, with an airy little laugh. "I'm a better one, when I put my mind to it."

"Are you? Perhaps, then, you should put your mind, and your hands, to it tomorrow. I daresay I would enjoy sampling your efforts and deciding for myself whether or not your claim is a valid one."

Ophelia's smug smile promptly vanished. She was trapped, and she knew it.

Will saw instantly what the captain was up to. "What a good idea!" he said loudly, earning a vicious glare from his sister. "You haven't cooked anything in ages, Ophelia! Why, I'll bet you're so out of practice that even the water won't remember how to boil for you!"

"I'm not cooking unless Millie helps me!"

"Do you mean that Mildred can also cook?" Charles murmured, raising his brows. "Dear me. I didn't know that either of you possessed such . . . talents."

"Of course I can cook! And I can make anything that Ophelia makes taste like slops in comparison!"

"I should like to see you try!" snapped Ophelia.

"Yes, so would I," mused Charles. "But since you are both so eager to prove your culinary expertise to me, perhaps Ophelia can cook tomorrow, and Mildred can have her turn the following day."

"I can't cook tomorrow, I have other things to do. Besides, *Amy* does all the cooking around here."

Charles smiled thinly. "Yes, so I've noticed," he murmured. And then, his voice hardening, "As well as all the baking, sewing, mending, cleaning, washing, weaving, marketing, and soap-making. Rather a lot for one woman, isn't it?"

Ophelia stiffened. Mildred sucked in her breath. Will coughed, Amy quietly went back to the sideboard for the gravy, and in the awkward, tension-filled silence,

Sylvanus decided it was high time to give blessing for the food.

"Dear Lord, we are gathered around this humble table tonight to give thanks for this meal and—"

"*I beg your pardon?*" said Lord Charles, still standing behind his chair and looking properly outraged.

Sylvanus's head jerked up. "Captain?"

"Your daughter has not yet taken her seat! Where, sir, are your manners?"

"I—uh . . ." Sylvanus reddened. Mildred and Ophelia stared at the captain as though he'd lost his mind. Will's lips twitched, and, as everyone watched, the boy got silently to his feet, went around to Amy's chair, and stood behind it as she took her seat, her cheeks pink with gratitude and embarrassment.

"Thank you, Will," she murmured, her gaze lowered.

Will returned to his seat.

The captain, finally, took his.

And after a rather stilted blessing, the meal was consumed in silence.

The following morning, Amy rose early and, creeping past the lightly snoring figure on his pallet, slipped out the door.

She quickly performed her morning chores, finishing all before the sun was even a red glow in the sky. Then, eager to make the most of her freedom before everyone was up and demanding breakfast, she hurried through a still-sleeping Newburyport and toward the Ashton's big Georgian house on High Street.

Mira Ashton was not exactly the sort of friend that the Reverend Leighton would have chosen for her, but as the daughter of one of Newburyport's most prominent citizens, there was little he dared say about it. The truth was, Mira—a scrawny, hot-tempered hoyden who dressed in her brother's clothes and swore like a sailor—

didn't give a hoot *who* Amy's real father was, accepting her as a friend when most people in Newburyport wanted little, if anything, to do with her.

This morning, Amy's heart could no longer contain the tumult that had been building within it since Lord Charles's arrival. She had to talk to somebody, and her outspoken friend was the only obvious choice.

She arrived at the Ashton's house just as dawn was painting its white clapboards in shades of rose. Inside, an argument was ensuing between Ephraim and his son Matt, and Amy could hear it clear through the heavy door.

No doubt, the neighbors could hear it too.

"I don't give a rat's *ASS* what you think, you ain't goin' down to Boston to join the rebels, you hear me? I need you around here, and besides, if ye're gonna go fightin' the Brits, I want you doin' it in a ship, not as part of a damned army!"

Old Ephraim was at it again.

"Don't you dare tell me what to do, you cantankerous old goat!" Matthew yelled back. "If I want to join the army, I will!"

"You go joinin' that army and the first thing ye're gonna do is git yerself kilt! I raised you as a seafarin' man and that's where ye'll serve America best!"

More yelling, this time Mira's voice joining in the clamor. Taking a deep breath, Amy reached up and banged the knocker.

Inside, the racket stopped and a moment later Mira herself opened the door, her board-straight hair hanging over one stormy green eye, her chin stuck out and her very stance belligerent. Behind her stood her brother Matt, his red hair wild, his face so angry that his spectacles were steaming up.

"Amy Leighton!" boomed Ephraim, coming around the corner. "Come on in and have some breakfast with us. Mira's made cornbread and there's plenty left over.''

Amy had no doubt that there was plenty left over; it was a known secret that Mira couldn't cook to save her life.

''Actually, I came to have a word with Mira—''

''It ain't about one of those bleedin' cats the two of you keep rescuin', is it?''

''No, Captain Ashton. Another matter entirely.'' God help her, what would he think if he knew it concerned one of the ''Brits'' he and his son wanted to kill?

''Just gimme a moment,'' Mira said, grabbing her brother's waistcoat and throwing it on over her shirt. No gown and petticoats for her; no jewelry, ladylike caps, or powder on *that* impossibly thick straight hair. Leaving her father and brother to their argument, she slammed the door behind them, and moments later, they were at the riverfront. There, gulls wheeled above their heads, their feathers gold in the rising sun, and the incoming tide sucked and burbled around the pier.

''All right,'' Mira announced, picking up a stone and skimming it out over the water. ''What's buggin' ye, Amy?''

''Can I swear you to secrecy?''

''I swear on my mother's grave, my father's ass, and every freckle on my brother's butt that I won't say a word.''

''Good.'' Amy sighed and sat down on the grass, spreading her checked linen apron over her petticoats and fiddling with the hem. ''Mira, you know that fellow Will brought home? The one who got hurt at Concord?''

''The one who nearly died fightin' those blasted Brits?''

''Um, yes.''

''Aye, of course. Whole town's been talkin' about him and waitin' for him to wake up so they can give him a hero's welcome.''

Amy cringed. "Well, he's woken up—but I don't think they're going to give him a hero's welcome." She tried to choose her words carefully. "And, he didn't nearly die fighting the king's men."

"No?"

"He *is* a king's man. A captain in the Fourth Foot."

"What?!"

"The brother of an English duke, in fact. He got hurt because he was trying to save Will's life, and Will felt so guilty and beholden to him that he switched his clothes with a dead rebel and brought him home thinking Sylvanus would know what to do."

"Holy *shit!*"

"Now that he's awake, he thinks Sylvanus should go before his parishioners and tell everyone who he is."

"Damn right he should! Bleedin' hell, I'll throttle Will myself for dragging him up here in the first place! A *Brit!* What in tarnal creation was he thinking?!"

"Mira, please!" Amy grabbed her friend's arm as she leaped to her feet. "Lord Charles is a good man. He's kind, and brave, and caring of others. He is also very much in a hell of his own already. He doesn't need you, or anyone else, going over there and causing him any more trouble."

"Oh, I'll give him trouble all right! I'll stick a gun against his ear and finish what was started at Concord!"

"Mira, he's blind."

"What?"

"I said, he's blind. Just as the doctor predicted he would be if he ever regained consciousness."

Mira's warlike stance relaxed. She was a patriot, but she wasn't heartless. With a sigh of exasperation, she flung herself back down on the grass beside Amy. "Well then, I guess he ain't much use to anybody then, is he?"

Amy would have disputed that, but she did not want, or need, Mira flying off in an ardent rebel huff, wreaking dissent and damage like a loose cannon. "Let's just say that he's no threat to America in the state he's in," she said. "But that's not what I want to talk to you about."

Mira wrapped her arms around her scrawny knees and cocked a brow at her friend.

"I've got this problem, you see, and I thought that maybe you'd know what I should do about it."

"Go on."

"He's"—Amy was blushing now, head bent as she rolled and unrolled the hem of her apron between thumb and forefinger—"he's terribly handsome, you know."

"You in love with him?"

Leave it to Mira not to waste words. "I . . . I think I might be."

"Bleedin' hell Amy, you *do* have a problem."

"I know. And the thing is, he's engaged to someone else. A colonial girl, down in Boston." She looked up at Mira, her eyes desperate. "I shouldn't be feeling this way, Mira. He's not mine to dream over, he's not mine to think about, he's not mine, period—and yet I can't stop dreaming about him, I can't stop thinking about him, and just being in the same room with him is torment because I find myself wanting to do all these lustful, wicked things with him. I'm wanton, Mira, the fruit of sin, and already I'm going the same route as—"

"Oh, not this again, I won't hear it."

"Mira, you know as well as I do that the circumstances of my birth are no secret! This—this wantonness is just what Sylvanus always predicted for me, and it's all because I've got the blood of a—"

Mira put up a hand. "You say he's handsome?"

"Yes."

"Kind?"

"Oh, yes—he defended me against my sisters, refused to let me slave over him, complimented me on my cooking, managed to trap Ophelia and Mildred into doing some work, and set an example at table last night over how he thinks I ought to be treated.''

"Well, hallelujah.''

"What?''

"And you wonder why the hell ye're havin' lustful thoughts about him? Bleedin' hell, Amy, if I was in yer shoes, had a family like yours, and a man treated *me* like that, I'd be all over him like cream on milk.''

"*Mira!*''

"Well, I would. And ye know something? I think that if he wants to treat ye nice, you damn well oughtta let him do it. Ain't no one else in that house who does, and maybe the rest of 'em will learn by his example. Hell, he might be a damned Brit, but if he can do that much for ye, then he's got my eternal gratitude.''

"So you won't say anything to anyone about him?''

Mira hooked her hair behind her ear and chewed her lip for a moment. "Aye, I'll keep my trap shut. But you'd better not let Sylvanus keep him a secret for too long, Amy. The truth'll come out eventually, and when it does, Sylvanus is gonna rue the fact he kept his silence.''

"Yes. That's what the captain said, exactly.''

Mira grinned. "Handsome, kind, *and* smart. I tell ye, Amy, if that girl down in Boston ever decides to let him go ye'd better get your claws into him post haste. I can just see it now. Amy Leighton, a lady! Amy Leighton, sister-in-law to an English duke! Amy Leighton, finally able to look down her nose at all the people who had nothin' to do with her all these years! Bloomin' tarnation, won't *you* have the last laugh!'' She grabbed Amy's arm. "Now, let's go. I've a mind to meet your captain and have a good gawk at him myself!''

Charles sat up on his pallet, rubbing the back of his ever-aching head and throwing off the last cobwebs of sleep.

He had been dreaming. About Amy.

Again.

In this one, she'd started by massaging his pain-wracked head . . . then his shoulders, his chest, and finally that part of him that was as hard as a brick every morning when he woke up, flushed, trembling, and drenched in sweat.

That part of him that was as hard as a brick, now.

He cursed and rested his forehead in the heel of his hand. His anger was not with her, of course, but with himself—and his own failure to meet his lofty standards of mental discipline. He ought to be dreaming about his fiancée, not this young woman he couldn't even see; he oughtn't even be *thinking* about her!

What does she look like? What color is her hair? Is it short or long, soft or silky, coarse and curly or fine and straight? Is she thin or plump, bird-boned or solid, flat-chested or buxom, pretty or plain?

He groaned as war raged within him, the higher planes of his mind fighting with the baser desires of his body. Those things didn't matter! He wouldn't *let* them matter! But the questions continued, fired at him from something deep inside of himself that he did not understand:

What does she feel like, how soft is her skin? What does she taste like, how does she kiss, and oh, God, would she be as ardent a lover in person as she is in my dreams?

And, some far more sobering thoughts: *Why does she hold herself in such low esteem? Why do those horrid sisters hate her so? Why is her father so apathetic, why does she call him "Sylvanus," and why does everyone treat her so badly?*

"Captain?"

He let his fingers slide from the back of his throbbing head. "Good morning, Reverend."

"Would you like some coffee?"

"Yes, thank you, but I smell nothing brewing."

"You will, shortly." Sylvanus pulled out a chair. "I just roused my daughters, and they'll be down shortly to get it started."

Charles raised a surprised brow.

"I, uh . . . got to thinking about what happened at the table last night, Captain. I saw what you were trying to do. You were right to take us all to task the way you did, though I admit, it was a bitter pill to swallow, at the time."

"The best medicines usually are," Charles said, carefully.

"My daughters—it's my fault they're the way they are, you know. When my wife died, I threw myself into my calling in an attempt to escape my loneliness. As a result, I didn't devote as much time to my family as I should've done, appeasing my daughters' pleas for attention with candy and trinkets, when it was obvious that what they really needed was love and discipline." He sighed, heavily. "It's no wonder they've turned out the way they have. No wonder they're now so spoiled that I'll probably never find husbands for them. I . . . just don't know how to handle them anymore."

Charles smiled, some of his hostility toward the reverend thawing. "Asking them to help Amy around the house is a start."

"Yes. A start, though I suppose that making them do it will be harder than getting eggs from a rooster. Still, thank you for showing me what's really going on under my own roof, Captain. And, for listening to the troubles of an old man." He rose to his feet and lightly touched the younger man's shoulder. "I'll let you get your morning in order."

He began to walk away, but Charles stopped him. "Reverend?"

"Yes?"

"There is a matter that has been troubling me. If I may speak freely?"

"Well, of course you may," said Sylvanus, sitting down once more and adopting his minister's voice as he prepared to hear Charles's problem.

Charles ran a hand through his sleep-tousled hair. "I understand that you mean to keep my identity a secret," he said, getting straight to the point. "I must ask that you tell your parishioners who I am, immediately. I cannot pretend to be someone I'm not, and I cannot abide the thought of what your neighbors might do to you and your family should a detachment of English troops come here to bring me back to Boston—which, given the fact that I have sent a letter to my commanding officer there, is not unlikely." He turned his sightless eyes toward where he knew the minister to be standing. "For your sake, Reverend, as well as that of your family, I implore you to confess the truth."

Charles could almost picture the reverend staring at him in dismay.

"But Captain, you don't understand . . . this is a rebel town, ardently patriotic, and if I tell them who you are—"

"They will appreciate your honesty, and admire you for your courage. Trust me, Reverend, it is far better to confront a problem straightaway than to hide from it, to take the offensive before it can sneak up and overwhelm you from behind." Bitterly, he added, "Had Parliament and our king only subscribed to such a theory, perhaps your people and mine would not be at war. There are lessons to be learned in history; I only pray that you heed them, as I wish that we had done."

Sylvanus was silent for a moment. "I will consider your advice, Captain," he murmured, deeply troubled, and left the room.

Charles sighed. He had done what he could. He lay

back on the pallet, staring up into the darkness, feeling the depression he'd tried so hard to keep at bay pulling him back into its abyss. His head still hurt. His thoughts were turning back toward Amy. Bored, frustrated, and with nothing else to do, he shut his eyes and willed himself to go back to sleep until Awfeelia and Mil-dread rose to make the coffee, which, if he were allowed a guess, wouldn't happen for at least another hour.

He'd just drifted off when the door banged open and footsteps came into the keeping room.

"Lord Charles?"

"Amy." He smiled sleepily and rose up on one elbow, the blanket sliding down one shoulder. "Good morning."

Temporary silence. Charles was unaware that Amy had a friend with her, and he was totally oblivious to the sight he presented to the two girls, his hair tousled by sleep, his pale blue eyes clear as aquamarine as a shaft of sunlight drove through the window and caught him full in the face. A sighted man would, of course, have squinted; Charles did not, and instead, Mira and Amy were treated to a brilliant, wide-open view of clear, intelligent eyes, romantically down turned at the outer corners and fringed by long straight lashes tinged with gold.

"Hell and tarnation above, Amy, ye sure weren't jokin'! He's bleedin' *gorgeous!*"

"Mira!" cried Amy, horrified.

Charles was hard pressed to hide his amusement. He knew, of course, or had at least suspected, that Amy had a girlish infatuation for him, and he'd tried his best not to embarrass her by calling attention to it. He determined not to do so now.

"And whom do I have the pleasure of addressing?" he asked, still supporting himself on one elbow and blinking the sleep from his eyes.

Mira, standing there with her mouth open, was transfixed by that slow, deliberate blink. In a heartbeat, she saw what Amy had seen: studied thoughtfulness, kindness, compassion. The way the man lowered those long eyelashes over those translucently clear eyes, then slowly brought them back up again, did something funny to her insides. Cripes, no wonder Amy was smitten!

"Mira Ashton, patriot," she announced. "I'm Amy's friend. She tells me ye're a blasted Brit who took it upon himself to be merciful to Will, so I guess I'll take it upon *my*self to be merciful to *you*. Besides, I hear ye're being nice to Amy, and since everyone else in this house treats her like donkey dung, I figger the least I can do is be civil to ye—redcoat or not."

"*Mira!*" Amy choked.

"Well, it's true. Where are those two bleedin' leeches, anyhow?"

Despite himself, and his irritation with both the girl's language and her rather vexing use of the word "Brit," Charles got to his feet, his spirits suddenly quite buoyed. If Amy had friends like this, maybe he shouldn't be worrying about her, after all.

"Still in bed, I daresay," he said.

"Good. Amy came up with an idea, and I'm here to see it carried out. We've decided we're gonna take you out sailin' so you can't sit here feelin' sorry for yerself."

"Take me *sailing*?"

"Aye, sailin'. My father builds ships, and I've got my own little boat. It ain't more than fifteen feet long, but it'll get us to where we wanna go."

Reluctantly, yet intrigued despite himself, Charles asked, "And where is it we wish to go?"

"That don't matter none. Now get your lazy carcass off that pallet, take Amy's hand, and come with me. I wanna get her outta here before those two bitches wake up and start hollerin' orders!"

Chapter 8

~~~⌒∽⌒~~~

Eager to escape the house before Amy's sisters rose, the three stayed only long enough to grab some bread and cheese from the larder, a jug of rum, and the blanket the captain had slept beneath, as well as a cloak for Amy and the new frock of warm blue frieze she'd made for their houseguest.

"It's likely to be chilly out on the water this time of year," Mira had warned, importantly.

Amy didn't know whether to be grateful toward or annoyed with Mira as, her hand tucked rather gingerly in the crook of Lord Charles's elbow, the trio left the house. She was horribly embarrassed by what Mira had said. And the captain himself was rather quiet. Was he still feeling unwell, going along with this scheme only for her sake? Had Mira's remark about his being "gorgeous" offended him?

Oh, Lord, maybe this wasn't such a good idea after all.

And now Mira, her stride faintly belligerent, was walking several paces in front of them, deliberately leaving Charles and Amy to their own devices.

Amy took the opportunity to stare up at the captain

as she strode along beside him, and felt her heart ache with unrequited longing. How easy it was to forget that he belonged to someone else. How tempting it was to pretend that he, a prince among men, a god among mortals, belonged to her, Amy Leighton, who was beneath the contempt of even the town's humblest bachelors. And how very, very proud she was to be on the arm of such a man as he.

Mira, as though knowing exactly what Amy was thinking, flung her an impish glance from over one shoulder, and immediately, Amy sobered.

I must stop this—he does not belong to me!

All too soon, they reached the banks of the Merrimack River. The tide was going out and the scent of salt hung in the air, mingling with the pleasant morning warmth. Gulls cried overhead. A cormorant, regal in its black plumage, coasted in the sparkling current, and then dived for a fish.

It was a lovely morning for a sail.

Mira, striding along with a self-importance that belied her small stature, headed straight for the pier.

"You two stay there while I go get the boat ready," she called over her shoulder.

They paused, and Amy self-consciously pulled her hand from the captain's, discreetly stepping away from him.

"Are you sad, Lord Charles?"

"What gives you that idea?"

"You're awfully quiet. We don't have to do this, you know. You've been ill, and perhaps I was wrong in thinking you had the strength for it. I thought the fresh air, and a chance to get outside, would do you good."

"My dear Amy. At risk of sounding vain, which I am not, do I look as though I haven't the strength to sit in a boat?"

"I'm sorry. I just don't want to cause you any more

distress than you've already suffered, and . . . well, Mira can be a bit brash.''

"Far too brash for my own tastes, yes, but she is good medicine for you, and this will be good medicine for *me*.'' He lifted his face to the early morning breeze. "I swear, if I'm forced to sit indoors for another day, let alone the next fortnight, I shall go mad. If nothing else, this may take my mind off things.''

Mira called from the boat. "Come on! I ain't standin' here all day waiting for ye!''

Charles offered his arm, and, taking it, Amy led them down the pier. Tethered to the supports at its end was a floating platform, and upon this Mira stood, hands on her hips, her eyes glinting with mischief and impatience.

Charles, of course, could not know that. He walked confidently beside Amy as they strode the length of the pier. But as they stepped onto the unsteady platform he immediately felt his balance fail him. He staggered, fell, and landed hard upon the sun-warmed wood, bringing Amy down with him. His face burning with humiliation, he allowed the two girls to drag him to his feet.

"Oh, don't look so sour, you silly nob,'' Mira scolded, releasing his arm. "Bleedin' hell, if you English weren't so darned stuck-up in the first place, we probably wouldn't be fightin' with ye.''

"I beg your pardon?''

Amy, catching her friend's impish grin, saw what she was up to and joined in. "Mira's right,'' she said, ignoring the captain's indignant scowl. "You need to learn to laugh at yourself, and now's a good time to do it. Life doesn't need to be so serious.''

"I do not find it amusing that I've been hauled to my feet by two girls who must be half my size. I do not find it amusing that I cannot see where I'm going, cannot see to walk a straight path, and cannot see to pick the splinter out of my palm.'' His mouth tightened. "Will you laugh at me when I walk straight off this confounded heap of wood and into the water?''

"Hell, *I* will," crowed Mira.

"That's not going to happen," Amy declared, opening his palm and gently extracting the splinter. "Now come on, cheer up. The sun's shining, the wind is high, and we're going to have fun."

"Fun," he grumbled.

"Fun," said Mira, gripping his other hand and, together with Amy, guided him toward the boat. Laughing, the two of them helped him down into it.

There Charles sat, hoping to God he wasn't going to be sick with the unsteady movement of water beneath him, the sudden vertigo he felt at not being able to see. But he did not want to disappoint Amy, who, he guessed, didn't get the chance to do things like this very often. She was sitting beside him, chattering happily to Mira, and already she seemed different than she had back in that oppressive house—brighter, more buoyant, more full of fun. He liked her this way, and he found her mood faintly infectious, despite himself. He would not spoil things for her by giving in to his own fears of shaming himself.

He heard a rope slipping, oars thunking about, and then felt water moving beneath the hull upon which his feet rested as the little boat slid out into the river. He tensed, not enjoying this feeling of being completely helpless and at the mercy of others.

Especially two young women.

"Gotta be careful of the current in this river," Mira said importantly, " 'specially when the tide's goin' out. People drown here all the time and ye gotta know what yer doin'.''

He hoped she knew what *she* was doing.

"Is it a big river?" he asked politely.

"Aye, probably as broad across as your Thames must

be in London," she said, eager to prove that an American river was every bit as good as a British one. "Of course, we ain't far from the mouth of it, so naturally, the Merrimack's quite wide here." He felt water rushing beneath him as she swung the tiller, and hoped his knuckles weren't white as he reached out and found the gunwale. "Amy, tell him what you can see. Paint him a picture instead of sittin' there like a bump on a preacher's ass."

She did. Charles, the sun warming his upturned face, the wind playing with his hair, settled back and began to relax as Amy's soft voice described their surroundings. She told him how the water, which was thirty feet deep out in the channel, was a rich cobalt blue, and how little whirlpools of current were trailing in their wake. She told him about the marshlands on the opposite bank of the river, and how the grasses there were glowing green and gold in the bright morning sun. She told him how they could see the steeples of Newburyport's churches from out here, and the Beacon Oak that guided mariners in from the sea, and, as he commented upon the ringing of hammers and growl of distant saws, of the shipyards that lined the Merrimack's banks, one of which belonged to Mira's father, where the Ashtons were building a fine new brig, *Proud Mistress*—

"So my brother Matt, who'll be her captain, can blow the tarnation out of you damned Brits," Mira supplied helpfully.

Charles merely smiled, refusing to be baited, and Amy went on describing the scenery that they were passing—the waders, sandpipers, and other seabirds near shore, feeding as the tide began to ebb; the broad mudflats laced with little channels; and there, off to starboard, the Joppa flats, where, at low tide, "you can dig the sweetest clams this side of Ipswich."

Clams? Charles felt sick. That was one food he vowed would *never* pass his lips.

"And that's Woodbridge Island coming up off to starboard, and beyond that, the mouth of the river and open ocean," Mira put in. "I think it's best to come about now, before—ho, what's this . . . *shit*!"

"What is it, Mira?" said Amy, scrambling toward the stern.

"Something's tangled around the bleedin' rudder! Quick, help me get the sail down!"

The boat lurched and rocked as the two girls tried to right the situation. And Charles, listening to Mira's increasingly potent curses, and Amy's sounds of dismay, had never felt more helpless in his life. He gripped the gunwales as the boat swung dizzyingly out of control, stared into the black slate of darkness, and decided he would have been better off staying home, safe on his pallet.

"You gotta knife on you, Brit?"

"No, Miss Ashton, unfortunately I do not. Why do you need one?" he asked, deliberately keeping his voice polite.

"There's a goddamned fishing net tangled in the rudder, that's why! We're driftin' downriver, and if I can't find a way to get it off we're in deep shit!"

As far as Charles could discern, they already were.

"Can you not steer it with an oar?" he asked calmly, as Amy finished lowering the sail.

"An oar? Are you joking? With *this* sorta current? There ain't no way an oar's gonna do a damned bit of good—"

"Mira, off to starboard!"

"*Cripes!*"

There was a bone-jarring crash and Amy was thrown violently across Charles's lap. He had a sudden armful of soft flesh, scrambling limbs, and a rounded derriere before she was up and off of him, scrambling toward the bow.

"It seems that we have landed. Somewhere," he murmured, hopefully.

"We're stuck prow-deep in the mudflats," Amy explained. "We're going to have to push off."

"Is it not wisest to stay here where it is safe, rather than be swept out to sea?" he asked, reasonably.

Mira snapped, "What, with the tide goin' out? Oh, what a sight *that'd* make, the three of us stranded in a mile of clammin' flats! If that happens, you can bet your ass that everyone in Newburyport'll be telling my bleedin' father I ain't got no business bein' in a boat after all, and then he won't let me go sailin' with Matt on his new brig! Grab an oar, Amy, and let's push outta here— if we're lucky, the current'll carry us onto Woodbridge."

"Or the tip of Plum Island."

Charles, sitting patiently as they struggled to get the boat out of the mud, raised a brow as he felt cold water coming into his shoes. "And what happens if we miss Plum Island?"

"You don't wanna know."

"Well, *you* might want to know that the boat is now leaking."

Even so, Mira had too much pride to change her mind. A moment later, they were out of the mud, and the little vessel was drifting helplessly downriver once more, Mira wrestling with the oars and cursing a blue streak.

"Why don't you let me take them?" Charles offered, positioning himself in the center of the hard seat. "Though I do not question your mariner's skills, Miss Ashton, I daresay I am stronger than you, and I may yet be able to get us to safety."

"Fine." She shoved the oars into his open palms. "If I tell ye to push hard on the right one, push hard; if I tell ye to push hard on the left one, you listen to me and listen good—and if I tell ye to back water—"

"Yes, yes, I do understand," he said tersely, trying to hide his impatience.

But despite his best efforts, Mira's hollered instructions, and the strength in Charles's arms, they missed Woodbridge Island. The sandy plate of land swept past them, and the river carried them ever further away from Newburyport, toward the turbulent mouth of the river, and beyond it, the open sea.

Plum Island was now their only hope.

"Hold up on the sta'board oar and push on the larboard!" Mira yelled. "Now!"

Charles could feel the tide fighting him, the ocean sucking the fast-flowing water past their boat and carrying it right along with it.

"Harder, *harder!*" cried Amy and Mira in unison.

With a lurching crunch, the boat hit sand, its stern instantly swinging around with the current.

Mira leaped out of the boat, nearly capsizing it.

"Hurry, Amy, help me get it onto the beach!"

Charles, feeling helpless, could only sit there as the girls tugged and wrestled the little boat further onto the sand.

And then all was still. Amy gave a little giggle. Mira joined her in a full-throated laugh. A moment later, the two of them were guffawing as though being stranded on some distant island was the funniest thing in the whole damned world.

"Now what?" Charles said irately, thinking this was not funny at all.

"Now we pull the boat onto shore, free up the rudder, and wait for the tide to come back in—and carry us with it."

Chapter 9

And stuck there they were.

Though Amy and Mira soon got the rudder freed, the boat was not seaworthy, and there was nothing they could do to make it so.

"Son of a bitch," Mira swore, kicking the hull.

Charles was vexed past his normal level of patience. He disliked Mira's belligerence, disliked her brash over-confidence, and mostly, disliked her unladylike language.

"Can we not walk back to Newburyport?" he asked tersely.

Mira turned on him. "This is Plum Island," she snapped. "*Island*. That means it's surrounded by water, namely, the Merrimack on one side, the Atlantic on the other, and Plum Island River in between. I don't know about you, but I sure as hell can't walk on water and I damn well ain't gonna swim it either!"

"Mira, *please*," said Amy, trying to mediate.

Charles took a deep breath. Despite his own anger, he was too much the gentleman to respond to Mira's in-flammatory tone. The situation needed immediate defus-ing, and trading insults with the girl was not the way to do it. Very calmly, he asked, "If we're near the mouth of the river, why don't we remain here on the beach and wait for a fishing boat or other vessel to spot us on its way out to sea?"

Amy saw what he was up to. "Yes, and we can have breakfast while we're waiting!"

"What if my bloomin' father hears of this?"

Charles gave a tight smile. "You can blame it all on me."

That satisfied the young hoyden. Within minutes, tempers had cooled and they were all sitting on the beach, eating bread and cheese and passing around the jug of rum. Twenty minutes later, the jug was half empty, the two girls were getting giggly, and Mira was bawling out sea chanteys whose verses were so ribald that Charles, keenly aware of the innocent Amy beside him, felt the tips of his ears go red.

"So tell us what it's like, growing up in a castle and havin' a duke for a brother," Mira asked, finally tiring of her bawdy solos.

"I have nothing by which to compare it, so I cannot answer such a question."

"I hear that you nobs grow up with nannies and governesses and tutors—that so?"

"Yes."

"What are yer other siblings like?"

Normally, Charles was very private about family. But the rum had made him feel pleasantly relaxed, these girls presented no threat or intrusion, and perhaps it would take his mind off Amy's proximity to his left shoulder—and the way that very proximity was affecting him—if he talked about the four people he missed most in this world.

Well, the four that he missed most besides Juliet, he thought, fiercely correcting himself.

He kicked off his shoes, pushing his stockinged toes

into the warm sand. "Well, first there's Lucien, the eldest," he said, visualizing Lucien's austere face with its smoldering dark eyes and flowing black hair. "He was quite young when he inherited the dukedom, and thus has a keen sense of responsibility—especially toward the rest of us. Unfortunately, he can also be an autocratic monster with a Machiavellian tendency to manipulate others for what he calls 'their own good,' a trait which does not make him an easy man with whom to get along. Or," he admitted with a rueful grin, "to live with. The people back in our local village of Ravenscombe call him the Wicked One."

"Why?"

"Because he's a lethal duelist, a master strategist, and the last man on earth you'd want as an enemy."

"Oooh, I'd *love* to meet him," Mira said.

"You just might, because the moment he learns of my fate, he'll be on his way over here to bring me straight home to England."

"Despite the fact there's now fightin' goin' on?"

"Yes. If my brother is determined to come for me, there is no force on earth that will stop him." He grinned confidently. "Mark me on that."

Amy, beside him, broke off a piece of cheese and pressed it into his hand, her fingers accidentally brushing his. "You have a sister too, don't you?"

"Yes, Nerissa. She's the youngest of us all."

"*I* wanna hear about yer brothers," Mira said. "Are they all like Lucien?"

Charles made a noise of amusement. "Thank God, no. I'm the second oldest, and then there's Gareth. He's the black sheep of the family and leads a group of ne'er do wells who've styled themselves after the Hellfire Club and call themselves the Den of Debauchery. Gareth is irresponsible and dissolute, and Lucien despairs of him ever making anything of himself besides a general public nuisance—but I have rather more faith in him than that.''

''And what do the villagers call *him*?''

''The Wild One.''

''He sounds fun,'' Mira said. ''Is *he* betrothed?''

Charles laughed. ''No mama in her right mind would want their daughter married to Gareth. His reputation is not undeserved.'' He leaned back, his elbows sinking into the sand, the sun warming his upturned face. ''And then of course there's Andrew, my youngest brother, who aspires to be an inventor and is, according to the last letter I received from him, hoping to construct a flying machine.''

''A flying machine?'' cried both girls in unison.

''Yes. A preposterous notion, isn't it? However, I suppose that if anyone can do it, Andrew can. He has a clever brain, and did very well at Oxford.''

''What's *his* nickname?''

''The Defiant One.''

''Why?''

''Because he is fiery and independent, and is ever at odds with Lucien.''

There was long silence. And then, softly, Amy said, ''And what did the villagers call you, Charles?''

Everything stilled inside him. He sat up, feeling a sudden rush of self-loathing and loss. ''The Beloved One,'' he said quietly. Head bent, he picked up a handful of sand, letting it trickle out through his fingers. ''Because I always did everything right, always lived up to what everyone expected of me, always succeeded at whatever I put my mind to—and never let anyone down.'' He turned his face toward the salty breeze. ''Until now.''

Even Mira, recognizing the pain in his voice, went uncharacteristically quiet.

Amy, beside him, reached out and touched his hand.

An uncomfortable silence ensued.

Mira got to her feet, making a big pretense of brushing the sand from her clothes. "Well, I think I'm gonna walk over to the other side of the point and see if any boats are goin' past," she announced briskly, realizing, perhaps, that two was company and three a crowd. "You two sit and chat for a while. I'll be back—whenever."

Charles waited until she had gone, and then rested his forehead in his hands.

"I'm sorry," he murmured, staring down into the blackness. "We were all having a good time, and now I've ruined it."

"No you haven't."

"All my life, everyone thought me perfect, confident, capable . . . and all my life I tried to be just that, so that I would not disappoint. People came to me with their problems, consulted me for advice, depended on me." He gave a bitter little laugh. "Do you know what Lucien told me the day my regiment left England to come to America?"

For answer, she reached out and took his hand.

"He wished me Godspeed—and then he said, 'Return to us crowned in laurels, Charles. You are a de Montforte. I expect nothing less than glory from you. *Especially* from you.' " He dug at the sand with his foot. "And instead of laurels, what will I bring back to my family? Shame. Pity. Embarrassment. I have failed them, and I have failed myself."

"You made an honorable sacrifice, Charles. You put the life of a young boy before your own."

"I fell and struck a rock. I seethe with humiliation when I think of explaining myself, and the circumstances of my injury, to my superiors—let alone my family, all of whom expected so very much of me." He made a sound of disgust. "Crowned with laurels! Indeed."

"Just because *you* have such high standards of perfection, doesn't mean everyone else does.''

"No, but they're accustomed to certain behavior and actions from me, and neither my behavior nor my actions give me any reason to be proud.''

"Well, *I'm* proud of you. You have more strength, more courage, and more determination than anyone I know.''

He allowed a grim smile. Of course she would say that; given the girlish infatuation he suspected she felt for him, such a defense came as no surprise. And there was no use arguing with her. When you were infatuated with a person, you always saw them as something more than they were, something almost superhuman. And Charles knew, more than anyone, that he was not superhuman at all.

Far from it.

They sat together, each all too aware of the other's nearness, each respecting the unspoken boundaries that forbid them to acknowledge secret yearnings, give in to forbidden desires. Finally, Charles sighed and, with his finger, began tracing patterns in the sand.

"Amy . . . may I speak to you as a friend?''

"Of course.''

"That first night after discovering I was blind, when I accused you of being your family's slave and you grew angry with me and told me to mind my own affairs—''

He sensed her going stiff beside him.

"Well, I cannot help but ask. Why do you allow them to treat you so shabbily?''

She was so silent that he thought for sure he'd offended her, and that she was going to get up and walk away.

Then, very quietly, she murmured, "Because I have to.''

"Why?''

"Because if I were to act difficult and contrary,

there's nothing to stop my sisters from asking Sylvanus to throw me out. And since I have no hopes of marriage, I just can't let that happen. I have nowhere else to go.''

"What do you mean, you have no prospects of marriage? You're young, charming, and no doubt beautiful. You have your entire life before you!"

"You don't understand, and I—I don't want to talk about this.''

"No, I don't understand, and how the devil *can* I, when every attempt I've made to have this conversation with you ends before it even begins?" Realizing that he was getting angry, he took her hands within his own and squeezed them, willing her to forgive him for his curiosity, his impatience, his interference. "I can't help but notice the way they treat you, Amy. I have come to care about you, and it hurts me. It upsets me. Can you not tell me why your sisters hate you so?''

"I'm not *really* their sister.''

"What do you mean, not *really* their sister?''

"Sylvanus is their father—but he's not mine.''

"So you're his stepdaughter, then?''

"Not exactly . . .''

"Then who is your father?''

She went silent.

"Amy?''

Her hands were trembling, and it was all he could do not to pull her into his arms, to comfort and hold and soothe her as everything inside of him screamed at him to do. Instead, he folded her cold hands within his and very calmly asked, "Can you not tell me who your father is, Amy?''

"I can, but . . .''

"But what?''

Something came into her voice; not quite fear, but shame. Deep shame. She whispered, "I'm afraid you won't like me anymore if I do.''

He smiled gently. "Does that matter?"

She swallowed. "Yes. It—it matters a lot."

Ah yes. That damned infatuation again. "My dear friend. There's nothing you can say or do that will make me dislike you, or cause me to forget all that you have done for me. If you want to tell me your secret, I vow I will keep it safe."

"That's just it. It's not a secret. Everyone in town knows about me, and they all have reason to treat me as they do."

"*Amy.*"

"Yes?"

He pulled his hands from hers and, bending his head, rubbed at the nagging pain in the back of it. "Please don't make me angry."

"I'm just telling the truth."

"No, you're putting yourself down and I don't like it. Do you like it when I put myself down? Do you like it when I refer to myself as helpless and blind?"

"No, of course not, but you're not helpless and your blindness may delay, but never deter, you from your potential, whereas I—"

"Whereas you need a good dose of self-confidence so that you'll stand up to people who treat you badly. How old are you?"

"Seventeen."

"And do you have a fair face, Amy?"

"No. I'm ugly."

"I suppose you're fat, toothless, and scarred by pox as well, eh?"

"Not yet," she murmured, but he heard the reluctant smile in her voice.

"So why do you think you're ugly, Amy?"

"I just am."

"You just are."

"Yes."

"Are your sisters ugly?"

"No. They're beautiful, both of them, with pale blond hair and lovely eyes and skin as white as milk. It's a good thing you can't see them, otherwise you'd probably forget all about your fiancée in Bos—" she stopped, horrified. "Oh, Charles, I didn't mean that the way it sounded!"

He shook his head. "I didn't take it the way it sounded. Now Amy. Since you have eyes that work, I want you to look at me. I'm missing part of my hair, I have a hole in my head, and my eyes must surely be staring into space. Do you think *I'm* ugly?"

"Oh, no, Lord Charles, they could shave off all your hair and give you a dozen holes in your head and do whatever they wanted to your eyes and you'd still be just as hands—"

She caught herself and gasped. The air between them turned suddenly warm.

He couldn't help grinning. "I'd still be just as what?"

"I can't say. I should never have said as much as I have. I've embarrassed myself and now I'll embarrass you—"

"I doubt that."

"Well, I was going to say that you'd still be just as . . . just as handsome, but I don't want you to think I'm trying to get under your skin as my sisters think to do. They—they look at you the way they look at dessert every night."

"Ah. And did they start thinking of me as dessert before or after they learned that my father was, and now my brother is, the duke of Blackheath?"

"After."

"Women." He sighed.

"You're kind, blue-blooded, and look like some warrior angel fallen to earth. You have to expect that women are going to throw themselves at you. Don't you find it flattering?"

"No, I find it damned annoying."

"Why?"

"I don't have time for it, am not vain enough to appreciate it, and have no use for females whose interest in me is predominantly based on the fact that my father was a duke." He pushed back a lock of hair that had come loose from his queue, began rubbing the back of his skull, and said wryly, "Perhaps now that I have a hole in my head and can no longer see, they'll leave me alone."

"I doubt it. You're still handsome, you're still brave, and you still have the same father."

He laughed. "Oh, Amy. Why is it that you can make the simplest statements sound so ludicrously funny?"

"Do I?"

"Yes." He smiled. "And don't ever stop."

They sat quietly together, he still rubbing the back of his head and trying to banish the pain that never seemed to let up beneath his skull. He didn't even realize he was doing it until suddenly her hand was there, her fingers encircling his wrist.

He stilled, one brow raised.

"I know you're in pain," she began, hesitantly. "Every time I see you doing that, all I want to do is try and find some way to make you feel better, but I . . ." she released his hand. "Well, you have a fiancée and I don't know if it's right to touch you." She swallowed. "*Is* it right to touch you, Charles?"

He frowned, considering the matter. "I suppose there's no harm in it, as long as my head is the only part of me you touch." He grinned. "We really don't need a repeat of what happened that night you, uh, helped me with my bath, do we?"

"Certainly not!" she agreed, with a nervous little laugh.

He bent his head, allowing her to do what she would. "Then go ahead, Amy. Make the pain go away, if you can." He shut his eyes, already anticipating the relief her touch would surely bring.

Amy, her throat suddenly dry, stretched her legs out in front of her, then smoothed her petticoats and apron over them.

"Is it, um, all right if you position yourself so that both of us are comfortable, Charles?"

"What would you like me to do?"

"Lie down, so that your head is, well, resting in my lap."

Again, he frowned; then, with a little shrug, he lay down in the sand with his back toward her, gingerly resting his right cheek on her leg and settling his left hand on her knee.

"How's that?"

"Perfect," she said—and it was.

With caring, ever-so-gentle hands, Amy untied his queue and drew her fingers through the shining waves of his hair. He sighed in what might've been content-ment, but was probably anticipation of relief. His fingers curled briefly around her knee, and then he began to relax as she started combing his hair with her fingers, knowing the gentle pulls against his scalp would be soothing in itself.

"I think I feel better already," he murmured.

"Do you want me to stop?"

"God, no."

She smiled and continued her ministrations, lightly drawing her fingers over his head and out through his hair, over and over again, carefully avoiding the still-tender scar and massaging his temple, his brow, his scalp, nape, and even his earlobe with a soft, caring touch. And as she worked, she gazed longingly down at him, wishing she could look at him forever. But he was not hers. He could never be hers. And soon now, he would be going back to those to whom he belonged. His oh-so-lucky Juliet. The family he so obviously loved. And probably to England, never to return.

Oh, why did it hurt so much?

Her chest constricted. Sudden tears made his image blurry, and she raised her head, blinking them away and desperately hoping that Mira wouldn't come back anytime soon and cut short this innocent intimacy that Charles had allowed them.

But Mira was nowhere to be seen, and now a breeze came up, ruffling his shirt and stirring his hair as Amy continued her gentle caresses. She hoped she was bringing him the relief he so desperately needed. She hoped he would let her do this again for him sometime soon. And she hoped that it really *was* all right to be doing it with respect to his pledge to Juliet, because the feelings that made her skin warm despite the nippy breeze, the feelings that made her breasts feel tight and now brought a raw, tingling ache to her most private of areas, were not all right at all, and she began to understand just how her mother might have felt all those years ago . . .

You'd better get up now, Amy. Enough is enough.

She opened her mouth to rouse him—and realized that his weight had grown a little heavier, that his fingers were loose and relaxed across her knee, and that he was taking the deep, rhythmic breaths of someone fast asleep.

Amy bit her lip. She hadn't the heart to wake him. Not now. Her gaze tender, she looked down at his firm, slightly parted lips, the long, pale lashes lying against his cheeks, the shoulders that rose and fell so gently. His breath warmed the top of her thigh through her petticoats. Her heartache intensified, the back of her throat felt raw. It was all she could do not to lean down and kiss his temple, but she would not, she could not do such a thing, it just wasn't *right*. Instead, she touched two fingers to her mouth, shut her eyes for a moment, and then, so softly that it might have been the whisper of a breeze, transferred the kiss to his lips. Her wistful gesture was enough to wake him. He took a deep sigh, slowly lifted his lashes, and, without moving his head, looked off over the river's broad blue basin, a broad blue basin that he might never see.

His face was not just relaxed. It was sad.

"Hmmm . . . Your touch put me to sleep, I think." He made no attempt to get up. "Thank you, Amy. You are very kind to me."

"You're not a hard person to be kind to, Charles. Besides, I've been no kinder to you than you've been to me."

"And I would say the same," he murmured, and let his eyes shut once more, though she knew he was not sleeping.

"Charles?"

"Hmmmm?"

She gathered her courage. "A few minutes ago, you told me how people treat you a certain way because of who your father was . . ."

His eyes slowly opened. "Yes."

"Well . . . people treat me the way they do because of who *my* father was, too."

He was quiet for a moment. "And who was your father, Amy?"

She took a deep, bracing breath, and her hands stilled in his hair.

"A red Indian."

Charles, his cheek still resting on her knee, waited for her to continue. She didn't. He waited another moment. She remained silent. He heard the wash of the sea against the beach, the roar of distant breakers, the high-pitched cry of a gull, and finally spoke when it became obvious that no more was coming from her. "Is that it, then?"

"Yes."

He pushed himself up. "You mean to tell me the reason your family treats you like a slave is because your father was an Indian?"

"Well, yes. I don't know what it's like in England, but here, Indians *are* treated like slaves."

"But—"

"I know, you're wondering how it happened, aren't you?" She gave a pained little laugh, trying, without success, to sound cavalier. "Everyone says it was rape, but it wasn't; Mama had been married to Sylvanus for five years when she met and fell briefly in love with my real father, a Mohawk, and the only reason people say it was rape is out of respect for Sylvanus's feelings. He let Mama keep me, but he always took care to remind me that I was the product of sin, just to make sure I tried twice as hard to do good, and not make the Lord any more unhappy with me than He already is."

"*What?!*"

"I'm the fruit of a terrible sin and that makes *me* unclean, don't you see? My mother was an adulterer. My father was a savage. Wanton blood runs in my veins. And that's why people treat me the way they do. It's not their fault that I am what I am—it's mine."

"I have never heard such complete and utter cod-swollop in all my life!"

"Don't you have a class system in England?"

"Well, yes, of course, but . . . for God's sake, this is different!"

"No it's not. We have a class system here, too, and Indians and people from Africa are at the bottom of it."

"I cannot believe that a man who calls himself a

Christian would raise you to believe you're responsible for something that has nothing to do with you!''

Her voice grew defensive. "You mustn't blame Sylvanus. He's a kind soul, and a forgiving one. He could've thrown Mama out, but he didn't because he still loved her. He could've thrown me out, as I must be a constant reminder of what Mama did, but he didn't. Instead, he took me in, gave me his name, schooling, and plenty of food to eat. No respectable man will ever marry me, but I have a home with Sylvanus for as long as he remains on this earth, and that's more than a lot of people in my position might have." Her anger faded when he remained still, shocked, and silent. "Honestly, Charles, my life isn't so bad. I am blessed. Really I am. Please don't look so upset.''

Upset? Charles felt sick to his stomach. Felt sicker yet by her blithe acceptance of her lot. And here he was, wealthy, privileged, blessed with every material gift that God could give a man, sulking because he'd lost his sight. At least he had everything else. What did this poor little mite ever have?

Nothing. Just gratitude for any scrap of comfort.

He pushed his fist against his brow, his heart feeling as though someone had dragged a rake through it.

"Charles?"

He lifted his head, staring blankly into the nothingness.

"Charles, are you all right?"

"No, Amy. I'm not all right. I feel a little sick by what you've just told me, that's all.''

"You don't need to feel sick, it's not your fault that I'm a dirty half breed—''

"Damn it, it's not your fault either, and you're not 'dirty,' so stop allowing Sylvanus and everyone else to convince you otherwise!''

"But Sylvanus is a man of God, he knows what he's talking about—"

"Sylvanus is a narrow-minded sod who's spent his life punishing *you* for something that isn't your fault!"

His words rang in the air, reverberating like the last clang of a bell. "I'm sorry," he said, shaking his head. " 'Sdeath, I'm sorry." He grasped her hand, holding it with a fierce strength. "Amy, listen to me. *Listen to me.* Don't you ever let them tell you you're ugly! Don't ever let them tell you you're dirty. You're a beautiful person, inside and out, thoughtful, sensitive and kind. I don't care what Sylvanus says, or what anyone else thinks. You'll find yourself a nice man to marry someday, and if your family's trying to convince you otherwise, it's only because they have an unpaid servant in you and they don't want to lose you."

He heard what sounded like a gulp, then a sniffle.

"Amy?"

"I—I'm sorry, Ch-Charles. No one's ever said anything like that to me before, and . . . and I j-just don't know what to make of it—"

"Oh, God, don't cry. I don't know how to deal with tearful females, truly I don't."

"I c-can't help it, you're being so nice to me, saying that I'm beautiful when really, I'm not, and—"

"You *are* beautiful, Amy, and don't you ever forget it."

"You can't say that, you've never even seen me!"

"Come here."

"I *am* here."

"Come closer, then, and let me judge the issue for myself."

She did.

"Now, place my hands on your face."

Sniffling, she took his hands within her own. Or tried

to, given that hers were half the size of his and dainty as a bird's foot.

And then she raised them to her face, placing one on each hot, tear-stained cheek.

The minute he felt her flesh beneath his, Charles knew this was a mistake. A big mistake. But to stop now would crush her.

"Ah, Amy. How can you think you're ugly? Your skin is so soft that it feels like roses after a morning rain."

"It's too dark. Bronzy. Not at all the color of Ophelia's and Mildred's."

"And who says skin has to be milk-white to be beautiful?"

"Well . . . no one, I guess."

He gently pressed his thumbs against her cheeks, noting that they were hot with blush, soft as thistledown, and that the delicate bones beneath were high and prominent. "And look at these cheekbones! I know women—aristocratic women, mind you—who'd kill for cheekbones like these. High cheekbones are a mark of great beauty, you know."

"High cheekbones are a mark of Indian blood."

"Amy."

"Yes?"

"Stop it."

"I'm sorry."

He continued on, tracing the curve of her brow, and the bridge of her nose. He had lost his eyesight, but it was amazing what his hands could see.

"You have a lovely nose," he said.

"It's too strong."

"No it isn't. Close your eyes."

She did. He could feel the fragile veneer of her eyelids, trembling faintly beneath his fingertips, and long,

long lashes that brushed those cheekbones he had so admired.

"What color are your eyes, Amy?"

"Brown."

"What color brown? Brown like conkers? Brown like nutmeg? Brown like black?"

"Brown like mud."

"Can you think of a more flattering word?"

"No."

His hands moved out over her face, learning its shape, before touching the plaited, pinned-up mass of her hair. It was straight, he could tell that much. Smooth like glass, as soft as a fern. He wished it was down.

Good God, man, whatever are you thinking?

"My hair's brown, too," Amy said, her voice now a tremulous, barely audible whisper.

"Brown like mud?" he cajoled.

"No. Brown like black. And when the sun comes out, it's got reddish undertones."

"It sounds very pretty."

"It's not, really. It's just hair."

"Just hair. Do you ever wear it down?"

"No."

"Why not?"

"It gets in the way of things."

"Don't you think that someday, a man will wish to drag his fingers through all this hair?"

"No . . . no respectable man."

He shook his head, his heart aching for her. "Oh, Amy."

He began to pull away, for this act was starting to feel anything but innocent, but as he did, his thumbs happened to brush the curve of her upper lip, the generous swell of her bottom one, and with a start, Charles realized he was only inches away from drawing her face close to his and kissing her.

Shaken, he pulled back.

"Are my lips all right, Charles?" she asked, innocently.

"Yes, yes, they're fine. Quite fine indeed."

"I wish they were more like my sisters' . . . Ophelia's and Mildred's are soft pink the way lips are supposed to be, but mine, well, they're just sort of a dark red—"

God help me.

"Amy! Lord Charles!" Mira's voice echoed over the dunes. "Get off your butts and get over here, quick! Old man Lunt is coming in off the ocean and he's seen me waving! We're rescued!"

Charles shut his eyes on a silent prayer of thanks.

Divine intervention. And not a moment too soon.

Chapter 10

⚜ ～⌒◯◯⌒～

Charles's warning had not been wasted on Sylvanus.

That Saturday—after Ophelia had grudgingly made (and burned) supper—he hastily rewrote his sermon, mustered his courage, and at the pulpit the following morning, announced to his stunned flock that Adam Smith was no farmer at all, but a king's officer and the brother of a mighty English duke.

By that afternoon, all of Newburyport came filing through Sylvanus's door. Or so it seemed. Some came merely to gawk. Some, impressed by the fact that Lord Charles was not only a friend of General Gage, but the heir-presumptive to an English dukedom, asked him to plead their grievances to such men of power in the hopes of preventing more bloodshed and settling the differences between colony and Crown before things got even worse. And a few—the hotheaded patriot Matthew Ashton included—were purposely rude to him, damning him for no other reason than the fact he was a "redcoat"— though their treatment of him improved when their insults and abuse failed to rouse anything from Lord Charles but polite sympathy for their complaints. By keeping a firm hold on his temper, by behaving like the gentleman he was, and above all, by proving he was not a vicious and unfeeling enemy but a man who had sincere compassion for their plight, he managed to keep the Leighton family out of trouble for taking him in, and defused a situation that might otherwise have become quite volatile.

Sylvanus, greatly relieved, came to him after everyone had left. "I can't thank you enough, Captain, for convincing me to tell them the truth. I feel as though a great weight has been taken from my shoulders. You were right all along."

Charles, sitting on his pallet and sharing a molasses biscuit with Crystal, simply shrugged. "It was for your own good, Reverend. Sooner or later they would have found out who I am, and then it would have been too late to save your reputation, let alone their trust in you. Because you were honest with them, they will continue to respect and admire you."

"And *I* will continue to respect and admire you, Captain. You may be 'the enemy,' but when it comes to courage, you've got more than any man I've ever met." He reached out to grasp Charles's shoulder. "After Lexington and Concord, I must confess that I didn't trust my neighbors not to do you harm."

But Charles had never had any fear of that. Indeed, the only thing he feared was the harm he was doing himself.

The incident out on Plum Island had unnerved him. If he'd thought his dreams were hot before, they were nothing compared to what they were now that he'd laid his hands on Amy's face and had as good idea as any what she must look like. He certainly knew what she *felt* like. Mornings found him hard with arousal. His body jolted to life the moment *she* walked into the room. Desperate to find escape, to find distance, to find the man he'd been before his life had been turned upside down, he gratefully accepted the walking stick Will made for him from the branch of an oak if only for the chance to get out of the house and away from the source of his distress.

"It's nothing fancy," the boy had said, "but maybe it'll help you get around some."

And it had. Soon, Charles could navigate every room downstairs as well as the back garden. He walked the route to the church, the road down to the river, and even the pier from which Mira Ashton had brought them on their calamitous escapade. He spent as little time as he could with the Leightons, distrustful of his thoughts, his reactions, and his desire for Amy. He was already engaged to Juliet, and he could not afford to make a mistake for which he could never, not in a million years, forgive himself.

After all, he could not marry both of them.

"For a blind man," said the people of Newburyport, amazed at his determination to overcome his handicap, "he sure does get around!"

Three weeks after his letters had been posted, the first reply arrived.

It was Amy who brought it to him, part of her excited for his sake, part of her dreading its contents. She hadn't seen much of him lately, and she almost wondered if he was avoiding her, so much time did he spend away from the house. And now this. She knew he wouldn't be with them forever, that he had a life beyond their little house in Newburyport, but still, the idea of saying goodbye to him—a rare friend who had somehow managed to make her sisters share the cooking, a friend who defended her, encouraged her, made her feel a little better about herself, and didn't judge her for the circumstances of her birth—filled her with unbearable anguish.

She heard him calling out as she entered the house. "Amy? Do you have the post?"

How hard he tried to keep the eagerness and anticipation from his voice. And how sad it made her to know that in a few days he might be gone. Taking a deep breath, Amy carried the letter into the keeping room.

There, Lord Charles, ever conscious of how his healing scar must look to those around him, ever careful not to offend others' eyes, sat on his pallet, tying the shining gold waves of his hair back with a black ribbon.

"Is there anything for me?"

"Oh, just a letter from Boston," she quipped, hoping the forced playfulness in her voice would keep him from guessing how low she suddenly felt.

He was on his feet in a heartbeat. "Go ahead, Amy, open it. Tell me what it says!"

Amy broke the seal, opened the letter, and began to read:

My dear Captain de Montforte,

I am sorry to hear of your fate, and am much aggrieved by the loss of your sight. I am sure I'm not telling you anything you don't already know, when I point out that an injury of this nature renders you unsuitable to the army that you have previously served so well. Given the tumultuous situation here in Boston, and the fact that you seem to be in very good hands where you are, I would advise you to stay with the Leighton family in Newburyport until such time as you might recover your sight, and your value to us. In the meantime, I convey my best wishes for a complete and timely recovery.

"Signed, Lieutenant Colonel Maddison," Amy murmured, her own guilty gratitude that Charles would be staying with them a bit longer dashed to ribbons when she looked up and saw the look of devastation, of stunned betrayal, on his handsome face. Immediately, she hated herself for her selfishness.

"I'm sorry," she said, instinctively reaching out to touch his hand.

He jerked back. And then he just stood there, not moving, not saying a word. He blinked, once, that slow, studied lowering of long lashes that was so oddly characteristic of him, and turned away, trying to hide the myriad emotions that shadowed his face—confusion, denial, hurt, and finally anger. Head high, he moved to the window, placing his hands on the sill and turning his face up to the warm sunshine that streamed through the panes.

"Well," he said quietly. "I guess that's that, then. It seems that you and your family are to be burdened with me for a few days longer."

She went to stand beside him. "No, Charles. You are never a burden. Please don't even think such a thing."

"I should have known they would do nothing to help me. I should have known that my value to them was determined only by my physical ability. I should have known . . . and yet, I had hoped otherwise." He gave a humorless little laugh and shook his head. "Silly me. Silly, silly me."

"*They're* the ones being silly, not you! Blind or not, I'll bet you're the finest soldier in the king's army! Why, if your Lieutenant Colonel Maddison knew you half as well as we do, he'd realize you're not 'unsuitable' a'tall! He's abandoned you, and I know you'd never have done such a thing to one of *your* men!"

"I would have died first," he admitted softly, and Amy knew then that he was thinking of the young soldier he'd been attempting to rescue, the bullets flying all about him, on that terrible day that had rendered him blind. "But you must not judge Maddison so harshly, Amy. He is merely seeing to the needs of his troops."

"What about *your* needs?"

"My needs cease to matter."

"This isn't fair!" she cried, her heart aching for him.

"What in life, is? I brought this on myself, Amy. It is my fault, not Maddison's, that I find myself in this predicament. Therefore it is I, not him, who must pay the cost for my clumsiness and stupidity."

"You *weren't* clumsy and you certainly weren't stupid! For God's sake, you saved the life of a child!"

His mouth tightened and with a little shake of his head he turned away, already weary of the argument. He would hear no more about it. And Amy knew him well enough to understand that to his mind, which tolerated nothing less than self-perfection, he was the one at fault, the only one to blame. He did not see his actions in saving Will as heroic. All he considered was that he had stepped backwards, lost his balance, and wiped out the rest of his life.

"I refuse to allow you to blame yourself for this," she said heatedly, wishing she could give this Maddison fellow a piece of her mind. "I refuse it!"

Very gently, and without facing her, he murmured, "Though you have been of great help and comfort, there are some things, Amy, that you cannot do for me. Clearing me of blame is one of them. I am sorry."

And with that he walked away, leaving her standing there all alone with the letter burning a hole in her hand.

She hurled it into the fire and watched the flames consume the offending vellum.

Take that, Maddison! she thought angrily. *He's worth far more to me than he is to you, anyhow!*

*   *   *

Most of Newburyport had good cause to hate the English army over the following weeks, each one devoid of letters for Lord Charles, but full of news from Boston that was downright horrible. Boston was a seething hotbed of horror, under blockade. And in June, the patriots made a stand on Breed's Hill, and hundreds of men on both sides—including the gentle, renowned Dr. Joseph Warren of the Americans, and Major Pitcairn of the king's forces, who had made a name for himself during the Concord expedition two months past—were lost. It was a long, bloody battle, and one that sent reverberations of hatred, sorrow, and grief rippling across the Atlantic and down through every one of the thirteen colonies.

What had begun as complaint had become conflict, and what had become conflict was now downright war.

Upon hearing the news about Breed's Hill, Charles sank even further into the depression that he'd been unable to throw off since receiving the letter from his commanding officer. Amy knew he was worried about Juliet, but she also suspected he was mourning the loss of friends, for rumor had it that the Americans, eager to wipe out enemy leadership, had focused their sharpshooting skills upon the bright coats of the British officers, dispatching those who wore them with deadly accuracy. Hearing this, Amy had shuddered violently, for it wasn't hard to imagine Charles out there with his peers, calmly giving orders one moment—and lying dead on the ground the next.

For the first time since he'd arrived here, she was almost thankful for his blindness.

And almost thankful that Lieutenant Colonel Maddison now found him "unsuitable." Although his pride had been dealt a stinging blow by the army's rejection, at least he was safe, and far away from the fighting that was tearing Massachusetts apart.

But the days passed, and no letters came from either Juliet Paige or his family in England. Though it was still early to expect a letter from the latter, Charles was sick with worry about his fiancée, tormenting himself with visions of her in a besieged and war-torn Boston, carrying the bastard babe of a hated English soldier and suffering the abuse of her patriotic neighbors. Sylvanus tried to relieve his distress by reminding him that Boston had been shut off from the mainland by the British troops, so surely the post going in and out of the town must be hampered as well.

But even such a rational explanation could not ease Charles's mind. Everyone noted the bleakness in his eyes, the pallor of his skin, the fact that lately, he would only pick at his food, and leave most of his meal uneaten.

And each and every one of them began to worry.

"He can't go on like this," Will told his father one day, striding purposefully into Sylvanus's study and shutting the door behind him. "We've got to do something, Pa."

Sylvanus, keeping his voice low so that Charles, who seemed to have very keen hearing, could not hear their conversation, murmured, "I can't make the post go any faster, Will."

"No, but you could let me go down to Uncle Eb's and bring him back a surprise."

"A surprise? What are you talking about, son?"

"Well, this morning, when the captain and I were out walking, Mira Ashton went past on El Nath, that mean-tempered black stallion of hers. She stopped and good-naturedly harassed the captain, as she usually does, about his being 'a Brit,' and while Lord Charles was a-standing there, stroking the horse's neck, I saw such a look of sorrow come over his face as you wouldn't believe. Next thing you know, that horse was rubbing its head all up and down his arm, and Mira was hollering about the horse being a traitor to the rebel cause, and Lord Charles was smiling a sad little smile and saying he'd never met a horse that didn't like him, whether it was a rebel horse or not.'' Will took a deep breath, looked his father in the eye, and said, "I think I know of a way that might make him happy again, Pa.''

"Well, you've got *my* attention,'' said Sylvanus. "What do you have in mind?"

"Remember that day he got hurt, and I took him to Uncle Eb's before bringing him here? Well, there was one thing that belonged to him that I had to leave behind.''

"Don't tell me,'' Sylvanus said, taking off his spectacles and rubbing suddenly-weary eyes. "His horse.''

"Aye, Pa, his horse.'' Will squared his shoulders and lifted his chin. "I'm a-wondering if I can go down to Uncle Eb's and bring it back. Besides a letter from his fiancée, there's probably nothing that'll cheer him up more than having his horse back.''

"But he can't ride it, Will,'' Sylvanus said gently. "Having it here will only remind him all the more of the things he can no longer do, and make him feel worse than he already does.''

"But he doesn't *have* to ride it, Pa. Amy can—Mira taught her how, and she can give it all the exercise it needs.''

"Amy has enough to do without exercising a horse, son.''

"Aye, she does. And this might not be my place, Pa, but I think it's high time that Millie and Ophelia did some of their own washing and mending.'' He raised his chin. "Amy never gets to have any fun, and it just isn't fair.''

Sylvanus sighed and gazed at the closed door, beyond which sat their silent guest. He knew his son was right;

he also knew that all chaos would break loose if he imposed such a ruling on his daughters, both of whom would object, and most violently at that. It had been hard enough just to get them each to cook a meal one day a week. He wished his Mary were here to guide him. He wished he had the patience and energy to stand up to their whining tantrums; and above all, he wished he could get them married off. Despite their beauty, despite the well-spokenness their gently-bred mother had insisted that all her girls possess, there had been no takers, and lately, he had begun to wonder if there ever would be.

Especially since they were no longer interested in Newburyport's eligible young men, but only in the handsome English captain, for whom they might as well not even exist.

Will was still standing there, waiting.

"Very well then, son. Go to my brother and fetch the horse, but you are to come immediately back, is that understood?" He levelled a warning stare on his son from over the top of his spectacles. "No stopping anyplace along the way, no joining any fighting, and no hobnobbing with the countryfolk. I have not forgotten the *last* time I allowed you to go to my brother's," he added, ruefully.

"I swear, Pa, I'll come right back. I've got no stomach for fighting anymore, I swear it, I don't."

"You don't need to *swear* to convince me. Just go, come right back, and be safe."

"Thank you, Pa—I just know this'll bring the captain 'round."

Will turned on his heel and made for the door.

"And Will?"

The boy stopped.

"One more thing. As you pointed out, Amy has enough to do around here. Therefore, you, not Amy, will be the one taking care of the animal. It will be your responsibility.''

Will raised his head and squarely met his father's gaze. ''No, Pa. 'Twill be the captain's responsibility. He may be blind, but there's nothing stopping him from taking care of his own horse.''

And with that he left, leaving his father staring after him.

He left for Woburn that evening. And the following afternoon, the two letters that Lord Charles had been awaiting for so long finally arrived.

Chapter 11

Sylvanus was off visiting a sick parishioner, Will hadn't been around since morning, and Amy had gone to market. Thus, it was the sisters who came back from town with the post.

"Why, Ophelia, would you look at this! Not one, but *two* letters for Lord Charles, and one all the way from England!"

Instantly, he was on his feet.

"And what a fancy envelope—do you think it's from the *duke*?"

"I don't know, Millie, but that sure does look like an impressive seal on the back ..." And then, Ophelia's voice dropping to a whisper, "Hurry, let's bring them to him now, before Amy gets back. Maybe if *we're* the ones to do him this small favor, he'll pay us more attention!"

They charged into the room. "Lord Charles, two letters have come for you and one's from England! Do you want us to read them to you?"

"Oh yes, please Lord Charles, you never let us do anything for you and we'd be honored to perform this small kindness—"

"Where is Amy?"

Ophelia made a scoffing noise. "In town, no doubt trying to decide between cod and flounder for tonight's stew."

Charles stood unmoving. The letters were personal and he didn't want anyone but Amy to know what was in them—especially the one from Juliet. But Amy was not here. Amy wouldn't be back for a while. And Charles knew, much to his dismay, that he had neither the will nor the patience to wait for her return.

He walked across the room and leaned against the open door, keeping his back to the two girls. "Go on then," he said quietly. "Open and read the one from England."

"What about the other, Lord Charles? Don't you want to know what's in that one as well?"

"I think I shall save that one for later."

He heard them breaking the seal, unfolding the letter, and Ophelia clearing her throat as she prepared to read. He swallowed, hard, overcome by such a flood of gratitude and relief that it nearly overwhelmed him. *Thank you, Lucien. And thank God for you. I knew that you would come for me . . . knew that you, and my family, would never let me down.*

He leaned his cheek against the cool wood of the doorjamb and closed his eyes.

And then Ophelia began to read.

"My dear Charles," she said, her voice sing-song with excitement, "You cannot imagine my distress and disappointment when I learned of your recent exploits and injury at Concord. As you well know—"

She paused abruptly.

"Go on," Charles urged.

"I, uh . . . don't know if you want to hear the rest," she said slowly.

He frowned and straightened up, turning on his heel

to face them. "Don't be absurd, of course I want to hear the rest. He's my brother, for heaven's sake."

Dear God, has something happened to one of my family?

Silence, and Charles could sense the two of them exchanging glances. Hesitating. Growing uneasy. A tingle of apprehension settled itself in the base of his spine.

And then Ophelia continued. ". . . as you well know," she read softly, "you have always been the pride of our family, the one upon whom rested our hopes of glory. When you left for those godforsaken colonies, I felt confident in knowing that you would do me, and our family, proud. But it was not to be. I am embarrassed by your performance at Concord, humiliated by your actions in battle, and disappointed that you—you of *all* people—have brought only shame upon us, when I sent you away with the highest expectations of honor. Had you sustained such a grievous injury whilst fighting a worthy opponent, I would be inclined to be more forgiving, but the knowledge that you brought on your miseries by your own clumsiness, poor judgement, and hesitation, grieves me to no end. I expected more from you, my brother. More from you than everyone else in this family combined. You have disappointed me, you have disappointed our family, and you have disappointed the village that sent you away with such pride and high hopes. In closing, I hope you can understand that while you will always have a home here at Blackheath, my own feelings are such that I cannot come personally to America to bring you back. I am sure you'll understand, and I wish you well in your recuperation. Until such time as we meet again . . ."

Charles stood frozen.

"Signed, Blackheath."

Silence, as Charles numbly tried to digest what he'd just heard. And then:

"He signed it *Blackheath*?!"

"Well, yes . . ."

Not Lucien. Not Luce. *Blackheath*. Crushed, he wiped a hand over his face and pushed himself away from the doorjamb, feeling as though everything he'd ever believed in had just been ripped out from under him. This was a bad dream. This could not be happening. Lucien would never do this to him, never, not in a million years!

"There must be some mistake . . ." He shook his head and took a few aimless steps, trying to deny the terrible words. "I cannot believe he would be so cruel . . ."

Mildred's voice gentled with sympathy. "I read the letter just as he wrote it, Lord Charles. Do you want me to read it again?"

As if he could bear to hear those damning words repeated! As if he could stand the pain of such a brutal knife to the heart all over again! "No," he ground out, pressing two fingers to his brow. "No, thank you, once is quite enough." And as he turned away from what he knew must be their curious stares, he felt a desperation that scared him, a raw torrent of pain clawing at his heart, making his throat so tight it ached with desperate, unshed emotion. *Amy.* God help him, he wanted Amy, needed Amy, with an intensity he could no longer explain or ignore.

He straightened up and it was a compliment to his self-control that he managed to keep his voice perfectly calm, his expression perfectly still. "Please—will you tell me when your sister will return?"

"Around five. But really, Lord Charles, why wait for her when we're here to read the other letter for you?"

He shook his head, desperate to escape before his rising emotions tore him apart and embarrassed him. Wordlessly, he held out his hand for both letters, shoved them into his pocket, and, pausing only long enough to pick up his walking stick, strode out the door.

"Lord Charles?" called Ophelia, her voice anxious with worry.

He didn't answer, wanting only to get away from them, to get away from everyone, and find a place to be alone until he could come to terms with what his brother had written.

He did not know where he was going. People yelled at him to get out of the street, to mind the carriages rushing past, to have a care where he was walking . . .

I expected more from you . . . than everyone else in this family combined. You have disappointed me, you have disappointed our family, and you have disappointed the village that sent you away with such pride and high hopes.

And that was the worst of it, because he had never disappointed anyone in his life, and the word hung suspended before him like a blazing sun on a hot summer afternoon:

Disappointed. Disappointed. Disappointed.

Cool wind now, and the scent of salt marshes as he neared the river. Gulls screaming, and the high-pitched cry of the sandpipers. And somewhere very near, the mighty river itself. Charles could hear it. He could smell it. A mile to the east, it widened into the broad basin in which Mira had come to such grief, swept majestically around the western side of Plum Island, and gave itself up into the embrace of the Atlantic. Or so everyone said.

He heard water surging against the pier, burbling and sucking around upright wood. The tide must be high. The cane swinging before him, he stepped out onto the pier and began to walk. His footsteps sounded hollow on the planking, and through his soles he could feel the swift outgoing tide thrumming against the supports as though trying to carry away the whole lot.

He walked as far out as he could go. When he reached the end of the pier he sat down, and, turning his face

into the salty breeze, pulled out Lucien's letter, the initial
tide of pain subsiding as he tried to understand why his
brother had treated him so cruelly.

He smoothed the heavy vellum. What could have
driven Lucien to be so lacking in compassion for the
one brother he'd always regarded as an equal, the one
brother who had never given him any trouble at all, the
one brother that had been groomed since birth to take
over as duke should anything happen to him?

And then it came to him.

Had his depression, self-disgust, and crushing sense
of failure—all things that the old Charles had never
known—come through in the words he'd dictated that
night in his letter to Lucien?

Probably. And if not, Lucien was more than capable
of reading between the lines.

"Why . . . you conniving *bastard*, you," he swore,
partly in admiration, and partly in mounting anger. The
devil take him, why hadn't he seen it before? Lucien,
with his manipulating games! Playing off people's emotions to get them to do his bidding! Was it conceivable
that he'd employ such tactics on him, Charles? *Would*
he? Lucien had never done so in the past, had never had
any reason to do so—but Charles had seen him practice
it countless times upon his two younger brothers, and
once or twice upon his sister, and now, as he sat there
on the pier and considered this new possibility, he became increasingly certain that Lucien was doing exactly
the same thing to him.

The knowledge stung.

It hurt.

And most of all, it insulted.

"How *could* you?" Charles crushed the letter in his
fist, anger blazing through him. "Do you think that by
wounding me with your insults, you can restore me to
the man I once was? I may be blind, damn it, but I can

see exactly what you're trying to do and I don't appreciate it!'' The anger moved out into his fingers, making them tremble; into his head, resurrecting the ache that was so easily called back during moments of stress. ''You and I have always regarded each other with dignity, friendship, and respect, but you have cut me to the quick with this, Lucien! I thought that you of all people would understand what I'm feeling . . . That you, of all people, would understand the hell in which I've spent the past two months.'' He drove his knuckles into his useless eyes. ''You have let me down, and this when I have never needed you more. The hell with you, then. *The hell with you!*''

Balling the letter in his fist, he hurled it far out over the water and buried his head in his hands. And as he sat there vowing never to return to England if this was a sampling of the treatment his older brother had in store for him, he heard someone calling him.

His head jerked up.

Amy.

Feelings he could neither explain nor rationalize crashed over him and in that moment, he wanted only the comfort of her touch, the balm of her presence, and God help him, God forgive him, the surrounding warmth of her arms. He rose to his feet as her light footsteps came running down the pier.

''Charles, what is wrong? What are you doing out here? Do you know how close you are to the edge?''

''I got a letter from Lucien,'' he bit out in a voice hoarse with pain and anger, and it was all he could do not to reach out for her, all he could do not to walk into the embrace he knew she would never hold back. ''He has rejected me. Insulted me. Affirmed the shame I've been struggling to overcome for the past miserable months . . .''

"Please, Charles, take my hand and let me lead you away from the edge."

He flung out his arm, palm up, preventing her from coming any closer. "No, Amy. I cannot touch you, for I have never needed you as much as I do in this moment, and God help me, if I touch you I may find myself unable to *stop* touching you, and if that were to happen I swear the guilt I already feel will be my undoing—"

"Charles, what are you saying?"

"It doesn't matter what I'm saying, Amy, sweet Jesus, forget I said anything and please"—he plunged his hand into his pocket, found the letter from Juliet, and held it out to her—"please, just read this before any more time passes, I beg of you, please read it and show me that someone in my life still cares for me and that this world has not been turned completely upside down, I beg of you Amy, read it and read it *now*!"

He drew back, trembling, hands pressed against his sightless eyes as he tried to get himself under control. He felt her hands against his shoulders, heard her soft voice only inches away.

"Charles, please, it's all right—"

"It's *not* all right, can you not see? My army has rejected me, my own brother toys with me in the name of *discipline*, and here I am in my darkest hour and who is it that I want to reach for, who is it that I want to hold, who is it that I need more than any other person on earth?"

"Charles—"

"It's *you*, Amy, can't you see it, can't you feel it, can't you understand that you are the very center of my existence?! You, not Juliet. You. God damn it, I need *you*."

He pushed away from her and bent his head to his balled fist, his mouth twisted in pain and self-loathing for these needs he could not control, these feelings he should never have.

"I'm sorry," Amy whispered, reeling with shock at what he'd just confessed. "I didn't know . . ."

"Juliet is the one I should want right now, not you," he was saying, hoarsely. "It is she who holds my heart, who wears my ring, who carries my unborn baby . . . Oh, God help me, Amy, read the letter. Read the damned letter now, so that I may be reminded where my heart lies, so that I may be reminded of my promise to the woman who loves me, so that I may be reminded of who I was and who I seek to remain. Read it so that I may know that *she*, at least, is still there for me when everyone on whom I thought I could depend, has abandoned me . . ."

Amy, trembling and afraid, put down her packages and silently took the letter from him. The shadows were long, the pier deserted, even the distant hammering from the Ashton Shipyards had ceased. Everyone had gone home for the night. She slowly broke the seal on the letter, scanned its contents, and, her eyes filling with tears, pushed a hand to her mouth.

No. Please God, no.

"Amy?" He stood there before her, his body rigid with anticipation, his mouth a slash of pain, his eyes fierce with a desperate hope. And Amy looked beyond his shoulder, at the wide expanse of water moving slowly toward and past them as it pushed its way out to sea, and suddenly felt a sense of menace. Dread shivered through her and she took Charles's hand. It felt stiff. Cold.

Like that of a man already dead.

He swallowed, and she knew then that he already suspected the worst. She squeezed her eyes shut on a film of silent tears. And then she quietly led him off the pier. Onto the soft bank that held back the river. Up the slight slope to a patch of grass, where she sat down and bade him to do the same.

She looked over at him. His face was totally expressionless.

"Go on," he said. "Read the letter."

She did.

Chapter 12

Dear Charles,

I know it has been some time since you wrote, and I hope you are still at the address you gave, for this letter to reach you. The time since we last met has been hell for me, and it has been as much as I have been able to do to keep body and mind together, never mind responding to your pitiful writings.

First I heard you were dead, then I received your letter from Newburyport and learned that you were blind. I am afraid that the shock of these several pieces of news led me to lose our baby, and I nearly died myself in the process.

The fact of the baby has not gone unnoticed, of course, and enough people have associated this news with the liaison I had with a king's officer, that my life, and that of my stepfather, has become almost unbearable.

I realise now that I no longer love you. You have ruined my life with the baby, I have lost the respect and the trust of our neighbours, and I have

no sympathy for the self-pitying letter you wrote
after your ridiculous accident at Concord. You are
not the man I thought you were.

In short, I intend to pick up the pieces and try
to make the most of what I have left, and I com-
mend you to do the same; however, do not make
things even more unpleasant for either of us by
trying to contact me again.

Juliet Paige

Amy lowered the letter.

And then she looked at Charles.

He sat beside her, his hair catching the last rays of
the dying sun, his lashes throwing shadows across
cheeks that had drained of blood. His face was fright-
eningly still. His fingers were interlocked in a sort of
double fist, the knuckles showing white; instinctively,
she reached out to touch them.

They were trembling.

"I'm so sorry," she whispered, wishing with all her
heart that she could take this pain from him. "About the
baby, about Juliet . . ." She squeezed his hand. "You
deserve so much better than this . . ."

His throat was working. He blinked in that painfully
slow, studied way he had and pulled himself to his feet,
where he stood swaying a bit, his gaze fixed on a horizon
he could not see.

"You're a fine man, and if Juliet can't see that, then
she's not worthy of you . . ."

He stood there, just staring emptily out over the darkening water.

"Please, Charles, say something—you're frightening
me."

He looked down at her then, blinked, and for a moment, she almost thought he could see her, so true, so

deep, was his gaze. There were tears in his eyes. He
smiled, gently—

And then, as though he could see exactly where he
was going, he began to walk toward the riverbank.

"Charles?"

And straight into the water.

"*Charles!*"

Amy leaped to her feet, grabbed up her skirts, and
charged after him. "Charles, no! *No!*"

He waded right up to his knees in the salty outgoing
tide, up to his thighs, staggering now, one arm thrown
out for balance, the opposite hand pressed to his eyes in
a futile attempt to hold back the tears. Amy plunged in
after him and made a desperate grab for his arm. He
gave one raw, choking sob, and then half fell, half threw
himself into the current, which quickly caught him and
began to sweep him downriver.

"Charles!" Amy screamed. "*Charles!*"

Terror gripped her. Heedless of modesty, Amy tore
off everything but her stays and shift, leaped onto the
pier, and pounded down its length as fast as she could
run.

"Charles!"

Without breaking stride, she flung herself off the pier
and far out into the river, where the current ran faster
than it did near shore and would carry her down to him
with utmost speed. Fighting her way to the surface, kicking furiously to speed her progress, Amy angled out
away from shore. Already the current was carrying her
down toward the dark blond head.

*Please, dear God, let me get to him in time . . . he's
lost everything, he doesn't know what he's doing—
please, God, he deserves better than this!*

The river bore her steadily down on him, frightening
her with the immense power of hundreds of tons of water all around her. Salt stung her eyes. Her skin ached

with cold. And now she was coming up to him, now he was thirty feet away . . . fifteen . . . closer in to shore than she was and not at the mercy of as much current. *Please, God, don't let it sweep me past him!* She struck out against the flow, swimming diagonally toward shore, crying, shouting, flinging out an arm in a desperate attempt to reach him. Her fingers hooked in his collar. Held. The rest of her body swept past him, so that she was caught on him like a boat at its mooring.

Both of them were going downriver now.

"Damn you, Amy, leave me be!" he shouted hoarsely.

"I won't let you die!"

"Damn you I *want* to die!"

"You can't die, because suicide is the same as throwing God's gift of life right back in His face, and I can't let you do that, Charles, I can't—"

She cried out as his shirt tore and she was swept away from him.

"Amy!"

The current caught her. Gamely, she tried to fight it. She snatched at the mooring line of a schooner as she was carried past, and missed. Beneath her was some thirty feet of water, and whirling, sucking tornadoes of current that were all going downriver with her.

"*Amy!*" he roared, striking blindly out towards her. "Amy, call to me, keep calling so that I know where you are!"

"Charles!"

Oh no, oh please God, no!

She tried to swim diagonally back toward shore, to work with the current instead of against it, but it was too strong for her. It pulled her braid from its pins and out past her fast-moving body; it dragged at her tiring legs and arms, bore her along like a leaf on the wind. She saw marshlands slipping past, a moored sloop, and envisioned herself being carried straight out past the mouth of the river and into the sea, never to be found, never to be seen again. *Oh, God help me, please God, help!*

"Charles!"

"Keep calling me, Amy, for God's sake keep calling!"

"Charles! *Charles!*"

She clawed her way around to face him, and there he was, ten feet away . . . five . . . an arm's length . . . reaching blindly out for her, his face a mask of desperation and terror that he would lose her. Amy, crying out, lunged toward him. Their fingers met, and were ripped apart once more. "Charles!" And then his hand lashed out and seized hers in a grip that nearly broke every bone in her wrist with the force with which he claimed her.

Together they struggled toward shore. Amy's strength was all but gone. Her lungs were heaving, her skin felt brittle with cold, salt water blinded her. But the grip Charles had on her wrist would've anchored any one of the boats that they were slipping past. A powerful swimmer, he angled straight across the swift outgoing tide and brought them safely toward shore.

And then there was mud beneath their feet, then grass, and he had her in his arms and against his chest as he waded out of the river, water streaming from his loose hair.

"Damn you for a little fool!" he rasped, staggering up onto the bank with her. And then, on a harsh, anguished sob, "What the *hell* do you think you were doing?"

His voice broke and Amy had no time to answer him, for his mouth came crashing down on hers and she was tumbling down to the soft bank.

"Charles!"

He buried his face in her shoulder, great, racking sobs convulsing his body. "Christ, to think I nearly just lost you as well . . . I need you so badly . . . you're the only one left to me . . . I don't know what I'm doing, I don't want to live anymore, I have nothing left to live for, I cannot go on—"

"Stop it!"

"I cannot fight this anymore, I just don't have it in me, it's too much, just too much . . ."

"Yes you *can*!"

She pulled his head down and wrapped her arms fiercely around the back of his neck. He struggled for the briefest of moments; then, with a harsh sound of defeat, he drove his mouth against hers, his hand plunging into the sleek wet hair behind her ear, his lips crushing hers with the desperation of the damned. Amy's head fell backwards, into grass and sand. She felt his weight come down alongside of and atop her, pressing her further into the damp earth, and now water was running out of his hair, down his cheeks, around and into their open, searching mouths. She tasted salt, and the tears of his anguish; felt the heat of his hand through her stays and the drenched cotton shift, and gasped as splinters of delight shot through her blood, bursting out in all directions, centering in a spot between her legs until she began to pant and writhe beneath him.

He tore his face away, his breathing as harsh as hers, his expression anguished.

"Dear *God*, what am I doing?"

She locked her arms around his shoulders as he tried to move away, fearing he'd throw himself straight back into the river. "Charles, please! I can't let you go!"

"You must, I need you—I *want* you—I fear my despair, I fear my need, I fear the control they have over me and my intentions . . . But oh, God, I need you . . . I want you . . ."

"I want you too, Charles."

"You don't know what you want, you don't know what you *ask*!"

"I love you, Charles. *I love you.*"

He gave a harsh sob, and then his mouth was against hers once more, kissing her hard and deep, his tongue thrusting into her mouth and plundering it ruthlessly. Her arms tightened around his shoulders, and then he was tearing his face away, only to drag fervent kisses down the salty, chilled skin of her jaw, her throat, the point of her collarbone. He had her stays unlaced, the soaked, boned garment ripped open before she knew what he was about, and now she felt his broad hand warming her flesh, cupping her breast, his mouth and tongue hot against her skin, moving lower and lower before finally fastening over her nipple and drawing both it and the gauzy wet shift up into his mouth. He suckled her hard. Amy arched upwards, a moan tearing from her throat as sensation exploded inside her. She drove her hands into his wet hair, holding him close, pushing herself wantonly into him. In seconds her skin was on fire, her insides a boiling cauldron, her breathing raw and raspy. And now his other hand was peeling the wet clinging cotton from her legs, driving between her thighs, caressing them up the inside and splaying fingers into the soft mound of curls between them, already slick with desire for him.

"Oh, God, Amy, please forgive me—"

His fingers plunged inside her. Amy gasped and bucked upwards, his name falling from her lips, her fingernails digging into his back. A raw, burning ache radiated out from where his hand was . . . from where his mouth was, gathering in a fierce, smoldering coil at the apex of her legs. She both fought it and strained toward it, not understanding it but knowing only that she must have it. Oh, heaven wasn't up in the sky; heaven was the feel of this man kissing her breast; heaven was his hand stroking her between her open thighs; heaven was the feel of his hot mouth against her nipple; his body against her own, the confession that he needed her—

Heaven was Charles.

And then she gave a muffled cry as his thumb, which had been stroking her so intimately *down there*, hit something she hadn't known existed and her senses began to splinter into a thousand pieces of glass. "Charles!" she half gasped, half sobbed, and then, as his fingers kept stroking, stroking, *stroking*, "Charles— *Charles!*"

"God help me," he rasped, and as she convulsed with pleasure, he fumbled with his wet breeches, groaned, and moved to cover her. Something hard stabbed at the inside of her thighs, at the hot and magical place he'd just shown her she had, and now his shoulders were blocking out the sunset, the red and orange clouds behind him, and he was moving into her, moving inside of her, filling her so full and stretching her so wide, that she thought she would faint with the feel of it. Wondrous pleasure. Hot, seething delight! She ought to stop him, she knew that she could, but no, no, oh please God no, this felt too good, this felt too right, and if she could give him no other gift than her love, if she alone could at least make him forget what the army, what Lucien, and most of all, what his heartless fiancée had done to him, then God help her she would, she would, she would, she *would*—

He thrust himself deeply inside her, impaling her virginity on the blade of his manhood and ripping a cry of surprise and pain from her lips. The world stopped. She clung to him, tears in her eyes, her legs wrapped around his straining loins. And then, slowly, he began to move his hips, to push himself deeper and deeper inside of her, until the pain dulled and became pleasure once more, until his breathing quickened and grew hoarse, until his lips came down on hers, kissing her desperately even as she flung out a hand and he found it and their fingers interlocked of their own accord, gripping, squeezing, knuckles whitening. Now he was thrusting, now he was pulling out, now repeating it, doing it again, each long, slow surge growing more rapid, more powerful, than the one before—

"Oh, Amy—"

"Charles, don't stop, *please* don't stop!"

"I can't—God help me, *I can't*—"

With a cry, he gave one last thrust, and she felt his seed warming and pulsing against the walls of her womb, even as she felt her own muscles contracting and convulsing around him with a force that left her gasping. He pulled back slowly, and thrust ahead once more before he collapsed, still deep inside her, bringing his mouth down upon hers in a final, tender kiss.

A moment later she felt his mighty shoulders shaking with grief for all he had lost—and wordlessly, Amy put her arms around him.

Holding him.

Just holding him.

There was nothing that either of them could say.

Chapter 13

~~~◯◯◯~~~

He pushed away from her, finally, and got to his feet. His back was toward her as he buttoned his breeches. The silence, which before had been appropriate, now became awkward and uncomfortable.

They had to walk upriver to retrieve Amy's clothes. She crossed her neckerchief around her neck and shoulders, filling in the bare skin, the swell of her breasts above the shift's neckline. She tied on her underpetticoats. Laced her wet stays over her equally wet shift. Donned her over petticoats, tied on her apron, slipped her arms into her open short-gown, and finally looked at Charles. He was standing a little distance away, staring emptily out over the darkening river. One look at his face convinced her that it wasn't a good time to talk to him. Instead, she picked up his walking stick, pressed it into his hand, and retrieved her nearly-forgotten packages.

He was still standing there, stone-faced, silent.

"Charles?"

He didn't answer.

"Charles, what is the matter?"

"I should be *shot* for what I have just done to you."

162

"What do you mean?"

He just shook his head, then turned away. Amy, wondering at his change in attitude and wanting only to comfort him, touched his shoulder, but he jerked back as if she'd burned him with the end of a poker. It was then that Amy realized the significance of what they had done—a realization that grew all the more sobering when she happened to glance up and see the distant spire of Sylvanus's church rising above the trees and glowing white against the darkening sky.

Would God be angry with her for what she had done? Was she a sinner, no better than her mother and the man who had spawned her? But if she had sinned, why had it felt so right? Why hadn't these feelings of apprehension and uneasiness affected her when she'd been about to commit the act, instead of now?

She felt her soaked shift and stays pressing against her body, the sea-salt drying on her skin, and a strange rawness between her legs. Her braid had come unpinned and now hung down her back in a long wet rope. Her lips felt swollen, her nipples still throbbed, and she knew she must look a sight.

Reality closed in, and with it, fear. Would everyone in Newburyport suspect? Would they point and snicker and whisper behind her back that she was no better than her mother? And what would happen when they got back to the house?

"Come, I'd best get you home," Charles ground out.

Side by side, but not daring to touch one another, they walked back toward the road in silence.

"Charles—"

"I do not wish to talk about it, Amy."

"But I just want to ask you a question . . ."

"Go on then."

"Do you think that when we get home, everyone will . . . will know? That it'll be written all over my face?

That"—she glanced down—"they'll be able to tell?"

"No."

"Are you certain?"

"Yes."

"But when a woman gives herself to a man, don't you think people can take one look at her and know what she's done?"

"No."

"But—"

"Amy, *please.*"

She paused, staring up at him in mounting confusion. A few moments ago he'd held her as though he'd never let her go. Now, he only wanted to get away from her. What had changed?

"Charles, will you please tell me what is wrong?"

He, too, came to a stop, but didn't turn around. "I am a disgrace," he snarled. "To my family, to my rank, to myself. I cannot forgive myself for what I just allowed to happen between us."

"For what *you* just allowed?" She gave an incredulous little laugh. "I was as much a party to it as you were." She blushed. "Besides, I thought . . . that you enjoyed it."

"Enjoyed it? Not only have I ruined one young woman and got her with child, I have just ruined a second and God knows, maybe got her with child as well! What the hell difference does it make whether or not I enjoyed it? I behaved abominably! I am disgusted and ashamed of myself!"

"You were upset, I offered comfort, you took it. Besides, I *wanted* to do what we did."

"No, Amy, you're too innocent to know what you want. It was a mistake."

"It was not a mistake."

"It *was*," he bit out through clenched teeth.

Amy lifted her chin, her eyes flashing with anger.

"You really do enjoy torturing yourself, don't you?"

"I beg your pardon?"

"What happened between us was beautiful. You made me feel loved and special and needed, and that's a feeling I've *never* had. Right now, everything inside of me is still singing with joy and it feels good. It feels wonderful. But you, all you want to do is ruin it. All you want to do is stand there and torture yourself with guilt and hold yourself up to some impossible standard of perfection that no one on God's earth can possibly hope to reach, let alone maintain. Well, Charles, I won't let you take this away from me. I *like* feeling good. I *liked* what we just did. You can regret it all you like, but I'm not going to." She shoved a stray bit of hair behind her ear. "In fact, it will become my most treasured memory."

"You're too young, and too naive, to know what you're saying."

"And *you're* too caught up in your quest for self-perfection to appreciate something good when it comes your way."

"And what if you're pregnant? Is that *something good*? I seem to be quite adept at impregnating virgins. It will be interesting to see if you're so cheerful if, a month or so from now, you find yourself kissing a chamberpot 'and wondering where your missing menses have gone."

"I'll worry about that when the time comes."

"I think you should worry about it now."

"I have other things to worry about."

"Such as?"

"The reception I'm going to get when I get home."

"Indeed." He gripped her arm and pulled her forward. "So let's stop arguing and get you back before it grows any later."

He was silent all the rest of the way home. With each

step they took, Amy's anger faded and her trepidation grew. Would Sylvanus notice her kiss-swollen lips and know immediately what she had done? Would her sisters take one look at her and see the truth in her eyes? And most worrying of all, what of Charles? Would Sylvanus throw him out of the house?

Or worse yet, force him to marry her?

Amy shuddered. She couldn't see that happening. What would Sylvanus do without her? Besides, Sylvanus would not play upon Charles's sense of honor by forcing his hand. He would not compel Charles, the impeccably bred, heir-presumptive to an English dukedom, to marry Amy, a half breed and daughter of sin, whose physical appeal couldn't hold a candle to the other women of Newburyport, let alone England's aristocratic beauties.

No, Sylvanus would not do that.

Would he?

They found the house in an uproar. Sylvanus was just about to go out searching for them. Will still hadn't returned from Woburn. Ophelia and Mildred, who had peeled a few potatoes but otherwise not lifted a finger to start supper, immediately rounded on Amy, savagely berating her for her tardiness and her failure to start the meal on time.

Charles turned on them. "Leave her alone. I took a walk, fell off the pier, and nearly drowned. *She* was the one who risked her life to rescue me. *She's* the one who nearly drowned, herself. Instead of standing there shouting at her, go get her a blanket and stoke up the fire."

"What?"

"*Now!*" he barked, his eyes blazing.

It was the voice of authority. His captain's voice. And heeding it, the two sisters slunk away to do his bidding.

Charles slammed from the room.

"What troubles the captain?" Sylvanus asked when

they finally sat down to supper an hour later. He shot a glance toward the parlor, where Charles had retreated and still remained. "He seems most upset."

Amy stirred her chowder without interest. She was trying hard to keep her face downcast in the hopes that no one would notice her kiss-reddened lips, or the guilty truth in her eyes. "He had bad news from both England and Boston," she said quietly. "I doubt he has much appetite."

Her sisters perked up. "Boston?"

"Yes."

"What was the news?"

Amy was reluctant to say anything, but everyone was gazing expectantly at her. "His fiancée has ended their betrothal and wants nothing more to do with him."

"Oh, good!"

Amy glanced up sharply. "Oh, *good*?"

"Well, yes," said Mildred, smugly. "Now *we* have a chance at him!"

Amy's spoon crashed down beside her bowl. "How can you be so cruel?! He's lost everything he owned, everything he loved, and all you can think of is what *you* might gain from his misfortune! You should be showing him sympathy and compassion, not trying to snare him in his weakest moment!"

"*Amy!*" sputtered Sylvanus, nearly choking on a bit of fish at this completely unexpected display of fire from the one member of his family that had never, ever, even raised her voice to him.

Mildred and Ophelia were staring at her in shock.

"Well it's true, Father!" Amy said angrily. "It's true and you know it!"

There was a moment of uneasy silence before Ophelia, looking Amy up and down with a look of raking contempt, finally spoke.

"Well," she said haughtily. "I'm sure Millie and I

can think of ways where we can show him *sympathy and compassion*, right, Millie?''

Mildred's eyes narrowed and her smile grew sly. ''Oh, absolutely.''

Amy had heard enough. Seething, she jumped to her feet, threw her napkin down on the table, and stormed from the room, leaving three pairs of surprised eyebrows raised in her wake.

''Well,'' said Sylvanus, stunned.

''Well, indeed! Are you going to let her get away with that, Papa? *Are you?*''

''As a matter of fact, I am,'' he said, wearily rubbing his brow. ''It's obvious she cares for the man and puts his welfare above her own. I see no need to punish her for it.''

Mildred's lips thinned. Ophelia's eyes narrowed. Both of them clenched their fists beneath the table.

''Furthermore, I am unhappy with the recent direction of this conversation,'' Sylvanus continued in the angry silence. ''The last thing Lord Charles needs or wants right now is feminine attention.''

''Don't be absurd, father, *all* men need feminine attention,'' snapped Mildred.

''Yes, it'll make him feel better, and reaffirm just how worthy he really is.''

''I said, leave him alone. The pain and suffering that man has endured over the past two months is enough to break anyone. He needs to be left alone. He need time to grieve. You're both to give him peace, do you understand me? *Peace.*''

Silence.

And then; ''Yes, Papa,'' the sisters said, but beneath lowered lashes, their eyes gleamed with malice and cunning.

*   *   *

Charles needed more than just time to grieve. That night, as he lay on his pallet—which had been moved upstairs into Will's room so that he might have more privacy—and stared into the ever-present darkness, he realized he'd sunk as far as he could go. For a man who had always tried to be perfect, to do everything right, to be all that—and more than—everyone expected of him, it was a bitter truth.

He had not learned from his mistake with Juliet. In a moment of passion, he had got her with child and ruined her life.

And now, he might well have ruined Amy's as well.

Oh, what had gone wrong with him? What had gone wrong with his life?

He thought back to the day he'd met Juliet. He'd been astride Contender, drilling his troops on snowy Boston Common. With that strange feeling of eyes on his back, he'd turned, and there she'd been, a dark-haired maiden peering at him from behind the window of a nearby store. And there she'd been every day thereafter, secretly watching him, until he'd finally entered the store on the excuse of a purchase so he could find out who the devil she was and why she was so interested in him. She had blushed wildly when he'd walked boldly through the door, dropped a sack of flour she'd been carrying, and began stammering foolishly—much to his amusement. He had vowed not to have anything to do with her, but he had. He had vowed not to strike up an acquaintance with her, but he had. He had thought he was above the carnal desires that made men do things they shouldn't— but he was not. Boston was a lonely place for an English soldier. Juliet Paige was pretty, sweet-natured, and eager to be in his arms. Within a week, she was. Within a month, he'd got her pregnant. He'd known from the beginning that she'd been infatuated with him, but he had wondered then, and had wondered rather uneasily many times since, if perhaps she'd been more enamored of the sight he'd made in his uniform than she'd been of the man inside of it.

Never in a million years had he thought she would betray him like this, but then, how well had he really known her? When he'd injured himself at Concord, they'd been acquainted for a mere four months. Their times together had been brief and, thanks to the explosive political tensions in Boston, spent in the utmost secrecy. Juliet had declared her love for him. But now, given the ease with which she'd thrown him out of her life, Charles wondered if maybe she hadn't loved him after all.

But did you love her?

Of course he had. Or so he'd always told himself. After all, he'd offered to marry her, for heaven's sake. But was that because of love—or of duty? When she'd come to him on the night of the fateful Concord expedition, with the news that she was pregnant, there was never any question in Charles's mind what he must do. His betrothal to Lady Katharine, planned for him by others and in place since his birth, had ceased to matter, for Katharine was three thousand miles away, safe, and he'd never loved her anyhow. Juliet Paige was right there in Boston and expecting his child. *His child.* Her needs, and their unborn baby's, were paramount. Katharine would find another suitor to marry; Juliet Paige, ruined by "the enemy" and carrying his babe, would not. As a gentleman, Charles had done the only thing he could do: offer to marry her.

But did you love her?

He wasn't sure, now. Nor was he sure if he was only questioning his feelings as a means of protecting his heart, and his pride, from the pain of her betrayal. Certainly, in comparison to Katharine, he had loved her. He had felt a need to protect her, to be with her, and to do right by her, even going so far as to instruct her to go to England and throw herself on Lucien's mercy in the event of his death. But had he mistaken the loneliness he'd felt in Boston—and then his overpowering sense of duty—for love?

His head was beginning to hurt. It was all too complicated, too confusing, and too wearisome to figure out. He had erred, though, and erred badly; that he *did* know. Always conscious of his betrothal to Katharine, he had lived his life free of romantic entanglements, and thus, didn't consider himself an expert in the area. Unlike his brother Gareth, he wasn't as seasoned a traveller along the highways and byroads of pleasure and passion. He had been pledged to Katharine, and that was that. With this aspect of his future already decided for him, he had seen no need to pursue it further, and thus, life's more serious callings had taken priority over any romantic entanglement that could only have ended in his taking a mistress at best, or hurting some innocent young woman like Juliet—*or Amy*—at worst.

Charles could not bear to hurt people.

He could not bear this sense of guilt and frustration at having messed things up so very, very badly.

And he didn't like to be hurt, himself.

There was nothing for it, then, but severing himself from the possibility of ever erring this way, again. It was obvious that he had a certain weakness where pretty young women were concerned; the fact that he'd deflowered not one, but two virgins was proof of that. And the way that Juliet, and now Amy, had reacted to him made him fear that there was something about him that women found attractive. Something that did neither them, nor himself, any favors when all was said and done.

I will never entangle myself with a woman again, he vowed. *In fact, I think I have had enough of relation-*

ships of any sort. Every attachment I've ever known— with my family, with Juliet, with my army—has brought me only hurt and pain. No more. Never again. I have always been self-sufficient. I have always done my duty to honor, integrity, and the expectations that others have of me as a gentleman. From now on, I shall shun all attachments, for they can bring me nothing but sorrow.

But then there was Amy. Amy who always treated him with respect, always believed in him, always brightened his day just by walking into the room, always found him worthy despite his shortcomings. She had seen him at his very worst, both physically, emotionally, and spiritually—and had not deserted him. She had stuck by him all these weeks when he'd been angry and hurting, a self-pitying wretch, a—what was it that Ophelia and Mildred had called him before they knew that his name was preceded by the word "Lord"?—"drain" upon her resources.

Amy was nothing at all like Juliet.

But no. Amy *was* like Juliet because she, too, was young and infatuated with him. And she, like Juliet, might let that infatuation get in the way of good judgement. Charles raked a hand over his face. He could not deny his desire for Amy, nor hers for him. It frightened him, the loss of control he'd experienced after he'd brought them both out of the river. That wasn't like him at all. He didn't want to get yet another woman pregnant. He didn't want to hurt anyone else. And besides, he didn't have a thing to offer Amy.

Not a damned thing.

If only there was a way to leave Newburyport, if only he could think of somewhere to go—for he knew in his bones that what had happened once, would surely happen again.

Soon.

For Amy—innocent, willing, naive, sweet-tempered Amy—was not safe from him.

And Charles wasn't safe from himself.

Chapter 14

Amy passed that night in vivid dreams.

In them, she was no lowly half breed, but a noblewoman in silks and satins, diamonds, powder and patches, a woman who was every inch Charles's social equal. In them, she'd been in his arms once again, comforting him, seeking comfort from him, loving him as he deserved to be loved, without feeling the guilt that she was not worthy of him, not worthy of even fantasizing about him. When she'd finally awakened to the pink light of dawn, her heart had plummeted upon the realization that it had all been a dream—until she'd stretched and felt the sudden, dull ache that still lingered between her thighs.

Her eyes had flown open. It had all been real then.

Blessedly real.

A thrill raced through her. Fired by the memories that they had made, reliving each moment of their lovemaking over and over again, she danced and twirled her way through her morning ablutions and all the way downstairs, careful not to wake anyone, her petticoats flying and her cheeks glowing with color.

She had just sobered and got the fire going when there

was a creak on the stair and Will came dashing into the keeping room, Crystal, her tail wagging, right behind him.

"Amy! I got back late last night and I've—"

"Shhhh!" She put a finger to her lips. "Everyone's still a'bed."

"I've got the horse!" he whispered, excitedly. "Come on out and see him!"

Of course; she'd almost forgotten that Will had gone down to Woburn for the animal. Oh, this if nothing else would cheer up Charles! Checking the fire to be sure it was safe, Amy picked up her skirts and ran outside to the barn with her brother.

"My goodness, Will, he must be all of seventeen hands!" she gasped, amazed. "How on earth did you ever get up on his back?"

"It wasn't easy," he admitted, patting the animal's sleek brown neck. "Isn't he a beauty, though? Oh, I can't wait for the captain to see him!" And then, realizing what he'd just said, he added, "Well, you know what I mean . . ."

"Yes. I know what you mean." Amy was still gazing up at the magnificent steed, who was stretching his neck over the stall door and sniffing the equally curious Crystal. Most of the horses she knew were sturdy, stocky, tough little animals as hardy as the New England land from which they came. Most were ill-proportioned and rather ugly. But this handsome stallion had obviously been brought from England—and looked as aristocratic as its owner.

His dark chestnut hide gleamed like glass. His legs were long, his neck proudly arched, his small ears set atop an expressive, intelligent head. His eyes were like velvet, and he had a perfect star in the middle of his forehead. With his deep chest, laid-back shoulders and sloping croup, he was obviously bred for speed and endurance. Amy could see him on a race track. She could see him galloping across an English countryside with the hounds in pursuit of a fox.

And she could see him carrying his master, splendid in his scarlet regimentals, into battle, and standing as still as a rock as the bullets flew around him.

She reached out and stroked the velvety nose. "He's a beauty, all right."

"Come on, let's go wake the captain!"

Together, they hurried back into the house, Amy waiting in the keeping room while Will, taking the stairs two at a time, went to get Charles. A few moments later the boy was bounding back down the stairs, a sleepy, tousled Charles a few paces behind him and stuffing his shirt down into his breeches.

Amy's throat went dry.

"The devil take it, lad, what *time* is it?" he grumbled, ruffling his hair and coming into the keeping room, where Amy felt herself melting all over again just at the delicious, sleepy-warm sight of him. "'Sdeath, I haven't even heard the damned cock crow yet."

"It doesn't matter what time it is, Amy and I have a surprise for you!"

"I dislike surprises. I've had damn well enough of them lately."

"But you'll like this one. Come on, let's go!"

Will grabbed his hand and Amy, after a brief hesitation, grabbed his other. Then, unable to conceal their excitement and laughing at his half-hearted protests, they dragged him out of the house, across the lawn, into the barn and straight up to the stall where the huge stallion stood.

The horse's head jerked up at sight of his master, and he began pushing his chest against the stall door in his eagerness to get to him. Will quickly opened the door and attached a rope to his halter. Then, eyes gleaming with excitement, he looked at Amy and nodded.

"Give me your hand," she said, pulling at Charles's fingers.

"Madam, you already *have* it."

"Yes, but let it go loose."

"For God's sake, girl, I don't have time for this nonsense—"

"Stop being such an old grouch, you have all the time in the world." And with that she pulled him forward, and touched his outstretched fingers to the horse's soft, velvety nose.

Charles froze, a look of stunned disbelief coming over his face.

"Contender?"

Amy and Will glanced excitedly between one another, watching, waiting, barely able to breathe.

"Contender, old boy . . . is that you?"

The horse began stamping impatiently, dancing in place and half rearing in excitement, only to be brought down by Will's firm hand. Then he whinnied and, lowering his head, drove it straight into Charles's chest, rubbing up and down in delight.

Charles closed his eyes, his face rigid with controlled emotion, his Adam's apple moving up, then down. And Amy, watching this emotional scene, felt tears shimmering in her eyes, and one or two of them sliding down her cheek as Charles stood there with his horse, never moving, only murmuring softly to him as he ran his palm alongside the animal's jaw, up around his ears, and down the long, crested neck, over and over again.

"Contender. Contender, old fellow." He continued stroking the animal's neck. "Pray tell, Will, where did you find him?"

"My uncle had him. I went down to Woburn and brought him back for you as a surprise."

"You should not have gone to such trouble on my behalf, Will."

"I wanted to. You've had such a rough time of it lately, and we all thought that having your horse back might perk you up a tad. Besides . . ." Will looked down and began kicking at a loose hank of straw. "It was the least I could do, after what I did to you back in Concord."

Charles, hearing the guilt in the boy's voice, reached out and found his shoulder. "Will," he said gently. "You owe me nothing. You never have. What happened to me at Concord was a direct result of my own actions, not yours. You did nothing to bring on my infirmity; instead, you acted as any Christian man would, putting aside the differences between your people and mine, and doing everything in your power to help me. Anyone else would have finished me off right there—or left me to the angry people of Concord. You did not. Instead, you chose to bring me home at great risk to yourself, and endeavored to save my life—for which I shall always be grateful."

Will swallowed hard and looked down, both humbled and a little embarrassed by the captain's words. "Thank you, sir." He was still kicking at the straw with one foot, a lock of unruly brown hair falling over his brow. "It makes me feel a whole lot better, hearing you say that."

"My only regret is that it should've been said sooner." He stood stroking the stallion's neck and pulling at the animal's forelock with gentle hands. "And that this horse, like its owner, is going to be yet another burden upon you and your family."

"Oh no, sir, he isn't a burden, I brought him back with Pa's blessings."

"Even so, he will eat you out of house and home, and I have no means of paying for his keep."

"Oh, don't worry about that, Captain. Pa said that as long as he can borrow him once in a while to make calls on his parishioners, he'll pay for himself."

But Charles's smile faded a little, and Amy saw the shadow of pain that darkened his eyes. Did he not want Sylvanus riding his beloved stallion? Was he feeling guilty that Will had gone all the way down to Woburn to bring the animal back? Coming up behind him, she touched his arm.

"Charles? What is wrong?"

That rueful little smile still in place, he bent his head, looking down as though he could see the beautiful animal whose broad brow rested against his chest, and whose ears were only a few inches from his nose. "I cannot ride him," he said softly, with one of his long, slow, blinks that lent him an air of studied sadness. "As much as he means to me, as much as I've missed him, he is nothing more to me than a pet, now—"

He never finished the sentence. As though he'd taken violent offense at his master's words, the stallion flung up his head, the blow catching Charles squarely beneath the jaw, snapping his head back and sending him reeling backwards into Amy's arms.

She staggered under his weight.

"Will, help me!"

Her brother rushed forward, and together they eased the captain down onto his back in the straw. His lashes lay against his cheeks. Blood gushed from his nose.

"Charles!"

Amy slid a hand beneath his nape and lifted his head just as his eyes fluttered open.

"Oh-h-h-h," he moaned, covering his nose with one hand and trying to stop the bleeding. "*Damn.*"

"Will, get some cold water, quick!" Amy urged. As her brother ran out of the barn toward the well, Amy helped Charles to sit up. Cradling him against her body and tipping his head back over her arm, she tore off her neckerchief and pressed it to his nose.

"You silly man," she said, in gentle admonishment. "I would've thought you knew your horse well enough to realize he doesn't take kindly to insults, either to himself or to his master."

"I didn't insult him." His voice sounded nasally and thick.

"You insulted yourself."

"I did not."

"You did. You said you couldn't ride him."

"I damn well can't."

"You damn well *will*. My brother didn't go to all the trouble of bringing him back just so you could do nothing more than groom and feed him."

"My dear Amy, please be realistic. I cannot ride him."

"Why not?"

"Because I can't *see*."

"So you can't. But there's nothing wrong with your legs"—she blushed hotly, remembering the feel of them hard and strong against her own—"or your balance, or anything else about you. You simply can't see where you're going. But Contender can."

"I shall not be able to guide him where I wish to go, pull him up when he needs pulling up, anticipate possible dangers to both himself and I."

"Then you can go out riding with Mira and me, and *we'll* anticipate those things for you."

"But I shall look the fool, up there on his back."

"You shall look splendid."

"Amy," he said in a patient, controlled voice, "you do not understand. If something cannot be done the proper way, it should not be done at all. Since I cannot ride him the proper way, I should not—"

"No, Charles, *you* don't understand. Sometimes there

is no right way to do something, but a whole parcel of varying ways. So you can't ride him the way you used to. You find a different way.''

''But—''

''You're doing it again,'' she scolded.

''Doing what?''

''Trying to be perfect. And taking yourself far too seriously. Stop it.''

He began to protest, then grinned and gave her a half-hearted salute. ''Yes, ma'm.''

At that moment, Will came running back in carrying a swinging, sloshing bucket of water. He set it down beside Amy, who rinsed the kerchief in it, wrung it out, and pressed it to Charles's nose.

Will knelt down before them, peering at the captain with anxious eyes. ''Is it broken?''

''It is not,'' Charles muttered, ''though I am not so sure about my jaw.''

''Shall I fetch the doctor?''

''The *doctor*?'' Charles scoffed, greatly amused. ''For a bloody *nose*?''

Amy saw the chance to rescue poor Will, who seemed at a loss for words. ''The *doctor*?'' she mimicked playfully, drawing out the first syllable as Charles had done. ''For a bloody *nose*?''

Charles's brows rose, as though he didn't know whether to laugh or take offense at Amy's exaggerated mimicry of his accent. He appeared to consider the matter for a moment before asking, with studied politeness, ''Are you ridiculing my accent, Miss Yankee Doodle?''

''Me? Never.''

''Good. Because you colonials are the ones who do not pronounce your words correctly,'' said Charles with a certain degree of hauteur, but a slow grin was spreading across his face, one that put a dimple in his chin and made his eyes seem to glow with inner warmth. He looked up in Amy's direction and Will, hunkered down nearby with his hands draped over his knees, saw that look, and the tender way his sister was returning it, and decided that he'd rather be elsewhere. Coloring a bit, he got to his feet.

"Er, uh, I'm going to go in and check on that fire," he said, taking Contender's halter and leading the big animal back into the stall. "What were you planning for breakfast, Amy?"

She looked up at him, blankly. "Breakfast?"

Will grinned. "Yeah. You know, *breakfast*."

"Oh!" Amy went as red as the side of the barn. "I was going to fry some eggs and have them with porridge—"

"I'll go get it started and put the coffee on to boil. You stay here with the captain and make sure he's all right. C'mon, Crystal, old girl!"

"I'm fine," Charles began, but the boy had already slipped away, leaving an awkward, expectant silence in his wake.

A silence where Amy became suddenly aware of the hard warmth of Charles's body, and the proximity of his lips to hers, and the way the morning sunlight made all the stubble on his jaw gleam like gold and begged her hand to touch it.

A silence where Charles felt the soft press of a breast against the side of his head, and remembered again, the taste and shape and silky-smooth texture of it beneath his lips.

This was not good. Not good at all.

"There. The bleeding's almost stopped," Amy said from just above him. Her voice sounded slightly breathy, a little nervous.

"Good."

"As nosebleeds go, this one was pretty bad."

"Was it? Surely, it could not have rivalled the one

my brother Gareth once gave me.'' He gingerly touched the side and bridge of his nose, neither of which, oddly enough, were sore at all. His jaw, however, and the entire top of his head, were another story. If Contender hadn't managed to crack a tooth with that blow, it would be a miracle.

''Why did Gareth give you a nosebleed?'' she was asking. ''I thought the two of you were close.''

''We are. But pugilism is all the rage with English gentlemen, and my brother has an exceeding amount of natural talent for it. We used to practice together.''

''Did you ever beat him?'' she asked, her voice sounding a bit calmer now that they were discussing something safe and benign.

''Never. But he never bested me at fencing, so I daresay we're even.''

He lay there for a few more minutes, content to be in the cradle of her arms, her breast warm against his cheek. Too content. He should get up. He really should.

He would, in just a few more moments. When the temptation to stay within these arms could not be denied, then he would get up.

''Amy, I er . . . that is to say, what happened between us yesterday has been preying on my mind, and my conscience. I hope I did not hurt you.''

''Oh, no, Charles. Not at all—''

''As you know, I pride myself on my conduct, my restraint, my treatment of others, and yesterday—well, yesterday I was not myself. I don't know what or who I was, but I was certainly not the man I am accustomed to being.'' He reached up, searching the empty space above him until he found her face, and let his fingers graze her cheek. ''Forgive me, Amy. I am making excuses for behavior that cannot be excused. Allow me to get straight to the point.'' He trailed his fingers down her neck, the outside of her arm, then found and raised her hand to his lips. "I have done you a terrible dishonor, and though I confess my intentions are based more on duty, fairness, and a care for your own future and reputation as opposed to any romantic inclinations I am reluctant to examine, I know, nevertheless, that I must ask."

"Ask what?" She sounded genuinely confused.

"Drat it, girl, what do you think?" he asked, trying to keep the frustration and impatience from his voice. "For your hand in marriage."

"*Marriage?!*" She nearly dropped him. "Good heavens, Charles, you can't be serious. I'm the very last person on earth you should consider marrying. You should go home to Katharine Farnsley, you should try to win back Juliet, you should find yourself some genteel English bride who'll do your name and rank justice." She gave a nervous little laugh. "Marry *me*? How silly. You cannot marry *me*!"

"I certainly can, if you'll have me."

"No, I will not have you. Please don't be angry with me, Charles. I know you're only offering this because you're a gentleman and feel guilty about what happened yesterday, but if I accept then *I'll* feel guilty as well, and then there'll be two of us feeling guilty, and that just won't do. Don't you see? Oh no, Charles. You're very kind for asking, and thank you for it, but I cannot marry you, I simply cannot."

"Amy, you are babbling."

"You've flustered me!"

"I am quite serious about this."

"And so am I, Charles, truly I am! But your heart isn't in this. You're only trying to make amends, but really, you don't have to, I don't expect you to, I don't want you to. Besides, you don't love me; you still love Juliet, and to marry me . . . well, that just wouldn't feel right."

"I don't *know* if I still love Juliet," he said tersely. And then, almost to himself, "I don't know as if I ever truly did."

"What?"

"She filled a large hole in my heart called loneliness," he said, trying to explain the feelings that he was just coming to recognize, and just beginning to accept. "She flattered that part of me called male vanity. She was kind and beautiful and practical and resourceful, but . . . well, it seems as though I didn't know her as well as I thought I did."

"Charles, what are you saying?"

"Only that sometimes it's easy to mistake need for love. I needed Juliet, yes, but now I cannot help but wonder whether I loved her the way I thought I did."

"Of course you did! You were devastated when you got her letter yesterday!"

"Yes—but was that because of a wounded heart or wounded pride?" He sighed and, picking up a bit of straw, began twirling it around his finger. "Of course you cannot answer that; I cannot answer it, myself. And now, I can only wonder if I am even capable of loving anyone at all, after all that has happened to me. You of all people will understand if I find myself frightfully reluctant to get close to another human being ever again." He tossed the straw aside. "I am better off alone, I think."

"Oh, Charles . . ." He felt her hands pushing the hair off his brow, touching the side of his face. "God didn't put us on this earth to be alone. You deserve happiness just like everyone else. Please don't lose faith in humanity."

"Humanity?" He gave a dry laugh. "Madam, I have lost faith in myself."

"You're allowing your blindness to ruin your life."

"My dear girl. It is not the blindness, but that partic-

ular defect in my character that will settle for nothing
less than perfection. The problem is not with humanity,
but with me. I expect too much. Not from others, but
from myself. It is only lately, when I observe the way I
have thought about, and behaved toward, you these past
two months, that I have come to realize that I'll never
meet my own rigid expectations of how I should behave.''

''You have behaved admirably. You have nothing to
be ashamed about.''

''Nothing to be ashamed about?'' He laughed without
humor. ''I deserve what Juliet has done. *She* deserves a
better man than me.''

''You're a wonderful man, Charles, and one that will
make some lucky girl very, very happy!''

''I am unfaithful, in thought if not in deed.''

''Charles!''

''It is true. Since the eighteenth of April, I have been
pledged to Juliet, but do you know, Amy, how often my
traitorous thoughts have turned to you instead of her
while I lay awake—let alone asleep—in the middle of
the night? Do you know how I've longed for the sound
of your voice, the touch of your hand, the cheerfulness
of your spirit when mine could do nothing but dwell in
the darkest depths of despair?'' He pressed his fingertips
to his brow in a gesture of defeat. ''No. You cannot
know. And you cannot know how very frustrated I have
been at my inability to turn my thoughts, and the baser
part of my nature, toward she whom I *should have* been
thinking about, instead of you whom I was helpless to
stop thinking about.''

''That doesn't mean you were unfaithful. Of course
you'd be thinking about me. I've been your eyes, your
confidant, your closest friend for the past two months.''

''Amy. Dearest Amy. Only I know the secrets of my
heart. And in my heart, I have been unfaithful, for I have

thought of you as more than a friend.'' He shut his eyes. ''Much more than a friend.''

Amy, hearing the unbridled pain in his voice, swallowed tightly. She wished she could make him realize that his thoughts were completely normal for a man in his situation, that he had done nothing wrong—nothing at all. But Charles was not like other men, and as she sat gazing sadly down at him, her heart aching for him and the pain he put himself through, she began to understand just what he'd meant. The rigid expectations he'd set for himself would allow him no happiness.

None at all.

Quietly, she took his hand and clasped it in her own, wishing there was a way to make him see that he was a far, far better man than he perceived himself to be.

''Amy, I want you to listen to me. To be practical here. You may, even as we speak, be carrying a child that will be a bastard if I do not wed you and give it its proper name. Perhaps I, with both my physical and moral shortcomings, am not fit to marry you, perhaps I am repeating the mistake I made before, but damn it, I cannot bear the thought of your raising a baby without a husband, a child without a father. I cannot bear the thought that I have taken your virginity and left you a ruined woman. And I cannot bear any more weight upon my conscience. I swear, I cannot.''

''But Charles, isn't that the same reason why you wanted to marry Juliet? Because she, too, was with child? It was a mistake then, Charles, and it would be a mistake now, because you're not sure you loved her, and we know that you do not love me!''

''Amy—''

''Besides that, it would never work because you're Quality, and I'm—''

''Don't say it,'' he warned, growing angry.

''Not Quality,'' she finished. ''You're the son of a

duke, I'm the daughter of an Indian, and besides, I can't marry you anyhow because if I did, then there'd be no one here to take care of my family. There'd be no one to watch over Sylvanus and make sure he had proper meals and clean clothing, no one to find his spectacles when he misplaces them, no one to help him with his sermons.''

"Amy, your family does not appreciate you! They do not appreciate you one iota as much as I would!''

"Charles, I can't do it!'' she cried forlornly. "It just wouldn't be right!''

She looked down at him. He remained staring angrily up at her, his empty gaze directed toward a spot just over her right shoulder.

And then something happened that she would never forget.

His gaze shifted, found her face, and something in his eyes came suddenly into focus.

They remained staring at each other for a tense heartbeat of a moment.

"A-Amy?'' he breathed.

"What is it?''

He had gone very still, but the focus in his blue, blue eyes was sharpening. "I—I think—oh, dear God, I think I am beginning to see you.''

Chapter 15

And see her he did.

Her image, and the rafters of the barn behind her, was shadowy. The entire left half of his vision field was still in darkness, but the right half was there, fuzzy, a bit dim, but there, and by God, he could see her.

He could see her!

Slowly, as though touching it might destroy the image, he reached up and put trembling fingers to her forehead . . . her cheek . . . her nose . . . her lips. The image did not go away. It did not waver. And as he stared in wonder and a sort of frozen disbelief, he saw the shyness and joy in the face that stared back at him.

A face that he was seeing for the very first time.

He saw a square jaw and high, prominent cheekbones that lent her a look of gauntness and strength; dark, velvety-brown eyes fringed by long black lashes; a shy and smiling mouth; full, dusky lips; and glossy hair the color of strong coffee, tightly braided and pinned in a coronet around her head. She was beautiful, even if not in the conventional sense, striking, slightly exotic, with flawlessly smooth skin of a slightly bronzed tone, not unlike that of a sailor whose life had been spent in the sun.

It was a lovely color.

A warm, toasted caramel color that made him want to put his lips to it and kiss her all over.

"Amy," he repeated, in a disbelieving whisper. "I can see you." He swallowed hard, and traced the shape of her mouth with his fingers. "*I can see you.*"

And he could also see something else. Mist in those huge, soft eyes—and a sort of awkwardness, if not fear, about his first visual impression of her.

"And just what is it you see, Charles?"

"I see a beautiful young woman"—he grinned—"garbed in the most singularly hideous gown imaginable."

"Oh, Charles," she cried, impulsively flinging her arms around him. He embraced her in turn. They remained like that, holding each other, both of them laughing and rejoicing and rocking back and forth in the straw.

"It was that damned horse!" he managed, setting her back to gaze into her rapt, mobile face. "The blow must've done something, must've jarred something loose inside my head. Don't you think?"

"Either that, or your sight was just plain destined to return anyhow. Maybe God simply decided that the time had come for you to have it back again."

"So that I could see you!"

"So you could write your own letters!"

"So I could find my way without a cane!"

Laughing with joy, he hugged her once more, then set her back, trailing his finger down her cheek, the edge of her jaw. Gently, he tipped her chin up so that her luminous gaze held his. "And look into the eyes of the woman who has become my dearest and very best friend."

And look he did; then, before he even knew what he was about, he closed his eyes and kissed her.

Unlike the last time, when relief had made them both desperate with passion, this was a slow, exquisitely sweet kiss, a tender meeting of lips, a gentle wedding of souls. His hand cradled the side of her face, holding her head close to his; his thumb caressed the hollow beneath one cheekbone and tested the dewy softness of her skin. Her mouth yielded beneath his; her tongue shyly came out, touched and tasted his, allowed him to touch and taste in turn. She tasted of sunshine, innocence and sweetness, smelled of bayberry and soap, and he lost himself in the kiss, the eager, but inexperienced feel of her lips beneath his, the way her hand went with shy uncertainty to his chest, and then his neck, gently curling around his nape and then sliding into the thick and shining waves of his hair.

Of its own accord, his hand drifted from her face and down her neck . . . down her bare collarbone . . . down over the lacy edge of her shift—

And froze.

What the bloody hell was he doing?

Charles jerked away. "My dear Amy—I *beg* your forgiveness!" he said with controlled anger, getting to his feet and shoving the offending hand behind his back.

She was still sitting in the straw, her petticoats spread out around her, her face tilted up to him. "Forgiveness for what, Charles?"

"Kissing you!"

She frowned, then she, too, got to her feet. She took a step toward him then stopped. As though she didn't know quite what to do with herself, she hugged herself, completely unaware that the motion only pushed against her breasts and made them swell all the more temptingly above her stays. Charles felt his throat go dry and had to look away.

"I don't see a need for you to beg my forgiveness for doing something I enjoyed," she said, a bit defensively.

"Don't you?" He shook his head and turned away, unable to look into those artlessly wide, innocently lovely eyes any longer. "I seem to demonstrate a remarkable inability to control myself when I am around you."

Needing to put distance between them, he walked a little distance away, grinding the heels of his hands into his eyes and trying to banish the memory of her sweet, trusting face. When he finally took his hands away, blinking, he saw that she was still watching him. He could see the compassion in her gaze, her quiet sympathy for his plight. It was nearly his undoing.

He cursed beneath his breath and went to stand beside Contender, whose head hung over the stall door.

"Charles?"

He shut his eyes as though in pain.

"Chaaaahles?" she said again, laughter brimming in her voice as she mimicked his accent.

He sighed. And then he turned, trying to be angry, knowing he could not be, steeling himself against all the feelings that came crashing over him just by looking at her.

This was the woman who had suffered through his surgery right along with him, who had pulled him back from the brink of death, and later, from the deepest pit of despair. This was the woman who had helped him learn to cope with his limitations, who had always had respect and compassion for his dignity and pride, who had done all in her power to give him the independence he had needed. She had stood by him when everyone else had deserted him, she had brought laughter and sunshine into the darkest days of his life, and now that he could see her he knew that his heart had no chance against the beauty that shone just as brightly on her outside as it did from within.

"Oh, Amy," he said, and shaking his head, he folded his arms, leaned back against the stall door, and looked down at her.

Just looked.

And Amy, smiling up at him, felt everything inside of her begin to melt as she gazed up into that clear, quietly observing stare. He had the warmest eyes. The warmest smile. The warmest hands. And, toward everyone but himself, the very warmest heart.

The Beloved One, indeed.

The power of her love for him nearly brought her to tears.

She sat there gazing up at him, growing a bit self-conscious beneath that keen stare. "If you don't blink your eyes once in a while, you'll wear them out," she murmured, in a little voice.

"I shall never blink again," he said softly. "I shall never sleep again. After all these weeks of darkness, I shall never close my eyes again. *Ever.*"

He said that now, but in her heart Amy knew that his recovery was the beginning of the end of what they had together—whatever that was. He was free, now. Free to stay, free to go, free to do anything he pleased. She didn't want to contemplate a life without him in it. She could not bear the thought of saying goodbye to him. But she was not so selfish as to chain him here, or to marry him just because he'd offered it, and that, only to satisfy his sense of honor and correct a wrong he thought he'd done her. Men like Charles were not to be found in Newburyport. He was priceless gold and he deserved to be amongst precious metals—not cheap tin and pewter. He was something that Newburyport had never produced, would probably never see again, and he did not fit in here, would never fit in here. She would not cry for what she had lost by the return of his sight.

Instead, she would enjoy what time she had left with him, and rejoice with him and for him.

Even if it broke her heart.

Affecting a cheer she did not feel, she pushed herself to her feet, took his hand, and tried to draw him away from the stall. "Then why are you wasting your time gazing at *me*? Come, Charles, let's go and put your restored sight to work."

"Amy, really, I—"

"Come, I want to show you everything! Our shipyards, our churches, our streets, and our people! The grand houses on High Street, the Beacon Oak, the tide coming in, the marsh grasses swaying in the wind, the sea gulls, the sandpipers, *everything*!"

He smiled fondly. "Everything?"

"Everything! Why, let's put a saddle on Contender, and bring him for a gallop along Joppa Flats where we can watch the sun coming up and painting the water blue, the skies pink, the masts of all the ships in the river, gold! Don't you want to see color, Charles? Don't you want to see everything there is to see? Hurry, let's go before it gets any later!"

Eagerly, she pulled him away from the stall.

"No," he said, with a rueful shake of his head, "I daresay I should like to walk, instead."

"Walk?"

"Yes."

"But, Charles!"

He raised his brows. "Yes?"

"You haven't ridden him for over two months—"

"I know."

"Don't you *want* to ride him?"

He shrugged, and when he spoke his tone was perfectly nonchalant. "Maybe tomorrow, Amy." And then, offering his arm but no explanation for his strange behavior, he escorted her out of the barn, turning his back

on the horse and ignoring the long, plaintive whinnies
the animal gave as it watched them go.

She had not pressed him about his reluctance to ride
Contender, and though he knew she had probably
guessed the truth, Charles did not bring the subject up,
either.

The sounds of the stallion's distress as they'd left the
barn had upset him more than he would admit, even to
himself. What was wrong with him that he didn't want
to get up on the animal's back? Why had he shunned
something that he—a de Montforte!—had been doing
since he was old enough to walk? The de Montfortes
were horse mad. It was in the blood. And yet he had
not wanted, had not been able to bring himself, to ride
the horse who'd been his most loyal friend for the past
decade.

*There is something very wrong with you, man. Some-
thing that goes a lot deeper than just the loss of your
sight.*

And with rising dread, he knew what it was.

He had lost confidence in himself.

He, the man who, if he could have chosen one word
to describe himself, would have said "capable," was
now a bundle of self-doubt, rejected by everyone and
everything he'd loved, plagued by the bitter knowledge
that he had let people down. He had thought that if he
ever recovered his sight, his insecurities would have
been banished along with the darkness. But now he
could see, even if not perfectly, and his confidence in
himself was no stronger than it had been last week.

He was frightened.

Very frightened.

And here was Amy beside him, another aspect of his
life that spelled a decided and distressing lack of self-
control on his part, dragging him down the street and

pointing out everything under the sun to him.

"Look, Charles, just there through the trees is the Merrimack River, and the fine brig that they're building for Matthew Ashton! And there is the little boat that we went sailing aboard! Oh, tell me, Charles, what do you think?"

He swallowed and tried to focus on his surroundings, but already, he could feel the resentment building within him. Resentment because the only thing he wanted was freedom to rediscover everything that had been denied him for so long; resentment because instead, all he could think of was his shortcomings, his fears, all the mistakes he had made, the people he had hurt, and most frightening of all, of the attraction he felt for this girl breezing along beside him.

"Charles?"

"Yes, Amy, I am looking . . . indeed, I am overwhelmed."

He tried to see beyond his own inner torment. He tried to take delight in the way the sunlight came through all the leaves of the maples overhead, illuminating each fragile vein, making each leaf glow from within; the way the marsh grasses all bent beneath the hand of a gentle breeze; the way the sun drew shadows beneath each clapboard of the timber-framed houses that lined this street. And since when had water showed so many variations of blue, from deepest azure to soft, pewter gray? He looked at everything—at the ships and boats in the river, the spartan New England churches whose spires rose majestically above this bustling seaport, the sun and salt-beaten piers, the humble colonial folk all going about their business in homespuns, cottons, woolens, and calicos. No priceless painting in Lucien's collection back at Blackheath Castle could rival the beauty of this world that Charles had rediscovered.

And no beauty presented to his starving eyes could

rival that of the girl who walked beside him.

He wanted her.

He could not help but want her, even though her drab clothes did nothing to flatter her toasted-honey complexion, even though Lucien would never, not in a million years, approve of her as his wife, even though his heart was still sore from the wounds Juliet had torn in it—which was reason enough not to want any woman ever again.

But he could no longer make his mind obey reason.

And worst of all, he knew that Amy wanted him as well.

That night at the supper table, as everyone celebrated the return of his sight, asking him what he thought of this or that, asking him how it felt to be able to see once more, and, in the case of the sisters, posing, preening, and doing everything within their power to gain his attention, Charles had had eyes only for Amy. She had had eyes only for him. The tension between them, the force of the desire each had for the other, was like an invisible thread growing tauter with every veiled look, every furtive glance. She watched him when she thought he wasn't looking; he did the same, noting that her dark gaze was mischievous one moment, laughing the next, and, on those occasions when she thought herself unobserved, wistful and adoring and maybe even a little sad. But Charles *had* been watching. Wishing. And wanting, more than anything, to unwrap those coils of dark, shining hair from around her head; to loosen and comb them out with his fingers; to find out just how long that hair really was—

And to see it spread out on a pillow beneath her.

By the time the evening ended, Charles was in hell.

Long after everyone went to bed, he left the house and walked down to the riverfront that he had visited so often in his prison of darkness. Under the faint glow of moonlight, he could see the broad surface of the Merrimack, and the low, dark hills of Salisbury, holding up the sky beyond it. The stars looked down on him, twinkling brightly, making him feel that there was no one else in this world but himself.

No one else in this world but himself.

The answer came to him.

He had never known the bitter taste of failure, but he knew it now—and he could not cope with it. He could not cope with its aftertaste of disappointment, he could not cope with the thought of letting people down, and he could not cope with the physical and emotional reactions he'd had toward Juliet, and now felt himself having toward Amy. They were feelings he could not control, feelings that made him feel weak and vulnerable and overwhelmed. As a man accustomed to having control over everything, it was a horrible and frightening thing to be buffeted about by such a mixture of passions. He was like Mira's boat that day the rudder had snagged and the tide had swept them nearly out to sea.

He was not the man he had once been. His confidence in himself, which he had always taken for granted, was gone. He would not regain it here in Newburyport. He would not regain it in Boston. He would not regain it in England, where Lucien's disappointment in him would probably end up killing him.

And he could not stay here and risk hurting Amy as he had hurt Juliet.

As soon as he was sure she wasn't pregnant, he would put a saddle on Contender, and go away.

Far away.

Where he hoped that God, and introspection, and most of all distance from all temptations and hurts, would restore him to the man he had once been.

Chapter 16

October 1776

Nearly a year and a half had gone by since Charles had left Newburyport, and for those he left behind, he seemed to have vanished without a trace.

He did not go back to England. He made no attempt to contact the family, the army, or the fiancée who had shunned him. Instead, he had bade a solemn goodbye to the Leightons, thanking them for all that they'd done for him and steeling himself against the tears in Amy's eyes before finally riding away, perhaps never to return.

He'd had no idea where he was headed. He had simply let Contender carry him where he might, looking for a place where he could come to terms with all that had happened to him, retreat from society, and avoid the hurt and suffering that relationships and attachments had brought him. Eventually—perhaps by accident but more likely by some hidden design—he'd found himself in Maine, the vast wilderness where Juliet had been born and raised. There, he had fallen in with a pair of French fur trappers and made a humble, lonely living. There, in the endless forests of cedar, pine, and fir, where granite boulders were the size of houses, and the trees were so densely packed that day became night, he had thought he might find peace. That his physical skills and mental resources would be tested such as to prove himself capable once more. That he would be able to forgive himself for all the mistakes he had made, for the disappointments which had reduced him to this wretched, insecure shell of the quietly confident, supremely capable man he had always believed himself to be.

And that there, if anywhere, he would forget about Amy.

But no. About the only thing he regained was the full use of his sight.

For Charles, an aristocrat raised to pomp and privilege in a gentle, mild country, had not been made for the brutally harsh climate of Maine. He had cursed its summer, filled with vicious swarms of mosquitoes, midges, and biting flies that plagued him both day and night. He had shivered his way through the longest and most bitterly cold winter he had ever known. He had lain awake in the darkness beneath the stars, his flintlock cradled in his arms, unable to sleep as he listened to the endless and eerie howling of wolves. And twice, because he had little sense of direction in the vast woods, he had to be rescued by the grinning Frenchmen when he didn't return to their camp by dark—a humiliation which stung him as a man, as a soldier, and as an Englishman.

The trappers tried to dissuade him and send him "back where he belonged," but Charles, angry with himself for his inability to adapt, stubbornly persevered. He lasted through another Maine summer, learning to live off a diet of venison and berries and, when they entered a town and sold their pelts, enjoying the finer things like decent meals eaten off equally decent china, before venturing off into the forest once more. And each time they left one of those little outposts of civilization behind and returned to the wilderness, Charles felt an increasingly larger part of him straining to stay behind. Wanting only to remain in those warm, cheerful taverns drinking cider and sugared coffee, instead of huddling around a smoking campfire slapping mosquitoes or trying to stay warm. Wanting only to sleep in a decent wood-framed bed with a feather or even a corn-husk mattress, instead of wrapped in a blanket with pine needles and moss and granite beneath him. And as the days began growing cold at the obscenely early date of mid-September, and he found himself hating this bearded, buckskinned, shamefully unkempt creature that he had become, he realized that clinging to this venture just for the sake of his pride was nothing short of insane.

When they reached Bangor, Charles bid a fond farewell to the two Frenchmen and headed south, still wearing his buckskins and a bitter cloak of defeat and blaming himself for yet another failure in a life that, of late, had been filled with nothing but. He didn't know what to do, where to go. But he knew that in March, the English army had finally evacuated Boston and gone to New York instead, and so it was there that he decided he would go, both anticipating a return to a life he knew, and knowing, deep inside, that he no longer had what it took to be an officer.

It took him several days to reach Falmouth. Portsmouth, whose inhabitants were busy fitting out privateers against his own country's navy.

Newburyport.

His good sense told him he ought to just take the ferry across the river and continue on, but when he saw Newburyport's white steeples rising high above the gold, scarlet and orange trees of autumn, he thought of Sylvanus, and he thought of Amy, and he thought that he really owed it to them all to stop. Surely he would be able to control himself around Amy now—after all, it had been a year and a half since he'd last seen her. His feelings for her had probably faded. And, for all he knew, some lucky sod had married her and given her a fine family by now.

Or so he hoped.

It was growing dark by the time he finally caught the ferry at Salisbury and crossed over the Merrimack to Newburyport. As he reached the shore, he could not help but remember how it had felt to make love to Amy on these very banks. He could not help but wonder what she was doing right now, at this very moment. Would she be happy to see him again? Angry that he had left in such haste?

With no small degree of trepidation, he rode Contender through the darkening streets. Work in the shipyards had ceased for the night. A church bell was tolling out the hour. Most people were home eating their suppers, but Charles knew he did not pass unobserved. Curtains moved at windows that already glowed with candlelight. A solitary carriage passed, slowing so that its occupants could get a better look at him. A few last people hurried home from market, and a group of swaggering, already-drunk sailors eyed him with a mixture of distrust and curiosity as he rode past. One of them called out a challenge, ridiculing his frontiersman's clothes and heavily bearded face.

The Charles of old would never have allowed such a challenge to go unanswered.

The new Charles continued on.

He rode through Market Square and headed up Fish Street. The scent of wood smoke lay on the cold, brittle air. There would probably be a frost tonight. As he approached the Wolfe Tavern there on the right, he found himself longing for something hot to drink, and it was all he could do not to dismount and go inside for a mug of mulled cider or even black coffee. But passions against England were far stronger now than they'd been when he had last been here, and he would instantly damn himself just by opening his mouth. He was an outcast, a man who no longer belonged anywhere, and as he came up to the tavern, the sound of revelry within made something inside of him ache and mourn for the days when he had been the most popular person in Ravenscombe . . . the most popular member of the de Montforte family . . . the most popular commander in the King's Own.

No more.

Never again.

He was just passing the tavern when across the street, a sound caught his attention.

It was a woman, cloaked and hooded, just coming out of an apothecary shop. Charles saw the pale oval of her face in the gathering gloom as she glanced about her; and then she hastily crossed the street, and, a parcel in her arms, hurried along as fast as she could.

The door to the tavern opened and a group of sailors, their voices raised in drunken song, stumbled out into the night.

"Bugger me arse, if it ain't the Leighton half breed!"

They had seen her. *Amy.*

She picked up her skirts and began to run.

The sailors were drunk, but not so foxed that they couldn't walk. Couldn't run. And run after her they did.

"Oy, girl! Come to ol' Jacko here! I'll show ye those legs ain't meant for runnin!"

Charles sent Contender galloping forward. Amy darted into an alley. The sailors, led by a towering, bow-legged wretch with a long black pigtail, charged in after her.

Charles was right behind them.

Too late, the last of the pack saw the huge stallion bearing down on them and shrank back. Contender's shoulder hit one of them a glancing blow and sent him sprawling in the dirt. Another dived out of the way a second before he would have been trampled. And there, just ahead in what was almost complete darkness, Charles saw the bowlegged seaman reach out, grab Amy's flying cape, and jerk her savagely backwards. She cried out and her little package went flying.

Immediately, the man was upon her.

"No! Get off me, you horrid beast!"

She was no match for him. He pushed her down hard, his laughter obliterating her screams even as one hand tore at her cloak and the other grabbed her petticoats and flung them high.

"Jack, watch out!" shouted one of the sailors.

But Charles was already off Contender, musket cocked as he ran toward the two struggling figures. He shoved the muzzle straight down into the seaman's nape.

"*Let the lady go.*"

Jack froze. Behind him, the other seamen skidded to a halt.

Slowly, Jack turned his head, his eyes glinting in the faint light as he gazed hatefully up at Charles. Beneath him, Charles could see Amy, her face pale with fright, her eyes wide and staring. She did not recognize her savior.

"*Lady?*" said Jack, with an ugly sneer. "Why she ain't no lady, she's nothing but a half breed slut who—"

He never finished. Charles sent his boot flying into the seaman's head and drove him, sprawling and unconscious, into the dirt. Behind him he heard curses, and then running feet as Jack's band fled, no doubt back to the tavern for reinforcements.

It was not, he decided, a wise idea to remain here.

Holding his musket aside, he bent and stretched a

hand down toward the young woman who lay in the alley staring up at him. She regarded his hand blankly for a moment. And then her gaze went to his face, and in that moment, Charles saw recognition, disbelief, and pure, unbridled joy fire her eyes as she tentatively reached up to grasp his offered hand.

"Charles? Is that . . . *you*?"

Chapter 17

With Amy before him, Charles slowed Contender up before the Leighton's house three minutes later. He sent the horse trotting around the house and into the back garden; there, safely out of sight from the road, he leaped down, pulled Amy from the saddle, and held her against his chest as though he'd never let her go.

He was shaking with fury.

"Amy." He felt the blood pounding in his ears. "*Amy.*" He rested his brow against the top of her hooded head and just held her for a long, emotional moment. "What the devil would have happened if I hadn't chanced to come along when I had?"

"Oh, they would've left me alone, eventually," she said, her voice muffled against his chest. "They just like to have a little sport with me, but I don't think they'd actually—"

"*Have a little sport with you!*"

"Well, not much. You see, last week Mira gave me a knife that I could've used if things got beyond my control—"

"I'd say they were already well beyond your control,

206

madam, when I happened along! Does Sylvanus know about this?''

''No.'' And then, with a little shrug of her shoulders, ''You know he probably wouldn't do much about it, anyhow. I—I am not Ophelia or Mildred.''

She said it without pity or sadness, just a simple acceptance of her place. ''Oh, poppet,'' Charles murmured, his heart aching for her, and reaching down, he pushed her hood back, cradled her face between his hands, and lifted it up to his.

She was lovely. The past sixteen months had further defined her already striking features, but otherwise, she was unchanged. The same huge dark eyes still gazed up at him. The same glossy hair was still parted in the middle, plaited, and pinned up beneath a little cap. The same sweet mouth still warmed him with its shy smile.

The same craving to kiss it still burned up his blood.

''Amy,'' he said softly, as he lowered his head to hers, and before he even realized it, he was kissing her with a hunger too long denied. She melted against him. Sweet, soft lips clung to his with a passion that rocked him to his boots. Her tongue came out to touch, to taste, his, and he felt her hand against his heart, where such a great swell of emotion rose that it nearly sent him to his knees. And somewhere deep inside of him, that part of him that he dared not listen to, and had tried to ignore all these long, lonely months, sang with joy and leaped with happiness and screamed that *this* was what he'd been searching for all this time, *this* was what he had needed to heal, this—this quiet love, this unconditional acceptance of all his flaws and weaknesses—was the key to finding his way back to himself, and the man he had once been. *Oh, Amy, Amy, Amy . . .*

So lost was he in the kiss, so lost was she in returning it, that neither saw the figure who appeared at the door and stopped short with a gasp.

Ophelia's eyes narrowed.

"Well, well, well," she said nastily, as her half sister jerked back, away from the disreputable character she'd been kissing with such wanton passion. "I send you to town to bring back some headache powder for poor Mildred, and what do you do? Return with this—this unkempt heathen who's as much of a savage as yourself. To think you'd stand here right on our very own lawn, throwing yourself at him like the shameless little whore that you are—*Lord CHARLES!*" Ophelia slammed a hand to her mouth, suddenly unable to breathe. "My g-goodness, I did not recognize you!"

And God help her, she probably wouldn't have recognized him even in broad daylight, let alone the gathering gloom! The bright hair she'd last seen carefully combed and clubbed now hung in rippling, unruly waves halfway down his back. His face was bearded, he wore a fringed buckskin coat, and leather breeches were molded to long, hard, handsomely muscled thighs. Ophelia could only stare, open-mouthed; why, he looked more like a wild frontiersman than the crisply mannered, impeccably bred aristocrat that she knew him to be! But any doubt she had that he was Lord Charles de Montforte, was banished without a doubt when he inclined his head and addressed her in that same cool, detached manner he'd always used when speaking to her and Millie.

That same cool, detached manner he'd never used with Amy.

"My dear Miss Leighton. It seems that you are forever putting me in the position of having to demand an apology on behalf of your sister."

"I—I thought you were someone else!"

"Did you? But I do not ask your apologies on *my* behalf," said Lord Charles, his mild tone belying the fact that his eyes had gone as cold as winter starlight.

"And while you might have mistaken me, and quite understandably so, for someone else, you knew very well who your sister was."

Indeed she had. And as Ophelia's gaze went to Amy, standing there with her lips looking dark and lush from kissing the man that she, Ophelia, had wanted so badly and tried so hard to get, the man that Amy certainly didn't deserve, the man that *should have been hers*, Ophelia felt a jealous rage so dark and violent that it set her to trembling right down to her toes. Her eyes narrowed to slits. How dare he defend that little slut; *how dare he*! And how dare Amy—dirty, vile, whoring Amy—triumph where both she and Millie had failed!

Ophelia's chin snapped up. "If you think I'm going to apologize to that half breed *bitch*, then you've sadly underestimated me," she snarled, raking Amy with a look of bitter loathing. "I will not apologize to her now, tomorrow, or ever, and why should I? She's nothing but dirt beneath my feet and I hate her! I hate her and I always have! *She's* the one my mother loved most, *she's* the one that everyone says is so kind and good when we all know she's nothing but a conniving little slut, and now *she's* the one you're kissing and holding when you should've been kissing and holding *me*, and this after all that Millie and I did to try to win you, after all the trouble we went through to keep you here with us. I can't believe you'd choose that disgusting little creature over one of us!"

"Ophelia!" cried Amy, aghast.

"Shut up!" screamed Ophelia. "You make me *sick*! I hate you and I hate *him* for choosing you when he should've chosen *me*!" And then, because she was past caring, because she was blinded by a vicious desire for revenge, because she wanted only to cut and wound and devastate Charles as he had cut and wounded and devastated her, she screamed out the terrible secret that she and Mildred had kept for the past year and a half. "And let me tell you something else, *Captain*! Those letters you wrote and the replies you got from the army, your brother, and your dear, darling Juliet? Ha! Well, they were ours! *Ours!* Millie and I read those letters you wrote, and we made up the replies so you'd stay here with us, fall in love, and marry one of us!"

At that moment Mildred came flying out of the house. She grabbed her sister's arm, desperately trying to quiet her. "Ophelia, stop! It's not worth it!"

"It is too worth it! *Anything's* worth it to punish him for choosing Amy over us! I've never been so humiliated in all my life!"

"What's going on here?" cried Sylvanus, hurrying out of the house with Will and Crystal right behind him. "What on earth are you girls screaming about?"

But Charles was staring coldly at Ophelia, his face completely devoid of expression, his eyes glittering with pale blue fire. And then, in a tone so dangerously soft that it sent chills up the spines of everyone present, he murmured, "Is it true, then, that the two of you have deceived me?"

Mildred felt all the little hairs on the back of her neck go stiff.

"*Have you?*"

Amy, Sylvanus, and Will regarded the two sisters in horror.

Mildred bowed her head. "I'm sorry, Lord Charles but—"

"Of course we did, you fool!" cried Ophelia, swiping angrily at her tears. "How often do you think girls like Millie and I get the chance to net handsome English aristocrats? We never posted those letters for you! We read them and listened in on your conversations with Amy and we made up the replies, but you never even suspected, did you? Oh, how that poor silly chit in Boston must've grieved for you! I wonder if she bore you a boy or a girl? I wonder if she found someone else to marry so it wouldn't be raised a bastard? I wonder if she even *survived* the news of your death, but oh, what difference does it make now, when you've long since forgotten her in favor of this—this whoring little savage!''

"*Ophelia!*" cried Sylvanus, but she turned and fled, sobbing, back into the house, leaving a shame-faced Mildred all alone with everyone staring at her in horror.

Sylvanus, looking as though someone had just punched him in the stomach, turned disbelieving eyes upon his daughter. "Is this true, Mildred? Is it true that you girls never posted those letters for Lord Charles, but made up false responses in order to keep him here?"

Mildred squeezed her eyes shut.

"Is it true that you willingly did this, and allowed him to think that everyone he loved, and who loved him in turn, had betrayed him?"

Mildred's entire face seemed to crumple before them; then, with a harsh sob, she pushed her fist to her mouth and fled into the house after her sister.

A terrible silence remained.

Sylvanus took a deep, bracing sigh, and as he released it, Amy saw, for the first time, anger coming into the eyes she had always known as kind.

"I am ashamed and embarrassed, Captain, by what my daughters have done. I can assure you that they will be dealt with severely. I'm sorry . . . if there's anything I can do—"

"There is nothing," Charles said stiffly, and then turned and walked a little distance away, his back to them all.

Sylvanus took a step toward him; then, thinking better of it, he went back inside, Will, with Crystal beside him, following sadly in his wake.

And Amy was left alone with Charles.

He took a few more steps, then sat down heavily on the edge of the watering trough, his head in his hands and his fingers splaying up through his hair. He remained still for a long moment, and when he finally raised his head, wiping both hands down his face and blinking once in that slow, thoughtful way he had, Amy nearly cried for him.

"So the letters were never sent," he whispered dazedly. "What a terrible irony . . . Dear God. Dear God, forgive me."

Amy quietly sat down beside him, but he made no move to reach out for her. He did not even look at her. And Amy knew that nothing she could say would take the pain away, or undo the wickedness of what her sisters had done. If he never trusted another human being again, if he never opened his heart to anyone else after this, she would not blame him one bit. He had suffered more in this past year and a half than any one person should have to suffer in a lifetime.

"How easily I have been deceived," he continued, head still in his hands as he stared at the ground at his feet. "Why didn't I realize that your sisters were capable of such treachery? That the situation was ripe for them to behave as they did? But no. In my despair, I never questioned the responses to my letters—and no one will have questioned what became of me."

Amy knew he was right. When Charles had fallen at Concord, apparently dead, the army had gone on without him. When Will had gone back for him, he'd switched his regimentals for the clothes of a dead rebel. And while the Englishman had been brought to Newburyport, the American had been buried in an enemy's uniform in a single mass grave near Concord. There was no reason for anyone to question the identity of the body that had worn Charles's clothes. There was no reason for anyone to think Charles hadn't died that terrible day eighteen months past.

Especially as Charles, forsaking those who had supposedly forsaken him, had made no further move to contact any of them.

To all intents and purposes, he'd simply vanished off the face of the earth.

To all intents and purposes he was dead.

He got to his feet, his face bleak with anguish. "The consequences of my supposed death are too horrific for me to even contemplate. The suffering that my family must have endured; the sorrow of poor Juliet . . . oh, what a fool I am for not suspecting deceit! Did I have such little faith in those who loved me that I believed everything I was told?"

Amy reached out and placed her hand over his. Ice might have been warmer. "Charles, you were blind. You could not see to read the letters, you could not have known they were false."

He shook his head, unwilling, unable, to forgive himself or make excuses for the fact that he had doubted and turned his back on his loved ones. "No, Amy. It is no use. I have made a grievous mistake in trust and judgement. I have erred badly, and in so doing, I have hurt the people I love. I could not see to read those letters myself, but I could hear the words they contained, and I should have had more faith and trust in those whom I held dearest."

"But you couldn't have known what my sisters did!"

"I should have suspected," he said coldly. "After all, I knew them to be selfish and conniving. And I should have known that my brother would never have turned me away, that Maddison would have brought me immediately back to Boston, that Juliet would never have behaved as she did. But no. I was so blinded by misery that I couldn't see through it to the truth. The truth being, that I let them all down—my fiancée, who was left to fend by herself in a town that had gone mad; my family, who must have spent a terrible eighteen months believing me dead; my troops, who had such faith in me and my judgement.'' He shook his head. ''My judgement. And all this time, when I thought everyone had betrayed *me*, the harsh reality is that I have betrayed *them*.'' He drew his hands down over his face and then lowered them, blinking. ''God help me. God help me undo this wrong that has been done, to ease those hurts that I have allowed to be done to others . . . I must leave for Boston at once.''

But Boston yielded nothing but memories of another lifetime. Others now inhabited the house where Juliet and her stepfather had lived. The general store where Charles had first met her was now the shop of a silversmith who sold plates, bowls, and engravings. The British army was gone, long since removed to New York, and the Common where Charles had once drilled his men, the streets that he had come to know so well, were ruled once more by the rebellious inhabitants who had once cursed and taunted his army into not only that debacle called the Boston Massacre, but this godforsaken revolution itself.

He knocked on doors and made his inquiries, only to receive cold looks and tight lips through which no information was forthcoming. Though he no longer resembled the elegant British officer who had once patrolled these streets with such confident aplomb, there was nothing he could do to change his prestigious accent, an accent that would take him far in class-conscious England, but which only brought him suspicion, distrust, and doors slammed in his face here. There was no disguising the fact that he was English, and high born at that. And there was no finding Juliet Paige as long as the people he contacted kept their silence about her.

It was only when he finally ran into an old widow named Murdock that Charles learned the horrible truth. Mrs. Murdock had known Juliet well, and she was all too happy to tell Charles just what had happened to her.

Juliet's stepfather Zachariah had been carried off by pneumonia last winter. And in March, when the British army and Loyalists had evacuated Boston, leaving it to the rebels, the unwed Juliet Paige had taken the bastard baby that had won her the ostracism of her friends and neighbors and gone with them, taking passage on a ship bound for England.

No one had heard from her since.

And as Charles stood on the wharf and looked out across Boston's cold, gray harbor to the horizon beyond, he knew why she had gone there. He had told her that if anything should happen to him, she was to go to England and throw herself upon the mercy and charity of his family. He remembered the dark premonition that he, like Gillard, had felt the night before Concord, and the letter he'd sent to Lucien, imploring him to take care of Juliet if ever he could not.

There was nothing for it, then.

It was time to return to his family.

It was time to claim the fiancée who had not deserted him after all.

It was time to go home.

My dear brother, Lucien,

I do not quite know how to begin this letter, especially knowing what you must believe—and what you will think of me after you have read it through. I hope to God my family has not wept for me, as I do not deserve your tears, your concern, not even your forgiveness. I have much to say, and much to explain as regards my absence and the unhappy fact that everyone seems to have believed me dead—but I dare say that a letter is not the place to do it, and there are things I would speak to you about only when I am back in England with my family.

To that end, I will be taking passage home in two weeks, and hope to be with you all for Christmas. Please discard all memories of the man you once knew me to be; illness and circumstance have made me but a shadow of my former self, and you should not expect too highly of me when next we meet.

I look forward to seeing you all soon. May God bless and keep you.

Charles

Chapter 18

Charles was back in Newburyport by that evening. He told himself he'd only returned because he needed to tell the Leightons what had become of Juliet. He told himself he couldn't just sail off to England without saying goodbye to these kindly people who had done so much for him. He told himself he owed Amy a last farewell. Then he would sever all ties to Newburyport, forcibly forget what he and Amy had shared, and pick up his life where it had left off eighteen months ago, even if that life was now guided only by duty—and not passion.

Unfortunately, things hadn't quite gone to plan.

Within an hour of his arrival, he learned that Sylvanus was punishing Ophelia and Mildred by assigning most of the chores that had been Amy's, to them. Subsequently, the sisters were treating her worse than they ever had, blaming her for their enforced regime and getting their revenge by ensuring that everyone in town knew of her "wanton seduction" of Lord Charles. As a result, Amy was now treated as though she had the plague. People crossed to the other side of the street when she approached. Shades were drawn shut within passing carriages. No one would even speak to her.

Her life had become miserable.

After supper, Charles went out to the barn to feed Contender. Amy followed him. She knew he intended to leave within the hour, and her heart was near to breaking at the knowledge that if she did not gather her courage and act, she would probably never see him again.

She looked at him, clean shaven once more, tall and handsome and leaning against the stall door as he watched the horse quietly munching his hay in the velvety gloom. His face was pensive. Unhappy. Bleak.

"Charles?"

"It's cold out here, Amy. You should go inside."

She joined him, respectfully keeping a safe distance between them as she rested her arms atop the stall door, her chin on her wrists as she followed his gaze to the quietly feeding horse.

They stood silently together, each lost in their own thoughts. Their private anguish.

"Charles," she finally said, picking idly at a sliver of wood in the stall door. "There's something I must ask you."

"We are friends, Amy. You can ask me anything you like."

Friends.

She took a deep, bracing breath. "You've known me for a long time, now. You've seen what my life is like and the way people treat me, and how much worse things are for me now than they were the last time you were here."

His jaw hardened in recognition of that fact, but he said nothing, merely staring absently at the horse, his thoughts far away.

Amy dug at the sliver of wood, trying to be strong, trying to believe that she really did deserve that for which she was about to ask. "As long as I stay in New-

buryport, the shame of my beginnings will always follow me, and things will never be any different. I have
no hopes of marrying, everyone in town shuns me, and
Mira, my only friend, is always off at sea in her brother's
brig.'' She bent her head, trying to sound cavalier instead of desperate, wanting only his help and not his
pity. ''Life has never been easy for me, Charles, but
lately . . . well, lately, it has become downright unbearable. I've often thought that if only I could get away
from here, and make a new start where no one knows
about my beginnings, that things might be different for
me. That maybe I might have the sort of life I've always
dreamed of having.'' She swallowed hard, feeling the
full weight of his gaze upon her. ''I—I hate to ask this,
Charles, but you're my only hope. You—and England.''

''Amy, what are you saying?''

She turned her head and met his piercing stare. ''That
I want you to take me to England with you.''

She saw him straighten up and wipe a hand down his
face, blinking once, as though her request had not only
surprised, but stunned him. Then he turned away, raking
a hand through his hair, putting a few steps between
them. ''Amy, I am promised to another. Much as I wish
to help you, I'm not sure this would be wise. You know
that I . . . that I have feelings for you, but I am honor
bound to keep my commitment to Juliet, and having you
near would only make things difficult. I'm sorry, but we
must try to forget all that has happened between us.''

''Oh, Charles, I would never hinder your plans or do
anything to jeopardize what is between you and Juliet.
After all that you've been through, you deserve to be
happy. But please don't leave me here to molder where
I'm neither loved nor appreciated; please take me away,
and let me have this chance at a new beginning, I beg
of you.''

''Doing what, Amy?''

"I would make a wonderful lady's maid."

He stared at her. "After all these years of catering to your sisters' every whim, is that what you *want*?"

"At least I'd be getting paid for it! At least there would be no shame in it, or in who I am! What other chance do I have, Charles? And even you must see that it's not an unreasonable request. Why, your sister could teach me all that I don't already know, and once I'm accomplished, I will leave, Charles. I'll go work for someone far away from you. I'll remove myself from your life so that I don't make things difficult for either one of us. But please, Charles, don't go off to England and leave me here, I simply couldn't bear it."

He kneaded his brow for a moment, tortured by this decision he wished he didn't have to make. Finally he gave a defeated sigh, his breath frosting the air, the wisdom of his head fighting a losing battle with the will of his heart.

In the end, he capitulated. How could he not? How could he go away and leave this woman who was so dear to him, who had done so much for him, to a life of servitude, misery and ostracism when he alone held the key to her happiness, her hopes, her very future?

What, really, would it cost him to bring her with him?

"Very well then, Amy. I'll go speak to Sylvanus about it."

"Oh, *thank you*, Charles!" she cried, and stopped herself just before she would have flung her arms around him.

He looked at her bleakly; then he turned and walked away.

Within the hour, Amy had packed the few things she had while her sisters looked hatefully on and heaped insult and abuse upon her head. She hugged her misty-eyed brother and bade a silent goodbye to a stunned

Sylvanus; and then, turning her back on the only home she had ever known, she'd gone with Charles to New York, where he'd met with his superiors, accepted a leave of absence, and arranged for passage on the first ship heading home to England.

The crossing took just over five weeks. For Amy they were wistful, lonely days, for Charles had arranged that she have her own cabin, and she did not get the chance to speak with him often. Sometimes she would see him on the quarterdeck, conversing with the ship's captain; sometimes she would see him at the rail, alone, the wind in his hair and the wide, cold expanse of endless blue sea spread before him. Her longing for him was a constant ache in her heart, but she knew that he wanted to be alone, and so did not seek him out.

She knew that he was avoiding her.

And everything that made her a woman told her why.

He did not love Juliet Paige. He might feel duty bound to marry her, he might feel responsible for her care and welfare, but he did not love the woman with whom he'd had a brief and impassioned romance two years past. He did not love Juliet Paige, and Amy knew, deep in her heart, that he loved *her*.

Knowing that this must cause him guilt and pain, she determined to do nothing to encourage things any further than they'd already gone. Charles had enough on his mind, and on his conscience, without the added anguish of trying to sort out his feelings for her. He was still betrothed to Juliet. He had a baby to take care of, a baby that he'd never even seen. There was no room in his life for a romantic entanglement with Amy, and Amy was not so selfish as to try to force him into one.

She would go to England, then, and seek employment as a lady's maid. As she had done before, she would love him from afar, doing her best not to make his life any more complicated than it already was. And if sometimes the memories of the brief interludes they'd shared became too painful, he need never know. If her heart broke when she saw him in the arms of his long-lost fiancée, she would smile for him and be glad that he was finally reunited with her. If she lay awake in her bed at night and burned with the memory of all the times he had kissed her, of what it had felt like to have his hands on her skin, her face, those areas of her body that no man had ever touched before—or since—well, she would treasure those memories in private. She would never have Lord Charles himself, but she had her memories, and those, she would forever keep close in her heart.

It was gray and gloomy when the ship dropped anchor in Portsmouth. Charles wasted no time in rejoicing that he was finally back in his beloved England; he wasted no time in appreciating how lush and green its grass was in comparison to the brown, weather-beaten turf they'd left behind in frozen Massachusetts. Now that he was here, he only wanted to get to Ravenscombe and to Blackheath Castle.

They hired a private carriage, and, with Contender trotting along behind, headed north. The sun did not come out once, and, looking at Amy's enraptured face— which had been pressed to the window ever since they'd stepped into the coach back in Portsmouth—Charles wryly decided not to tell her to expect it to. At least, not until April.

That was the way of an English winter.

Thoughts of his family were paramount on his mind. Had they received his letter? What would his homecoming be like?

Unreasonably, a thread of nervousness coursed through him. He turned his face to the window, gazing out at the downs as he tried to dispel it. How lovely and

silent they looked beneath the brooding, darkening sky—
timeless, changeless, majestic. A glaze of white frost
cloaked them, and, bare of trees as they were, their noble
brows blunted by time and the elements, they looked
invincible.

Like Lucien.

His wiped suddenly damp palms on his breeches. He
had no reason to feel this strange tension, but he did,
and it was growing stronger the closer they got to Blackheath. At dusk, they passed through Lambourn with its
familiar taverns, shops, and buildings. There, the carriage broke an axle, forcing them to hire another to take
them the rest of the way. Charles's apprehension settled
in the pit of his stomach. They continued on through the
downs, and now he felt strange palpitations in his chest
as his heart began skipping beats. He told himself he
was merely excited. But he knew it was something else.

And there, far out across a darkening valley and commanding the countryside for miles around, was Blackheath Castle. Even from here, Charles could see the
pennant, tiny with distance, that flew above it. Lucien
was home. In a few minutes, he would be reunited with
his family—and the fiancée who had loved him so
dearly and so well back in Boston.

Was that the reason for this strange, unfathomable
nervousness? The idea of seeing Juliet again?

Didn't he *want* to see her?

All too soon, the wheels of the carriage were crunching on the great drive of crushed stone . . . moving past
the ancient walls with their ivy-cloaked crenelations . . .
through the gatehouse and over the moat, past stands of
copper beeches and now, pulling up at the massive door,
its thick, medieval oak strapped with iron and looking
as imposing as the castle itself. Twin lamps burned
above it, throwing a faint glow on the stone steps beneath.

The carriage came to a stop.

"Here ye be, sirrah!" called the driver from the box. Charles stepped down, reached back inside to help Amy out, and paid the driver. He was a local from Lambourn and his name was Paul Bosley, and Charles remembered the man's damp eyes when he'd sent his son John off to join Charles's regiment—but Bosley did not remember him. His gaze was blank as he took the fare, touched his hat, and sent the coach back off down the drive, leaving Charles staring after him in disbelief and no small degree of confusion.

Did he look that much different than he ever had?

Of course not! He was not dressed as richly or as elegantly as the old Charles would have been, but he was neat and clean in his white linen shirt, knee breeches, and coat of dark blue frieze; his hair was carefully combed and queued, and there was no reason why Bosley shouldn't have recognized him.

But he hadn't.

They stabled Contender. "What magnificence," Amy was saying, jolting him from his thoughts as they walked back to the castle. She had paused, and was now staring up at the twin crenelated towers that seemed to hold up the gloomy sky itself. "Did you really grow up here, Charles?"

"Yes. Though it seems a lifetime ago, now." He picked up her trunk and carried it up the stairs. "I daresay it has not changed as much in five hundred years as I have in twenty months. Come. Let's go inside."

The familiar door with its massive oak timbers and iron hinges loomed before him. For one brief, insane moment Charles almost raised his hand to knock; but that was ridiculous. He was the long-lost son, come home at last. Everyone would be ecstatic to see him. He, of all people, did not need to knock!

And so he turned the latch and pushed open the heavy

door, and there was the Great Hall's high, vaulted ceiling of carved stone that he remembered so well; the tapestry on the wall, the suits of medieval armor, the primitive weapons and shields, the mullioned windows rising magnificently from floor to ceiling—and a liveried footman, already leaping to his feet at the sight of Charles and Amy. His face was tight with disapproval and indignation. "Sir! This is a *private* home, the residence of His Grace the duke of Blackheath, and you have no business—"

Charles removed his three-cornered hat. "Simmons," he said gently. "Do you not recognize me?"

The footman came up short, frowning. And then his eyes widened and he paled to the color of milk. "Lord Charles!" he gasped, bowing deeply. "Is it really you?"

Charles, relieved, smiled warmly. "It is what remains of me, Simmons. I have come home at last."

"You—you're several days earlier than the family expected you—"

"Yes, I know. Is the duke about?"

"Well yes, he's in the dining room with your brothers and sisters—"

Charles smiled. The man was obviously befuddled, as he had only *one* sister. But he didn't wish to embarrass the poor fellow, or upset him any more than he'd already done by his untimely arrival. "In the dining room, you say? I shall go to him, then."

"Please, my lord! Let me summon him for you!"

"Come now, Simmons—I hardly think that is necessary."

"B-but my lord, it is on His Grace's orders. I will return for you in but a moment."

And with that he hurried off, leaving Charles staring after him in confusion and a slow sense of mounting anger.

Let me summon him for you . . . it is on His Grace's

orders. There was no need for Simmons to *summon* anyone! What the devil was going on here? Why was Simmons treating him like a visitor in his own home? And acting so damned nervous? Bugger this! He wasn't waiting for anyone! Bewildered and upset by this strange treatment, this total lack of fanfare when he'd expected everyone to be joyous at his arrival, he offered his arm to Amy and strode across the polished marbled expanse of the Great Hall, the empty suits of armor staring silently at him through the black slits of their visors as though in silent disapproval.

"Charles," Amy murmured, hurrying to keep up with him, "perhaps we *should* wait . . . after all, maybe your brother has a surprise in store for you and doesn't want you to spoil it by rushing in unannounced—"

"My brother is treating me with the formality due a visitor and I dislike it. Come along, Amy, I wish to get this over with and I wish to do it *now.*"

His buckled shoes beating a clipped tattoo, he strode down the shadowy corridors. As he passed them, servants stared at him with wide eyes. "Hello, Puddyford. Hello, Rawlins," he heard himself saying, and though he greeted them warmly, the smiles they offered him in return were nervous, and there was an obvious tension at his early return.

By the time he reached the double doors of the dining room, closed, unwelcoming, and stiffly guarded by Cooper, a normally stone-faced footman whose eyes shot wide with surprise before he schooled himself back into the deference expected from a servant, Charles was quietly furious. Why this tension in the air, this formal treatment, and this pins-and-needles behavior from servants with whom he'd always had an easy, informal relationship?

The devil take it, he would find out what was going on and he would find out now.

"Open the door please, Cooper."

"But my lord—"

"Open it *now*."

Visibly tense, Cooper turned and was just about to push open the great doors so that Charles could join his family, when the left one opened from within and Charles found himself eye to eye with the brother he hadn't seen in well over two years.

"Lucien!" he said abruptly, unable to keep the hurt from his voice at this treatment that had been bestowed upon him. "By God, what the devil is going on here? What is this business about my having to be announced, and to you my own brother, in my own home? Why would you keep me from joining you all in the dining room?" He clenched his fists, unable to keep the anguish from his rising voice. "Do you all hate me now? Am I so terrible that you cannot forgive me for the mistakes I have made?"

His anguished cry echoed down the corridor. *Mistakes I have made? . . . Mistakes I have made? . . . Mistakes I have made?*

Lucien only stared at him, as though he could not quite reconcile this desperate, emotional stranger with the crisp and confident officer who had taken his troops off to America. And though Charles knew he was coming apart before Lucien's very eyes, he couldn't recover himself, couldn't stop this spiralling freefall into pathetic behavior, couldn't ignore the deep and indescribable pain in Lucien's black and suddenly sympathetic eyes which told him that his brother no longer admired, but pitied him.

"My dear Charles," he said gently. "My long-lost and much beloved brother." He reached out and laid his elegant white hand on Charles's arm. "It is not a question of whether or not I can forgive you," he murmured, "but whether or not you will forgive *me*."

"I beg your pardon?"

"Prepare yourself," Lucien said simply, and turning, pushed open the great carved door that had swung shut behind him.

Chapter 19

But nothing could have prepared Charles for what he found in the dining room.

The first thing he saw was the candelabra, glittering at the ends and center of the table and drawing the eye away from the friezed ceiling he remembered so well, the carved mantelpiece of Italian marble, the centuries-old portraits, the drapes that fell in great sweeps of burgundy velvet from ceiling to floor, all of which seemed impossibly dark in comparison to the faces, glowing in the flickering light, that turned toward him in stunned surprise. It took Charles a moment to recognize each one. He never knew that Lucien came quietly up behind him.

In that brief, fleeting moment that would remain amongst the most shocking of his life, ranking right up there with when he'd woken to discover himself blind, he saw Nerissa, the sister for whom he'd always had a soft spot, looking up at him with tears of sympathy in her pretty blue eyes. He saw Andrew, tall and handsome now, his brows raised in surprise before he slowly put down his napkin and looked nervously toward Gareth; and there was Gareth, for once not smiling, but looking almost sick with uncertainty and embarrassment as he stared at Charles and then, with a subtleness that did not escape his keen gaze, reaching out to cover the hand of the woman beside him with his own.

A woman with dark hair and fine green eyes.

A woman Charles had not seen in nearly two years.

A woman who, as she slowly rose to her feet and stared mutely at him, her face paling, one hand pressed to her lips, could not conceal the fact that she was heavy with child.

"*Juliet?*" Charles whispered, his stunned brain trying to absorb what he was seeing and sort it out into something he could understand . . . trying to reason why she was still pregnant when she should have delivered the baby months and months ago . . . trying to put together the pieces of this puzzle that made absolutely no sense. "Juliet, will you not come and greet me?"

As though for approval, she glanced toward Gareth, who had also risen and now stood almost protectively beside her. And as Charles's confused and uncomprehending gaze went from Gareth's hand, which now supported Juliet's elbow, to his fiancée's swollen belly and finally, to the high chair drawn up beside her which contained a toddler whose curling hair was as bright a gold as Charles's own, he began to understand.

It felt as though God had slammed a fist into his stomach.

"No," he murmured, shaking his head in denial and stepping backward, his gaze still fixed on Juliet's gently rounded abdomen. Involuntarily, his fists clenched and he was suddenly afraid that he was going to call out Gareth, his own brother, right here in front of everyone, for what he had done to her. "No, I . . . this cannot be—"

And then Lucien was there, his hand like a vise on Charles's arm as he firmly turned him around and began

dragging him out of the room. Charles resisted, trying
to twist his head around, unable to take his disbelieving
stare from Juliet's belly, from her face, from her eyes,
which met and held his in a silent plea for forgiveness,
but Lucien only tightened his grip and pulled him away
from the table. Away from the others.

Out the door, which he shut behind him.

"Now you know why I did not want you to charge
unannounced into this house," he said quietly, as
Charles walked a little distance away and leaned his
brow against his forearm, and his forearm against the
cold stone wall. There he remained, head bent, totally
undone by the confusion and despair of his discovery.
"I am not angry with you, and there is nothing to forgive. But since you were unaware of the situation, and
Juliet is obviously in a delicate condition, you can be
sure that I would do everything in my power to protect
you both from shock and upset. I am sorry that you had
to learn of things this way."

When Charles made no move to acknowledge him, he
turned to Amy. "Who are you?"

Amy had stepped up beside Charles, who stood with
head bent, shoulders quaking. "My name's Amy Leighton," she answered. "I'm a friend of your brother's."

"How close a friend are you?"

"Well, that's hard to say, really, because—"

"She's the only person in this bloody world who
hasn't betrayed me!" Charles shouted hoarsely, his face
still buried against his arm. And then his raw, choking
sobs reverberated throughout the hall.

Lucien stood there for a moment, his mouth tight,
studying this wretched creature before him with a flat,
expressionless gaze that revealed none of the heartache
such a completely unexpected sight brought him. This
was definitely not the brother he knew. The Beloved One
was falling apart before his eyes, and any moment now

the door behind them would open and everyone would see this shocking, pathetic sight that shook Lucien to his very soles.

That would not do.

"Come along, both of you," he snapped, and roughly seizing Charles's sleeve, dragged him away from the wall. His brother jerked angrily out of his grasp and tried to charge back into the dining room, but Lucien anticipated it and nodded to the footman, who moved to stand in front of the door.

"Let me through! Damn you to hell, let me through so I can give that—that bastard what he deserves!"

"*Charles.*"

Lucien's voice was like ice. His brother stopped short, his eyes bleak with anguish.

"I would prefer that you do not make a scene," Lucien said in a quiet, controlled voice. "At least, not until after you hear me out. Come, let us go to the library."

And with that, he extended his hand, indicating that Charles precede him, and Lucien's astute gaze did not miss how this Amy Leighton, who proclaimed herself a friend, discreetly closed the distance between herself and his brother, there if he needed her, but allowing him the dignity of his own private grief.

He made a mental note of that. And he made a note of something else as Charles, his head bent, turned on his heel and started off down the hall. His brother, who'd always been so capable, so confident, so easily able to handle problems no matter how large or small, had always walked with a quietly authoritative stride even before he'd bought his commission and entered the army. But now the proud shoulders were slumped, the back no longer straight, and there was an air of defeat and despair about him. Of insecurity. Whatever had occurred in America must have been terrible indeed. Lucien set his jaw. He would learn exactly what had happened to turn

Charles into this emotional wreckage—and then he would endeavor to find a way to glue the broken pieces that had been his self-assured and admirable brother back together again.

He ushered them both into the library, shut the door behind him, and after bidding Miss Leighton to take a seat, went straight to the decanter of brandy resting on a table before the fireplace. He filled a glass and offered it to his brother, who was walking silently back and forth, his fingertips pressed against his bent forehead.

"Take it away," Charles said.

"Drink it, it'll do you good."

Charles merely paced the room once, then came to stand before the fire, his elbow propped on the carved mantelpiece, the heel of his hand shoved against his bent brow. His back was toward them both. "Gareth," he snarled. "That bastard, he got her pregnant, didn't he? I should have known such a thing would happen. He's always been the Wild One, recklessly out of control, priding himself on leading that confounded Den of Debauchery and getting up to all sorts of mischief. Now he's had his way with the woman I sent to you for safe-keeping, the woman who deserved your protection, and it's *his* babe that's in her belly, isn't it?" He twisted to glare at Lucien. "Damn you to hell, Lucien, how could you allow such a thing to happen?"

"Sit down, Charles, and drink your brandy."

Charles turned from the fire and threw himself into a chair. He picked up the glass of brandy and drained it. He would not look at Lucien.

But Lucien was watching him, and most shrewdly indeed. Not much got past his enigmatic, heavy-lidded stare. Now, he poured two more drinks, one for himself, and one for the young woman whose dark, anxious eyes flashed briefly to his before returning once more to Charles. Lucien saw the way she was looking at his brother, and the way his brother had taken the chair nearest hers, and suspected there was more between the two of them than just "friendship." Two years ago he would not have approved of Charles being involved with a woman so far beneath him in rank, and a Yankee at that. But Lucien had, after Juliet, learned a thing or two about American women, and he was not so ready to write off this young provincial as he might have once been.

Especially as she might be useful in his plans for Charles.

He offered her a glass of brandy, picked up the other, and turned his enigmatic black stare on his brother.

"You are not the man I once knew," he said abruptly. "You have changed since I last saw you, and you have changed in a way that brings me great sorrow and distress. I will hear all about what happened to you in a moment. But I think it best that I satisfy your curiosity about what has transpired on this side of the Atlantic, before I satisfy my own as regards what transpired on the other."

Charles merely sat there, staring mutely, angrily into space.

"I said but a moment ago that you have changed, Charles, but your brother Gareth has changed as well. He is no longer the wild, irresponsible young man who gave me daily headaches, spent his time in drunken debauchery and always came out the worse in the inevitable comparisons with you. He is no longer the black sheep of this family, the never-ending source of despair and embarrassment. He now owns a very lucrative estate in Abingdon which he won back for this family through his own courage and sacrifice, is a much respected Member of Parliament, and is a father, a husband, and a man worthy of the de Montforte name. I am very proud of him."

Still, Charles said nothing, merely staring at the book-
cases with their ancient, leather-bound tomes without
seeing them.

Lucien moved forward to refill his brother's brandy.
"When Juliet—at your bidding, I might add—came to
us last April, I saw a woman who was the complete
opposite of Gareth. I saw a woman who was steadfast
where he was impulsive, who was practical where he
was reckless, who was grieving where he was full of fun
and laughter. I also saw that she was greatly in need of
a father for her little baby."

Charles slowly turned his head, his expression going
cold as he met Lucien's black stare. "No. Don't tell me
that you're behind this, Lucien. Don't tell me that you,
with your infernal machinations and manipulations, en-
gineered this damnable union."

"I'm afraid that is precisely what I did. You were
dead, or so we thought. Your charming fiancée needed
not only a husband who could give your daughter her
proper name, but someone to pull her out of her grief.
In Gareth, I saw a man who was capable of doing both.
She needed to laugh again, and he needed someone to
teach him the meaning of responsibility. The two of
them, as I was quick to discern, brought out the best in
each other. Of course I"—he tapped a finger, once,
against his pursed lips—"*arranged* things so that the
two of them ended up together. How could I not?"

Very slowly, Charles put down his brandy. "And just
what was it you did?"

"It is not important."

"It is to me."

"Very well, then." Lucien affected a weary sigh. "I
told the girl that I could not make baby Charlotte my
ward. Her pride was most grievously injured, and so she
left, just as I suspected she might do. Meanwhile I allowed Gareth, who had pushed me beyond the limits of

my patience with a certain act of public vandalism the night before, to think that I had banished her. He was already half in love with her, and determined to do right by both the young lady and the child of the older brother that he had so loved. He went after her, and had what he thought was his revenge on me and my apparent cruelty by marrying her—just as I suspected *he* might do. It was all very neat and simple, really, and I am most pleased with the consequences of my . . . manipulations. There is nothing that will make a fellow grow up faster than a little responsibility, and with a wife and baby to look after, I daresay Gareth had more than enough.''

Charles, who had gone very, very still, held up a hand. "Do you mean to tell me that you sent a young woman with a tiny baby off, alone—and then sent *Gareth* of all people, to rescue her?!"

"My dear Charles. Do not be so upset. I was in complete control of the situation—"

"I cannot believe you would take such an unpardonable risk!" cried Charles, leaping to his feet. "When I bade Juliet to come here should anything happen to me, I thought *you*, not Gareth, would be responsible for her! Gareth can't even be responsible for buckling his own shoes for God's sake, let alone a wife and baby!"

Lucien had been previously content to suffer Charles's anger, but now his expression hardened. "You are judging your brother most unfairly, Charles, and I will not tolerate your abusing him in this manner. He would be much wounded if he were to hear you speak of him so. I know that Gareth was once irresponsible and dissolute, but he has made much of himself, Charles. He is a loving husband and a playful, adoring father, and his days of debauchery are far behind him. Go ahead and be angry, as you have every right to be, but do not be angry with him. If you must assign blame to anyone, assign it where it is due. That is, assign it to me."

"Yes, you and your infernal meddling! I hope you're damned proud of yourself!"

"I was—until I got your letter saying you were not dead, after all. But really, Charles. Even you must admit that Gareth, with his light heart and carefree spirit, is much better suited to Juliet, who is as serious-minded as you are. My only regret is that something has reduced you to this pathetic wreckage I see standing before me, and I was not there to help you. But as sorry as I feel for you, Charles, I will tell you this. If you do anything to sabotage your brother's and Juliet's newfound happiness, I assure you I will be most irate indeed."

"Don't be ridiculous," Charles muttered, crushed that Lucien would even think him capable of doing such a thing. "I may be a *pathetic wreckage*, but I still have a heart."

Lucien gazed for a long moment into his brandy. "Do you?" he asked quietly. "I wonder, then, why you allowed the family that loves you so to believe all this time that you were dead."

The words were softly spoken, without rancor, without accusation.

"I know it stings your pride that the brother you always pitied for his inadequacies is now happily married to your Juliet," Lucien continued. "I know that you are shocked and angry and upset, and I will not judge you harshly for that." He looked up then, turning that ruthless black stare on Charles. "But do you think that these past eighteen months caused us any less anguish than what you must feel right now?"

"No," Charles admitted, walking slowly toward the window. "I have made a mess of things. I, the perfect, invincible, oh-so-beloved one, have bungled things, and bungled them badly. I do not expect nor deserve your compassion—"

"Please, my dear Charles, dispense with the self-pity. It does not become you."

"I beg your pardon?"

"The brother I knew would never behave this way."

Charles set down his brandy, his eyes glittering with anger. "The brother you knew is dead. *Dead.* And I am in no mood to discuss any of this. Good evening." With a short bow to Amy, he strode angrily from the room. She rose to her feet, determined to follow him, but the duke raised his hand.

"Sit, sit, my dear child. Your Beloved One needs time to sort out a few things, don't you think?"

Amy gazed into those fascinating, all-knowing eyes, and felt a sudden flutter of nervousness. "There is nothing between your brother and me," she murmured, even though she knew her sudden flush of color betrayed her.

"No?"

Amy gulped. "No. Well . . . that is to say, there is no future between us. There cannot be. I . . . came here with him so that I could learn how to be a lady's maid."

The duke raised one brow. Amy's insides began to shrink. He looked at her for a long, contemplative moment, letting his hooded stare flicker down the length of her body; then he turned to gaze out the window into the night. He was an incredibly handsome man, Amy decided. And a rather intimidating one as well. She sensed that there was much more going on behind those black, black eyes than anyone could guess.

"Do you think he loved Juliet?" he asked, almost conversationally.

Amy thought very carefully about her answer. "I think, Your Grace, that he convinced himself that he did. He got her with child. He felt obliged to marry her. He's angry now, I think, because his pride has suffered a terrible blow. But for a man who professed to love someone, he didn't speak of her all that much . . . and, well . . .''

She was turning quite red, and she knew it.

"And, well, what?" prompted the duke, turning around.

"And, well . . . he—he kissed me, in those rare moments when he let down his guard. He was good and kind and protective of me when everyone else, even my own family, would never have exerted such efforts. And every so often, I used to hear him talking in his sleep," she said, hoping that this austere, omniscient man would not judge his brother too harshly. "While he was convalescing, he slept on a pallet downstairs by the fire, you see . . . I used to watch over him at night, though he never knew it. He used to talk in his sleep, Your Grace, and . . . it was not Juliet that he spoke of."

"It was you."

Amy bowed her head, reddening. "Yes."

"And do you love him?"

She blushed wildly. "Oh, yes, Your Grace, I love him more than he could ever love himself, and I would do anything to bring him back to the man I know he must once have been, anything to make him forgive himself for the mistakes that he has made, anything to make him accept that he's not the god of perfection that he tries so hard to be, but a human, just like the rest of us."

"God of perfection. My, my, you know him well, don't you? If he is still that, my dear, then perhaps he has not sustained as much damage as I had feared." The duke smiled, but behind the gesture was a discerning sharpness that made Amy feel as though he could look right through her and know every thought that went through her head. "Are you in any hurry to get to bed tonight, Miss Leighton?"

"Not if I can help you find a way to help Charles."

"My sentiments exactly, and help me, you will. But

first some supper for you,'' he said, tugging on a bell-pull, ''and then we shall talk. Something very terrible must have happened to my brother to turn him into what I saw tonight, and you, being the perceptive young woman I think you to be, are surely the best person to fill me in on just what has brought him to such a deplorable state.''

''Starting with the events of April, 1775?''

''Starting before that, if need be.''

''Then I'm afraid it's going to be a very long evening, Your Grace.''

Again, that benign little smile. ''Ah. But my brother is worth it, don't you think?''

Chapter 20

The dining room had gone as quiet as a tomb after Lucien had, thankfully, dragged Charles out.

"My God," Andrew said, speaking for them all. His face, in contrast to the dark auburn hair that framed it, was still a bit pale. "I wonder what the devil happened to him?"

"He looked terrible," Gareth agreed.

"And it is totally unlike him to carry on so," said Nerissa, putting down her napkin. She rose to her feet. "I must go to him."

"No. Let Lucien handle it," Gareth said, waving her back down into her chair. "After all, it was his meddling that brought on such a complicated mess."

None of them voiced what was also uppermost in their minds: just who was the woman with the dark eyes and high, striking cheekbones?

And then Nerissa, noting that Juliet had gone silent, reached out and touched her sister-in-law's arm. "Are you all right, Juliet?"

Juliet, who had lost all appetite, nodded. Tears burned beneath her eyelids, but she would not, could not, let them fall. The husband that she so loved had suffered enough heartache over the years by being constantly compared to his perfect, saintly older brother. If she cried now, he might think that she was crying because she wanted Charles—when nothing was further from the truth.

She had not seen Charles for nearly two years. She had loved him, once, but when he'd charged into the room she had felt nothing. No. That was not true. She had felt something, and it was the complete opposite from the almost worshipful admiration that she had once harbored for him.

Pity.

The tears grew closer. *Oh, don't let them fall. For Gareth's sake, don't let them fall.* If she sobbed, it was because pregnant women often did, she told herself. If she sobbed, it was because the anguish she had seen in her former lover's face had totally annihilated what had remained of her self-control. And if she cried, it would be for Charles himself, for all she could think of was the steely-eyed, confident British officer he had once been, so godlike and untarnished up there on his horse as he'd drilled his troops, so above the cares of the everyday world. Such a man might as well have died and been buried at Concord, for the one who had pushed his way into the dining room tonight was a shadow of that proud English officer who'd been so full of confidence and elegant aplomb. *Oh Charles, Charles... what has happened to you?*

"Juliet?"

Gareth must've seen the telltale glassiness in her eyes. He reached down and gently, drew her to her feet. "Shhh, my love. None of us could have been prepared for what we saw tonight, least of all you. I know Lucien warned us that he might not be all that he had been, but you have every right to cry for him . . . We all do."

She turned her face against his chest. "But I don't

want you to think my tears are because I want him back, or that I have regrets about which brother I actually married.''

He cradled her to him, tenderly. ''I don't.''

''It's just that seeing him the way he is now . . . it has upset me. I was not prepared . . . Oh, Gareth. Please know that what I once felt for your brother is dead. It is you, *you*, that I love.''

''I know that, dearest.'' He tipped her head up and wiped away her tears with the pad of his thumb. ''Come. You are upset, and I think it is best we go on up to bed.'' Reaching down, he picked Charlotte up and held her to his chest. Juliet looked at him and felt a raw ache at the back of her throat. And what would become of their fourteen-month-old baby? Would Gareth have to give the daughter that he'd loved as his own back to the brother that had made, but never even seen, her? Would Lucien come down on their side or Charles's? Would Charles's return threaten all that they both held most dear?

No, Juliet vowed. Charlotte, no matter who had sired her, was Gareth's daughter. Gareth's! Gareth had nearly lost his life for the two of them, and there was no question in Juliet's mind about who her little girl belonged to.

She moved close to her husband and, drying her tears, allowed him to lead her from the room.

Gareth, sending away Juliet's maid, undressed his wife, helped her into bed, and stayed with her, gently stroking her hair, until she finally fell asleep.

And then he rose and, determined to tell Charles just what the lay of the land was, went looking for him.

Gareth's heart was in turmoil. He had always respected and admired his brother, had always thought him pretty much infallible. And who wouldn't? There had been nothing that Charles could not do. No problem he could not solve, no challenge that was too daunting for either his mental, physical, or emotional capabilities.

But now . . .

Charles was not in his old bedroom. He was not in the Gold Parlour, the dining room where Andrew and Nerissa still sat talking quietly, or in the library. But Lucien was, and as Gareth entered the domain of his brother the duke, he saw that Lucien was standing quietly at the window, gazing out over the night-enshrouded downs toward the twinkling lights of Ravenscombe in the valley below.

"Hello, Gareth," he said, knowing, without even turning, that it was Gareth who had entered. "I have been expecting you."

Six months ago, Gareth would have taken offense at such words and bristled. But now . . . Well, he'd changed a lot since meeting and marrying Juliet. Now that he had an estate to oversee, business headaches, and responsibilities toward not only his wife and daughter, but to his home, his tenants, and his parish, crops to put in, livestock to purchase, a community image to maintain and of course, his challenging and varied duties as an elected Member of Parliament, he had more respect than resentment for Lucien, who had always managed to handle those sort of concerns, and then some, without so much as a second thought. But Gareth had not always respected his brother so. There had been a time not so long ago that he had hated him. Of course, he didn't want Lucien meddling in his business anymore, but over the past six months he had come to understand his brother, to comprehend the reasons why he was the way he was, and to see him as the infallible being that most people who knew him perceived him to be.

Lucien would straighten Charles out.

Gareth was sure of it.

He went to the decanter and poured himself a drink. "So," he said, leaning against the mantel. "What are you going to do about him, Luce?"

Lucien remained unmoving, a tall, slender figure in black. "Me?"

"Yes, you. You 'fixed' me, surely you can fix Charles as well."

"Hmm. Yes. I am not sure, Gareth, if I shall do anything."

"You have to! He's a wreck!"

Lucien turned around. "Do you think I don't know that? But if I had not manipulated events so that you felt obligated to marry Juliet, he might not be such an emotional mess. I am not sure it is wise of me to interfere this time."

Gareth shook his head and gave a disbelieving little laugh. "Really, Luce. Can you honestly stand there and tell me this and expect me to believe that you *won't* interfere? You are very good at arranging circumstances and events so that things come out exactly as you would wish. You are very good at finding the strengths and weaknesses in people and then using them to bring about desired results. You are very good at playing games with people's heads, and doing it in such a way that they never even know what you're up to. If anyone can help Charles, *you* can."

"I am not so sure of that, Gareth. Despite the warning in his letter, I must confess that I did not expect him to be so damaged. Miss Leighton told me everything, you know. He was seriously injured at Concord, then left for dead. Her brother brought him home. They trepanned him—ghastly thought, that, especially as the surgery was performed by a colonial doctor. And when he came to his senses, it was only to find himself completely blind, dependent upon people he thought were his enemy, and sadly, almost completely lacking in that spirit of self-confidence with which we have always associated him.''

Lucien gazed thoughtfully down into his brandy, swirling it a little in his glass. ''He had Miss Leighton write letters to Juliet, to his commander, and to us, but they were intercepted and destroyed by her two sisters before they could be posted. Apparently they had designs upon Charles, and sought to keep him neatly trapped with them in the hopes of winning him for themselves. They fabricated responses from all of us that were guaranteed to hurt him, to turn him away from everyone he loved, never to trust anyone again.''

''And he *believed* such rot? Why didn't he try to pursue things and see for himself how we all felt?''

''He believed it because he could not see to read the false letters; they were read to him either by Miss Leighton, or the sisters who had fabricated them.'' Lucien was silent for a moment. ''And as far as his failure to pursue these matters, I suspect that *that* is what he cannot live with.''

''You don't think it's the fact that I've got Juliet, then, and he doesn't?''

''No, Gareth. I don't believe that's the problem at all. Your brother, who never put a foot wrong in his life, has not only put a foot wrong, he's walked straight off the damned path. He is in uncharted territory, and his only companion is guilt at having made such a botch of things. He is a perfectionist. He is not accustomed to, and cannot accept, the fact that he is as flawed as everyone else. That he makes mistakes just like the rest of us.'' Lucien took a sip of his brandy. ''Of course he's angry, but it is not because Juliet is married to you. No, I suspect that he is genuinely angry with himself. Or with me. But not with you. Never with you.'' He smiled. ''After all, are you not the brother he always loved best?''

"And now I'm the brother who has betrayed him."

"No, Gareth. You picked up the pieces of the mess he made. And I suspect that he just can't tolerate the idea that you, the brother he last knew as irresponsible and dissolute, the one he tried to teach by example and take under his wing, have been the one to fix his mistakes. Though Charles loves you, I do believe that he always pitied you in some small way, especially as it seemed destined that you were never to make anything of yourself whereas he was destined from the start to go far. You know as well as I how much he hated the comparisons between the two of you, his guilt that he always came out on top. And now look. Now you are the one who's a Member of Parliament, who has an estate, who has a wife and daughter and more admiration than you know what to do with. You're the one who has everything that he once had . . . whereas now, he's the one at the bottom looking up. Now he's the one who is pitied and despaired of. For someone like himself, can you not see how such treatment would completely demoralize him?"

Gareth nodded, slowly.

"And to complicate matters even further, there's Miss Leighton. She cared for him when he was ill, gave him some sense of independence and worth, and captured his heart, though I daresay he may not realize that, and certainly won't admit it."

"Guilt over supposedly betraying Juliet?"

"Of course."

"And what does she think of him?"

"My dear Gareth. Charles may be broken, but he is still handsome, gallant, and kind—enough to make any young lady sigh with wanting. As she strove to give him dignity and independence when he had neither, so he strove to give her confidence in herself, and to defend her from a family that, from all accounts, quite despised her. What do you *think* she thinks of him?''

"Given that she followed him across the Atlantic, I should think she's quite in love with him," Gareth said wryly. "I should also think that, because she's a commoner, and because Charles has been engaged since birth to Lady Katharine, you will crush any hopes of a romantic union between them."

"On the contrary," Lucien said smoothly. "For one thing, Lady Katharine has recently accepted an offer from Viscount Bisley, so her engagement to our brother is off. Furthermore, I have learned a thing or two about American women since Juliet came into all our lives. Amy Leighton is exactly what Charles needs, and I will do all in my power to get them together."

"The best of luck to you, then. Charles is smarter than me, and far more perceptive. He'll know what you're up to when I did not, and he will know immediately."

Lucien gave a benign smile. "My dear Gareth. Do you have such little faith in me as all that? He will not discern my hand in this—just as you didn't." He put down his glass and, hands clasped loosely behind his back, returned to the window, where he stood gazing out over the silent, starlit downs. "And he will not discern my hand in anything else, either. It is time for me to play God, I think. To find some sort of challenge that will restore our brother's confidence in himself and his abilities. To begin the Restoration . . . of Charles."

Chapter 21

⟨⟨◦◦⟩⟩

After Charles stormed out of the library, he felt an overpowering need to get out of the house, away from his family and the guilt, shame, and confusion that dogged him like a shadow.

He slammed out of the castle.

Outside, the night was damp, skeins of cloud trailing past a dim moon and spitting out a few drops of rain. He felt it on his face, sweet, cool, and misty; he heard the English wind moving through the copper beeches, just as it had always done. He stood there for a moment, looking back at the castle with its twin towers, and Lucien's pennant fluttering high up there in the darkness, scraping the ceiling of scattered cloud. A glow of light came from Gareth's room. He thought of his brother up there, probably with Juliet, the woman that he, Charles, had once lain with and thought he'd loved, the woman he still owed an explanation to, the woman he had grievously wounded. His ears burned. They were talking about him, he knew it. Discussing him, perhaps lamenting how much of a—what was it Lucien had called him?—*pathetic wreckage* he'd become.

He wiped the mist from his face with the back of his wrist. Pathetic wreckage indeed.

He strode angrily toward the stable.

Inside, a row of equine faces all turned to look at him as he passed by each stall. There was Crusader, Gareth's horse and a full brother to Charles's own Contender. There was Nerissa's gray mare, Andrew's hunter, and Lucien's fierce black Armageddon, desert-bred, desert-born, and brought back from Egypt during the duke's travels.

And there in the last stall as though he was an outcast, the horse who'd crossed the ocean with him twice— Contender.

Safe, loyal Contender, who would demand no explanations, who cared not what he'd become, who was a non judgmental and steady friend. Charles opened the door, shut it behind him, and sat down in the straw beside his horse, his back against the wooden partition that separated this stall from the next. Contender moved close, blowing softly, and dropped his head to nuzzle his shoulder. Staring into the darkness, Charles reached up and stroked the velvet nose.

He didn't know how long he sat there, wondering how he would ever find the courage to go back inside and face them. It was certainly long enough for the moon to move into the square of the window and bathe the stall in bright silver light. It was certainly long enough for his anger to fade to a dull, throbbing ache, content to join the others that already lurked within the scarred chambers of his heart. And it was certainly long enough for someone to come and find him.

Someone did.

"Charles?"

Relief and gratitude swept through him that that someone was Amy. She had come, just as he'd known that she would.

He heard her approaching through the darkness, passing each horse and looking for the only one that was familiar to her. A moment later, the stall door opened, and she was there, the moonlight in her hair, in her eyes, casting shadows beneath those dramatically high cheekbones.

"What *are* you doing out here?" she asked crossly. "It's cold, it's wet, and everyone has long since gone to bed. You haven't even had any supper. What are you trying to do to yourself?"

He raised angry, mutinous eyes to her. She was beautiful, despite the drab, straw-colored jacket and petticoats which did nothing to flatter her—and she had come for him. She understood him. And tonight, there was a strength about her, a certain something that had never had a chance to shine back in that oppressive house in Newburyport, and he found himself drawn toward it, needing it, when his own strength seemed to have deserted him.

She moved forward, the straw whispering about her feet, and sat down beside him. She took his cold hands within her own, and his fingers curled around hers.

He stared mutely at the opposite wall of the stall.

"So, did he interrogate you the way a general might a prisoner-of-war?" he finally asked, bitterly.

"Who, Lucien? He was . . . thorough, yes. But he was also kind. He said I could stay here at Blackheath as his guest for as long as I liked." She paused. "He's worried about you, Charles. They all are."

"They should hate me."

"No they shouldn't, and they don't. You're being absurd, and you know it."

"But I've failed them. I doubted their love, allowed myself to be deceived by letters I should have *known* were false, and caused them untold grief and sorrow . . . and now I have compounded that by coming back and showing them just what depths I've sunk to. How ashamed they must be of me. How ashamed I am of myself. What must they think?''

"They're your family, Charles. You don't need to impress them, or pretend you're something you're not. If you can't be yourself around them, and be accepted for the man that you are, then who *can* you be yourself around?''

"You," he said bleakly. "I can be myself around *you*. I tell you things I've never told anyone else, I feel completely at ease around you, but then, you know all of my secrets and I have nothing to hide from you. You have seen inside my head''—he gave a bitter little laugh—"literally. 'Sdeath, why shouldn't I feel comfortable around you? You can see right through me.''

"And you think that Lucien cannot?'' she asked, smiling and raising one brow. "Really, Charles. You are underestimating him.''

"Lucien is accustomed to seeing capability and confidence from me. He was disappointed in me tonight. Disgusted.''

"Worried, perhaps, more than disappointed. Never disgusted.''

"No, he was disgusted. He spoke to me the way he once spoke to Gareth. *'If you do anything to sabotage your brother's and Juliet's newfound happiness, I assure you I will be most irate indeed,*' '' he quoted, his jaw clenching with hurt and anger. "To think he'd feel he has to tell me such a thing! That he'd think me capable of robbing either one of them of happiness!''

"Lucien can have no way of knowing how you feel about your brother and Juliet being together,'' Amy pointed out. "He can't know until you tell him.''

He rested his elbow against one drawn-up knee, and his brow against the heel of his hand. The silvery light inside the stall began to fade as more clouds moved in over the moon.

Amy wrapped her arms around her knees. "You're not jealous of all that Gareth's accomplished since you last saw him, are you?" she ventured.

"No. It's just the reversal of roles; I don't know what to make of it. How to act."

"And his marriage to Juliet? Do you have any resentment toward them?"

"None." He picked up a piece of straw, twiddling it distractedly between his fingers. "I resent Lucien for the way he interfered in their lives, and put Juliet and Charlotte at risk, but I bear no ill will toward either Gareth or Juliet. In fact"—he tossed the straw aside—"it shames me to admit this, and I would never say as much to Juliet, or anyone else, but I'm rather relieved that Gareth married her. It lets me off the hook. And though it's embarrassing that Gareth of all people was left to clean up *my* mess, I wish the two of them only happiness. He loves her far better than I could ever have done."

"You felt nothing for her, then?"

"I felt something, but it wasn't love. It was regret for what I have done to her. Anger with myself for ruining her life. And that baby sitting beside her . . .'Sdeath, I don't even want to think about it. The infant was the spitting image of me. *Of me.*"

"You're going to have to talk to her," Amy said gently. "I think that once you have, you'll feel better. In fact, I know you will."

"I doubt it."

She sighed. "Why do you do this to yourself?"

He only shook his head, unable to answer her.

"Charles, you have something I never had: a family that loves you very much. They're not ashamed of you, they love you and only want to help you."

"I am no longer worthy of that love."

"What, simply because you made a mistake or two along the way?"

"Yes. Horrible, injurious mistakes. I cannot forgive myself for what I have done to them."

"Do you think they've forgiven you?"

"Well of course they have, they *would*."

"Precisely. And do you think God has forgiven you?"

"Probably."

"Well then, if your family can forgive you, and God can forgive you, why can't *you* forgive you?"

Charles frowned, confused by the sense of her logic, which was at odds with the feelings that slashed at his heart. He knew she was right, but that didn't mean he could accept the simple truth of her words. He wanted to accept it—but he could not. It just wasn't that easy.

"I don't know," he admitted. "Maybe because I've never really had to forgive myself for anything. I . . . this might sound awful, pompous, even, but I just didn't make mistakes, Amy. And I don't know how to deal with the repercussions of them, now that I've made several monstrous ones."

She took his hand, running her thumb over the ridge of his knuckles. "Well, the way I see it, you have two choices. You can either stay angry with yourself even though no one else is, and make your life miserable because of it, but even you will see that there's really no point in *that*."

He didn't say anything.

"Right?" she asked, playfully.

He sighed. "Right."

"Or, you can look at things differently and be thankful for what *did* happen. Everything worked out perfectly for both Juliet and her baby, and for Gareth, too. They are well-suited and happy together and you just said yourself that you're relieved you don't have to marry her because you didn't love her the way you thought you did. So why keep tormenting yourself? Theirs is a story with a happy ending, so let it go. As for you, you're a free man. You have your sight back, you have the love of your family, you have your army career if you want it, and you have this magnificent castle to call home. Can't you see that you have the world at your feet?" She pressed his hand to her cheek and gave him an encouraging smile. "All you need to do is forgive yourself, and believe in yourself once again—as I believe in you, and as I suspect your family believes in you. The only thing standing in your way is yourself."

He grinned, a little sheepishly. "I am a difficult obstacle to remove."

"Yes, you are. But you're as human as the rest of us, and the sooner you can accept that, the sooner you're going to find the happiness you deserve." She lowered his hand and squeezed it. "You are still loved, Charles. There are people around you who still care for you. You've changed, yes—but that doesn't mean you're rejected."

"Amy." He looked at her with his heart in his eyes. "You say the wisest and most understanding things . . . What did I ever do to end up with someone like you?"

She grinned, playfully. "You lost your balance and hit your head on a stone wall, remember? You made a mistake, Charles, which has worked out better than anything you could have planned. I just wish you could see it that way for yourself. Now—how about coming inside, hmm?"

From somewhere above their heads came the sound of rain beginning to fall on the roof. It was a light, gentle sound, full of comfort and healing.

"Yes . . . I suppose I should," Charles murmured, but made no move to get up.

Amy didn't pursue the issue. Truth be told, she was in no hurry to go back inside, either. Once there, Charles would go to his apartments, she would go to the bedroom that Nerissa had assigned her, and they would be alone and apart. She was not homesick—she was too excited about being in England, too eager to begin the rest of her life to waste any time in missing America. But she didn't want to leave Charles, who, it seemed, had grown awfully quiet.

She walked over to Contender, who was gazing down at the two of them, wondering, no doubt, what his master was doing out here at two o'clock in the morning. "You're beautiful, you know that?" she said, stroking his soft muzzle. "And you know what else? You gave Charles a bloody nose that we'll never forget! He can see because of you, Contender, and I love you so much."

Impulsively, she put her arms around the horse's neck, then looked over her shoulder at the man still sitting with his back and shoulders propped against the wall. He was watching her quietly, smiling, and looking much less angry and tense than he had when she'd first come into the stable. Amy gave Contender a last hug, then returned to Charles and sat back down beside him in the straw.

He reached for her hand.

She slid her fingers between his.

Their shoulders touched.

She asked, "Feeling any better?"

"Yes . . . yes, I suppose I am. What you said makes sense, though I must confess I would not have thought to look at things in the same way. But you're right— things did work out for the best. I must . . . I must try to get on with my life, I think." He smiled faintly, his gaze and thoughts far away, and Amy watched as his long lashes came down, so slowly, in that gentle way she'd come to recognize. He blinked so carefully, it seemed as though he treasured his eyes more than ever.

"Things worked out for the best for everyone," Amy affirmed. "Why, the only people who must surely be complaining are Mildred and Ophelia!" She couldn't help a little grin, as she thought about how things must have changed for them since Charles had rescued her from their cruel clutches. "I guess they must be washing, mending, and ironing their own clothes now, to say nothing of cooking the meals and picking up after their father! I know I shouldn't laugh, but somehow the idea of Mildred trying to make soap, or Ophelia trying to darn stockings . . . why, it's just too funny!"

The long, slow sound of breathing made her look across at him, and she saw that Charles had closed his eyes and finally succumbed to the fatigue of their journey, the traumatic events of the evening, and the lateness of the hour. He was sound asleep. A rush of warmth swept through Amy and gently, carefully, she lifted his hand and cradled it to her heart. Seeing him thus reminded her of those early days back in Newburyport, almost two years ago now, when Will had first brought him home and he'd discovered he was blind. How many evenings she'd spent with him, caring for his needs, talking to him, and, as now, watching over him while he slept.

How many hours she'd spent fantasizing about him, and wishing that he was hers.

And here they were, still together, three thousand miles away in England—*England!*—where *he* had brought her. She shivered with excitement at all that lay before her. Was she really here with him at his ancestral home, where there was nothing, really, standing in the way of their own possibilities except Charles's self-imposed torments and the fact that Amy was only a colonial nobody? She shook her head. No. No! She couldn't let herself even *think* such a thing, let alone dream it. The duke would never allow it, she herself did not deserve it, and Charles ought to marry some fancy lady whose family was as old, whose blood was as blue, whose—

"Amy . . . ?"

She started to answer, but then she saw that his eyes were still shut, his head still resting against the wall behind him—and that he still talked in his sleep. Amy smiled fondly.

"The soap," he mumbled thickly, and then gave an involuntary shudder. "Soap . . . itches . . . wipe it off . . ."

So, he hadn't forgotten that first evening, either, when he'd come to her, blind, soapy, and damp, and innocently, perhaps naively, asked her to wipe the suds off. Even now, she remembered how she'd responded to his nearness and virility . . . and how he'd grown hard with arousal beneath his breeches, despite the fact he'd called it nothing more than a "physical reaction."

He had wanted her, then. He had wanted her many times since, and had told her as much—but only once had he let himself prove it. Only once had he shown her the pleasures she'd never believed would be hers.

And now, looking down at his dear, dear body twitching a bit in a shared, remembered dream, Amy saw that he wanted her now.

And wanted her badly.

Between them, it had never been, and would never be, just a "physical reaction."

She swallowed, hard. His hand jerked, the long fingers brushing Amy's thigh, and her own flesh answered his unconscious touch with a sudden tingling warmth. The temptation was too much. She would wipe the soap off, then, if only to give him peace in his dreams—if only for the excuse to touch him. *Oh please, Lord, just to touch him.*

His blue frock coat was unbuttoned, as was the pewter-buttoned waistcoat of dark gray wool he'd brought from America. With gentle fingers, Amy teased them apart. She caressed his chest through his linen shirt, recreating, for his dreaming mind, for her own wistful memories, the sensations she had unwittingly given him that long-ago evening. How solidly muscled he was beneath the shirt's loose folds . . . How warm was his chest, how taut and hard was his stomach, how splendid the length and power of his thighs! Unbidden, memories of that day on the riverbank, when he had made her a woman, swept over her and she trembled with a savage longing. If only to be in his arms, to be cherished and loved and made love to, to once again experience that bliss, that delight, of a man who wanted her so much, *and oh, if that man were Charles!*

She covered his heartbeat with her hand and gazed down at her splayed fingers, her eyes misty with a sudden wistfulness. "Oh Charles, my love—my Beloved One. Will we ever be together?"

"We are together now, dear Amy."

Her gaze flew to his face, for she hadn't realized that he'd woken and was now watching her from beneath half lowered lashes. "I thought you were sleeping!"

"An impossible pursuit, I think, given the circumstances," he murmured with a little smile. He had his far leg drawn up, the near one outstretched in front of him, and now he took her hand and rested it on the hard thigh of the latter, covering it with his own hand. Amy caught her breath, but his expression was kind, even a little teasing. He looked down at himself, and at her hand, imprisoned beneath his and resting so near to his arousal, and raised one brow ever so slightly, as though he wasn't sure whether to be amused or concerned about his very noticeable reaction to her. "Hmmm. I recall that we have acted out this scene before," he mused.

"I'm sorry," she breathed, trying to pull away.

"Are you? I'm not." He kept her hand where it was, resting solidly atop his right thigh, and stroked the back of her knuckles with his thumb. "I daresay I was rather enjoying that."

"You were talking in your sleep. Dreaming, I think, about that night you asked me to wipe the soap from your skin."

"Ah, yes. I remember that night well, Amy." His head still resting against the wall behind him, he turned it ever so slightly and looked at her, his down-tilted, sleepy eyes romantic in the scattered moonlight, in any light. "Do you?"

She smiled, her face suddenly warm. "Of course."

"And do you remember all those nights we used to sit up and talk together, long after everyone went to bed?"

"I do."

"And the way you bullied me into eating that stew when I wouldn't dine in front of others for fear of making a fool of myself?"

"How could I forget?"

He smiled and gazed once more at her hand, still caught beneath his, resting oh-so-close to that ever-growing bulge beneath his white leather breeches.

"Amy," he said softly.

"Charles?"

"That talk we had earlier . . . I have been thinking. Thinking about what you said, as compared to my own standards of perfection, my own belief that if something isn't done correctly, it isn't worth doing at all."

"Yes?"

"Well, I beg your forgiveness for what I am about to ask, that is, for what I am about to suggest . . . and this, out here in a rather damp winter stable, certainly not the most comfortable of settings, certainly not perfect by anyone's stretch of the imagination, least of all mine—''

''Charles, what *are* you trying to say?'' she chided with a little laugh, though everything inside her tensed with expectation, with hope, with desperate, fervent longing—

''What I am trying to say, Amy, is that I would like to make love to you.''

Chapter 22

He added, almost apologetically, "It will not be perfect, of course . . . I would far prefer to lay you down on a soft mattress . . . to have a candle by the bedside so that I could see your face, your lovely, tawny skin . . . a damp stable is not quite what I envisioned, but—"

"But it will be all the more wonderful for what it is, not what it isn't," she said, and reaching out, touched his cheek.

Her hand was shaking.

She saw his slow smile. He had once admitted that he was not a worldly man when it came to bedplay, that he had been betrothed since birth and thus, had never seen a reason to stray—but was he as nervous as Amy suddenly felt? Her own experience was limited by what he had taught her, and what her womanly instincts bade her to do. He was relaxed, yes—she could see that—but was he also, given his strident sense of perfection, worried that this wouldn't be done right?

"You're trembling, Amy."

She blushed. "I'm a bit nervous, suddenly . . ."

"Why?"

"Why?" She gave a little laugh. "Because for nearly two years I've dreamed of this moment—of having you in my arms, all to myself. Now that I do, I . . . I just don't know what to do!"

"You could start by touching me, if you like."

"Yes, I think I'd like that."

"You see, I am a bit nervous, as well."

"Are you?"

"Well, tense. I could do with being touched." He smiled, still lying totally relaxed with one leg drawn up, his shoulders and head propped against the wall behind him. He looked devastatingly attractive. A little bit wicked. "I like to be touched, Amy."

She touched him. First the soft, wavy hair that swept back from his brow, then his temple, then his cheek, slightly rough beneath her palm, a man's cheek. His skin was warm, the faint light making his hair seem darker than it really was. He was splendid. Unbearably handsome. Beautiful in a very masculine sort of way. Oh, Lord Gareth with his good looks and easy charm, he was handsome, too. Lord Andrew with his defiant eyes and warm russet coloring—he would turn any woman's head. And Lucien, the duke—enigmatic, fascinating, everything about him emanating danger, power, omniscience—there was no word to describe him. But Charles . . . none of them, as far as Amy was concerned, held a candle to the Beloved One.

"And I like touching you, Charles," she breathed, her fingers grazing his mouth, which now curved up in the faintest of smiles.

"You weren't just teasing me, were you?"

"About what?"

"About your having wanted to do this for nearly two years?"

She paused, her fingertips still against his lips, and gazed into his eyes. "No, I wasn't just teasing you. I once told you that I've always loved you, Charles. But I would never, ever have acted on that. Not with you betrothed to Juliet.''

''And how do you feel about me now that I am a free man?''

''I still love you. Of course.''

''Would you marry me if I asked you?''

''I . . . I don't know, Charles. You were born to something I will never know, can never be. I'm afraid that I could never fit into your world. That you would, eventually, come to resent me.''

''Juliet was not of my world either. Do you think I would have resented her?''

''Yes, but for different reasons.''

''Well then, do you think that Gareth will come to resent her?''

''I don't know,'' she said honestly. And then, in a little voice: ''*Are* you asking me to marry you?''

''I . . . I am asking myself if I am ready to ask you to marry me. Does that make sense, Amy? With all my heart I want you as my wife, as my lifelong companion, as my best friend forevermore—but I am so afraid, after all that has happened to me, that I will let you down. That I am not worthy of you. You think you don't deserve me, because of the differences in our backgrounds. Well, I don't think I deserve *you*, because I'm but a mere shell of the man I once was, and you are entitled to far more than that.''

''Charles—''

''No, please. Hear me out. When I feel confident in my abilities again, when I am once again the man I was before that fateful day in April, then . . . then, Amy, I will feel worthy of you. Then I will ask you to be my wife, and by God, you had better accept.''

She shook her head and gazed at him with a mixture of love, frustration, and affection. ''Oh, *Charles.*''

"What?"

"You're doing it again. Being the perfectionist, all or nothing."

"I know." He grinned. "But you're doing it again, too."

"Doing what?"

"Belittling yourself."

He gazed up at her through his long, down-tilted lashes, one brow raised, a little smile tugging at one corner of his mouth. She grinned back at him; then, laughing, she playfully swatted his chest with a handful of hay. "Very well then, you've made your point, *my lord*!" she said, her body responding to the deliciously seductive picture he made, reposing so carelessly in the straw. "Now take off your frock, then lie back and close your eyes."

He lifted a brow, but did as she asked.

"Amy, my dear, what *are* you doing?"

She slid her hands beneath his open waistcoat. "I'm taking your clothes off."

He opened his eyes. "I say, I'm supposed to be undressing *you*—"

"You'll get your turn in a moment. Now how does one untie this thing?" She leaned over his chest, her heart beating with erratic, fragile little pulses of growing excitement, and fumbled with his cravat, the only concession he'd made in his humble American clothing toward high style. "I'm glad that we women don't have to find ourselves choked by one of these things!"

"Oh, but it is far preferable to the stays and hoops that you have to wear," he said, grinning as she finally got the knot loosened. Holding it by one end, she pulled the expensive length of lace from his neck, then slid her hands beneath his shirt and found the bare, warm skin of his chest. Beneath it, the muscles were tense and hard, his heart almost pounding, and as she began to caress the ridges and valleys of bone, muscle, and sinew with her palms and fingertips, he lowered his lashes and gave a soft moan of delight.

"Relax," she said.

"I am relaxed."

"No you're not, you're hard as a slab of marble."

"Am I?"

"You are," she laughed, bending her head to place her lips against his warm skin.

"Well, I have never been seduced before," he said pensively. "I don't quite know what to expect!"

"And I have never before seduced anyone," she murmured against his throat, "so I don't quite know what to do. But isn't that half the fun?"

For answer, he only curved an arm around her neck, then ran his hand down her shoulders, her back, and out over her bottom. Oh, it felt good, that broad, warm, hand of his against her body, even if her petticoats still separated it from her skin. No, it felt better than good; it felt delicious. Oh, more. More!

His hand explored the curve of her bottom. She kissed the base of his throat, where his pulse was beginning to beat quite rapidly now. She was not unaffected herself. She heard her own heartbeat in her ears. Felt a strange shortness of breath, and a feverish glow kindling in her blood, making her skin feel warm, making all her nerve endings tingle, making the heretofore chilly air feel blessedly cool against her skin.

"Charles?"

"Yes?"

"Do you mind that I'm doing this?"

"No, it is rather . . . novel."

"And do you mind if I touch you all over?"

His voice was deep, a little husky. "You may touch me wherever you please, Amy."

"Wherever?"

He smiled up at her. "Wherever."

She drew back and looked at him lying there, watching her every move from beneath lazy, half-lowered lashes. His left arm rested across his abdomen; she picked it up and, raising his fist, undid the buttons of his sleeve while he watched her with a patient mixture of interest and amusement.

The sleeve gaped open, then slid all the way to the elbow, exposing his taut, lightly haired forearm to Amy's gaze. He had strong, hard arms. Wonderful arms. She saw the tendons just beneath the skin, and, defined in the moonlight, the beautiful play of muscle. And still he lay quietly watching her, his shoulders propped against the wall, content to let her do as she wished to him and promising with his eyes that he would do the same to her. In time. All in good time. Still holding his fist in her hands, Amy smiled down into his eyes, lifted the underside of his wrist to her lips, and pressed it to her mouth.

She feathered her lips against it, and lightly, lovingly, touched it with her tongue.

She saw the exact moment something changed in him. His eyes darkened. His lashes lowered. A slow, easy smile lifted one corner of his mouth.

Still kissing the underside of his wrist, Amy picked up his other hand and repeated the procedure. She undid the button, and allowed the sleeve to whisper down his raised arm. She put her lips against the slightly salty skin, then lightly ran her tongue all the way from wrist to elbow, chasing the sleeve and kissing, tasting, and licking as she went.

He swallowed, hard, and she saw that his smile had widened until a dimple appeared in his chin. Beneath those long, sweeping lashes, his eyes were crystalline and gleaming with interest.

"Why, Charles. I haven't seen you looking this relaxed since that day we got you half drunk out on Plum Island!''

"I daresay I was not nearly as drunk then, my dear, as I am now." His gaze held hers, steady, deep, and oh-so-warm. "And this time, I *far* prefer the intoxicant."

Amy's own eyes glowed with answering warmth, and then she bent her head, feeling suddenly powerful in an entirely feminine sort of way. As she released his hand and began to pull his shirt free of the waistband of his breeches, she felt a tugging sensation in her hair.

She glanced up, brows lifted in surprise.

"Your hair," he murmured, setting aside the little muslin cap he had just removed. "Only once have I seen it down, and then, when it was wet and bedraggled after our little escapade in the river. You just told me how long you have waited for the chance to touch me as you're doing . . . well, Amy, that wait was no less difficult for me. For nearly two years, I have fantasized about freeing your hair from its pins and running my hands through the entire length of it. For nearly two years, I have tormented myself with wondering just how long it really is, how silky it must really feel, how thick and shining it might really be between my fingers. Please—do not deny me."

He pulled a pin from her hair, and part of her pinned-up braid sagged against her ear.

Amy cocked her head and looked up, as though she could see the damage he'd just wrought. "Well, if you get to undo something, then so do I."

"You've already undone something. In fact, you are several steps in front of me, my dear, and it's only fair that you give me the chance to catch up." He drew another pin from her hair, and dropped it against the wall behind him, where Contender would not step on it. "There. One pin for one sleeve." He withdrew another, and the heavy, coiled mass of Amy's hair began to droop. "A second pin for the other." Grinning, he reached up and drew one, two, three more pins from her hair, and with a whispery little sigh, the entire mass came tumbling down around her shoulders, around her breasts, around her waist, and to the straw in which she sat in a gleaming fall of sleek, nearly black satin. He reached out and touched it, combing out one long, long skein with his fingers and admiring it with his eyes, with his hand, with his lips. "And there. That, I think, makes us even."

"Not quite."

Returning his grin, she pushed her hands beneath his shirt and slid her palms up the flat, hard expanse of his stomach. He was deliciously warm, and she thrilled to the feel of silky male hair around his navel, of the concave tautness of his belly, of the curve of his ribs. Here, a small bump; there, what felt like a tiny scar. She splayed her fingers and spread her hands wide, running them further up his torso, trying to touch all of him, all at once. Hard, slightly bulging pectorals. Soft, wiry hair fanning across his chest and under his arms. Tiny nipples that beckoned exploration, and warm, wonderful skin that begged her never to stop touching it.

"Mmmmmm," he murmured, his eyes drifting shut before he dragged them open once again. "Your hands feel wonderful, Amy."

And then, reaching up, he caught a length of her hair and trailed it over his bare stomach.

"You're shivering, Charles. Are you cold?"

"No, Amy." He shook his head from side to side, slowly, and never took his steady gaze off her. "I am not cold. I am not cold at all."

She drew back, bringing her hands back down his chest as she went, feeling the tiny, involuntary shudders beneath her palms, beneath her fingertips. And as she returned to an upright position, her hands came once more over his navel—and stopped, just at the top of his breeches.

There she let them remain.

He gazed up at her. Watching. Waiting.

She gazed back down at him.

And then, her face growing warm—not with embarrassment or maidenly modesty, but with the fire that was already burning hot through her own blood—Amy let her fingertips whisper over his waistband. Down over the top button of his drop front. And now, up and over the huge, hard bulge just beneath the butter-soft leather, where she let them remain.

"Oh," he said, taking a deep breath.

"I thought you liked to be touched."

"My dear—*like* is not quite the word I would use to describe the pleasure you are currently bringing me."

She smiled, and, still holding his gaze, exerted the faintest of pressure against him.

"Oh—oh, blimey," he said, on something of a surprised gasp.

Amy's lips twitched on a helpless, giddy giggle, and beneath her fingertips, she felt his arousal straining, swelling, craving her touch with all the concentrated desire that was in its owner. He said that he liked to be touched. He said that this brought him pleasure, but his heavy-lidded expression, the sudden dampness on his brow, and the hoarse, shallow little breaths he was beginning to take made her wonder how much of this he could stand. How much of it he would permit.

No sense backing down now. After all, he said he liked it.

She opened her hand fully, and, hardening her palm, pressed it against the swelling ridge, then traced its shape with her fingers. He winced, and a soft groan escaped him. He was very hot beneath the soft leather of the breeches. He felt as hard as rock. Did it hurt, to be contained so completely by the straining leather? Was he uncomfortable? Guided by compassion and instinct, she found the pewter buttons that closed his dropfront, pushing first one through its hole, then another. He was breathing more raggedly now, and she realized, belatedly, that so was she.

"Amy—what *are* you trying to do to me?" he asked, in a hoarse, strained voice.

"I'm trying to make you more comfortable, Charles. You must be in pain, all bundled up like that . . . I mean, we wouldn't want to cut off the blood supply or anything . . . You don't mind, do you?"

"Mind?" He gave a little half laugh. "No, no, I certainly don't mi—" He sucked in his breath as she undid the last button and his hard, hot flesh sprang free against her hand. "Mind at all . . ."

"Do you still want me to touch you, Charles? Does this part of you enjoy it as much as the rest of you?"

"Amy . . . yes . . . that part of me enjoys it more than all the rest of me combined, which is why—*oh*—which is why . . . dear God! . . . which is why you really cannot p-play with it the way you're doing . . ."

"I'm not trying to play with it, Charles, I'm just rubbing it to restore the circulation since it was pushing so hard against your breeches that it now looks a little blue."

He made a strangled sound. "Rubbing it to . . . to restore the circulation . . . will, I think, put a premature end to this act—*oh-h-h-h*—Amy—Amy, I think I must ask you not to do that."

"Do what?"

"What you're doing . . ."

"You don't want me to rub it, then?"

"It's not that I don't want you to, it's that I'm about to crack a tooth with the force with which I'm clamping my jaws shut. Please . . . I am not strong enough to hold

out against such . . . such sweet torment, I swear, I am
not . . .''

''What happens if your strength gives out?'' she
asked, cupping her hand around his hot flesh and ex-
ploring the tip with her thumb. ''What happens if you
just let yourself go?''

''Amy . . . I want to make this special for you . . .
magical . . . last time it was rushed, desperate, over too
quickly. If you—,'' he groaned beneath her ruthless caresses and, shutting his eyes, let his head droop sideways
against the wall, his teeth bared with the effort it took
to control himself, ''—if you show me just a little
mercy, I can make this last much longer . . . much longer
indeed.''

Amy, learning for the first time that a simple touch
could bring him to this, learning for the first time the
extent of her own feminine power over this strong and
virile man and revelling in the use of it, had no intention
of stopping—or showing him any mercy whatsoever.
She went right on rubbing him. ''But we have all night,
Charles,'' she said with false innocence. ''And you *did*
say I could touch you, anywhere.''

''I . . . think perhaps that I . . . that I . . .''

She ran her fingers down the hard, hot length of him,
caressed the twin sacs nestled in their bed of wiry hair,
lifted them gently in her hand.

''That you what?''

''That I . . . that I . . .'sdeath, I don't know.''

Amy, stroking him with her fingers, sucked in her lips
against threatening laughter. She was making him mindless, and she loved this magical hold over him. But even
as she secretly rejoiced, she knew that down there beneath her petticoats, and high up between the junction
of her thighs, she was feeling awfully hot and tingly as
well, and that part of her ached with a prurient fire that
wanted only to be filled by him, and filled soon. But

they had all night. They really did. And now she lightly squeezed the velvety knob of flesh until his entire body was rigid and tense, his cheek pressed against the wall behind him, and a muscle was quivering in his jaw.

"I . . . I don't know—'struth, I cannot take much more of this," he groaned. "God help me, I cannot!"

"Then I think you should just stop fighting it and let come what may."

He nearly choked.

"Just sit back and let me touch you, Charles. I know you enjoy it. You know I'm enjoying it. Besides, you *did* say I could seduce you, so for just once in your life, stop trying to control a situation and just let what happens, happen."

He had drawn his leg up once more; she pushed it gently off to the side, running her fingers up the inside of his thigh, and now Charles squeezed his eyes, his fists, his jaw shut in a last, Herculean effort to resist that which she was pushing him towards.

"Amy—"

And felt her warm little fingers caressing his damp and throbbing tip.

With a hoarse cry, he felt the barrier of his self-control break, and a second later, his seed was pulsing out of him, leaving him gasping and shocked and completely mortified that he had not been able to stop himself. His eyes opened, and, flinging an arm across his feverishly hot brow, he looked up at Amy, who was gazing down at him with an expression of satisfaction and amusement.

"You were right," she quipped. "You certainly *do* like being touched."

He swore and shut his eyes.

She lay down beside him, facing him with her weight on one elbow. He felt her playing with a lock of his hair, felt her lips brushing his temple, his cheek, his neck. Her hair was glassy smooth against his arm, his neck. He could smell the soft fragrance of her skin, the muskiness of his own desire, and he could feel the blood returning to his member, could feel himself rallying once more.

"Good God," he said, half surprised, half grateful, as he opened his eyes.

"That was fun, Charles."

"Probably more so for me than it was for you."

"Oh, I don't know about *that*!"

"You were not offended?"

"Of course not. Should I have been?"

"No," he said, pensively. "No, you should not have been. I think you are a very . . . a very bold and intuitive lover, Amy. I daresay I like that in you."

"It was fun, to make you lose control like that. I felt so . . . so *powerful*!"

He raised his brows, amused by her innocence, the wicked delight she'd found in her discovery. "Yes, well. A woman's feminine power will make her the victor every time, when it comes to testing the strength between the sexes."

Her hand traced little circles atop his stomach, every so often roving down into the curling bed of hair from which his manhood sprang and was, even now, starting to harden once again.

He reached out and caught her hand.

"Oh, Charles," she giggled, kissing the base of his throat. "Let me make you all confused again, let me make you lose control, let me touch and love and stroke you."

In one fluid motion, he rolled over onto his side, pushing her down on her back as he went. "No, Amy," he murmured, arranging her long, heavy tresses in the straw around her head. "It is my turn to touch and love and stroke *you*."

"But—"

"Shhh," he said, and silenced her with his mouth.

Amy had no wish to fight him, none at all. Her eyes slipped shut as his mouth came down upon hers, and with a little sigh, she slid her fingers around his nape and up into his hair, cupping the back of his head, holding him to her as though she'd never let him go, and meeting his kiss with fervent, building passion. She kicked her shoes off, first one, then the other. His tongue slipped out, running along the soft swell of her bottom lip once, twice, before coaxing her mouth apart and slipping inside. She met it with her own, first shyly, then with increasing eagerness to return these most intimate caresses. She felt the gentle touch of his hand against her cheek, her jaw, now moving down to slowly pull her neckerchief out from beneath her stays, slowly pull it off her neck altogether, until deliciously cool air swept against her collarbone, the top of her chest, the pushed-up swell of her breasts. She moaned, her body quivering with anticipation. Already, his big, warm hand covered her breast, his fingers lightly caressing it and the nipple that had gone hard beneath stays and shift.

"Charles," she gasped, breaking away.

He merely smiled wickedly down at her. "Ah. This is vengeance of the sweetest sort, I think." And then, kissing her once again, he opened her jacket, unlaced her stays, and pulled both garments from her trembling body, leaving them both on the straw behind her. Beneath the thin cotton glaze of her shift, her breasts were tight, heavy and aching with need, on fire everywhere the fabric touched them.

Oh, touch me, Charles, please touch me!

"The shift too?" she whispered, staring up at him.

He smiled down at her. "The shift, too."

She sat up, and he pulled the loose, sheer undergarment over her head, exposing her naked breasts to his warm gaze, then putting his hands on them, all over them, while Amy sighed with pleasure and felt everything below her waist beginning to melt.

"The petticoats too, my dear."

"Everything?"

"Everything."

He untied both the heavy outerpetticoats of wool, and the softer underpetticoats of linen, pulling them off and spreading them out in the straw. Then, with an easy strength, he scooped her up and into his lap, cradling her shoulders against his right arm and caressing, kneading, firing her breasts with the other hand.

She shut her eyes, feeling his lips brushing her hairline, the sensuous drag of his fingers combing and pulling all the way down through her hair. "You are the most exotically beautiful woman I have ever met," he whispered against her forehead. "Don't ever leave me, Amy. I beg of you, never leave me."

"I couldn't Charles, not even if I wanted to."

And then he was kissing her lashes, the bridge of her nose, and finally, her lips once more. He lifted her slightly beneath the shoulders, putting an arch in her body, bringing her breasts shamelessly up toward his mouth; a moment later he was hefting one of them in his hand and drawing a taut, swollen nipple into his mouth.

Amy squirmed and sighed with pleasure.

He pulled back, his eyes gleaming with amusement. "My dear Amy. I am pleased to see that I'm not the only one who enjoys being touched."

"Oh, no, Charles. You're not the only one at *all*."

His hand left her breast, moved down her bare stomach, just grazed the top edge of her feminine curls, came slowly back up.

Teasing her.

"Oh . . ."

He brought her a little higher, readjusting her so that

her shoulders were cradled in his right arm and her legs, still in their stockings and garters, were draped over his left thigh. She wore nothing else. Nothing.

Oh, oh *dear* . . .

Back down went his warm, broad hand again, this time moving out over her silken mound, just skirting the damp, aching center of her, skimming out over one inner thigh and gently pushing it aside. Amy shuddered.

"Does that please you, Amy?"

"Yes. Oh yes, Charles!"

"Shall I continue?"

"Yes!" she moaned breathlessly.

His hand still caressing her leg, he untied the garter, hooked his forefinger beneath the top of her stocking, and slowly peeled it all the way down her leg.

Slowly, gently, peeled off the other one.

Amy, completely bare of clothing, was now trembling so violently she couldn't keep still, and it had nothing to do with cold. "Charles, please . . ."

His eyes heavy-lidded with passion, his pupils very dark, he bent his head, drawing her nipple up into his mouth once again and suckling it with a strong, steady pressure that soon had Amy moaning in wanton, feverish delight. She felt his hand moving back down her belly, down to the drenched, silken curls of her femininity— through them. And still he suckled her nipple. Her head began to writhe against his arm, damp tendrils of hair to cling to her brow, her cheeks, her throat. Oh. Oh, she could not *bear* this! Her head fell back, lifting her breasts all the higher, and as his fingers slid between her legs, the coiled, building heat there burned with a restless ache and she squirmed, trying to relieve the pressure, trying to seek relief.

"Charles . . . these feelings . . . is this what I brought to you?" she managed, with what little air she was able to bring into her lungs. "This prickly heat, this unbearable thing that feels like pain but is not, this . . . oh!''

He raised his head, dragging his mouth across to the other breast, his fingers still moving through her damp, feminine curls, now finding the soft folds and gently parting them. ''Yes, Amy, it is indeed. Get used to it, dearest, because I plan to ensure that you experience these feelings on a *very* frequent basis.'' And with that, he drew the other nipple into his mouth, slid his fingers between the hot flesh that guarded her femininity, and with his thumb, began stroking the velvety softness.

''Oh . . . oh, Charles,'' she gasped, and involuntarily tried to close her legs against this sweet, but not unwelcome invasion.

''No, Amy. Open for me,'' he murmured, coaxing her thighs apart, his big hand deliciously hot against her skin. He raised his head, gazing down at her flushed face before turning to look at his own fingers where they touched and stroked and kneaded her. ''I want to look at you, as you have looked at me. I want to touch you, as you have touched me. I want to rub you, as you have rubbed me—''

She sucked her lip between her teeth and heard a strange noise that wasn't quite a sob, wasn't quite a gasp, coming from her own throat as he slowly kneaded the soft petals of her womanhood between his fingers—

''And by God, I want to taste you.''

''*Taste* me?''

He lifted her from his lap, and in the next moment, he'd placed her on the petticoats spread out in the hay, and his hands were lifting her bottom and his jaw was rough against her inner thighs and his mouth, his lips, his tongue, were *there*—

''*Charles!*''

He buried his face in her equally hot curls, kissing her hard and deep and open-mouthed. She felt his lips moving against her, and now his tongue—*his tongue!*—

slipping out to press here, there, to begin a long, slow, torturous stroke, over and over and over again, that caused her head to whip back and forth, and her hand to claw madly at the straw, and a sobbing, whimpering cry to rip from her throat even as she began to thrash in mindless frenzy with the sensations that were rushing down on her. He held her thighs wide, never letting up with that long, slow, licking stroke, and as Amy began to thrash with the first waves of pleasure, he pressed his tongue against a hidden button of flesh, and her world blew apart.

She bucked and writhed, but still he held her against his mouth, until she was wailing and clawing and moaning like some rabid creature brought in from the wild. He brought her toward her peak once more, patiently, skillfully—and then, when she was nearly over the edge, when he, too, was breathing hard and shaking with need, he covered her with his body, and, clearing the wild, damp tangle of hair from her face, kissed her madly even as he drove himself to the hilt inside her.

He came with an explosion that tore her name from his throat, that drove his seed up into her womb and caused her to climax with such force that her convulsions wrung every last bit of strength from his body. And afterwards, long after the last tremors finally quieted and she lay depleted beneath him, Charles eased himself out of her, covered her with his coat and a possessive arm and fell, exhausted, into sleep beside her.

Chapter 23

~~~∽~~~

Charles awoke shortly before dawn.

They had both put their clothes back on during the night, though Amy hadn't bothered with her stays. Now she was snuggled against him, still asleep and shivering beneath his frock. Charles got to his knees, slid his arms beneath her slight body, and picked her up. She never woke. With his free hand he collected her stays and then, holding her close to his chest, he carried her out of the stable and across the still-dark lawn toward the castle.

He saw the great, iron-banded medieval door looming out of the darkness, and, knowing there would be a footman stationed just beyond it in the Great Hall, decided against going in via that route. He did not want Amy to be the subject of servants' gossip. Instead, he followed the castle's silent, looming walls and, hoping he wouldn't run into Juliet, entered via the servant's entrance.

Amy stirred as he began carrying her up the stairs.

"Mmmmm . . . Charles?"

"Go back to sleep, poppet," he murmured, pulling her long fall of hair up over his arm so that he wouldn't

280

trip over it. His shoes made little sound on the stairs and as he emerged onto the top floor, he paused for a moment to listen. The house was quiet, and far down the end of the west corridor, where tired, dwindling sconces painted the ancient stone walls in flickering shades of gold, he saw a servant dozing in a chair. Cradling Amy to his chest, he continued on, past the austere portraits of his ancestors, his feet moving silently over priceless carpets, until he finally reached the Blue Bedroom.

He carried her inside. She sighed and clung to him as he peeled back the covers and gently lay her down in the bed, stripping her down to her shift. As he caught sight of her rosy areolas just beneath the gauzy fabric, the nipples still pert and pebbled, he felt himself growing hard once more. Chastising himself for his lusty thoughts, he brought the covers up so as to cut off the sight from his prurient gaze. It was all he could do not to join her in that huge bed, but he would not, he could not. Ruefully, he touched her hair, leaned down to kiss her cheek, and, after putting another log on the fire, strode from the room, gently closing the door behind him.

Beyond the castle's great leaded windows, it was starting to grow light. He could just see the copper beeches, their branches tossing a bit in the wind, beginning to take shape, and a few jackdaws flying about the ancient stone gatehouse that guarded the moat. Beyond, the downs, sugared with frost and standing in silent, timeless dignity, tumbled down and away toward the village of Ravenscombe, still cloaked in mist at this early hour. Charles turned from the window and went downstairs, intending to sit in the dining room and have an hour or two to himself before everyone else rose.

An hour or two to prepare himself for the inevitable meeting with his family—

And Juliet.

But as he pushed open the great double door, he saw that there was someone already in the dining room. A solitary figure, still wrapped in shadowy gloom, sat at the table, his arm stretched out on the table before him, a goblet of pale amber liquid held loosely in his hand, into which he was gazing. He glanced up at Charles, who had paused just inside the door.

"Charles. Come in."

Charles, caught in emotions he could not understand, and did not know how to address, almost made an excuse and retreated. "Hello, brother," he finally said, trying for lightness in the hopes that Gareth would not discern his sudden, and unreasonable, nervousness. He directed a pointed glance at Gareth's goblet, thinking that Lucien had been dead wrong about Gareth, and that Gareth was as dissolute as ever. "Bit early to be getting soused, isn't it?"

The Wild One looked at the glass in his hand. "Apple juice."

Charles flushed, suddenly feeling very small. "Oh."

"Though *she* calls it cider."

"I am familiar with it."

Gareth gave an unsure little laugh. "The things those Yankees drink . . ."

"Yes. If you think that's vile, you should try their ribwort tea some time. Damnable stuff, that."

"I think I'll stick with our fine China blends."

Charles ventured into the room—and saw then that Gareth was not alone. Cradled in his left arm and smiling adoringly up at him was Charlotte, the little girl that Charles had sired—and who would grow up calling Gareth "Papa" instead of him.

Gareth noted the direction of his suddenly unsure gaze.

"Want to hold her?"

Charles swallowed, hard. "I-I am not sure."

"Here." Gareth stood up and walked around the table. "Take her."

After all, if things had gone differently, she'd have been yours.

Charles tensed as his brother placed the baby in his arms. He looked down into eyes as blue, at hair as blond as his own, and in that moment Charlotte screwed up her face and began to cry. Struggling in Charles's arms, tears running down her cheeks, she reached for Gareth in a desperate plea to be rescued by the only father she had ever known.

Gareth took the child back, making a lame and embarrassed comment about "having to get used to them first," while Charles stood back, a bit hurt but strangely relieved that the episode was over so quickly. He had expected to feel overwhelmed by love and perhaps even jealousy when the baby was placed in his arms, but no. There'd been nothing. It had been like holding a stranger's child, not his own flesh and blood. She might look like him, but the baby was Gareth's, not his. She would always be Gareth's.

And now Gareth felt badly about it. It was evident in his face.

"Don't be upset, Gareth," he said quietly. "I wasn't ready to be a father yet, anyhow. And it's obvious that you're the apple of her eye."

"Still . . ."

"Besides, it would have made things even more complicated than they already are," Charles added.

Gareth reclaimed his seat, his face troubled. An awkwardness settled over them. The temptation to make his excuses and leave the room was overwhelming, but Charles stayed. He would not take the coward's way out. Not this time. But he could not sit down companionably with his brother, either, not yet and with so much between them, and so he walked a little distance away, keeping his back to Gareth and the child.

"We heard all about what happened to you over there," Gareth said from behind him, his voice guarded, slightly uncertain. "About the surgery, and your blindness, and the way those two horrible creatures deceived you." He paused. "I don't know how you managed it, Charles."

Charles didn't turn around. "Managed what?"

"Why, to survive such an ordeal. It would've driven me to drink, if not worse." He gave a little laugh. "But not you. You've got too much strength. You survived, and here you are, back with us at last. I wish I had half your courage and resolve."

Charles, uncomfortable with such praise, bent his head and made a pretense of examining his thumbnail. "From what I understand, *you're* the one who deserves to be admired. Lucien tells me that you've done quite well for yourself since we last saw each other."

"I'm doing all right."

"Got yourself an estate now, eh?"

"Yes. Swanthorpe Manor, up in Abingdon. Do you remember it? It used to belong to our family way back in Grandfather's time, but he lost it over a card game. I won it back, last summer."

"At cards?"

"No, pugilism."

"Pugilism?" said Charles, finally turning around.

Gareth shrugged and looked down, absently toying with the stem of his goblet. "Yes. Everyone thought I was so useless, so I determined to make something of myself—not only to support my new family, but to prove something to Lucien." His finger smoothed the glass. "I turned to fighting for a living."

"Good God, man!"

"I did quite well in the end, even became a champion." He looked up, grinning. "Though Luce nearly had my head."

"I can well imagine."

"Well, I *was* always good with my fists."

"Yes, certainly better than me," said Charles.

"But *you* were better at swords." He paused. "You were better at almost everything."

"No. It only appeared that way." Charles was quiet for a moment. "You probably never knew it, but I wouldn't do anything I wasn't good at. Why do you think I never had any sparring matches with you after you beat me that time?"

"You couldn't bear the thought of losing?"

"No, I couldn't."

Gareth gave a little laugh. "You're right. I never knew."

Charles went back to examining his thumbnail. A few feet away, Gareth gazed down at the baby cradled in his arm, and tenderly brushed aside a lock of pale blonde hair that had tumbled over her forehead. A silence fell between them. Finally, Gareth blew out his breath. "I'm sorry about how everything worked out for you," he said. "Hell, man, if I'd known you really weren't dead—"

Charles held up a hand. "No. You mustn't blame yourself. It's my fault. I made a mess and you were gallant enough to pick up the pieces. It—it all worked out for the best."

Gareth's finger was moving agitatedly over the base of the glass now. "You're not angry, then? You don't resent what I've done?"

"No. I have no reason to resent you."

"If it's any consolation, she missed you terribly when she first came here."

A shadow fell over Charles's face. "I am sorry to hear that." He went to the window and looked out at the brightening downs, so green beneath their mantle of frost. Very quietly, he murmured, "It seems that there is no end to the number of people I have hurt, is there?"

"You would never have hurt anyone intentionally, Charles. Least of all those who love you."

Charles took a deep breath, steeled himself, and looked at his brother. "And did *she* love me?"

Please, please. Tell me that she did not.

Gareth's blue eyes, heavily lashed and tilted down at the outer corners in a sleepy, romantic look that mirrored Charles's, lifted to regard him. "She was young, Charles," he said quietly. "It was a long time ago."

"Yes. A long time ago."

And then, hesitatingly: "Did you love *her*?"

Charles looked back out over the downs. "I thought I did. Once. But it is possible for affection to masquerade as love, especially when loneliness and naiveté are there to help it along." He paused. "I . . . I do feel a need to speak with her, though. To close the book on that chapter of my life." He turned and looked at his brother. "What are your feelings on that, Gareth?"

Gareth shrugged and looked down, veiling his expression with his long lashes. "You know I've always felt, well, second best in those awful comparisons everyone always made between the two of us. I'd be lying if I said I wasn't just a little bit . . . well, tense about it. But you do what you have to do, Charles."

"I feel nothing for her, Gareth. I'm sorry if my behavior last night might have indicated otherwise. I saw that she was with child, and drew the wrong conclusions. I hope you can forgive me."

Gareth grinned. "Hell, if the shoe was on the other foot, and I'd come to the same conclusion, I probably would've taken your head off. There's no need to apologize."

Another awkward, uncomfortable silence. And then

Charles sighed and pulled out the chair opposite Gareth.
He propped his elbows on the table, rested his forehead
in the heels of his hands, and, pushing his fingers up
through his hair, stared down at the table.

Gareth resumed sipping his apple juice.

"I see you've brought a friend back from America
with you," he said, after some time.

"Yes. Amy. She's been my polestar, and my salva-
tion."

"She's striking. Quite exotic, if I do say so myself."

"Yes, she is."

Another pause. And then, Gareth asked impulsively,
"Do you love her?"

Charles dragged his head up and regarded his brother
with what was almost a smile. "Yes." He looked beyond Gareth's shoulder, out the window, and over the
downs, his gaze fixed on some distant point that only he
could see. "And this time, it is for real, I think."

"You ought to marry her."

"I can't."

"Why not?"

"I am not ready to be anyone's husband." As Gareth
started to protest, Charles murmured, "She deserves
more than a washed-out shell of a man whose courage
and confidence are in tatters, who can't offer her much
of anything, who is less than perfect."

"What a load of bollocks."

"I beg your pardon?"

"I said, what a load of bollocks. Really, Charles, you
haven't changed a damn bit, have you?"

"I don't know what you're talking about."

"Look at you, striving to be perfect, just as you ever
were. Won't do anything unless you can do it to your
own ridiculous standards of excellence. Well, let me tell
you something. Being a husband means learning as you
go along; you don't go into it already knowing every-

thing there is to know, and can't expect to. You make mistakes, and you learn by them.''

''I dislike making mistakes.''

''So what are you going to do, live your life in a cage for fear of making any?''

Charles tightened his jaw. He knew his brother was right, but it was hard to hear a lecture from a younger sibling, and the one *he'd* always had to lecture, at that.

''Don't look so perturbed,'' Gareth said lightly. ''And for God's sake, stop taking life so damned seriously, would you?'' He drained his glass and stood up. ''Now come on. It's early, and we have the whole morning to catch up on things. I want to hear all about America and how you met Amy. I want to tell you about the flying contraption that Andrew's working on. And I want to talk to you about Swanthorpe, because there are some problems I need your advice on.''

''Need *my* advice on?''

''Yes, regarding the sort of things I just don't have a head for, you know, things like how to sort out disputes between staff, and what to do about the poachers that have been nicking my pheasants, that sort of thing. I'm no leader of men, like you!''

''Well, I—''

''And just to get our blood going first, what do you say to a horse race, just like old times? First one down to Ravenscombe and back wins!''

Charles shook his head, but he was already getting to his feet. ''Really, Gareth, *you* haven't changed a damn bit, either.''

''Not in any of the ways that matter. Now come on, let's go. If we're quick we'll be back by sunrise!''

Chapter 24

Amy stretched, yawned, and opening her eyes, found herself in the most beautiful bedroom she had ever seen.

She sat straight up in bed. *How did I get here?*

And then she remembered. A night of heated passion. Falling asleep in Charles's arms. And later, much later, the sensation of being picked up and carried somewhere . . .

Here.

She gazed about, her eyes wide with wonder. Sunshine streamed through the floor-to-ceiling windows, making the room so blindingly bright that she had to squint against it. There was so much gilt in here—what with the ornately worked frame of the mirror, the paintings, the elegantly turned legs of the furniture—that the room itself seemed to glow. Amy reached out and touched the powder-blue hangings of the bed, the gold tassels that trimmed them, the silky-soft fabric of a sheet, then let her gaze travel up the nearest wall, rising some fifteen feet up to that ornately plastered ceiling.

What a fairytale place! And what a fairytale man who had brought her here! She shivered with delight as she relived the feel of his arms around her, his hot kisses, his ardent lovemaking. *Oh, Charles . . . How I love you!* Eager to see him, desperate not to waste a single moment of her new life in England, she jumped out of bed clad in nothing but her shift, her bare feet sinking into a plush rug that probably cost more than Sylvanus's house. Humming, she did an excited little pirouette on the ball of her toe. Then, suddenly realizing how foolish she was acting, she giggled and, wrapping her arms around herself, scampered to the window, where she climbed up onto the window seat and looked out.

There, far off in the distance and racing over the downs toward the castle, were two horses. One was a dark red, the other a tall liver chestnut. They were too far away for her to see the faces of those who rode them, but she would know Contender—and his rider's bright gold hair—anywhere.

She smiled, feeling suddenly happy. Oh, what memories they had made last night! She hurriedly brushed her hair and washed her face, reveling in the luxurious, lavender-scented soap at the washstand. Dressing quickly, she was just putting on her short-jacket when there was a soft knock at the door.

"Come in!" she said breathlessly, hoping it was Charles.

The door opened and a young woman of about Amy's age poked her head in. Amy instantly recognized her, though the two of them had not yet been formally introduced. "Good morning, Miss Leighton. I'm Nerissa—Charles's sister." She pushed the door fully open, revealing another woman standing just behind her. "And this is my sister-in-law, Juliet. May we come in and visit for a few moments?"

Amy, flustered and caught by surprise, dipped in an immediate curtsey. "Yes, yes of course," she said, but all the while her mind was racing. Had they found out that she and Charles had spent most of the night making love out in the stable? Had Nerissa come here to reprimand her, to tell her to stay away from her brother and leave him to his equals? And oh, how mortifying to meet Juliet now, the woman who may or not be her rival, when she was totally unprepared for such an encounter!

But Nerissa did not look angry; if anything, she looked a bit amused by Amy's sudden discomfiture. "I trust you slept well?"

As pale a blond as Charles, she was dressed in a shimmering gown of white, silver, and gold, and with the room's bright light surrounding her, she looked like some beautiful earthbound angel.

"I did, my lady."

"Please—just Nerissa." She smiled. "I hate formality, don't you, Juliet?"

"Can't stand it," said the other woman, her familiar New England accent as out of place in this magical castle as Amy herself felt. Gareth's wife had moss-green eyes and lovely dark hair drawn loosely, but becomingly, back from her exquisite face. Neither her coiffure nor her clothes were as fancy as Nerissa's; she had an air of no-nonsense about her, of Yankee simplicity that Amy instantly recognized and responded to. She smiled a little shyly, wondering if Juliet was discreetly studying her as she was discreetly studying Juliet.

Just don't think about the fact that she once lay with Charles. Don't think about the fact that her daughter is really Charles's flesh and blood. Don't think about that, and everything will be just fine. I hope . . .

And now Juliet came forward, her eyes mirroring the same wary hesitation that Amy herself felt, her smile a little unsure. "I understand you're from Massachusetts, too," she said, trying to be friendly.

"Yes, Newburyport."

"I'm from Boston—and Maine before that."

"Yes, I know," Amy said, and instantly clapped her hand over her mouth. "I'm sorry—I didn't mean that the way it sounded. I really *don't* know everything about you—oh, you must think me terribly rude!"

Nerissa, grinning, wandered into the adjoining dressing room, tactfully giving them a few moments alone.

"No. Not at all," Juliet replied. "Of course you would know more about me than I would about you, so please don't worry, Miss Leighton—I am not offended." She regarded Amy with her steady green gaze. "I know that things seem a bit awkward between us right now, given the fact that I knew Charles, but I want you to know that that is all in the past, and that is where it will stay." She smiled then. "I do hope that we can be friends."

"I think we already are. And please, call me Amy. *I* hate formality, too!"

"Amy, then." Juliet relaxed, and her soft smile became a grin. "Goodness, it *will* be nice to have one of my countrywomen here! These English are a strange sort. Why, do you realize that they play cards and drink and make merry on the Lord's day, doing things that we'd *never* be able to do back in Massachusetts? But never mind, you'll find all that out for yourself. Now tell me, are you homesick at all?"

"Oh, no, I'm far too excited to be homesick! So much to see and do and learn . . . I can't wait to start work. Do you think the duke would temporarily employ me as a lady's maid or cook or housekeeper or something?"

"What?" said Juliet, slightly taken aback.

"Well, I *do* need to find a position right away, so that I can earn my keep. After all, that's the only reason I came to England, so that I could make a new start and actually earn money for all my hard work!"

Juliet frowned and looked at her as if she had two noses. Then, recovering herself, she glanced toward the dressing room into which Nerissa had gone, and changed the subject. "Speaking of His Grace . . . how did you hold up during the rigorous interview I assume he subjected you to last night?"

"You—you knew about that?"

"Yes, but only because he subjected *me* to one the night I arrived, as well. It was dreadful. Gareth had rescued my stagecoach from highwaymen and gotten himself shot in the process, and I was covered with his blood. Lucien showed me no mercy whatsoever though, and forced me to sit there in the library and answer every one of his questions, and this after I'd only just met him and must've looked like the loser in a gladiator fight! I thought him quite the rudest, most arrogant man I'd ever met." She shook her head. "I hope he wasn't as overbearing with you."

"No, he was actually quite kind."

"*Kind?*" Juliet raised her brows. "He must be up to something, then."

"Yes—the Restoration of Charles, as he called it."

"I rather suspect he's up to far more than that," Juliet said, cryptically.

"Such as?"

"Oh, never mind. It's only a thought, and not worth voicing."

"Well, he *was* a bit intimidating."

"A *bit*?" Juliet laughed. "We're talking about a man who conceals a rapier in his walking stick, who appears to be as omniscient as God, who faithfully practices his duelling skills every week, and who loves nothing more than to move and manipulate those around him as he might the pieces in a game of chess. Add to that the fact he is one of the most powerful—and dangerous—men in England, and I fear that *intimidating* doesn't even begin to describe him! But he loves and is very protective of his family, I'll give him that. If you could have seen him when he found out that Gareth had taken up pugilism for a living . . .''

Humming to herald her imminent arrival, Nerissa reappeared, all smiles.

"Well, well, I see that you two Yankee Doodles have found something to talk about!"

"Yes, your infamous brother," Juliet said wryly.

"Lucien? He wasn't unkind to you, was he, Amy?"

Amy nearly laughed. "I don't understand why everyone thinks he's such a monster!"

The other two exchanged knowing glances. "You will," they chorused.

"Is he *that* difficult to work for?"

Nerissa stared at her. "What do you mean?"

"Amy came here looking for work," Juliet supplied, with a glance at Nerissa that spoke volumes.

"Work? Why, that's preposterous. She's not going to work, Charles would never allow it and neither will Lucien. I've never heard of anything so silly in all my life."

"Well, of course I have to work," Amy said, greatly confused and a little chagrined. "After all, I do have to eat . . .''

But Nerissa was studying her jacket and petticoats, both faded to the color of beach sand; her impossibly long fall of sleek dark hair, her shoes, her work-roughened hands. "You don't need work, you need a maid."

"No, you don't understand, I came to England expecting to be someone *else*'s maid—"

Nerissa gave an airy wave of her hand. "Nonsense. You must have a maid. You must have new clothes. And you must have a ball gown, which is why you're going to London with me this afternoon so we can visit my dressmaker."

"London? A *ball gown*?" Amy couldn't help her

burst of laughter. "That's the last thing I need!"

"On the contrary," said Nerissa. "Lucien is throwing a ball next Friday in honor of Charles's homecoming, and he wants you to be there."

"Wants?"

Juliet drawled, "*Demands* is more like it."

"It's his way of thanking you for all you've done for Charles," Nerissa added. "He wants to give you a magical, Cinderella night-at-the-ball as his way of expressing his gratitude for saving Charles's life."

"But—but I *can't* attend, I—I don't even know how to dance!"

"Then you will learn," said Nerissa, blithely.

"And . . . I don't know the correct things to say to people, or how to address them properly . . . or—or . . . anything!"

"We will teach you."

"And I can't afford fancy new clothes, let alone a ball gown!"

"Ah, but I can, and I would be very offended if you do not accept them as a small token of my appreciation for saving my brother's life," intoned a smoothly urbane, aristocratic voice. Gasping, Amy whirled to see the duke of Blackheath standing in the doorway, an amused little smile playing about his otherwise severe face.

Amy sank in a curtsey. "Your Grace!"

"My dear girl. Are you giving my sister trouble?"

"No, but I really can't go to a ball, I'll look the fool and I've got no business being there anyhow and—"

"Do you want to go to the ball?"

"Well of course, it'll be magical, wondrous, but I'll feel like a chicken amongst a flock of peacocks!"

The duke folded his arms and leaned negligently against the door jamb, his black eyes holding her captive. "Do you remember the conversation we had last night . . . about helping Charles?"

That soft, suave tone was enough to make Amy's heart still. "Well yes, but I don't see how this has anything to do with him . . ."

"Of course you don't. And so I will tell you. Nerissa wants a new gown for the ball. As a lady's maid, you will want some new clothes. And *I*"—he gave a silky smile—"I will want Charles to ride alongside your coach to provide safe escort to and from London." He smiled, but the gesture was just a little bit sinister. "It would benefit him greatly to feel . . . useful, don't you think?"

And Amy, standing there feeling nervous and drymouthed and very, very intimidated indeed, suddenly understood. By sending the girls off to London and asking Charles to go along as protection, Lucien was setting things up so that Charles would have opportunity to regain some of his feelings of confidence and self-worth.

She only hoped he wasn't lining up a highwayman to rob them, as well!

She returned the duke's smile, suddenly feeling like a co-conspirator instead of a scared ninny. "Yes, Your Grace. I quite understand."

"Good. I knew that you would." And then, with a furtive exchange of glances with Nerissa, he bowed deeply to the three women and continued on his way.

Charles returned from his race with Gareth, flushed and in higher spirits than he'd been in a donkey's age. It had been just like old times, the two of them pushing their eager horses to the limit, leaving the cares of the world behind and rebuilding the deep friendship they'd always had. They had galloped all the way down to Ravenscombe and back, slowing their mounts a half-mile away from the stables to give them a chance to cool down.

"Damn good run you gave me, Charles," said Gareth, patting Crusader's neck before dismounting and handing him into the care of a waiting groom. "You might've beat me today, but by God, I'll have my revenge tomorrow!"

"Is that a challenge?"

"It is indeed!"

"Very well then, I accept it." Charles grinned and also dismounted, and watched as the groom led both animals away. His brother was still standing beside him, his cheeks a bit flushed from the winter wind, his eyes bright.

A silence fell between them as they headed toward the castle.

They'd taken only a few steps when Charles paused and, reaching out, caught Gareth by the shoulder. "Gareth, I . . . I just want to say thank you."

"For what?"

Charles thought for a moment. "For being yourself," he finally said.

Gareth grinned. And then he looked hard at Charles, and his blue eyes began to twinkle. "And thank you too, Charles—for being *your*self," he said cryptically.

"I beg your pardon?"

"Never mind," Gareth said, his eyes warm with brotherly love. "Come on, let's go inside. It's cold out here!"

They were just approaching the front entrance when the great iron-banded door opened and Lucien came out. He had his walking stick in his hand, and his two dogs circling his heels, eager to be off on their morning run.

"Ah, Gareth," he said. "I do believe your daughter is crying for you. Why don't you go see to her?"

Gareth opened his mouth to protest, but something in

Lucien's eyes made him suddenly think better of it. Making his excuses, he left his brothers standing together on the drive.

Something clenched in Charles's gut as he remembered his deplorable behavior of last night.

Thankfully, Lucien chose to ignore it.

"My dear Charles," he said, expansively. "I wonder if I might ask a favor of you?"

"What would you like?"

"Nerissa and Amy wish to go to London, and I simply don't have time to go along as escort. You wouldn't mind going instead, just to ensure that they come to no harm, would you?"

"What do they need to go to London for?"

Lucien gave a dramatically heavy sigh. "Oh, female pursuits, of course. Shopping, gossip, maybe a visit to that infernal French dressmaker of Nerissa's. You know how your sister just has to have the latest fashions from the Continent." He raised his brows as Charles eyed him narrowly. "But of course, if you don't feel . . . up to it, I suppose I could always send Andrew instead."

"What do you mean, if I don't feel up to it?"

"Oh, nothing. I was just thinking about our little conversation last night. The one where you made it quite obvious that you are no longer, shall we say, capable of the things you once were. But never mind. I'm sure that Andrew will be delighted to lend his protection to the girls, instead. He has become quite a handsome young lad, don't you think?" His black eyes gleamed. "I *do* wonder what your little friend will think of him . . ." He whistled for the dogs and raised his walking stick to Charles in mock salute. "Good day, Charles. I will see you at teatime, I hope."

And then he moved off, leaving Charles staring after him in rising fury, his hands balled into fists and a little muscle ticking in his jaw.

What the *devil* was that all about?!

And was that thinly veiled insult payback for what had transpired between them last night?

Well, one thing was for sure. Andrew was *not* going to be the one escorting the girls into London! Charles marched into the house, striding as though he was still a captain in the King's Own. He went straight across the Great Hall, through the length of the castle, out into a far wing, up a flight of stairs, and found the youngest de Montforte brother right where he expected to find him: in the great chamber above the ballroom that Andrew had long since adopted as his laboratory.

Charles's anger cooled the moment he stepped into the room.

The last time he'd been here, there'd been a dazzling array of bottles containing an even more dazzling array of chemicals and solutions filling the tables, the shelves, even the window sills. There had been open books and scholarly papers strewn about on both floor and tables; notes and mathematical equations that Charles didn't even try to begin to understand scrawled across the blackboard; weights, scales, and measures; evil-looking concoctions simmering in various tubes and beakers; and Andrew, commanding this chaos like some mad scientist. All of those things were still here.

As well as—

"What in God's name is *that*?" Charles expostulated, staring at the strange contraption that dominated the wooden floor. Shaped like a giant arrowhead, it appeared to be constructed of a bamboo frame filled in with yards of tautly stretched red silk. Beneath it, Charles could just see Andrew's stockings and shoes protruding; the rest of his brother was somewhere beneath—

"My flying machine," said Andrew, sliding out from beneath the thing in question on a wooden dolly. Lying on his back, he cocked a grin up at Charles, obviously quite pleased with himself. "Or rather, the Contraption, as they mostly call it round here." He got to his feet and brushed himself off. "What do you think?"

Charles, shaking his head in amazement and disbelief, walked a slow circle around Andrew's latest invention. He had no doubts about Andrew's brilliance, but a flying machine? It was . . . impossible!

"It looks like a giant kite," he finally said, hoping Andrew did not see the doubt in his eyes.

"But it's not." Andrew kicked the dolly out of the way and clapped a hand behind Charles's shoulders. "I say, Charles, I'm devilish glad you're home, because there are a few things I need some advice on. I'll need to form a company to produce these things . . . I'll need to attract investors . . . and I want to consider whether there's a military application, which you're obviously the best person to advise me on."

"Why is everyone coming to *me* for advice?"

"Are they?"

"Yes," said Charles, frowning. "Gareth wants to bend my ear about some of the problems he's having with his estate, and now you . . ."

"Well, I don't see anything unusual about it," Andrew said, shrugging. "We always came to you for advice before you went away, so why not now?"

"Because . . . oh, never mind." He shook his head. "That reminds me, what *are* you doing about your army career? Isn't there a war going on?"

"I'm on an extended leave of absence, which was rather necessary considering that someone else had already been promoted into my place as company commander. I'll probably end up resigning my commission, anyhow."

Andrew screwed up his face. "Whatever for?"

"Because—oh, forget it, it's not important." What was he supposed to say, *because I lost my nerve, my*

confidence, and am no longer capable of leading men?
He forced a smile. "Come, I wish to know more about
your invention. Will it really fly?"

"Damned if I know. Haven't tested it yet, and I
won't, until that bastard Lucien conveniently decides to
go off to London or something." Already, Andrew's
eyes were beginning to flash. "For six months he's been
insulting me, taunting me, and quite confidently declar-
ing that I'd never succeed in building it, let alone getting
it to work. I'll tell you, Charles, there's nothing that
would bring me more pleasure than to make him eat his
words, every last damned one of them!"

So, Lucien and the Defiant One were still at odds;
some things never changed.

"I'm sure that day will come," Charles said, reaching
out to touch one silk-clad wing, then bending and peering underneath, where there was a crude leather harness
attached to the frame at the center. "How does it
work?"

Andrew, eager to discuss his creation, promptly forgot
about his enmity with Lucien. Brightening, he pushed
back a stray bit of dark auburn hair that had come loose
over his forehead and squatted down beside Charles.
"Well, that there is the harness that will keep me
strapped in. These are the wings—I've spent all summer
and autumn studying the shape of bird's wings, and the
ratio of length to weight so I could get it just right—
and these extra supports here are for strength."

"I see. And how do you intend to steer it?"

"I'm still working on that bit."

"Hmmm."

"It's meant to ride on air, much as a boat rides on
water, but I haven't yet worked out the best way to get
it airborne. It's all a matter of finding enough speed to
give it lift, which rather limits my choices. I have two,
as far as I can determine."

"Oh?"

"I've been thinking that the least dangerous way of doing it would be to hitch a carriage to our two fastest horses, squat atop it with the Contraption on my back, and then make the horses gallop as fast as they can go. When there's enough speed, the craft should lift and *voila*, I shall up and fly like a bird!"

"Uh . . . yes," Charles said, dubiously. He rubbed his chin. "And the other method of getting it airborne?"

Andrew grinned. "A catapult."

"Good God, man!"

"Want to see it?"

Charles blinked. "Well, I—"

Andrew seized his arm. "Come on, I've got it set up on the roof."

His face alight with excitement, Andrew led Charles out of the laboratory, up the stairs, and onto the roof. Up here the wind was gusty and fierce, the view spectacular, the moat below sparkling in the sun. Andrew was oblivious to all of it. He swept his hand forward— and sure enough, there it was.

A giant catapult.

Charles felt his mouth go dry. "Uh, Andrew . . . this is a little high, isn't it?" he asked, a sudden nervousness on behalf of his brother's safety making his palms go damp and a sick feeling to settle in the pit of his stomach. Andrew was not foolhardy; either he had more than enough faith in his creation, or his desire to prove something to Lucien was making him reckless.

"Not as high as the tower," Andrew said cheerfully. "This is perfect, really. And if things go wrong, I've taken into account both the force of the catapult and the weight of me and the machine, and I've calculated it so that I'd land in the moat. It's perfectly safe, I can assure you."

"I'm glad you won't be testing your invention any-time soon."

"Well, I *was* going to wait until Lucien's gone, but you know something, Charles? I'm so confident that this thing is going to make history, so confident that it's going to make me famous, and so confident that I'm *finally* going to be able to rub Lucien's nose in my brilliance, that I'm going to hold a demonstration at the end of next week."

"Next week?" Charles asked, faintly.

"Yes. And everyone will be there. You do know about the little party that Lucien's throwing to celebrate your return, don't you? Not only is he inviting everyone for miles around, he's sent off a special invitation to the king himself."

"*The king?!*"

"Yes, the king." Andrew's eyes gleamed. "Just think, Charles, what it will mean to have *him* there to endorse my entrance into the history books! His Majesty will grant me royal patronage! I'll be rich beyond my wildest dreams!" Hands on his hips, he gazed out over the downs, his expression already triumphant. "And Lucien will rue the day he *ever* mocked me!"

Charles was still staring at him, trying to digest all he'd just been told. A demonstration? A little party? *An invitation to the king?*

Andrew grabbed his arm. "I say, it's bloody cold up here. Let's go back inside so you can help me figure out how to start this company of mine!"

Chapter 25

After meeting Amy Leighton, Juliet walked slowly back down the corridor toward Gareth's old apartments, which she and her husband were sharing during this sudden Christmastide visit to Blackheath Castle.

Her heart was heavy. Troubled. Though Lucien had prepared them all for Charles's imminent arrival after receiving the startling news that he was actually alive and coming home, it had still been a dreadful shock to see him in the flesh. It had been an even more dreadful shock to see what he had become in the nearly two years since she had known him. Juliet had not lied to Gareth about her feelings for Charles, and she would not trade Gareth for the world—or for Charles, for that matter— but she was mature and honest enough with herself to accept that old memories died hard. Seeing Charles again had reactivated a score of them. He had been her first love—and her first lover. You couldn't make a baby with a man and accept his offer of marriage, and then cast him out of your heart just like that.

Even if there *was* someone else you loved a hundred times better.

She paused at a window which looked down on the lawn and the graveled drive below. Lucien's coach, polished until it shone like jet, was already being brought round, the clouds floating across the bright blue sky reflected in its glossy paintwork. She was glad that her pregnancy gave her an excuse not to go to London with the others. Already, liveried footmen awaited Nerissa's and Amy's arrival, and in a few moments, a groom would bring Contender out—the magnificent animal she'd first seen Charles mounted on, so many months ago, so many miles away, on Boston Common.

Something began to ache in Juliet's heart and she turned away from the window, continuing on down the west corridor.

Last night still haunted her. Every time she closed her eyes, she could still see Charles barging into the dining room, stopping short when he'd seen her with Gareth, his shocked gaze going to her rounded belly, his blue, blue eyes so full of hurt.

She bent her head, watching the floor as she walked, her eyes stinging with unshed tears. Her guilt knew no bounds.

Oh, where was absolution? Forgiveness for what she had done—and how she now felt?

Even though she'd thought that Charles was dead, it had taken time for her heart to let go of the dashing officer with whom she'd had a few stolen moments and not much more, really, than that. It had taken time for her to stop wearing the miniature of him, painted shortly before Concord, that had long occupied a place around her neck. And it had taken time for her to realize that she'd been in love with an icon. An image. An idea. But Gareth was none of those things. She loved him to the fullest extent of her being, and though it was painful to admit, given the guilt she felt about Charles and the way she had inadvertently hurt him, she was very, very glad that the Wild One was the brother she'd married.

But what had that done to Charles?

If Charles could find happiness with anyone, Juliet hoped it would be with that soft-spoken young woman whose bright sense of whimsy would go far toward soothing his hurts and healing his ravaged heart.

She only hoped that Charles would allow himself the freedom to love Amy in return.

"Now Charles, there's no need for you to escort us to *every* shop," Nerissa chided, poking her head out the window as the coach came to a stop in front of Madame Perrot's and her brother swung down from Contender. "And we're going to be *ages* in this one. Maybe you ought to go off and visit your club or something. You can meet us back here at, say, three o'clock, and then we'll head home."

"*Three o'clock!*" Charles expostulated, as a footman lowered the steps. He moved forward, handing first his sister and then Amy down from the coach and walking them to the door of the shop. "Why do you need three hours in a single shop?"

"Because we're women, that's why," Nerissa returned, as though that explained everything. "I need a new gown for the ball and it will take time to select suitable fabric and colors. Hmmm. I wonder if I will go with an ice-blue silk? Or perhaps a frosty mint-green satin trimmed with silver thread and delicate, matching brocade around the skirts—"

"Right. I'm off then," Charles muttered, much to Nerissa's secret delight. As he bowed to them both, Nerissa noticed that his eyes caught and held Amy's—and that Amy's cheeks instantly darkened with color. Nerissa grinned to herself. *Ha, by the time* we're *through with her, you won't be able to take your eyes off her!* she vowed in silent amusement, thinking back to the conversation she and Lucien had had in the library shortly before leaving . . .

The duke had given her explicit instructions.

"Remember what I told you, Nerissa. Spare no expense when it comes to dressing her. I want her *out* of those hideous colors and fabrics she's in now, and into something that will show her coloring to greatest advantage."

"Silks, satins, velvets?"

"Yes, and the finest, most expensive ones Madame has." Lucien's enigmatic black eyes had gleamed with sly delight before he'd turned away and, his forefinger tapping his lips once, twice, continued on. "And dramatic colors only—no pastels for that girl, no more washed out yellows and wretched browns that only make her look sallow and ill. She's no English rose and shouldn't be dressed like one. No, I want her in blazing scarlet, brilliant turquoise, emerald green, magenta— loud, startling hues that will flatter her exotic coloring and make every man at the ball unable to take his eyes off her." He'd given a dangerous little smile. "*Especially* Charles."

Nerissa had returned his grin. "Especially Charles."

"Just take care, my dear, that he does not learn of the purchases you'll make for the girl at Madame Perrot's. Let him think the shopping trip is for you, and that Amy is along as . . . as training to be a lady's maid. Ah, yes. That will throw him off the scent quite nicely, I think— as well as make him seriously begin to question, if he has not already, whether he wants her to be a lady's maid or *his* lady." He had grinned then, as delighted with his machinations as he must've been when he'd brought Gareth and Juliet together. "It is imperative that he is, shall we say, *pleasantly surprised* when he sees his little friend at Friday night's ball. . . ."

Even now, Nerissa's eyes gleamed with a co-conspirator's delight. Oh, she was all too happy to help Lucien play matchmaker! Wouldn't it be wonderful if Charles could find the same happiness that Gareth had found? Wouldn't it be wonderful if she had *two* sisters-in-law that she just adored? All Charles needed was to see Amy outshining a backdrop of English beauties and heiresses, and he'd be completely undone. All *Amy* needed was some confidence and self-esteem. To Nerissa's way of thinking, gorgeous clothes, jewels, and some lessons in comportment would go far toward making her feel every bit as worthy as the women with whom she'd be competing on Friday night.

Grinning, Nerissa linked her arm through Amy's and pulled her into the shop.

The trip to London was hell for Charles. Hell because they'd had to stay at coaching inns on the way out and back and he'd had to sleep alone—which was torment in itself after the wild night he'd spent with Amy. Hell because she was in the carriage and he was on Contender and they were separated.

I want her. I want her so damned *badly.*

Hell because they were now heading back to Blackheath Castle, and the inevitable and all-too-necessary confrontation with Juliet that awaited him there.

He dreaded that confrontation with all his heart, yet he knew it needed to be put behind them both. He had seen the anguish in Juliet's eyes when he'd charged into the dining room the other night, and it upset him greatly to think she might still hold a candle for him. Would she expect him to still have feelings for her? Would she *want* him to still have feelings for her? And would it hurt her to learn that he—the man who had once offered her marriage—had no feelings for her at all beyond affection and a sincere wish that she find happiness with Gareth?

He thought of what Gareth had both said and left un-said—that when he and Juliet had known each other in Boston, her love had been that of an impressionable young girl enamored of a man in a dashing uniform. She had grown up since then; her heart was with Gareth now. But was it, truly?

He had to know for himself before he could proceed with the rest of his life.

Before he could even think about having a life with Amy.

It was drizzling and growing dark by the time they finally rode into Ravenscombe, nestled at the foot of the downs. The village was silent, its inhabitants eating their suppers and preparing for bed, the silence, combined with the soft whisper of the rain, contriving to weigh down Charles's already flagging spirits. But as the carriage, with Contender prancing along beside it, passed the statue of Henry VII on his rearing horse, doors and windows on both sides of the street began to open, and the villagers came running out of their cottages, some waving, some cheering, all rushing forward.

"The Beloved One—he's back!"

"Lord Charles! Bless you, Lord Charles, you've been returned to us!"

"Hip hip, huzzah! Hip hip, huzzah! Hip hip, huz-zah!"

The cheers were deafening. They swarmed the carriage, and Contender. Charles, taken aback and more than a little embarrassed, saw Amy's startled face at the window and then, before he knew what they were about, the villagers were pulling him down from the horse and hoisting him above their shoulders, laughing, singing, and cheering him to the black and misty sky.

"Please—I do not deserve such accolades!" he protested, thinking of his inglorious performance in battle, but his words were drowned out by cheering.

Moments later, they were carrying him on their shoulders toward the Speckled Hen, where the grinning proprietor, Fred Crawley, had thrown wide his door and was wildly beckoning everyone inside.

"Free ale all around, to celebrate Lord Charles's return!"

And Nerissa, watching from the carriage with a speechless but delighted Amy, hid her own little grin and wondered if Lucien was behind this as well.

One thing she did know: Charles wouldn't be home for a while. Probably a long while.

She rapped once on the roof to signal the driver to continue on to the castle.

Chapter 26

❧

As it was, Charles didn't get home until nearly one in the morning. He had always been well liked by the people of Ravenscombe, easily mixing with the villagers despite their social differences, and that, at least, had not changed in the slightest.

They'd wanted to know what had happened to him in America. They'd wanted to know why he was believed dead. And they'd wanted to know who the pretty young woman he'd brought back from America was—for after all, many of Lucien's servants lived here in the village, and gossip travelled fast.

Everyone knew she was at the castle.

Who *was* she?

"A friend," Charles said evasively, gazing down into his ale so they wouldn't note his sudden flush and start teasing the truth out of him. At the very thought of Amy—and what the two of them had done out in the stable the other night—he felt a stab of heat that manifested itself squarely beneath the drop-front of his breeches. "I brought her to England so she might have a better life."

"A better loife, eh? 'Ere's 'opin' ye'll be the one to be givin' it to 'er!''

"Aye, another Yankee bride for another de Montforte brother!''

"Hear, hear!''

"Ah, leave 'is lordship alone, 'e wants 'is privacy, can't ye see?''

There was laughter all around and Charles felt his cheeks going uncomfortably warm. He grinned and accepted another ale.

"So tell us wot 'appened to ye, m'lord!''

Charles did not find it easy to talk about himself, but after that second drink, he was able to tell them what the situation had been like in Boston. A third, and he was able to explain what had happened to make everyone think him dead. A fourth, and he was actually able to poke a bit of fun at himself as he related his embarrassingly inept performance at Concord, this alien, self-deprecating humor surprising no one as much as it did himself. And all the while, they were urging him on, pressing more drinks into his hand and making him feel as if maybe, just maybe, he hadn't erred so badly, after all.

"So ye saved the little lad's loife, did ye?''

"Sacrificed yer eyes, an' wot could've been yer loife, just so's the boy could live!''

"That's our Beloved One!''

More cheering, so loud that they could probably hear it all the way up at the castle. And then the villagers had told him all the news that had occurred in his absence, who had been born and who had died and who had got married, before finally dragging him off to the church, where they'd all celebrated the ripping down from the wall the plaque that had proclaimed his date of death. And later, as he had walked—or rather stumbled—back to the Speckled Hen and Contender, his heart had felt curiously light, his mind, which had been troubled for so long, still and at peace.

To them, you're still the Beloved One. To Amy you're the Beloved One. Everyone is still asking for your advice, just like they always did. Nothing has changed. Maybe you are still the same as you used to be....

Maybe.

So why don't I feel that I can live up to that, and be the man I used to be?

He swung up on Contender, blinked away the raindrops that pattered down from the branches, and made his way home.

Morning dawned cold and gloomy, with a brooding gray sky that engulfed the downs in mist and seemed to sit heavily atop Blackheath's ancient towers.

It was a morning to stay inside. A morning to curl up beside a fire with a book, or to drink chocolate in bed, or to snuggle up beneath the covers with a lover.

Charles awoke in his old bedroom, feeling cold and, not surprisingly after last night's indulgence, hungover. His rod was a pillar of stone. Also not surprising. He lay there kneading his brow and remembering all those weeks when his head had ached, and that time on the beach at Plum Island when Amy had massaged the pain into something bearable.

Ah, God help him. Wouldn't it be nice if she was here right now, rubbing his brow?

Or anything else, for that matter ...

He sat up in bed, knuckling his eyes. He could hear the rain falling softly just outside, and the distant tinkle of a pianoforte from somewhere downstairs. His sister was probably in the Gold Parlour, entertaining everyone with her talent, of which she had much. His grin faded. He felt suddenly excluded.

I can't live like this.

Best to go down and join them, then, and try to pretend that his uncharacteristic outburst the other night hadn't occurred. That nothing had ever happened between himself and Juliet, who would surely be down there with the others. That he was the same man he'd always been, as he'd been able to believe if only for a little while when the villagers had made so much of him last night. Rising, he summoned his valet, and a half hour later, was washed, shaved, and dressed.

But as he moved down the west corridor and started to turn the corner to descend the staircase, he heard voices on the landing, hushed, excited.

"Oooh! I just felt him kick again!"

"Now Juliet, how can you know it's a 'he'?"

"I know because I'm not nearly as sick as I was with Charlotte. Boys are easier to carry than girls, you know. Or so they say. Oh!" An excited little squeal. "Put your hand right there, Gareth."

"Here?"

"Yes, right there—do you feel it?"

A tense, expectant silence. And then, "Oh, *Juliet . . .*"

Charles froze, feeling as though a bucket of ice had just been thrown over his head. Afraid of being caught eavesdropping, he began backing up. He did not want to intrude upon this tender scene. He did not want to do anything to wreck his brother's and Juliet's happiness. He turned around—

And nearly collided with Lucien, who had come silently up behind him as he'd stood listening to a conversation he should never have heard.

"Why, hello, Charles. Fancy finding *you* standing here."

On the stairs, the voices immediately hushed. Lucien's eyes gleamed, and in that instant Charles knew his brother had wanted Juliet and Gareth to know that he, Charles, had overheard their private conversation. He felt a swift flood of anger.

"I was contemplating going down to breakfast," he bit out.

"Strange place to contemplate such a matter, don't you think?"

"If you will excuse me."

"Actually, I will not. There is something I wish to discuss with you, if I could have a few moments of your time."

"What is it?"

"Andrew. I am . . . worried about him, and this confounded Contraption of his. You do know that he wishes to test it during the ball and in the presence of the king, don't you?"

"*I* know, yes, but you weren't supposed to."

Lucien smiled thinly. "My dear Charles. I can assure you, there is nothing around here that I do *not* know. But never mind. You appear to be in a rather foul mood this morning and, well, we all know that you're not the man you were. Pity! And here I keep forgetting . . . Perhaps I shall ask your brother's assistance instead." Casually straightening a white ruffle at his wrist, he raised his voice slightly. "Gareth?"

As Charles stood fuming at both the insult and the way Lucien had deliberately chosen Gareth's assistance over his, Gareth, looking a bit pink in the cheeks but otherwise as euphoric as any father would be who'd just felt his child moving in his wife's womb for the first time, emerged from around the corner, a slightly sheepish Juliet in tow.

She looked at Charles, and then averted her gaze, pretending to be absorbed in a painting that hung on the wall.

Charles glared at Lucien, who pointedly ignored him.

"Gareth, I am concerned for Andrew's safety. The

idea of our brother catapulting off the roof in what appears to be an untethered kite is causing me no small degree of worry. Would you mind accompanying me into his laboratory? As he's gone down to the village, I should like to take the opportunity to examine this Contraption for myself, and, since you are no stranger to daredevil stunts, get your opinion on it as well.''

Gareth glanced uncertainly at Juliet, still pretending to be absorbed in the painting, and then at Charles, who was visibly furious.

"Uh, I'm sure, Luce, that Andrew knows what he's doing—''

"Andrew may be gifted when it comes to intelligence, but he is no . . . perfectionist, as some of us are. He doesn't always get things right, and in this case, a mistake might be fatal.'' Again, Lucien gave a benign little smile that was not benign at all. "Will you accompany me, Gareth?''

Charles knew he had been baited. *Perfectionist.* "*I'll* go with you,'' he said through his teeth.

"No, no, Charles,'' murmured Lucien, with a casual wave of his hand. "You go downstairs and have some of this breakfast you've been uh, *contemplating.* I'm sure that Gareth and I will manage just fine.'' Then, bowing to Juliet, he drew Gareth with him back down the hall.

And Charles, incensed, was left with Juliet.

Alone.

She was still examining the painting, but he knew she wasn't really seeing it. It would be so easy to just excuse himself. To put this off for another day.

Unbidden, the advice he had once given to Sylvanus Leighton came back to him. *It is far better to confront a problem straightaway than to hide from it, to take the offensive before it can sneak up and overwhelm you from behind.*

He took a deep breath.

"Juliet—"

"Lucien, he—he is up to his usual tricks, I fear," she said shakily, still without looking at him. "It is cruel of him to taunt you so."

She pulled back from the painting, wiping damp hands down her skirts, her eyes nervous. He cleared his throat. She gave a quick, fleeting smile, her almost desperate gaze following Gareth, who appeared to have no concern at all about leaving her with the man she had once loved. He rubbed at a nonexistent itch at the corner of his eye.

"Yes. He never used to, you know."

"He's worried about Andrew, I guess. It would be terrible if Andrew demonstrates his Contraption at the ball and embarrasses or injures—let alone kills—himself in front of the king."

"He won't kill himself," said Charles.

"You have faith in him, then?"

"More than Lucien does."

"I . . . I think that Lucien probably has faith in him too, but is just trying to bully him into being successful. Andrew seems to need constant prodding to follow through with his ideas—or so Gareth and Lucien tell me." She plucked at the edge of her sleeve. "When I f-first came here, Lucien told Andrew that he'd never even build his Contraption, let alone get it to fly."

"Oh, I suspect it will fly," said Charles. "The question is, how far?"

She looked down, the toe of her slipper rubbing at the floor with obvious agitation. He wished he could spare her this apprehension, this awkwardness, and that this conversation he was not looking forward to any more than she, was already behind them.

"So. What do you think of England?" he ventured, after a few moments.

"It is grand."

"Do you miss Boston?"

She shook her head. "I'm happy here. The grass stays green all winter, and there are no mosquitoes in the summer. And I'm sure that so much has changed in Boston since I was last there."

"Yes, as so much has changed here, as well," Charles said, offering his arm to her. After a moment's hesitation she took it, her fingertips barely touching him, her entire body stiff with nervousness, as though she feared he might ravish her, or that she was doing something wrong. His heart hurt for her, for such feelings were needless.

He began walking back down the hall, adjusting his pace so that she did not have to labor to keep up. Relief was already starting to spread through him. Hard to believe that if he hadn't fallen against that wall, he'd be married to this woman. Hard to believe that he'd made a baby with her. Hard to believe that he felt such a curious absence of desire for her now, and that his mind recoiled from the memories they had once made like two magnets placed pole to pole.

Pray God that she felt the same way.

"*Has* your home changed so?" she asked, giving him the impression that she wanted to make small talk, and avoid the deeper issues that lay between them.

"Yes, it has." He guided her into a small sitting room that looked out over the gardens, and half shut the door behind them. He wanted them to have privacy, but he didn't want her to feel that he was closeting her in here with him. "When I went off to America with the army, I left behind one brother who did not seem capable of bringing his scientific ideas to fruition, and another who did not seem capable of behaving as an adult." He smiled as he saw the spark of anger coming into her eyes, and instantly banished it with his next words.

"Now, I come back to find the first ready to take to the skies in a flying machine, and the other married, leading a responsible life as a Member of Parliament, and proving himself to be the best father in England." He smiled, putting all of the warmth in his heart in the gesture. "I would never have thought it possible."

Pain darkened her eyes and she walked a little distance away from him, wringing her hands. "Are you angry, Charles?" she asked, her voice little more than a whisper. She raised her anguished green gaze to his. "Have I hurt you beyond repair?"

"You? Hurt *me*?" He gave a bitter laugh. "Madam, it is *I* who have done the hurting."

"*You* weren't the one who went off and married someone else."

"And *you* weren't the one who died and then came back to life, expecting everything to be the same as before. I'm the one who's caused all the hurt, Juliet."

"But not intentionally, Charles. You wouldn't."

"No, I would not. But that doesn't make me any less sorry for the pain I've brought to both you and my family. I'm glad that all has worked out so nicely between you and Gareth, and that your love has transformed him into a very different man than the one he once was, but I regret that I was taken in by the deceit of Amy's sisters, and that I believed the letters they had written, including the one that was supposedly from you."

She gave a nervous laugh. "But as you say, everything worked out nicely . . ."

"Are you happy, Juliet?"

She gazed up at him, and he saw the pain in her eyes, the warring emotions. And then she came toward him and hesitantly placed her hand in his. "I am happy, Charles." She bit her lip, trying to choose the right words. "Probably—and I beg you not to take this the wrong way—happier than I might have been with you."

She gave a tremulous grin, trying to soften her words. "You and I are too much alike, both too serious minded, and too cautious, to have ever made a good go of it."

Charles shut his eyes and released his pent-up breath. He squeezed her hand and then let it go. "Thank you. Thank you, madam, for saying that."

"It doesn't hurt you to hear that?"

"No, Juliet. It relieves me of much of the guilt I've been carrying."

"What do *you* have to feel guilty about?"

"Me?" He shook his head. "Guilt for being taken in by those letters. Guilt for the fact that you were left to fend for yourself. Guilt for the grief you must have suffered in thinking me dead. Guilt for . . . for the feelings I now have for another."

She smiled, some of the pain leaving her eyes. "Thank *you*, Charles, for saying that."

"That doesn't hurt *you*?"

"No." Her smile deepened. "It relieves me of much of the guilt *I've* been carrying."

Their gazes met, warm and understanding, before she blushed and he looked away, clearing his throat.

"Juliet, you and I—that is to say, I was . . . very fond of you once, and I meant everything I ever said to you, but I did not understand the feelings I had for you at the time. I thought I was in love with you. Now—and I beg *you* not to take this the wrong way—I realize my love was not as strong as it might have been. As it should have been. You and I were different people, two years ago. I was far from home, and lonely—"

"—And I was young and impressionable."

"And I should have known better than to dally with a pretty young Bostonian."

"And I should have known better than to try to catch the eye of a handsome English captain."

He caught her grin and returned it, feeling the tension

and guilt he'd been carrying since coming back to find her here easing out of him by degrees.

"You really *do* forgive me, then," she said, her eyes suddenly misty with tears.

"I do, but with the fervent hope that you really forgive *me*."

"Of course I do. You have been cruelly used, Charles, and dreadfully wronged. No one blames you for what happened, least of all me."

He looked down into her eyes, no longer troubled, but shining with relief and gratitude for what he had told her. They had set each other free. "I hope you love my little brother with all the strength of your heart," he said, gazing deeply into her eyes. "Gareth has suffered much pain in his life, and he deserves no less than what I know you can give him. He deserves someone like you, Juliet."

"I do love him, Charles." A tear slipped from the corner of her eye, and began a slow path down her cheek. "I do love him, and I pray that you find someone to make you as happy as he has made me." She swiped away the tear. "But I think you already have."

He smiled, gently. "Yes . . . I think I have."

And then she reached deeply into her pocket and drew something out which she held tightly in her closed hand for a long moment.

"I've been keeping these for you. Waiting for the right moment to give them back to you. They once belonged to you, but they really should be hers now."

And then she held her hand over his and dropped two objects into his palm. One was the miniature he'd had painted two years ago in Boston. And the other was the signet ring with which they had sealed their betrothal that fateful night in April.

Her smile was a little watery. "You're a free man

now, Charles. Take these and be happy.'' And then she closed his hand around the two objects, stood on tiptoe to kiss his brow, and turned, walking from the room without a backwards glance.

Chapter 27

～～♡♡～～

Yes, he was free.

But during the week that followed that liberating conversation with Juliet, Charles certainly didn't feel free. He felt buffeted on all sides.

Though his friendship with Gareth was as strong as it had ever been, though he and Juliet had managed to clear the air between them, though Andrew asked his help in getting the Flying Contraption removed to the roof in preparation for tonight's demonstration, Charles's relationship with Lucien—which had always been amiable and mutually respectful—was in tatters.

It was obvious that his brother no longer respected him, and though Charles found it hard to admit, even to himself, he was hurt by the fact that where Lucien had once turned to him for advice, assistance, and friendship, he now turned to Gareth.

And to add insult to injury, there was the matter of Amy.

Every morning right after breakfast, Nerissa and her maid, Hannah, had spirited Amy off, depriving Charles of any and all time spent alone with her. It was almost as if his family knew what had happened out in the

323

stable, and were contriving to keep them apart until Amy could be safely packed off to some new employer as a lady's maid.

And now, with the ball only a matter of hours away, they had taken her off yet again, teaching her how to dress another woman, how to arrange the hair of another woman, how to make herself indispensable to another woman, another woman who would be having all the fun while Amy, who had never had any fun, watched wistfully from the wings. Charles wanted to hit something in his frustration. True, he had brought her to England so she could have a better life, and now that Nerissa was preparing her for a position that would carry no small degree of prestige in itself, he was beginning to realize that perhaps that wasn't quite what he wanted for Amy after all.

Back in America, when he'd allowed her to come to England with him, he might have told himself it was, but now, with no promises to Juliet to bind him, with nothing standing in his way, it wasn't—and he knew it. He did not want her to leave Blackheath. He did not want her to leave *him*. Yet what excuse did he have to keep her here?

The dilemma chipped away at the peace his conversation with Juliet had given him, made him feel restless and impatient and compelled to act in a way for which he was not prepared: To offer a marriage proposal to Amy. But that was impossible, of course. He might be the heir presumptive to a dukedom, but he was still the second son with no means of income besides his army career—which he wasn't so sure he wanted to return to. He couldn't afford a wife. But that was an excuse, and he knew it. The problem wasn't his lack of income; it was himself. Others might think he hadn't changed, but he knew, even if they did not, that the courage and confidence that had once come so easily to him had been lost on a rock in a foreign land, on a cold April afternoon. He was unworthy of being anyone's husband.

"My lord?"

He looked up from his absent contemplation of a cup of tea. It was Dawson, his valet, standing respectfully outside the door.

The servant bowed. "My lord, it is getting late. I must know what you plan to wear tonight so that I might ready it for you." He smiled. "May I suggest your dress regimentals?"

"My dress regimentals?"

"Why, yes, my lord. Your Colonel Maddison sent them back to us upon confirmation of your supposed death. They have been in storage."

Charles turned toward the window so that the valet would not see the sudden pain in his eyes.

He was not worthy of wearing the king's coat. He did not want to make Juliet remember things he wanted her to forget. And he did not want to remind himself of the man he had once been.

Wearing the coat would be a sham.

"I think my suit of plain blue silk will suffice, Dawson."

The guests would begin arriving soon.

The duke of Blackheath sat wrapped in a special gown to protect his fine clothing, his head bent to accept the white powder his valet was currently applying to his hair. Though he followed fashion, he abhorred wigs, and it was his own midnight-black mane that had been carefully dressed, rolled and powdered, the back drawn into a queue, tied with a velvet bow, and left to hang between his shoulders.

"That's it, Your Grace," said the hairdresser, stepping back. As Lucien got to his feet, his valet removed the powdering gown and a third servant came forward with a mirror.

Lucien lifted his chin and made a tiny adjustment to his stock, fastened behind his neck with a diamond buckle. He surveyed himself with a coolly critical eye. Then he left the room and made his way toward the separate wing of the castle that housed both the ballroom and Andrew's laboratory on the floor above it.

There were two sets of doors, one just after the other. Behind the first was the staircase, enclosed by old panelling, that led up to Andrew's laboratory—and the roof above that, where the flying contraption waited. Lucien paused for a moment, resisting the urge to go up there and have a last look at the thing. But no. He had to trust Andrew, though he could never let Andrew know that. After all, Andrew would never even have completed the thing if it were not for his fervent desire to show Lucien up—which was why Lucien kept taunting him.

And would keep taunting him until his little brother got the fame and recognition Lucien would drive him to get.

He pushed open the doors to the ballroom.

Servants bowed and curtsied to him as Lucien, in a suit of blue velvet so dark it looked black, toured the room. The theme of Christmas was everywhere. Fragrant branches of pine, tied together with red ribbons, framed the doorways. Silver and gold bunting hung above the floor-to-ceiling windows and was entwined around the heavy drapes. The refreshment tables were decorated with white tissue that glittered like snow; in a few short hours, those tables would groan beneath the weight of silver punchbowls and a host of delicacies from the kitchens. His musicians were already setting up their instruments in the far corner, tuning them, and servants were putting out chairs for the ladies. A maid was replacing the candles in the wall sconces, another was dusting the great, gilt-framed mirrors that would reflect the whirling dancers, and still others were lowering the great chandelier so that it could be filled with candles. When raised, it would dominate the room.

Lucien smiled to himself. There had not been a ball at Blackheath since before Charles had left for America, and this one promised to be spectacular—in more ways than one.

The Restoration—what an amusing little play on words, he thought, considering that the other Restoration had also centered around a Charles—was going exactly to plan. His barbed insults were making Charles increasingly angry, and hopefully, driving him to prove Lucien—and himself—wrong, which was, as far as Lucien was concerned, the only way to restore Charles's confidence in himself. Lucien had faith that Charles was the same man he'd always been; Charles was the one who needed convincing. And how well everyone was playing their parts! They had all contrived to keep Amy and Charles apart so that neither could learn that Lucien was not only subtly manipulating things, but playing matchmaker as well.

Again.

Still smiling, he decided it was a good time to have a look at his creation.

Amy was, at that moment, standing before a full-length mirror in her new shift,—*chemise* Nerissa insisted she call the garment—stockings and garters, trembling with nerves and excitement as Nerissa's maid Hannah, supervised by her mistress and Juliet, helped her into her new corset.

"Now stand still, miss, and let out yer breath so Oi can lace it up the back," she instructed, from just behind her.

Nerissa was watching the proceedings with an eagle

eye. "Not too tight, Hannah. Her waist is small enough as it is. A few rough yanks and I daresay you'll end up breaking her!"

Their charge burst out laughing at the same time Hannah yanked, which ended her guffaw on a choking gasp. Nerissa, grinning, exchanged furtive glances with Juliet. Her sister-in-law sat in a chair nearby, her advanced pregnancy politely concealed by a loose gown of rich, pine-green velvet. She too was in on the secret, and so, of course, was Gareth.

"Do you remember everything I taught you about the proper use of fans, Amy?"

"Oh, yes—I can even flick one open now without accidentally flinging it across the room!"

"And you're comfortable with all the dance steps that you practiced with Gareth?"

"Well, I no longer tread on his feet . . ."

"And you know what to say if someone with whom you're not comfortable asks you for a dance?"

"Yes, but . . . Nerissa, was it *really* necessary that I learn all this simply as training to be a lady's maid?"

"Yes, absolutely. If you want to go out in the world and make yourself invaluable to your future employer, you have to know how those things work. After all, you will be your mistress's friend as well as advisor."

"I see," said the young woman, frowning. "But I still don't know why the duke spent so much money just to make me look nice for tonight . . ."

Nerissa knew, but she certainly wasn't going to confess it. "It's just as he told you. You saved Charles's life and now he wants you to have your Cinderella night at the ball. It's the very least he could do!"

And as Nerissa also knew, it was the very least he had done. Amy might believe that she was getting a "night at the ball" and a few simple "maid's dresses" to prepare her for her future life at some distant country house, but she had no idea just what the duke had really bought for her when he'd sent her and Nerissa into London last week!

The clothing had already begun to arrive, and what fun Nerissa and Juliet had had going through it! There were ten new chemises, including this one of soft white linen, its triple tiers of exquisite French lace dripping from the elbow like angel's wings. There were several new corsets, twenty pairs of silk stockings, ribboned garters and even a rather wicked little night-shift trimmed with scarlet ribbon, a nightcap, three hats, four caps, hooped petticoats, and several underpetticoats, two made of cambric, one of dimity, and, the other, for colder weather, of quilted cotton lined with silk.

And that was just the underwear!

There were also handkerchiefs, slippers, gowns for dress, gowns for undress, shawls, fans, cloaks, several pairs of long, butter-soft gloves, silk aprons, and an ermine muff for her hands. Nerissa couldn't wait until Lucien's plan came to fruition and he had a legitimate excuse to give Amy these things he intended as a bridal gift.

These things that were, for the moment, hidden away.

"How's that, m'lady?" asked Hannah, stepping back and looking to Nerissa for approval.

"Perfect."

"I can't *breathe*!" gasped Amy, putting a hand to her chest, which now swelled to admirable, nearly scandalous proportions above the corset. "I'm so tightly trussed that my shoulder blades must surely be touching!"

"Good," said Nerissa.

"Good?"

"That's the way a lady of leisure and breeding is supposed to be laced. But don't look so concerned, Amy. Why, if you swoon for lack of air, then some gallant gentleman will be obliged to carry you outside to revive you!"

"Yes, perhaps even with a kiss," added Juliet.

Nerissa noted the sudden wistfulness on Amy's face, and knew what she was thinking. The only gallant gentleman Amy wanted was Charles, though she probably thought she could never have him.

We're going to make sure *you have him!*, Nerissa thought gleefully.

Moments later, Amy was in her hoops, and Hannah and Nerissa were lifting the shimmering, peacock-colored gown from the bed.

"Raise yer arms, miss," said Hannah, holding the gown up and then letting the magnificent creation whisper down over Amy's slim body in a rippling fall of silk. Hannah smoothed it over the hooped petticoats and stood back, beaming, while everyone in the room sucked in their breaths in awe.

"Oh, *my*," said Nerissa, when she could speak.

Juliet, smiling, murmured, "Would you just *look* at her."

So caught up were they in admiring Amy's new look that no one heard the knock on the door.

"I don't think we can *help* but look at her," murmured an urbane voice, and gasping, all three women turned to see Lucien standing in the doorway, arms crossed and his black eyes gleaming in the candlelight.

He lifted his hand. "Turn around, my dear," he said, giving a negligent little wave. Her eyes huge, Amy slowly did as he asked, staring down at herself in awe and disbelief. The gown, an open-robed saque of watered silk, shimmered with every movement, a vibrant purplish blue in this light, a vivid emerald green in that. Its robed bodice opened to show a stomacher of bright yellow satin worked with turquoise and green embroidery, and it had tight sleeves ending in treble flounces just behind the elbow, which, combined with the chemise's triple tiers of lace, made Amy feel as though she had wings. She smoothed her palms over the flounced and scalloped petticoats of royal blue silk, and then, with impulsive delight, threw back her head on a little laugh, extended her arms and spun on her toe, making gauzy sleeves, shining hair, and yards upon yards of shimmering fabric float in the air around her.

Hannah, who did not think such behavior was quite appropriate, especially in front of a duke, frowned, but Lucien was trying hard to contain his amusement. He couldn't remember the last time he'd made anyone so happy, and it touched something deep inside him that he'd long thought dead. He exchanged a look of furtive triumph with Nerissa.

"Oh! Is it really *me*?" Amy breathed, reverently touching her sleeve and then raising wide, suddenly misty eyes to her small audience.

"It is really you," Juliet said, smiling.

"Only someone with your coloring could wear such bold shades and make them work for instead of against you," said Nerissa, coming forward to tie a black ribbon around Amy's neck. "Lud, if I tried to wear those colors, I daresay they would overwhelm me!"

"Speaking of overwhelmed . . ." Amy turned to face the man who still lounged negligently in the doorway, his fingers trying, quite unsuccessfully, to rub away the little smile that tugged at his mouth. "Your Grace, I don't know how to thank you," she whispered, dabbing away one tear, then another. "No one has ever done anything like this for me before and I . . . I feel like a princess."

"My dear girl. Don't you know?" His smile deepened and she saw what was almost a cunning gleam come into his enigmatic black eyes. "You *are* a princess. Now dry those tears and if you must thank me, do so by enjoying yourself tonight.''

"I will, Your Grace."

"Yes," he said, on a note of finality. "You will."

And then, with a bow, he continued on his way.

Amy's tears finally spilled over. "I . . . I just don't know what to say," she managed. "His Grace is the kindest man in England to do this for me . . . to give me this one night of magic, to buy me such a generous gift, to make me feel like Cinderella at the ball. What my sisters would say if they could see me now! How happy my Mama, God rest her soul, would be for me . . . Oh, Nerissa, how can *anyone* think your brother is cunning and devious and manipulative?"

Juliet coughed.

Nerissa flushed and cleared her throat. "Well, um, yes," she said, turning away. But her own heart was pounding with glee, for if all went according to plan, Amy would soon know *exactly* how cunning and devious and manipulative Lucien could be.

And, she thought with a grin, his little sister as well.

Chapter 28

⟨~⟩⟨○⟩⟨○⟩⟨~⟩

The guests began to arrive shortly thereafter. A long line of elegant carriages stood out in the drive, waiting to discharge their equally elegant passengers. The king and queen were the last to arrive, and as soon as they had been announced, Lucien, the duke of Blackheath, officially opened the ball.

All across the vast and crowded ballroom, fans were fluttering, people staring, whispers flying.

"Who *is* she?"

"I don't know."

"*I* heard that she's some Indian princess from America with a vast fortune."

"An Indian *princess*! Why, where did you hear that?"

"From the duke of Blackheath himself," said the dowager countess of Brookhampton, who was Blackheath's closest neighbor. She tugged at her sleeve, preening with all the smugness of one privileged to know such information. "Apparently her people wish to help us defeat the Americans in that silly war, and she's here to speak with the king himself about it."

"You don't say!"

"I hope she's not looking for a husband . . . my Chloe

is going to have a difficult enough Season . . .''

Completely satisfied by the rapid spread of the rumor he'd started, Lucien, resplendent in dark velvet and an embroidered waistcoat of Italian silk, moved amongst the guests, making polite conversation here, complimenting a lady on her appearance there, and always keeping a discreet eye on his young charge, who, equally overseen by Nerissa, seemed to be holding her own quite nicely. He was very pleased with the past that he had fabricated for the girl; when she finally *did* marry Charles, at least she would be accepted as an exotic foreigner and forgiven any little social *faux pas* she might make. Now, she was being swung through a dance with Perry, Lord Brookhampton, who was the dowager countess's son, Gareth's best friend, and the current leader of the Den of Debauchery.

Good. Perry was following instructions, too.

Not that he needed any encouragement, given the sensation the girl was causing. For all the good it was doing! Charles had disappeared before Amy had made her appearance.

Lucien was quietly furious. And now the king was approaching him, his face flushed with pleasure. "Fine show you put on, Blackheath, fine show indeed," he said, saluting his host with a glass of sherry. "Been far too long since you've had any excitement out here and I'm damned pleased you finally have a good excuse to throw a party, what? Not every day you get a brother back from the dead!" He watched the dancers swirling about the ballroom. "Where is the guest of honor, eh? Haven't seen him since you opened the ball."

Lucien did not know where Charles was, though he had sent two servants to investigate that very question. He inclined his head. "I daresay he must be with his brother Andrew, Your Majesty, preparing his flying machine for its impending demonstration."

"Yes, yes, I *am* looking forward to seeing history made tonight, Blackheath!"

But Charles, at that very moment, was roving the house in search of Amy. He had stayed at the ball only long enough to claim the first dance with his sister; then, when the dancing was in full swing, he'd melted into the crush, strode through the doors leading back to the main part of the castle, and gone looking for Amy.

But she was not in her rooms. She was not in the dining room, the library, or wandering the halls. It wasn't until he strode into the Gold Parlor and found Juliet—who would not, of course, be attending the ball in her advanced condition—quietly working on a piece of embroidery, that Charles got the first clue to her whereabouts.

He bowed to his sister-in-law, who looked up at him in some surprise.

"Why, hello, Charles. What are you doing out here? You look most annoyed."

"Amy. I can't find her anywhere, haven't seen her all day and I'm sick to death of everyone monopolizing her time. You haven't seen her, have you?"

Juliet looked at him peculiarly, then lowered her needlework, a little smile touching her lips. "Actually, I have. You might try checking the ballroom."

"She wouldn't be in there."

Juliet's eyes sparkled with mirth. "Oh, I wouldn't be so sure."

At that moment Gareth, who was dividing his time between his wife and the ball, entered the room, fashionably splendid in raspberry silk, tight breeches, and shoes sporting huge Artois buckles. In his hand were two glasses, one of sherry, the other of cider, the latter of which he handed to his wife. He had caught the tail end of the conversation.

"Yes, you really *should* check the ballroom,

Charles,'' he said, his own blue eyes twinkling.

Was there some damned conspiracy going on here? Thanking them, Charles strode out of the parlor. He should have just stayed in that hot and stifling ballroom then, and searched her out in the maid's area where common sense told him she would have been all along. He headed toward the great double doors, which were respectfully opened by a bowing servant, stormed into the ballroom—

And stopped in his tracks.

No. Yes. *Good grief.* It couldn't be . . .

"*Amy?*" he breathed.

Two dancers, caught up in the dance, didn't see him standing there and collided with him, nearly knocking him down.

"Lord Charles! I *beg* your pardon!"

But he never heard them. He never saw them. He had eyes only for the stunning beauty who was being swept around the dance floor by Gareth's friend Perry. She was a ravishing young woman in shimmering peacock and royal blue whose beauty commanded the eye, the attention, the heart—and made every other woman in the room pale to insignificance.

Charles's mouth went dry. His heartbeat cracked his chest and he forgot to breathe.

Another set of dancers collided with him, knocking him to his senses. Angrily, he stared into the amused eyes of Gareth's friend Neil Chilcot, another Den of Debauchery member who was partnering a grinning Nerissa. "Gorgeous young woman, isn't she?" quipped Chilcot, sweeping Nerissa past. "You should've stuck around to see her announced, Charles. Not that you'll ever have a chance of claiming a dance with her now, what with all the young bucks before you already waiting . . ."

Charles had heard enough. But as he stalked across the dance floor, he heard even more.

"Well, His Grace told *me* she's an heiress . . ."

"Not just an heiress, but a princess from some vast Indian nation in America . . ."

". . . came here to offer her tribe's help in the war against the Americans . . ."

Charles clenched his fists. *Lucien.* No one else could have, *would* have, started and circulated such a preposterously crazy rumor! What the hell was his brother trying to do, get Amy married off to some handsome young swain and out of Charles's life forever? *This* was no training for a lady's maid, that was for damned sure!

His jaw tight, he stormed across the dance floor toward Amy. He saw her hooped petticoats swirling about her legs and exposing a tantalizing bit of ankle with every step she took, the laughter in her face even though she kept glancing over Perry's shoulder in search of someone, the studied grace in her movements that, a week ago, he would've sworn she didn't have.

She had not seen him yet, and as Perry, a handsome man who had something of a reputation with the ladies, led her through the steps, Charles felt a surge of jealousy so fierce, so violent, that it made him think of doing something totally irrational.

Such as calling Perry out for dancing with *his* woman.

Such as killing Lucien for whatever little game he was playing.

Such as making a spectacle of himself and claiming Amy for his own.

For once in his life, Charles didn't care what anyone thought of his behavior. He marched straight up to Perry, tapped him on the shoulder, and jerked his thumb to indicate that Perry had better relinquish Amy to him.

Now.

Perry, grinning, bowed and backed off. At the same

time, Amy turned her head and saw Charles, her face breaking into such an expression of joy that he was nearly undone. "Charles!" she cried, and he knew then that if they weren't in the middle of a crowded ballroom, with everyone staring at them, she would've thrown herself straight into his arms. As it was, she stumbled such that he had to catch her and set her on her feet, a move that he managed to carry off such that she barely missed a step. "Oh, Charles, I've been waiting all evening for you to arrive! Where have you been?"

"Looking for you." He stared at her. "Amy, you look . . . ravishing," he said, and it was all he could do not to claim those smiling, carmine-rouged lips and kiss her senseless.

"For once in my life, I actually *feel* ravishing! Oh, Charles—will you look at all these powdered heads, the jewels and silks and satins, everyone having such a good time! Isn't it just wonderful? Isn't this just the most magical place on earth?"

He swung her through the steps. "Amy, I do not wish to spoil your enjoyment, but exactly *what* are you doing?"

"I'm dancing!" she said, her cheeks flushed, her eyes sparkling as he led her through the steps. "Oh, Charles, this is such *fun*! Your brother was so kind to give me this night . . . I feel like Cinderella!"

"What?"

"Lucien! He was so grateful for what I did for you back in America that he gave me this night, this gown, a new identity, and . . . and, even these diamonds at my ears! Well, he didn't actually *give* them to me, I understand that they belonged to your grandmother but he said that only someone with my coloring would be able to carry them off . . ." She blushed. "Charles, you don't think everyone's staring at me because I'm the only one here with unpowdered hair, do you? Lucien said that I really should leave it natural, and—''

''No, Amy,'' he said tightly, realizing that everyone *was* staring at her, and it had nothing to do with her hair.

It was because she was the most strikingly beautiful woman in the room and one couldn't *help* but stare at her.

''Charles, are you angry?''

''Yes, Amy, I am angry, quietly furious, in fact, but not with you.''

''Then with who? Certainly not Perry I hope, because he's now dancing with your sister—she has a *tendre* for him, you know.''

''And where did you learn that word, Amy?''

''Oh, Nerissa taught it to me. I understand it is quite the thing to know some French. Oh, Charles, please don't be angry with Perry, he did nothing wrong—''

''It's not Perry I'm angry with, it's Lucien.'' The dance ended. ''And by God, I'm going to give him a piece of my mind.''

His gloved hand capturing hers, he all but dragged her back through the crush, uncaring that everyone in the room was staring at them, the men elbowing each other, the women's fans fluttering wildly. He saw Andrew and the king, accompanied by three of his entourage, going out the double doors, no doubt heading upstairs for a private viewing of the flying contraption before the big event. And there was Lucien, elegant in darkest-blue velvet, standing near the refreshment tables and conversing with his barrister friend Sir Roger Foxcote. Slowly, as though he'd been expecting it all along, he turned his head to regard Charles's approach—and in that enigmatic black gaze, Charles saw a swift blaze of triumph before it was quickly veiled.

''Why, Charles. How good of you to finally rejoin

us,'' his brother drawled, taking a sip of sherry and watching Charles from above the rim of his crystal goblet. "Everyone was wondering about you, you know. Damned rude of you to hide from your own ball, no?"

Charles, bristling with anger, responded instantly to the challenge. "I wasn't *hiding*, and I'll thank you to stop interfering in people's lives, especially Amy's! How dare you lift her up only to throw her down, how dare you give her a taste of something she can never have again, only to toss her back into obscurity! I don't know what you're up to, but I won't stand for you hurting her so, Lucien, by God I will not!"

Around them, people hushed.

Amy, standing in confusion beside Charles, went very still.

And Lucien raised his brows and pretended to straighten the ruffles at his sleeve. But he could not hide the faint smirk that touched one corner of his mouth, and Charles suddenly understood what Gareth must have felt like, all those times that Lucien had goaded and taunted and insulted him into wanting to pull back and place his fist in it. Lucien was enjoying this.

And enjoying it immensely.

"My dear Charles," he murmured, placing his empty glass on the tray of a passing servant and turning a benign, infuriating little smile on his brother. "Given the fact that you no longer possess even the courage to jump your horse over a hedgerow, I really don't think you should challenge me so. It could be rather . . . hazardous to your health."

"Lucien," said Charles in a very cold voice. "You have just insulted me one time too many. If you weren't my brother, I'd call you out right here and now."

"Pointless, Charles. You would only lose. For that reason, I would never accept the challenge." Dismissing Charles, he took Amy's hand and raised it to his lips.

"My dear Miss Leighton. Are you enjoying yourself to-night?"

"I am, your Grace. This has been the most magical night of my life and"—she looked at Charles—"now that your brother's here, it just got a hundred times better."

"Have I misled you in any way, disappointed you in any form?"

"No, Your Grace. I don't know what Lord Charles is so upset about."

"There. You see, Charles? There is no harm done. If you truly cared about Miss Leighton, you wouldn't begrudge her the chance to enjoy herself—and perhaps make an advantageous match. It's obvious that *you* don't have the courage to make an immediate offer for her, but I daresay there are many here tonight who would."

Charles's eyes narrowed; he had caught the wicked little gleam in Lucien's eyes, and suddenly, belatedly, he understood.

"You conniving wretch," he said, his eyes blazing as he began to see how neatly he'd been manipulated.

Lucien, knowing the game was up, only raised a brow and smiled.

"You set this all up to try and force my hand, didn't you?"

"Now, really, Charles. What reason would I have to do that?" He looked up as Gareth approached through the throngs. "Why hello, Gareth. Your brother here has just accused me of interfering in Amy's life. Have you ever heard of anything so ridiculously absurd?"

Gareth's mouth dropped open; he was caught in the middle and he knew it.

Lucien straightened one glove. "And here I was having *such* fun watching her enjoying herself. Really, Charles, the look on your face when you first saw her in that gown was worth more than all the tea in China—"

Sudden screams reverberated throughout the room.

His head jerking up, Charles saw it all. A young serving maid, just setting a Christmas pudding soaked with flaming brandy onto the refreshment table, had turned to laugh at something one of the footmen had said—and in so doing, suddenly tripped. The pudding flew from the tray and instantly both the girl's petticoats and the tablecloth were on fire.

Panicking, she leaped to her feet and ran, shrieking, for the door, where the flames caught the bunting that hung there and whooshed toward the ceiling.

"Help, somebody help me!"

The music crashed to a stop and people began to scream.

"Help, *help*!"

Charles, with Gareth right behind him, was already sprinting through the crush after her, shoving stunned dancers out of the way, grabbing up a tablecloth as he raced past and sending china crashing to the floor in his wake. "Gareth! Dump the punch, get the cloth off that other table and stamp on it! And get everyone out!"

Chapter 29

⌒◯◯⌒

The old authority was back in Charles's voice.

But even as Gareth saw his brother tumble the screaming maid to the floor and smother the flames consuming her skirts, even as he and Perry worked to put out the burning tablecloth, even as he saw Lucien calmly escorting the queen and her attendants outside, he knew it was too late. The fire had already spread to the bunting, to the decorations, and to the heavy floor-to-ceiling drapes.

In moments, the room was on fire.

An exodus of people surged toward the door that led outside, some crying out to loved ones, some coughing, the musicians running past carrying violins, cellos, and other instruments. A few loyal servants began pulling priceless art from the walls, but already Charles, with the sobbing young maid in his arms, was shouting orders.

"Leave them! Get out of the room and onto the lawn! Everyone get outside on the lawn and *stay there*!"

He carried the girl outside, relinquished her into the care of Nerissa and Amy, and, coughing from the smoke, grabbed Gareth's arm. "Get a bucket brigade started!

Keep the area around the door wet until we get everyone out!'' Pressing his handkerchief to his face, he raced back into the ballroom.

The room was rapidly dimming. Inside, the settee and chairs were on fire. The screens that had been erected to give people a private place to talk were aflame. Fire was racing up the walls, engulfing the paintings, roaring up the drapes. Looking up, Charles saw thick black smoke gathering along the ceiling, banking back down, bringing a wave of intense heat with it that felt like a blast from an open oven. He could no longer see the great chandelier above his head.

Eyes watering, the handkerchief pressed to his nose, he hurried around the room, dragging the last people out and shouting for Gareth, lost in smoke over by the door, to keep the bucket brigade going. And now the heat was building, beginning to parch his face, to dry his eyes and the inside of his nose. It was getting hard to breathe. Impossible to see.

I've got to get out of here.

''Is anyone left in here?'' he shouted at the top of his lungs. He worked his way along the edges of the room, desperately searching among the chairs and remains of screens. The fire was roaring now, nearly drowning out his voice, the smoke stinging his eyes, filling his nose and mouth and throat. ''If anyone's left in here answer me!''

''Charles! Come on out, I've got the last of them!''

Disoriented, coughing so hard he could barely draw breath, he sprinted toward the sound of his brother's voice. Every breath was agony. Black smoke was halfway back down the windows now, meeting ugly yellow-gray smoke coming back up. And there was Gareth's hazy form, still directing the bucket brigade and keeping the exit door wet until Charles could come safely through. He grabbed Charles's arm and hauled him roughly outside, slamming the door shut behind him and dragging him away from it and onto the cool grass.

"You sure everyone's out?" Charles managed, through retching coughs.

"I think so; Lucien just sent riders off to Ravenscombe to call out the villagers, we need all the help we can get!"

"What about the other door, from the ballroom to the main wing? Did anyone close it?"

"Bloody hell——"

" 'Sdeath, we've got to shut it so the fire doesn't spread down the corridor to the main part of the castle!" He shouted to the bucket brigade, standing outside now but still feverishly hurling water at the door, around whose edges sinister tongues of flame were already licking. "Stop!" He ran forward and grabbing arms and shoulders, manhandled people away from the door. "The main building!" he yelled, trying to be heard over the shouting, frightened guests. "*The main building!*"

They looked at him uncomprehendingly; then, Charles yanked the last of them back just as a huge ball of smoke and flame exploded every window in the ballroom and hurled shards of glass and wood everywhere. The force of the blast threw him against Gareth and both brothers went down, but Charles was instantly on his feet, hauling the bucket brigade to theirs, never stopping to consider that by pulling them away from the door, he had just saved their lives. Calling them to him as he had once done his soldiers, he ran back around the burning building, his feet slipping on broken glass, never slowing as he tried desperately to reach the other door before the fire did.

He charged in through a servant's entrance and sprinted headlong back toward the ballroom. Every step brought him closer to the fire roaring behind the door— it was shut, *thank God*—like a furnace in hell. Behind him, the bucket brigade came running, some with sooty faces, one or two men cut and bleeding.

"Soak the door, and then the hallway!" Charles shouted. "Start a line from here to the moat. *Move!*"

Gareth was right behind him. Frantically, they both grabbed buckets, each load of water hissing up in steam as it hit the smoldering door, working against time, working against fate, and then Lucien was there, shouting to be heard over the terrible roar of the fire on the other side of the door.

"Gareth!"

"Lucien, *get outside*!"

"*Gareth!*" Pointedly ignoring Charles, Lucien yanked Gareth out of the line. "Listen to me! The king is still upstairs with Andrew, do you hear me? *The king and Andrew are still upstairs!*"

The king, his three attendants, and Andrew had all been up on the roof, examining Andrew's Contraption, when the fire broke out. They never heard people screaming two floors below. Never knew what was happening down in the ballroom. By the time they did know, it was too late.

"I say, Andrew, I *am* looking forward to seeing your invention in action!" the king was saying as he watched Andrew crank back the giant catapult and position the flying contraption for its impending display. "The medieval catapult idea is most ingenious, what? So let me make sure I understand this. All you have to do is strap yourself into the harness, release that lever, and bang, you're off, eh?"

"Well, yes . . . something like that, Your Majesty. Perhaps you'll come back down to my laboratory, where I can show you the drawings so you may see exactly how it works?"

The little group headed back toward the stairway that

led down to Andrew's laboratory just above the ball-room.

The king sniffed and drew out his handkerchief. "Speaking of medieval, I really must speak to your brother about updating his kitchens. I fear his chimneys must not be ventilating properly. What a damned lot of smoke is in the air tonight, what?"

They went down the stairs, opened the door to Andrew's laboratory, and froze.

The room was hot. Unnaturally, terrifyingly, unbearably hot. And as Andrew, horrified, looked around, he heard an angry, rushing roar, faint shouts from people outside, and saw that all around the room, ominous black fingers of soot were creeping up the walls.

"Dear God—"

At that moment, a giant explosion rocked the building itself, throwing them all to their knees and sending row upon row of volatile chemicals and solutions crashing to the floor. Flames burst forth and Andrew knew only one thing:

He had to get the king out.

Now.

He grabbed the old wool coat he often wore when it was chilly up here, threw it over the king's shoulders, and, apologizing for manhandling him, helped him to his feet. The attendants assisting His Majesty on the other side, they all made their way toward the door.

"By God, Andrew, if this is your idea of a joke I am *not* amused!"

"I can assure you, Your Majesty, this is no joke. The building's on fire and we must get you out!"

Already the room was clouded with smoke, and Andrew dared not think of what would happen when the gases from his burning chemicals mixed and began filling the air, dared not think what must be happening below, dared not think about his poor, poor flying machine on the roof just above, dared not think of anything beyond getting the king out of here, down the stairs, and to safety.

He reached the door. Found it shut and barred. Damn! The explosion must have sent the bar he used to keep Lucien out when he was working, crashing down. His eyes stinging with smoke, unable to see what he was doing, he tried to remove it but it was stuck fast in its slots. He threw his weight beneath it and shoved with all his might.

Horrible, noxious fumes came roiling up from behind him.

We're going to die, Andrew thought—and at that moment, the bar gave beneath his frantic shoves, the door crashed inward, and a figure came stumbling in through the smoke.

It was Charles.

"You can't get out that way!" his older brother shouted. "The stairway's on fire!"

Charles, who'd instinctively charged up the stairway before Gareth could even react to Lucien's words, now stared past Andrew. Somewhere off in the billowing, poisonous smoke behind him, bottles were exploding, great timbers were beginning to crash down, part of the floor already starting to give way. Charles sank to his knees, crawling through the smoke as he fought to reach the stricken king.

"Your Majesty! I beg you to forgive me for suggesting such a thing, but please, get down, get down on your knees and crawl! The air is cleaner down here, cooler, and you'll be able to breathe better! Now follow me! We've got to get you out of here!"

With an arm around the king to support him, the three attendants coughing and gasping just ahead and beside him, Charles, on his hands and knees, fought his way back to the door. Great torrents of dense black smoke were rushing back up the stairway from which he'd just come but if they were lucky, they might be able to get back through before the fire entirely blocked off their escape.

He could hear Lucien downstairs, somewhere beyond the smoke, shouting for him.

"Charles! This way!"

"God help me, I can't see, I can't breathe," the king cried, "I can't breathe!"

Charles, with the attendants' help, managed to get the king down the first step, then the next. The fire, growing hotter by the second, baked him through his hot clothes, seared his nose, sinuses, trachea, and lungs with every agonizing breath. He half fell, half stumbled down each step, trying, as best he could, to shield the king from falling debris as he went. A chunk of burning wood glanced off the back of his neck, branding his skin like a hot poker; beneath his gloved hands, the stone was blistering hot. And there, finally, just visible through the smoke, he could just see Lucien and Gareth, charging up to meet him.

"Well done, Charles, well done!" said Lucien, leading the coughing, gasping king out of the stairwell and to safety, the heavy woolen coat slipping from the royal shoulders. Charles, coughing violently and unable to see beyond the burning agony in his eyes, felt Gareth grab him and half carry, half steer him out of the stairwell and into the smoky but untouched corridor, still under siege by a rapidly growing bucket brigade.

Lucien, who had relinquished the care of the king into his gathering entourage, turned back toward the stairway, frowning.

"Charles, where is Andrew?"

"Right behind me—" He was seized by a racking spell of coughing. "He . . . came down the stairway . . . right behind me."

"No, Charles. He did not."

Charles dragged open burning, watering eyes, shook his head to clear it, and stared at Lucien. His brother's face had gone very still. Very pale. And then Charles saw something in that black stare that he'd never thought to see, something that was reflected in his own suddenly cold bones.

Fear.

"I'm going back in after him," Gareth vowed, spinning on his heel.

Lucien's hand shot out and seized Gareth's shoulder. "No. You stay here with your brother. *I'm* going back in."

Gareth's eyes were wild. " 'Sdeath, Lucien, the whole stairway's on fire, you'll be killed!" he cried, struggling to tear free.

"I will not leave Andrew in there, and I will not allow you to risk your life in an attempt to save him. You have a wife and family to think of, Gareth. I do not. Now do as you're told, damn it!"

He shoved Gareth away from him, sending him sprawling to the floor. As Gareth stared up at him in hurt surprise, the duke of Blackheath turned his back on both brothers and strode toward the closed door, determined to meet his own death, if need be, with all the courage and dignity that had marked generations of ancestors before him.

"Lucien," Charles gasped, trying to stagger to his feet. "Wait. *Wait!*"

But Lucien did not wait.

Charles was on his feet. Gareth, behind him, was already getting up. The two younger brothers exchanged glances; then, as one, they ran toward Lucien, who never turned around, who ignored them as he did the heat and choking black smoke that came surging down out of the stairwell as he opened the door.

Charles seized the duke's elbow, yanked backwards with all his strength, and hurled him violently into Gareth's waiting arms. The force with which he threw Lucien tumbled both his brothers to the floor.

"Hold him there, Gareth, and don't let him up," Charles ordered, his eyes blazing into Lucien's as he donned the wool coat that had been on the king's shoulders, seized a pail of water from one of the bucket brigade, and raising it high, poured it over himself. "And if he tries to follow me, hit him. *Hard.* Do you understand me?"

Gareth's eyes gleamed. "I understand perfectly—*Captain.*" And then, holding Lucien with one arm locked around his neck, he watched Charles walk away, his pride and admiration in his brother renewed.

But Charles never saw it. The dripping coat pulled up and over his head, he was already through the door and heading back up through the smoke.

It was like stepping into a furnace.

Smoke clogged the stairwell and banked down and around him. Already, the ancient panelled wood of the stairway was charring, and by the time Charles got halfway up the stairs, it was on fire.

"Andrew! *Andrew!*"

No answer.

He held the wet coat over his head, trying to give himself a pocket of air to breathe, trying to keep the blinding, stinging, smoke from his eyes. Growing dizzy, unable to see, he reached out to get his bearings. Just as quickly he jerked his hand back, cursing with the pain. "Andrew! By God, where are you?"

He charged up the rest of the stairs. Behind him, flames were already licking, blocking the way out, chasing him up the stairway. The heat intensified, sucking the water from his coat, baking him inside of it. His earlobes must surely be on fire. His eyebrows were shrinking up into tiny singed knots. *By God, Andrew, where the devil are you?* Had his brother bolted back into the laboratory and barred the door? Had he fled to the roof, desperate to save his precious flying machine? Had he jumped out a window to dubious safety?

Please, God, let me get to him in time!

He ripped open the door to the laboratory, staggered inside, and slammed it shut behind him, trying to buy just a few more seconds, knowing that way of escape was now permanently blocked.

"Andrew!"

Nothing but the savage roar of the fire, all around him.

"An-*dreeeeeew*!"

It was like being blind all over again, only a hundred, thousand, million times worse. Coughing, wheezing, unable to see through the smoke, Charles fell to his hands and knees and began feeling along the floor, so hot now that it was roasting his palms through his gloves. Horrible, toxic chemical fumes mixed with smoke and pushed into his face, up his nose, trying to drive him back, trying to drive him toward unconsciousness and death. He shoved a fold of the damp coat against his face, strained the air through it, and continued searching the floor, his palms blistering, his knees screaming with the agony. And there! His desperate hand found a leather shoe; a silk-clad calf. A still arm.

"Andrew!"

Whether dead or merely unconscious, his brother didn't answer him. Cursing, Charles grasped Andrew around the shoulders and began dragging him across the floor toward where the windows must surely be.

Slow, painful progress. The terrible roar of the fire, the crash of falling timbers beyond the door, sections of the floor going up in colored flames, weird, horrible, chemical smells. Chunks of burning plaster rained down from above, and his nostrils flared with the acrid stench of singed hair, smoldering clothes. His lungs contracted with the heat, refused to expand, and his eyes, his nose, his throat began to close up.

We're not going to make it.

He couldn't breathe. He couldn't see. *Keep crawling!* Dizziness made him reel. *Keep crawling, damn you!* His chin struck the floor as he fell, his lower teeth clipping the tip of his tongue. Blood filled his mouth. He dragged his head up, dragged himself up, kept going, *keep going!*, one elbow locked around Andrew's chest as he pulled himself along with one hand and burning knees, unable to hear even his own cries of pain, of desperation. *It's no use.* A burning timber crashed down ten feet from his face, brilliant orange through the black smoke. He shoved his face into his sleeve, trying to draw breath. *Keep going!* But there was nowhere to go, no way out, and when he fell a second time, then a third time, he knew he was fighting a battle he could never win.

A strange, not unpleasant euphoria came drifting over him, lulling him down into darkness, calling him away from the agony against and inside him, and the horrible death that now seemed imminent. The horrible death that neither he nor Andrew would escape.

With the last of his strength, Charles fell over Andrew, trying to cover him with his body, to shield him from the flames until the very end.

And as he lay there with his arms around his brother, the fire all around them, unconsciousness beginning to draw him down, down into its seductive net, his dying brain ran desperately, frantically back through a lifetime of memories . . . and he was once again in the proud regimentals of the King's Own, galloping through a wooded field in faraway Concord, bullets raining all around him.

He was once again carrying Ensign Gillard to safety, with no thought for himself.

Once again falling against a rock—and failing everyone, most of all himself.

Pathetic wreckage . . . pathetic wreckage . . . pathetic wreckage . . .

"Charles!"

Someone was calling him, forcing him back to himself, to reality. Dazedly, he raised his head. The fire was all around them now. His arms tightened fiercely, protectively, around Andrew.

"Charles . . . get off me . . . I can't breathe."

Andrew . . . oh, God, why did you have to wake up?

"Charles? The Contraption . . . it's our only chance."

"What?"

"It'll get us out of here . . . if you can only get us up onto the roof. You can do it, Charles. I know you can. They all know you can—even Lucien. Come on, Charles, get up . . ."

"Damn you, Andrew," he croaked hoarsely, and then he was on his hands and knees, one hand locked around his brother's in a grip that even death would never break, calling on all of his strength, all of his determination, all of the things that had made him the officer he had once been—and hauling them both toward the door to the roof.

He stumbled over debris and yanked the door open. A blast of cold night air laced with rain swept in, making the fire roar all the louder, causing the tears rushing down his face to change to ones of gratitude. Andrew in tow, he dragged himself through the door, and, somehow managing to get his brother into his arms, carried him up the stairs and onto the roof.

And there it was.

Andrew's flying machine, which had never been tested, which had never been flown, which offered them their only chance of survival. It lay silent and waiting, a fragile, flimsy, winged thing poised in a huge catapult that was already cranked back and ready to hurl its occupants toward death—or the history books.

He set Andrew down.

And now flames were licking up through the roof, smoke curling and rising like little snakes beneath Charles's grimy, blackened shoes. He felt a terrible rumbling beneath him and knew the floors were falling in, and down below on the lawn, so far, *far* down below on the lawn, he could see hundreds of people, some holding torches, some pointing up toward the roof, all yelling, shouting, "Jump! For God's sake, Charles, *jump!*"

He backed up, turned, and when he looked at Andrew, he saw that his brother had dragged himself to his invention and was looking expectantly up at him.

"Come, Charles—time is running out."

"But Andrew, it's only designed to carry one person . . . you calculated it could reach the moat if something went wrong but that was for one, not two people . . . there's twice the weight between the two of us, we'll never make it!"

But Andrew only shut his eyes on a tired little smile. "Go on, Charles, buckle us in," he whispered. "I had faith in you . . . now have a little faith in me."

I had faith in you . . . now have a little faith in me.

His knees quaking like the roof beneath him, Charles squatted down and buckled the harness around himself, his fingers shaking so badly that Andrew had to do up the last catches. Around him, the flames were roaring up through the roof now. Sweat pouring from his face, he wrapped his arms around Andrew, who in turn reached up to grasp the leather handholds sewn beneath the Contraption's wings, glowing eerily now as the fire punched through the roof all around and behind it.

"Oh, God," said Charles, squeezing his eyes shut. "Oh, God help us . . ."

"You ready, Charles?"

At that moment, the roof began to cave in, flames shot up into the black sky—

And Andrew pulled the lever.

Chapter 30

It was a demonstration that the king, standing outside with two hundred people and staring up at the roof, would never forget.

At the very moment that the building began to cave in, something that looked like a giant bat shot out from the top of the duke of Blackheath's roof, blazing across the sky like a comet. Two hundred voices rose in a single horrified scream. Ladies fainted and horses bolted and hearts stopped in frozen chests.

The Contraption was coming down.

Coming down in a graceful, gliding arc.

Coming down from a height of nearly a hundred feet—straight toward Lucien's lawn.

If the hand of God intervened that night, and everyone there would swear that it did, it was apparent not once, but twice.

The first miracle was the rain that suddenly came pouring out of the sky, aiding the bucket brigade in their eventually successful attempt to contain the fire to the ballroom and thus save Blackheath Castle.

The second was the fact that at the very moment the flying machine began to dip its nose toward the lawn, carrying Lord Charles and Lord Andrew to their certain deaths, an immense, roaring fireball roiled up and out of the collapsing building behind them, lighting up the night and creating a violent blast of turbulence that rocked the air for several hundred feet around.

Fortunately for Charles and Andrew, that same blast of turbulence was enough to propel the Contraption another sixty feet. Its wings afire and trailing ribbons of smoke, it sailed straight over everyone's heads, straight over the waiting carriages, and down into the moat.

"Bravo!" cried the king, clapping. "Bravo!"

Charles and Andrew, of course, were not clapping. Death by drowning was only marginally better than death by fire. As everyone ran toward the moat, it was Lord Gareth who dived into the ice-cold water, swam to the rescue of the stunned victims, and pulled them out of the wreckage. Swimming back to shore, he gave Andrew into the care of a relieved Lucien, and Charles into the arms of his Indian princess.

Around them, everyone was cheering.

"*Never* have I seen such selfless courage!" cried the king, his voice hoarse from the smoke as he rushed over to where Charles lay, pale, drenched, and shivering, in Amy's arms. "Not only did you save my life, you saved your brother's, you saved everyone in the ballroom, and you saved the duke's home. Bravo, Charles! Or should I say *Major* de Montforte, now?"

Charles dragged open his eyes. "I . . . beg your pardon?"

"Major de Montforte! From now on I want you here in England, not wasted off across the ocean fighting those damned rebels! An appointment at Horse Guards is just the thing, and a hefty cash grant from the privy purse as well, what? Fine show you put on tonight, Major! Fine show!"

He went to Andrew and congratulated him as well.

"Keep up the good work, Andrew—glad I didn't have to try it myself!" Then, after a private word with Lucien, who managed to look unruffled and unscathed by the near-catastrophe, the king departed for his waiting coach, his party of attendants trailing in his wake.

The excitement over, the rain beating down, the guests also put the sizzling wreckage behind them and began to leave for their carriages.

Affecting a heavy sigh, Lucien accepted a blanket from a servant, walked up to where Charles lay, and draped it over him. Then, folding his arms across his chest, he tilted his head back, and thoughtfully regarded the blazing ruins of his ballroom.

"Pity," he said, with a rueful little smile, still gazing at the conflagration. "But I suppose that part of the house was due for renovation anyhow. I think I shall have it redone in the new classical style . . . what do you think, Major?"

"I think that's the *last* ball of yours I will ever attend."

"Now really, Charles. You wound me." He knelt down, and, lifting one of Charles's hands, turned it palm upward, shaking his head as he examined the blistered red flesh through the burned-out glove. "And you have wounded yourself. How fortunate that you have someone to take such good care of you." His black eyes, which gave away nothing, found Amy's as he stood up. "You *will* take care of him, won't you, my dear?"

"Oh, I'll take care of him, Your Grace," she vowed, tenderly smoothing Charles's singed wet hair from his face. "After all, I've done it before, haven't I, Charles?"

"You certainly have." He shut his eyes, pulled her head down to his, and found her lips in a deep, searching kiss. And when he finally broke it and looked up, there was everyone gazing down at him, grinning so fiercely he thought their faces would split. Lucien, one brow raised, but otherwise as composed as ever. Gareth and Juliet, standing arm and arm, their eyes shining. A battered Andrew, Nerissa, Perry, Chilcot, the villagers, and everyone else whom Lucien must have used—either directly or indirectly, knowingly or unknowingly—to prove to Charles that he was not only forgiven, but loved, respected, and admired. They were all there, too.

And at that moment Charles's thoughts raced back to the time he'd lain blind and helpless in Sylvanus Leighton's house, with only Amy to look after him in his days of darkest despair. He recalled how many moments they'd shared together, how much they'd come to mean to each other, and a huge knot of emotion closed the back of his throat as the full magnitude of his love for this woman nearly crushed him beneath its weight. He could never live without her. Ever. And this time, of course, he had no guilt over Juliet, no feelings of self-doubt, and absolutely no reason this side of heaven not to give in to his most fervent desire: to be with Amy, always.

He had come full circle, then.

He was the man he had always been.

The Beloved One.

Charles tilted his head back within Amy's arms and, looking up into her eyes, saw such a wealth of love for him there that he thought his heart was going to come bursting right out of his chest.

He lifted her hand to his lips. "Amy. My dearest, precious Amy. I love you. Will you marry me?"

Her eyes suddenly misty, she looked up at Lucien.

He only smiled. "I believe, my dear, that the traditional reply is 'I will.' "

Epilogue

～～⚬✺⚬～～

Lucien's wedding gift to the bride and groom was nothing short of magnificent.

Built of honey-colored stone and commanding several hundred acres of fields and pastures, Lynmouth Park, just ten miles southwest of London, was all that a promising young major and his lovely wife could have wanted. Now, in September, the air smelled spicy, the sun was hanging lower in the sky, and the willows ringing the ornamental pond dropped leaves that lay curled and yellow in the grasses and floated upon the still, cold water below. Geese gathered and began to migrate; hawthorn shed vibrant red berries; the air grew cooler and thistledown drifted in the wind, floating lazily over fields of wheat long since harvested.

And in an upstairs bedroom of the elegant house, the newest de Montforte was being born.

Charles was as distraught as Lucien had ever seen him, pacing back and forth in the drawing room while above, Amy screamed in pain as another contraction seized her.

Charles blanched. Droplets of sweat beaded his brow.

"Do sit down, Charles," Lucien murmured, not looking up from where he sat calmly writing a letter. The duke, along with his siblings and Juliet—whose presence Amy had specifically requested—had arrived a fortnight ago so they could all be together for the grand event. "I daresay you're expending as much effort on delivering this child as Amy is."

"Yes, I wonder which one will be more exhausted when it's over?" teased Gareth, lounging on a nearby sofa and bouncing a leg over one bent knee.

Charles kept pacing. "I won't sit down, I can't sit down, I can't rest, I can't eat, I can't *think* until I know that both of them are all right!"

Gareth, with his new son Gabriel in his arms and Charlotte playing on the floor nearby, fought hard to contain his laughter. Having recently gone through the same hell as Charles was currently experiencing—and behaving just as abominably—he considered himself quite the expert on such matters. He looked at Charles and grinned.

"Yes, Luce is quite right, Charles. All you're doing is wearing a hole in the carpet. Amy will be just fine."

"But those screams! I cannot bear to hear them!"

Lucien dipped his quill in the ink bottle. "Then go outside, my dear Charles, so that you do not *have* to hear them."

For answer, Charles only threw himself down in the nearest chair. Raked a hand through his hair. Jumped to his feet, poured himself a drink, and continued his pacing.

Moments later, a particularly harsh scream came from above, followed by the thin, lusty wail of a child. Charles dropped his glass and bolted for the stairs, taking them three at a time as he sprinted to his wife's aid.

In his wake, Gareth and Lucien merely exchanged amused glances.

"A girl," said Gareth. "I'll bet you ten pounds on it."

"No, no, Gareth. It will be a boy. It has to be a boy. I hope to *God* it's a boy, since it seems that the next heir to Blackheath is going to have to come down through Charles, not me."

"Come now, Luce, you have plenty of time to marry and get an heir of your own."

Lucien arched a brow. "What, and put myself through the hell that you two go through every time you become a father? I think not. . . ."

Upstairs, Charles was running headlong down the corridor toward the closed door of Amy's room. Nerissa stood just outside, arms folded, barring his way. She saw his panicked face, his wild eyes, as from behind the door, the baby's wailing intensified. "Really, Charles. Are you all right?"

"Never mind me, are *they* all right?!"

His sister smiled with infuriating sweetness. "Why don't you go in and see for yourself?"

He lunged for the door.

Nerissa grabbed the handle, laughing. "Ah! Sedately, brother dear!"

He willed himself to calm down, his hands, his body, his very nerves, shaking. His throat felt dry and he feared his knees were going to give out and he had to take several gulping breaths to get himself under control.

Nerissa, smiling, opened the door.

And there was Amy, propped up on pillows, her face pale, wan, exhausted—radiant. Juliet stood beside the bed, sponging her brow and grinning as the midwife wrapped the tiny, squalling bundle in a blanket and placed it on Amy's chest. The old woman raised her head as she saw the lord of Lynmouth standing there, looking as though the gods had just struck him to stone with a bolt of lightning.

"Congratulations, m'lord. You 'ave a little girl."

Charles stood frozen, afraid to come any closer. Amy turned her head on the pillow and smiled at him, her eyes suddenly misty beneath their fan of thick black lashes. For a long moment the two gazed at each other; then Charles moved forward, toward the bed, toward the crying child. He never noticed that Juliet and the midwife stole from the room.

"Amy," he breathed, staring down at the tiny, wailing bundle that their love had made. "Oh, Amy . . ."

"Want to hold her?"

Charles paled, unable to forget when Gareth had asked him much the same thing before placing Charlotte in his arms. He remembered the terrible awkwardness of that moment, the crushing love he'd thought to feel for the toddler but hadn't, the mixed hurt and relief when Charlotte had suddenly started crying and reached for Gareth. Now, he stood frozen and uncertain, desperately wanting to hold the baby, desperately afraid to for fear that it would be a repeat of the last time he'd held his own flesh and blood. Especially as this one was a red-faced, black-haired, puckered bundle of screaming misery.

"Go ahead," Amy prompted. "She won't bite."

Swallowing hard, Charles reached down.

Put his hands around his tiny daughter.

And gingerly picking her up, cradled her tiny body to his chest.

Instantly, the baby stopped crying—and Charles felt as though the mallet of the gods had just smote him across the heart. A tumult of emotion nearly cracked his chest and closed his throat, and for a moment he could do nothing but gulp back the huge lump there as he cupped the baby's head in his palm and stared reverently down at her. With a shaking hand, he touched one curled, tiny fist. Smoothed the downy-soft hair. Kissed the red and wrinkled brow and then, moisture sparkling on his own gold lashes, he looked over at Amy, whose eyes were dark with love as she watched the two of them together.

"I think she's going to be Papa's little girl," she said softly.

"Oh, Amy," he blurted, in a raw, hoarse voice. "Oh, dearest, the world itself is not big enough to hold all the love I have for you . . . for this little girl. Thank you for making me the happiest man in England—not just once this year, but twice." Still cradling his daughter, he got down on his knees before the bed, took Amy's arm, and, kissing her palm, pressed it to his cheek to stop the sudden flood of emotion.

A droll *ahem* came from the doorway.

"My, my, have you ever seen such a nauseatingly tender, sickeningly domestic, scene?" drawled a voice that was, despite the words, ripe with amusement. Turning, Charles saw Lucien, with Gareth, Nerissa, and Juliet standing beside him. "Congratulations. And what will our newest de Montforte be named, eh?"

"Mary," said Charles, getting to his feet. "After both our mothers."

"Mary Elizabeth," Amy added, gazing at her husband and daughter.

"A girl, then," murmured Lucien.

"A girl." Charles came forward, holding a fold of the blanket back so that everyone could see his daughter. He was beaming with excitement. Bursting with pride. "Isn't she just beautiful? Have you ever seen anything so precious? Look at her little fingers! Look at that head of black hair! Look how perfect, how sweet, how *exquisite* she is—"

Lucien shook his head, secretly amused that something so tiny could reduce not only a de Montforte, but an army major, to *this*. With a heavy sigh, he raised a brow and looked at the Wild One. "It would seem, my dear Gareth, that I owe you ten pounds after all," he murmured, with a rueful smile that could not disguise his delight in having yet another niece to spoil. "Though how you knew it would be a girl is beyond me."

A sudden gust of wind lashed the window, peppering it with rain. "*That's* how I knew," said Gareth, handing Gabriel to Juliet and picking up a squirming Charlotte. "With a storm on the make, how could we have expected anything *but* a female!"

Laughter rang around the room at his wry observation. Congratulations and well wishes were said, and Mary Elizabeth de Montforte was passed around so that all could see her. After inspecting his new niece, Lucien, feeling more than a little smug for his part in getting yet another brother set to rights and safely married off, moved to the door.

"I say, Luce, where are you going?" Charles asked.

Lucien smiled. "Well, *someone's* got to tell Andrew," he said. And then, bowing to the ladies, he left the happy throng behind him and made his way downstairs.

Outside, the wind was picking up. Donning his coat and pulling his sleeves straight, Lucien paused at a window, already streaked with rain. The sky was growing dark, spreading its dire gray gloom across a lawn that had been, just an hour before, bright with sun. And there, strolling beneath a row of ancient chestnuts, was Andrew. Aside from a paleness that lent him an almost otherworldly quality, he appeared to be quite normal. But Lucien knew differently.

There was nothing "normal" about the Defiant One at all.

And now, as a flock of starlings was buffeted across the brooding gray sky, Lucien saw his brother, a notebook in his hand, pause to stare up at them. The wind tore at his hair and made the branches above his head bounce and claw at the roiling clouds. Andrew jotted something down, then moved on, writing as he went. A second later a branch as thick around as Lucien's thigh crashed down where he had been, missing him by inches.

Andrew, head still bent as he wrote, merely kept on walking.

Nothing normal about the Defiant One at all.

For a long moment, Lucien stood there, watching that slim, preoccupied figure moving across the lawn. Then, he took off his coat, went to Charles's desk, and pulled out another sheet of vellum.

It was time to face reality.

Time to seek help.

Time to write the letter he'd been putting off for far too long.

He dipped his pen in the ink and began to write.

Dr. Salcombe,

Your name was given to me by an acquaintance who informs me that you have vast experience in the field of strange and startling phenomena. Nine months ago, my youngest brother Andrew survived a fire that badly injured his lungs and caused his family, in the ensuing months, to fear that his every breath would be his last. Though my brother is no longer in need of medical attention and to the naked eye seems to be quite recovered, it is obvious that the cocktail of burning chemicals he inhaled that day has left him permanently changed in a way that I can only describe as . . . strange.

If you would be so kind as to come to Black-heath Castle near the Berkshire village of Rav-enscombe at your earliest convenience to observe

my brother without his being aware of your inter-
est, I am sure you will find the challenge both sci-
entifically—and financially—rewarding.

> *Blackheath*

Lucien folded and sealed the letter.

And then, picking up his coat once more, he went outside into the gathering storm.

Author's Note

Well, well. A second de Montforte brother all straightened out, squared away, and happily married off. Lucien must be quite proud of himself! Now that the scheming, manipulative duke has done it twice, will he find Andrew to be his greatest challenge yet?

And speaking of Andrew, just what *did* that strange mix of chemicals do to the Defiant One . . . ?

Many thanks to all of you who wrote to tell me how much you enjoyed *The Wild One*, and were eagerly anticipating Charles's story. I must confess, that when I sat down to write *The Beloved One*, I wasn't exactly sure myself what would happen to him! I suppose that, aside from hearing from our readers, that's one of the nicest things about being a writer—often, we're in for surprises ourselves. Still, I hope you've enjoyed meeting the characters first introduced in *The Wild One*, and also this early glimpse of feisty Mira Ashton, who was the heroine of my 1992 Avon release, *Captain of My Heart*.

The Beloved One is my eighth novel for Avon. For more about my books, most of which are interrelated, visit my web page at *http://members.aol.com/dharmon2*— where you can read synopses and newsletters, view covers, sign my guest book, and even vote for your favorite "Harmon Hero." You can also write to me either by e-mail at *Dharmon2@aol.com* or old-fashioned "snail mail" c/o Danelle Harmon, P.O. Box 6091, Newburyport, Massachusetts, 01950. I love hearing from my readers.

Happy reading, and until next time!

Danelle Harmon

We've got love on our minds at

http://www.AvonBooks.com

Vote for your favorite hero in
"HE'S THE ONE."

Take a romance trivia quiz, or just
"GET A LITTLE LOVE."

Look up today's date in
romantic history in "DATEBOOK."

Subscribe to our monthly e-mail
newsletter for all the buzz on
upcoming romances.

Browse through our list of new
and upcoming titles and read
chapter excerpts.

Dear Reader,

As you're getting deeper and deeper into the holiday hustle and bustle, don't forget to take some time out for yourself—by indulging in an Avon romance! Is there any better way to enjoy a precious few moments of time for yourself?

Avon's Romantic Treasure for December comes from Karen Ranney, whose emotionally intense and wildly passionate love stories are sure to warm up the coldest December night! In *Upon A Wicked Time* a young beauty transforms a wicked English duke into a man worth loving. This is a story that will go straight to your heart!

Contemporary readers won't want to miss Patti Berg's delightful *Looking for a Hero*. What would you do if a devastatingly handsome man washed up on your beach and into your life? And what would you think if he insisted he was a real, live 18th Century *pirate?* Fans of warm, wonderful, magical love stories won't want to miss this "keeper!"

Readers just can't get enough of *The MacKenzies* by Ana Leigh, and the latest MacKenzie is here—*Peter*. These heroes are hot, and Ana Leigh's writing is filled with the passion and humor—and western setting—I know you all enjoy!

And if you like your romance stormy and sensual, then don't miss Margaret Evans Porter's *Kissing a Stranger*...where a beautiful heroine travels to Regency London, desperate to marry for money. But she ends up with more than she ever bargained for...

Until next month, happy reading.

Lucia Macro

Lucia Macro
Senior Editor

AEL 1198

Discover Contemporary Romances
at Their Sizzling Hot Best
from Avon Books

ANNIE'S WILD RIDE *by Alina Adams*
79472-1/$5.99 US/$7.99 Can

SIMPLY IRRESISTIBLE *by Rachel Gibson*
79007-6/$5.99 US/$7.99 Can

LETTING LOOSE *by Sue Civil-Brown*
72775-7/$5.99 US/$7.99 Can

IF WISHES WERE HORSES *by Curtiss Ann Matlock*
79344-X/$5.99 US/$7.99 Can

IF I CAN'T HAVE YOU *by Patti Berg*
79554-X/$5.99 US/$7.99 Can

BABY, I'M YOURS *by Susan Andersen*
79511-6/$5.99 US/$7.99 Can

TELL ME I'M DREAMIN' *by Eboni Snoe*
79562-0/$5.99 US/$7.99 Can

BEDROOM EYES *by Hailey North*
79895-6/$5.99 US/$7.99 Can

Avon Romances—
the best in exceptional authors and unforgettable novels!

THE HEART BREAKER   **by Nicole Jordan**
78561-7/ $5.99 US/ $7.99 Can

THE MEN OF PRIDE COUNTY: **by Rosalyn West**
THE OUTCAST   79579-5/ $5.99 US/ $7.99 Can

THE MACKENZIES: DAVID   **by Ana Leigh**
79337-7/ $5.99 US/ $7.99 Can

THE PROPOSAL   **by Margaret Evans Porter**
79557-4/ $5.99 US/ $7.99 Can

THE PIRATE LORD   **by Sabrina Jeffries**
79747-X/ $5.99 US/ $7.99 Can

HER SECRET GUARDIAN   **by Linda Needham**
79634-1/ $5.99 US/ $7.99 Can

KISS ME GOODNIGHT   **by Marlene Suson**
79560-4/ $5.99 US/ $7.99 Can

WHITE EAGLE'S TOUCH   **by Karen Kay**
78999-X/ $5.99 US/ $7.99 Can

ONLY IN MY DREAMS   **by Eve Byron**
79311-3/ $5.99 US/ $7.99 Can

ARIZONA RENEGADE   **by Kit Dee**
79206-0/ $5.99 US/ $7.99 Can